In Fine Form

THE DOYLE FAMILY

SHANNYN SCHROEDER

Ebook ISBN: 978-1-950640-63-8

Cover created by The Killion Group

CHAPTER

One

"Hey, asshole, you up?"

"I am now." Declan Doyle rolled over on the couch and eyed his best friend, who looked far too happy considering the sun was barely up.

"I have an early start at the shop, and I wanted to talk to you before I head out."

"What's up?" Declan stood and stretched. He'd been sleeping on Tyler's couch for a week and the springs were killing him.

"Frankie is getting a little irritated with you being here. He thought you were staying for like a day, and that's on me." Tyler pressed a hand to his chest. "I thought I made it clear you needed a place to stay. I'm sorry, but I got something else for you."

"Look, I appreciate the place to sleep." Not so much the uncomfortable couch. "I can make my own way." He'd left his brother's house knowing he needed a change, but going without a plan wasn't working so well.

"No. Really. This is a win-win situation."

"What is?"

"My sister needs some help with that crappy house she bought. She drove me crazy when I was there because she needs all this work done, but she can't afford a lot, and I'm not into construction. Give me an engine to work on, and I'll do it all day. But a piece of wood or drywall? Hell, no."

"Are you telling me Rennie wants me to move in?"

"First, you know she hates when you call her that."

He did know. It was why he did it. If he couldn't treat his best friend's older sister like his own, what was the point?

Tyler continued, "Renee needs someone to guide her through what she should do first and if that someone can do some of the work for cheap, say free room and board…She'd really appreciate it."

Declan laughed. "Your sister doesn't appreciate anything about me. I don't think she even likes me."

"She likes you just fine. Except when you call her Rennie."

It was a silly childhood thing. He'd known Tyler since the third grade and Renee was in seventh. She was too cool to hang out with them, so it had been their duty to torment her. "Why did she buy a crappy house if she doesn't have the means to fix it?"

Tyler shook his head. "Ever since the divorce, everything that happened with Graham, she needed to start over. The divorce pretty much bled them dry because Graham's an asshole, and crappy was what she could afford. But it's livable. And you'd have your own bedroom."

"I don't know. I need to get a job. How am I supposed to fix her shit and work a job?"

"Do some of her stuff while you look. Anything's an improvement. Plus, Sadie adores you."

"I am pretty adorable. That's why all the ladies like me."

"Yeah, whatever. So you'll do it?"

Declan shot his friend a look. "What's in it for you?"

"Besides you getting off my couch? It gets her off my back. Like I said, win-win."

"The idea of win-win isn't supposed to be about you."

"I take what I can." He pulled out his phone. A moment later, Declan's phone pinged. "That's her address and number."

Declan narrowed his eyes. "Did you already tell her I'd do this?"

"Maaaybe."

"Asshole. What if I said no?"

"I had faith that I'd talk you into it. I was prepared with pics of Sadie and everything." He waved his phone in front of Declan.

"Like a cute little kid would make me change my mind."

"What time should I tell her?"

"You mean I'm supposed to go now?" Declan looked around the room, where his few belongings were scattered.

"She works from home, so why not?"

"Fine. Tell her I'll be there by lunch. I want to shower and get my stuff together."

"Cool. Meet for beers tonight?"

"You're buying." He grabbed a T-shirt from the arm of the couch and sniffed it.

"You got it." Tyler grabbed his keys and left.

Declan sank back to the couch, T-shirt in hand. Working on Renee's house couldn't possibly be that bad. He'd survived a couple months living with Ronan who didn't cook, rarely had groceries in the fridge, and had no furniture. Renee might be a cranky chick, but he knew she'd have the basic comforts. And it would afford him time to figure out his next moves while giving him more experience. Living with the wicked witch wouldn't kill him, would it?

Renee scrolled through the spreadsheet double checking her figures. She knew it was right. This was more like triple-checking. Her phone bleeped with a text from her brother.

> Declan will be there by lunch.

> He better be able to really do the work. I'm not playing.

> Do you ever play? He grew up with brothers who do construction and he redid Ronan's kitchen. He's the best you can afford.

She made a face at her phone even though he couldn't see her. She didn't like the truth he was spewing. She sighed and looked around her kitchen. She'd love to redo this room first, but she wasn't sure if it was the best use of her limited funds. She wasn't thrilled with the state of her new house, but it was hers. Graham had no part of it and there were no memories of him in it. So no matter how rundown it was, it was worth it.

The thought made her smile.

A moment later, Sadie came running into the kitchen. "Can I have a snack?"

Renee sighed. Growth spurts were going to kill her. Sadie was back to eating nonstop. "You can have an apple or grapes. It'll be lunchtime soon."

"Grapes."

She gathered a handful of grapes and put them in a bowl for her daughter. As she handed Sadie the bowl, she said, "Declan will be here around lunchtime. Remember I told you he might be coming to stay with us for a while?"

"He's funny." She snatched the bowl and ran back to the living room.

Funny. That was one way to think of Declan. Renee closed her laptop and checked in the fridge to decide what to make for lunch. "Hey, babe. What do you want for lunch?"

"Chicken nuggets!"

She should've guessed. Sadie was in a pattern of eating the same food over and over for days on end. Renee was fine with it, but she had no desire to eat chicken nuggets again. She turned the oven on and grabbed the chicken and a pizza from the freezer. While the oven preheated, she pulled out her notebook where she kept all of her ideas and thoughts about the house. She wanted to be able to have a starting place for Declan.

As she thumbed through the pages, she created a mental list of work she needed to finish by the end of the week. It was hard to believe that her baby was starting kindergarten. When Sadie was an infant, it felt like it would take forever for her to get to school age. Now, she was there, and Renee wasn't sure she was ready to let go.

When the pizza and chicken nuggets were ready, she set plates on the table and called Sadie. They settled in for their usual lunch routine, where Sadie told her about her morning as if Renee hadn't been there with her. It made sense when Sadie was coming from preschool or one of her classes when she was on her own.

But Renee let her chatter on about the cartoon she watched or the game she played with her toys or the city she built with her Legos. Mostly, Renee just needed to smile and nod and ask an occasional question.

"School now?"

Renee sighed. "I told you, school on Monday."

Sadie bounced in her seat in excitement.

"But we can go pick out a backpack today if you want." Renee had already bought all of the other school supplies and painstakingly wrote Sadie's name on every little thing. She almost hadn't because who cared if someone stole a pencil or crayon? But she knew Sadie would notice if other kids had their names on everything, so Renee followed the instructions the school had emailed.

She checked the clock. Still no word from Declan. Was she supposed to sit around all day and wait for him?

She sent a text to Tyler since no one had thought to give her Declan's number.

> He's still not here. I have shit to do.

> So go do it. He'll get there eventually.

She gave him until she had lunch cleaned up and Sadie ready to go. No Declan, so they went to the store. Sadie had to try on nearly every backpack before settling on the first one Renee handed to her.

"Can I wear it home?"

"You can wear it until we check out and you can hold it in the car. It can't stay on your back. It's not safe."

Sadie squinched up her face and nodded, her light

brown curls bouncing around her face. They held hands as they walked through the store toward the registers. After paying for the bag, they drove home, Sadie playing with the zippers on her bag, testing them repeatedly.

"Who's that?" Sadie asked as Renee was parking.

"Who?"

"On our steps."

Renee put the car in park and looked through the window to their front porch. Sure enough, a man was lying on the stairs, legs outstretched, his head resting on a bag. A moment of panic hit her, but then she remembered Declan. She honked the horn. He sat up and pushed his sunglasses to the top of his head. He squinted at her and smiled.

"It's Declan."

"Yay!" Sadie unbuckled herself, grabbed her bag, and flew out the door. "Declan!"

How the hell did a guy who they hadn't seen in almost a year get a reception like that?

Renee climbed out of the car and locked up. By the time she reached the house, Sadie was showing Declan how awesome her new backpack was. He looked different than she remembered. He was one of those people who were frozen in time in her mind. Although she'd seen him in recent years, he was always seventeen in her head. Cute, but annoying like a little brother.

He looked at her over Sadie's head and shot her a grin. That smile had always been a killer and seeing it on a guy who was definitely more man than boy was quite the hit.

"Hey. How are you? It's been a while." He stood and leaned over to kiss her cheek.

For some stupid reason, it made her blush. "I'm doing okay."

She pointed to his scruffy jaw. "That's—" *Sexy*. "New."

He rubbed his hand over the close-cut beard. "Yeah. Ronan had one for a while because he didn't want to look like our dad. I figured I'd give it a try."

She'd never met his dad. He went missing right before Ty and Declan became friends. She wasn't sure if it was a sore subject. "Ty said you were gonna be here by lunchtime."

He shrugged. "It's only like one-thirty. That's still lunchtime, right?"

She sucked in a deep breath. "Let's go in and get you settled." She looked around. "Is that it?" she asked pointing to the duffel he'd been resting on.

"Yep. I travel light."

She walked past him to the door, unlocked it, and ushered Sadie in. "Go put your backpack away. I'm going to show Declan around."

Declan followed them in as Sadie ran off to her room, bag thumping at her side.

"Your room is this way, toward the back of the house on the other side of the kitchen." She led the way, looking at her house the way he might see it. It was a little dingy and had an old lady vibe, but she was working to change that. "Here you go."

She gave the bedroom door a shove and stepped back toward the kitchen. He tossed his bag on the bed and turned in a circle.

"Nice place."

"If you say so."

"I slept on Ronan's attic floor. This is furnished and everything."

"Your brother made you sleep on the floor?" She couldn't keep the shock from her voice.

"He lives alone and didn't have much furniture to begin with. But he bought a mattress, so I wasn't on the bare floor." He lifted a shoulder again as if he didn't have a care in the world.

To be so laid back.

"Should we see what needs work?"

"We will. But first, some ground rules."

"Shoot." He sat on the edge of the bed and gave a bounce. Then he patted the mattress beside him. "Take a seat."

She waved him off. She was better when standing. "First, no parties, no women."

"You mean here, right? Like you don't expect me to be celibate. Just don't bring them here."

"What you do out in the world is your business."

"I would never be so disrespectful to bring another woman into your house. What do you think of me, Rennie?" He put a hand over his heart and looked at her with wide clear blue eyes.

"Second, do not ever call me Rennie. It annoys me."

He huffed out a breath. "I'll try."

"Three, you're welcome to eat or drink anything in the fridge. I cook or pick up dinner most nights. I'm willing to get you something specific when I do the grocery shopping —within reason."

"Whatever you have, is good with me. I'm not picky."

"Four, I expect you to treat this like a job. No sleeping all day and then working at midnight. Sadie has a regular bedtime and I don't want work noise to keep her up. Plus, she's starting school next week, so her routine is shifting. It's going to be hard enough without adding lack of sleep. Any problems?"

"Got it. Don't be a douche. Get the work done."

She cringed. "And maybe try to curb the language. I really don't want to have to explain to a five-year-old what a douche is."

"Again, I can try." He stood up. "My turn."

"For what?"

"My rules."

CHAPTER
Two

What the fuck was he doing? Declan said the words even though he knew better than to mess with Renee. But there was part of him that couldn't help it.

Her crossed arms and arched brow reminded him of how little bullshit she was willing to put up with. But now she was waiting to hear his rules.

As if he ever had any rules?

He stood and took a step closer. "I work cheap, but beer in the fridge would be nice."

"Easy enough as long as you're not drunk while you work. Anything else?"

"Yeah." Another step closer. He studied her face. She was a beautiful woman. Her sharp brown eyes were so expressive. "I don't need you to take care of me. I'm all grown up."

They stared at each other for an uncomfortable beat. He wasn't sure what exactly caused the tension. It wasn't anger. But something was simmering. Something in the way she looked at him, like she had on the porch when she commented on his beard. He just couldn't pinpoint the feeling.

The corner of her mouth lifted and he thought for a moment that she was going to laugh at him. Instead, she said, "I'll try to remember that."

He shifted to step around her to go back to the kitchen, but she stopped him with a hand on his forearm.

He looked at her hand and then into her eyes.

"Ty told me you guys had a memorial for your dad. I'm sorry."

"It's all good. It was a long time coming." He brushed off her sympathy. Part of why he left Ronan's house was his need to escape thinking about his father. One stupid letter from a dead man had shifted everything he'd ever thought about his dad. He shouldn't have to think about it here. "Let's go see what we're working with."

He stepped through the doorway and back into the kitchen. He hadn't looked at anything on the way to the bedroom.

"Um, not to sound like a bitch, but how are you going to work without tools? All you brought was one bag."

Glancing over his shoulder, he said, "I have tools. I just don't carry them with me."

"You can use the garage or the basement if you want. I don't use either except for storage."

"Okay," he responded, but he was studying the cabinets. They had to be from the seventies. The doors were plain and had been repainted a number of times, but the cabinets themselves were solid wood. He opened and closed a few doors. The counter had to go. It was green Formica. He looked down at his feet. Yellowish vinyl tile that at one time had a design swirling through it but had been worn away. "Did the last owners do any work over the last fifty years?"

Renee leaned against the counter and blew out a breath. "I don't think so. They were an old couple. I had the place inspected before I bought. The guy said the house was in good shape. It mostly needs cosmetic stuff."

He reached over and unlocked the window above the sink and gave it a shove. It was a wood window. Old, like everything else, and it barely budged.

"Have you thought about what you want to do first?"

"I'm hoping you can help with that. I'm sure there are things that should be done first. Things that are more important than a pretty kitchen."

He should've known better than to think Renee would be anything less than practical. "If all the windows are like this one, I suggest you start there."

"Yeah, I already got an estimate for the windows and that's gonna have to wait. Maybe by spring, I can get that kind of money together."

"You'll lose money this winter with these. Who gave you an estimate?"

"I Googled window companies and called three. They were all out of range."

He shook his head. "That's because they're marking up the cost of the window and screwing you on the labor. I can get the windows wholesale for about two hundred each except the picture window in front."

"What?"

"I don't have an account set up, but I'm sure Ronan does." He smiled at her. "It pays to know people."

"And you know how to install windows?"

"If you don't believe I know how to do anything, why am I here?" He was used to people underestimating him, but this was getting ridiculous.

"I thought you would paint and maybe put in some tile

or something. I don't know what's required to replace windows."

"Once I measure the windows, I'll get an estimate. You'll have to pay someone to do the capping. I don't have the tools or experience for that. Plus, it's too tedious for me." Based on the look of confusion on her face, he explained. "The metal around the outside of the windows. I spent one miserable summer with my brother doing windows, and while I don't mind the installation, the capping is frustrating. We can find someone to do it as a side job, so it'll be cheaper."

"Okay. Windows." She opened a drawer and pulled out a small notebook and pen. "What else? I want to get a list and figure out a budget."

"I'm not a plumber or HVAC guy so if you have anything more than a clogged toilet or a furnace filter that needs to be replaced, you need to pay a professional."

"The furnace and AC are newish. Certainly not as old as the kitchen."

"Cool. Then let's do a walk-through."

They went from room to room, Renee scribbling notes on everything he said. Sadie joined them on the tour and insisted on showing him all the cool parts of her room. Then she followed along as he checked the avocado-green bathroom. "Why exactly did you fall in love with this house?"

Renee laughed. "The price was right. I wanted Sadie to have a house with a backyard. Ugly can be fixed. It'll just take time."

"What about your ex? Couldn't he do some of this for you? I thought he was a plumber."

Silence greeted him and he turned to Renee. Her face

was tight and her lips pinched. *Note to self: don't mention the ex.*

He looked at Sadie and said, "What color do you think we should paint your room?"

"I can pick? Any color?"

"Uh..." He was afraid to look at Renee. He'd probably fucked up again.

"Within reason," Renee cut in. "One color. No rainbow stripes or polka dots."

Sadie giggled.

"I don't know what you're talking about," Declan said. "I think rainbow stripes and polka dots and maybe a unicorn!"

"Yeah!" Sadie yelled.

He scooped her up and flew her down the hallway, trying to think of ridiculous things kids liked. "Maybe a mermaid?"

"Or a superhero?"

"Anything is possible."

He set her down at her doorway.

"You know you created a monster," Renee said. To Sadie, she said, "You can pick one color."

"It's only paint, and if it makes her happy, what's the big deal?"

"I can't cave to every whim." But there was something in her expression as she watched Sadie pull books off her small bookcase and flip through pointing at colors and pictures, getting more excited with each page.

"But sometimes kids need a win," he said.

Declan's words hit home. He should know nothing about raising kids, but since he spent most of his childhood without a father, he had some insight.

"We'll see," she grudgingly agreed. "Are you staying for dinner?"

"Is that an invitation?"

"Just a question so I know how much to make."

"Can we have pizza tonight?" Sadie asked from her floor.

"We can't have pizza every night."

"Pizza is pretty much the perfect food," Declan said, and Sadie's eyes lit.

Renee sighed. "Fine. But you need to have a salad or fruit with it."

"Okay," Sadie answered excitedly.

"On that note, since I now have extra time because I'm not cooking, I'm going to get some work done. Do you need anything from me?" she asked as she headed back toward the dining room which was acting as her office.

Declan shook his head. "I'll measure the windows and see if I can get a quote. It's kind of late in the day, so it might be tomorrow."

"That's fine. Just let me know when you get a price and I'll figure out the finances." She paused in the living room. "Remote is on the table if you want to watch TV. Or there's a TV in your room if you prefer. No cable, but I have streaming services."

"Hey, sorry about bringing up your ex. Ty never mentioned not to."

"It's not that the divorce was bad." She looked over her shoulder toward Sadie's room. "He's just unreliable. When I asked him if he would come look at this house with me to inspect it, he refused. Said I wasn't his problem. Since I wanted to be on my own, I should learn to handle things."

The memory of the conversation still burned her. She'd spent years with him, helping him build his own business.

"Asshole. Even if he didn't want to do it for you, his kid lives here."

She blew out a breath. Pretty sad that someone who was barely a friend was more concerned about her daughter than Graham was. "Anyway, I do my best to not talk about him in front of Sadie. He loves her and she adores him. I don't want to get in the way of that."

She went to the dining room table and opened her laptop. Declan disappeared into the bedroom and returned with a tape measure and one of her notepads. He moved around, measuring and scribbling.

Even though she was keenly aware of his presence—she was so used to being the only adult here—she focused on work. She'd been dreading working on this client's account. He was old school and had been fighting her on using spreadsheets. Instead, he continued to use a ledger—like an honest-to-God green book with accounts payable and receivable. They met once a month at a coffee shop and he handed her the book. She shouldn't complain, but it never failed that in transcribing the information, she made mistakes and had to comb through the pages multiple times. At least he paid well. He was one of her first clients as a freelancer.

"Sorry to interrupt," Declan said.

She looked up from the ledger and checked the time on her laptop. Damn she'd been at it for over an hour. She raised her eyebrows at Declan.

"I can't get to the windows in here. I did all the rest in the house."

"Sorry. I was absorbed in work." She pushed back from the table and stood.

"I know you said windows, but are you sure you don't want me to price a new patio door? The one you have going to the back yard has seen better days."

"That's for sure a next-year problem." Closing her laptop, she added, "I'll go order pizza while you do this."

He glanced down at the ledger. "That's a lot of numbers."

"I'm an accountant. Numbers are kind of my thing."

He shifted the table a little and leaned toward the window. "So you really were one of those math-loving weirdos, huh?"

She laughed because Ty and Declan had always teased her about being a nerd. It never bothered her because it was true. "Yeah, I guess I am."

"Ronan's girlfriend Chloe manages a bar. She probably does the same kind of stuff."

"I'm not that kind of accountant. Present workload aside. This has been paying the bills. I'm a forensic accountant."

"I have no idea what that means."

"I'm kind of like a financial detective. I figure out why the numbers don't add up."

His arms stretched across the window and he scribbled in the notebook. Then he measured the height. She watched as his muscles rippled through the thin T-shirt he wore. As long as she'd known Declan, having him here now felt almost like having a stranger in the house. She wasn't uncomfortable, but something was off—different. Not necessarily bad, either. She went to the kitchen to call for pizza.

By the time the pizza arrived, she was bleary-eyed from

creating the spreadsheet from Larry's small, blocky writing. If she powered through, she might have it all done tomorrow. She carried the pizza to the kitchen table and yelled for Declan and Sadie.

They each emerged from their rooms and ran toward the table as if they hadn't eaten all day. Maybe Declan hadn't, but she knew Sadie had. If she kept this up, the girl was going to outgrow the new school clothes they just bought.

"Smells delicious," Declan said.

"It's my favorite," Sadie said earnestly as she climbed into the chair beside Declan. "Mom gets extra sauce and pepperoni."

"Pepperoni? No way. That's my favorite, too. Corner or inside pieces?"

"Inside. I don't like the crunchy crust."

"Dude. We're like a match made in heaven. I love the outside pieces."

Renee listened to the conversation with a smile. She had no idea if Declan was telling the truth or just entertaining Sadie, but it was nice for Sadie to have someone new to talk to. When he took a plate, Declan loaded it with edge pieces.

Sadie leaned over and whispered something to him.

He scoffed. "If your mom wanted the little triangle pieces, she should've moved faster. You snooze, you lose." To prove his point, he shoved one of the corner pieces in his mouth.

Sadie's eyes popped wide.

"Since you're a guest, I'm going to let that slide. This time."

He smiled and took a bite of another slice. His phone buzzed and he pulled it from his pocket. "Why does Ty think he needs to check on me?"

"Why are you asking me?"

"I told him he was buying tonight, but he's making sure everything's okay."

She dropped her pizza on her plate. "How is it that you move into *my* house, but he's buying *you* drinks? Shouldn't he be taking me out?"

"I think he's worried you'll scare me off, and I'll end up back on his couch." He shot off a text and returned his attention to his pizza.

"Am I really that bad?" Graham had been telling her for years that she was too strict, too bitchy, too stubborn—too everything except fun.

"Nah." He paused. "Well, when we were younger, yeah. But you've mellowed in your old age."

"Old, huh?"

He straightened in his chair and looked up over her head. She turned to see what he was looking at.

"I think there's some gray hair. Definitely a sign of old age."

"Shut up! I am not going gray already. I'm not that much older than you."

Sadie sucked in a breath. "You said shut up."

"I'm sorry. I shouldn't have. I wasn't saying it in a mean way, though. Declan knows I was kidding." She glared at him. Having Declan in her house might make her regress to her angsty teenage attitude.

"That's right, Sadie. Sometimes your mom has a hard time holding her temper. We'll help her by reminding her when she messes up, right? She should be nicer to me." He winked at Renee.

At this rate, being told to shut up might be the nicest she could offer.

CHAPTER
Three

Declan walked into the small neighborhood bar that was about halfway between Renee's house and Tyler's apartment. It was pretty crowded, so he made his way to the bar first and ordered beer for him and Tyler. While waiting, he texted Tyler to see if he'd arrived. As the bartender set the bottles down, Tyler responded that he was at a table near the back. With bottles in hand, he moved through the crowd, smiling at pretty women as he passed. Too bad he'd agreed not to bring anyone back to Renee's. He actually had a bed there.

He sighed at himself. He'd decided he was going to figure out his life. Getting laid was not top priority right now.

Tyler saw him and waved. Declan set the bottles on the table.

"Hey, I said I'd buy. I got you one," Tyler said as he slid a bottle in front of Declan.

Declan picked it up and took a swig. He shrugged. "It was crowded, so I grabbed a couple. Not like we won't drink 'em."

"So how'd it go with Renee?"

"Fine." Declan looked at his friend with suspicion. "What are you not telling me?"

"Nothing. She was a little testy earlier today when you weren't there by her lunchtime. I figured she might've been bitchy by the time you actually showed."

"Nah. We're good." He took another drink. "Sadie's gotten big, man. It hasn't been that long since I've seen her, but she's like this cool little person, not just a cute kid."

"She is pretty awesome. Too bad Graham doesn't see it."

"What do you mean?"

Tyler leaned his elbows on the table. "Look, you didn't hear this from me."

Declan cocked an eyebrow.

"Part of the reason I suggested you move into Renee's is because I know you'll keep an eye on her."

"Why?"

Tyler sighed. "The divorce did a number on her."

"I thought they split a long time ago."

"They did. But he dragged the divorce out forever. He's an asshole."

"If you're that worried about her, why didn't you stay?"

"I love my sister. I really do. But I can't live with her. We make each other crazy. And she does need work done that I can't do."

"You're telling me. That house looks like no one's done shit in decades."

"I know, but like I said, it was what she could afford. She's happy with it, I think. She needed something that was hers, you know?"

Declan nodded, even though he didn't really get it. Owning a house meant committing to being in one place for the long haul. He'd never considered it. "What do you need me to watch her for then? Did Graham do something?"

Tyler shook his head, a flash of anger crossing his face. "He's treated her like shit for a long time. Now that the divorce is done, I figured it'd be better. Sometimes she still lets him get under her skin, though. Especially when it comes to Sadie."

"He's an asshole to his daughter?" How could anyone be mean to a five-year-old?

"Not directly. But he'll blow off his visitation if something better comes up. He's late with child support all the time. That's part of the reason for the house. She needed to do it all on her own without counting on anything from him."

"That's all shitty, but what do you want me to do?"

Tyler shrugged. "She gets in her head and forgets about living. Just let me know if she's not okay. I don't know how to explain it."

"I get it. Nessa's picked some real winners, too."

Tyler barked out a laugh. "Nessa can handle her own. I've seen that girl downright brawl. I can't imagine some guy making her feel the way I've seen Renee act."

"I think you underestimate your sister. She can put the fear of God into a guy if she wanted."

They finished the beers in front of them and ordered another round. They talked about old friends and work, not that Declan had a job. After the next round, Tyler looked at him with serious eyes.

"Hey, you know, we haven't really talked since the funeral."

"We've talked. I lived with you."

"You know what I mean."

Yeah, he did. He hadn't talked to anyone. What was there to talk about?

"How are you?

He shrugged. "Fine. It's not like having a funeral changed anything. He's always been gone."

"No other news about what happened?"

Declan had told Tyler about his brothers' investigation into their father's disappearance. Although Brendan and Ronan wanted to keep it quiet, Declan knew he could trust Tyler not to tell anyone. "They don't tell me anything. If I wasn't living with Ronan, he wouldn't have said anything to me. I would've been just as in the dark as the rest of my siblings."

"It's gotta feel different, though. Having confirmation that he's dead. That he didn't run off."

Declan inhaled deeply. Yeah, it felt different, but he didn't know how to explain it. He spent his life thinking his father didn't want them. "It's making me re-evaluate my life choices, that's for sure."

"How so? Were you planning on working for the Cahills?"

At the mention of the company his father worked for, the very man that confirmed his dad's death, irritated Declan. "No. I can't believe Ronan is staying on. He must have one hell of a poker face to look at Danny Cahill, knowing his father took secrets about our father to the grave."

"How much can he see Cahill? I heard he was running for alderman. I thought that meant he wasn't working for the construction company anymore."

"Hell if I know. Like I said, my brothers aren't too forthcoming."

"So then how are you rethinking life?"

"Unlike a lot of little kids, who want to be like their dad when they grow up, I made the choice to be nothing like him. He worked hard at the same job for years, bought a house, had a family, and then left. Like it was too much. I spent years having fun and making it all up as I went. But now, I don't know." He paused, searching for the words. "It wasn't his choice to go."

Tyler smiled. "So now you're ready to settle down and be a family man? Many Chicago hearts will be broken."

He chuckled. "I'm not quite there yet. But I'm at least trying to figure out what I do want long-term. A plan for the future. A regular job. A place to live."

"Aw, our little boy is growing up."

"Shut the fuck up, asshole." He held up his empty bottle. "Now you owe me another."

"No problem. I can do that because I *do* have a job."

"Still an asshole."

Tyler went to the bar to get their drinks. Declan was glad Tyler had decided to move back to Chicago. He'd missed him over the last couple of years. He had a pretty wide circle of friends, but they were drinking buddies, not guys to have a serious conversation with. No one who had known him as long as Tyler. Ty was family.

As much as he'd avoided commitment, family like this was different. They didn't depend on him. He could enjoy having the connection with people who cared about him without them expecting much of him.

Except now, Ty needed him to keep an eye on Renee. And Renee was counting on him to fix her crappy house.

His life was already changing.

AFTER SHE GOT SADIE TO BED, RENEE SAT AT ON THE COUCH with a glass of wine, her laptop sitting in front of her. She scrolled job boards looking for something steady. She'd freelanced for years, but now that Sadie would be in school for half a day, she could pay for after-school care and get a regular part-time job. Hopefully, one that would become full-time next year.

She missed forensic accounting. Digging through the financials of a business or individual, finding out all their secrets. It was better than watching a movie. She didn't mind doing regular bookkeeping or even helping people with taxes, but it was so repetitive. Forensic accounting wasn't glamorous or exciting, but it wasn't boring either.

On the sidebar of her computer, an ad for a dating site flashed. She looked at it for a few seconds. She didn't even remember the last date she'd gone on. Although she and Graham had been separated for more than a year and a half before the divorce was finalized, she hadn't had it in her to think about wading into the dating pool. Maybe it was time.

She sighed. But it took such effort. And she had so much going on right now. Did she really want to add another variable to her life? Not a good plan. She refocused on the job board.

Noticing the time, she realized why she was so sleepy. It was near midnight. When Declan left, she hadn't thought about how late he'd be gone, and she hadn't given him a key. But he was with Ty, who did have a key. She texted her brother and told him to give Declan his key to get in. Then she closed her laptop and turned on the TV. She needed something easy for her brain before bed.

She put on some sitcom but couldn't get into it. Her mind kept wandering to the thought of a new job. Maybe she could take a class or two online to brush up on her skills. It had only been a few years, but things changed. That might give her the edge she'd need for someplace to ignore the fact that she'd stayed home to be with her daughter.

For the most part, she didn't have regrets about that. Her mom worked while she was little, and she remembered feeling lonely every time her mom left for the office. And she had Ty, as annoying as he was. She worried about Sadie because she was an only child. Not that that had been her plan. She'd been ready to try for a sibling a long time ago. Graham had his own ideas, though.

She drained her glass and set it on the table. Pulling a blanket onto her lap, she scrolled to find something that would be more interesting.

RENEE JOLTED UP ON THE COUCH AND LOOKED AROUND. SHE must've fallen asleep. But the TV was off. She rubbed her eyes and glanced at the table. Her wine glass and computer were gone. What the hell? Tossing the blanket aside, she stood and heard movement in the kitchen. As she passed the dining room table, she saw her laptop plugged in. She leaned on the doorway to the kitchen, where Declan stood at the sink rinsing her wine glass.

"You didn't have to clean up after me," she said.

"Sorry. Did I wake you? I debated if I should wake you but figured if you crashed on the couch, you were probably really tired."

"I don't know what woke me, but finding the TV off and my stuff moved was weird."

He turned and looked at her with a wide grin. "If you can't handle your alcohol, maybe you shouldn't drink."

"Very funny. It was just a long day. One glass of wine isn't enough to do me in."

"How much would it take?"

"What?"

"How much wine is needed for you to loosen up, lose control?"

"It's been too long for me to remember. I'm not twenty-two anymore. My life doesn't lend itself to losing control. Thanks for cleaning up. I'm going to bed. See you tomorrow."

"Yes, boss."

She shook her head and laughed. Declan poked at her because that was what he did. But he had a point. It was time for her to make some changes and get her life back. Not that she'd consider losing control as Declan suggested, but she deserved to have some fun. So tomorrow, she'd think a little more about getting on a dating site. Maybe make plans to do something more than book club.

CHAPTER

Four

Declan didn't sleep well after his night out with Ty. He had so much on his mind, and he felt a little overwhelmed trying to figure out what he should do when. He didn't even know where to start. It didn't help that he looked at the people around him and they all seemed to have their shit together.

Ronan and Renee both had their own houses. Sure, they were older than him, but if he considered where they had been at his age, they still would've been way ahead of him. Even Ty, who just moved back to the city had a steady job and a place to live.

After tossing and turning well into the morning, he lay in bed and heard Renee and Sadie making noise in the kitchen. Then it got quiet again. Part of him felt like he was hiding out, and he didn't really know why, but he wasn't ready to hang out with them. He was too lost in his own head. When it quieted again, he got dressed and left without a word.

He decided the least he could do was focus on getting things done at Renee's while he figured out the rest of his life. And if he wanted to start work, he'd need the tools that he'd stored at his mom's house. He hopped a bus to get there, figuring he'd take a ride share back so he wouldn't have to try to juggle all his tools.

As he walked down the block toward his childhood home, he looked around the neighborhood. It was a good neighborhood, the kind of place where people knew each other and made lasting friendships. He'd never thought about it much, and he hadn't lived in a place like this since, but there was comfort in coming back. He paused in the middle of the block and let memories wash over him. Even with the shadow of his dad's disappearance, he'd had a great childhood.

He continued his path and realized that Ronan's truck was parked in front of the house. Maybe he wouldn't have to pay for a ride back to Renee's after all. He climbed the new concrete steps and swung the door open. "Hey, Ma!" he yelled.

He heard shuffling coming from the kitchen and then his mom was standing in the doorway, stern look on her face, as always when he entered the house like that.

"Why must you all yell to announce your presence? It's a wonder they never threw me out of this neighborhood."

He neared her and wrapped her in a bear hug. "Nah, they love us here."

Ronan sat at the kitchen table drinking coffee. "What are you doing here?" he asked.

"I came to pick up some of my tools."

Ann leaned back from his arms. "You have a job?"

He smiled. She was always hopeful. "Kind of. I'm staying with Renee Kane—Griggs, Tyler's sister. Her house needs some work. Speaking of," he said, turning to Ronan. "I need to start with her windows. Do you have an account set up somewhere so I can get them wholesale for her?"

"Sure. You need me to place the order?"

"No. I've got the measurements and everything. I just need to use your account."

"You sure you measured right? I can stop by later if you want."

Declan swallowed his irritation. He knew Ronan wasn't questioning him to be a dick. He didn't see Declan as anything but his screw-up little brother. "I got it. I know how to measure."

Ronan pulled out his phone, scrolled for a minute, and then Declan's phone buzzed with a text.

"That's all the info you'll need." He smiled. "And if you talk nicely to Lindsay, the girl who usually mans the phones, she might give you a little extra discount."

"I'll charm her so good you'll get the discount on the next ten orders you have."

Ann walked past him shaking his head. "You should learn to use that charm for good instead of evil."

"This is good. I'm saving Renee money. She needs all the help she can get."

His mom put a cup of coffee on the table. "Sit. I have some cake. Unless you'd rather have some eggs and toast."

"I don't need you to cook anything, Mom."

"It's no bother."

"You didn't offer to cook me breakfast when I came in." Ronan said.

"You looked like you already ate."

Declan reached over and tapped his brother's hard abdomen. "Maybe it's time for a diet, bro."

Ronan swatted his hand away.

A moment later, their mother was sliding a piece of coffee cake in front of each of them.

"So what are you doing at Renee's besides windows?"

"I'm not sure. The house is rundown. And she's pretty broke, I think. The windows are the most important. Then, probably paint. I don't know what her budget is for big projects like the kitchen and bathrooms. You should see this house. I swear, her house was last decorated by someone Mamó's age," he said referencing their grandmother.

"That bad, huh?"

"Yeah. I think she wants to do the kitchen, but she's being practical and doing the things that need to be done first."

"I'll let you know if I come across extra material."

"Thanks. Every bit will help." He drank his coffee and swallowed the coffee cake. They chatted about Ronan's work, carefully avoiding any conversation about where his investigation into their dad's disappearance was heading. Declan didn't want to talk about it anymore. He was still sorting his shit about that revelation.

After finishing a second piece of cake, he stood. "I'm going to grab my tools from the basement. Can you give me a ride back to Renee's? I can wait if you're not done here."

"I can do that. We can head out whenever you're ready."

Declan went to the basement to the side of the house opposite to where his mother had her at-home salon set up. Over the years, this entire half of the basement had become storage for all of them as they moved out but still wanted to cling to parts of their childhood.

Unfortunately, none of them were great at keeping things organized, so his stuff was mixed in with everyone else's. Whenever one of his siblings came to unbury what they wanted, something else became buried.

He'd moved about five boxes in various directions when he heard someone coming down.

"You need help?" Ronan asked.

"If you're offering."

Ronan stood next to him, staring at the stacks of boxes and crates. "What are you looking for?"

Declan squinted his eyes in thought. "I'm pretty sure there are boxes with my name scribbled on the side. Not a hundred percent sure. I was moving in a hurry."

He'd broken up with Sheila—no Shelly—and she'd flipped out and started throwing his stuff all over the lawn. He'd had to scoop up things quickly before they walked off.

He had a sudden thought. "No. Wait. The tools are in old milk crates."

His clothes made it into boxes, but he'd used crates for tools since they stuck up all over and wouldn't fit neatly in a box.

Ronan sighed and hefted some boxes out of the way. It took into the third row for them to find the crates. At least all three of them were together. They yanked them out and reset the boxes they'd moved.

His brother looked in the crates and grunted.

"I don't need your criticism. I haven't needed most of these tools in a while and like I said, it was a fast move. I usually take better care of them." At least he would if he had a place to keep them.

"These aren't the best tools."

"Some of us can't afford the best. We get what we can that'll still get the job done."

"These won't last the duration of a rehab. Good quality tools cost more upfront, but they last longer so you're not wasting money replacing them. Not to mention the frustration when they don't work." He grabbed a crate and headed toward the stairs. "We can stop by my house. I have some extras you can borrow or have."

"I don't need your charity."

"You're my brother, and I have extra."

As much as he wanted to do things on his own, Declan started to see that no matter what, Ronan was always going to be his big brother. He and Brendan were kind of hard-wired to take care of their younger siblings. "Thanks. I appreciate it. I'll borrow them and return them when I'm done."

Another grunt. Declan didn't understand how Chloe figured out how to interpret Ronan's various grumbles and grunts. They pushed through the old door at the top of the stairs and set the crates in the kitchen.

"Where's Chloe?" Declan asked.

"She went to church with her parents and then they have lunch."

"Weren't you invited?" Ronan always said Chloe's parents didn't like him, but that was cold, seeing as he was right across the street.

"She invited me. I wasn't up for the whole church thing."

Their mom shot them a look from the sink where she was washing dishes.

"I get that. So is she moving in?"

"That's the plan. As soon as her lease is up."

"Maybe you should make an honest woman out of her," Ann said.

"She's as honest as they come. She doesn't need my help."

Declan hooted a laugh.

"You know damn well what I mean."

"Yeah, I'm teasing, Mom. We'll get there. I can't think about that until Brendan and I find the answers about Dad."

Mom's face brightened at the admission of an inevitable wedding. Declan shook his head. "How the mighty have fallen. I never would've guessed you'd be the first to settle down."

"What the hell is that supposed to mean?"

"Come on. Brendan? Sure. Gavin? Definitely. Even Nessa. But you? You've always been...I don't know restless."

Ronan huffed. "You're one to talk."

"That's what I'm sayin'. I'm not the one hearing wedding bells."

"I didn't expect it either. Shit just happens."

Not to Declan it didn't. He'd led his life to avoid such traps.

SUNDAY BREEZED BY AND NOTHING HAD CHANGED IN THE house, other than having an extra person around, which felt odd. It wasn't as if Renee had expected Declan to show up and magically alter her house, but she at least wanted a plan.

She gave him the weekend to settle in. He, however, went out Sunday. She hadn't heard him come in, so she wasn't a hundred percent sure he even came back home. But today, they needed to develop a to-do list so she could plan her finances.

After showering and dressing, she went to Sadie's room to wake her. Her little girl had been so excited for her first day of real school, she'd had a hard time falling asleep. Renee had read her three stories and rubbed her back and snuggled her until she'd finally drifted off. Renee hadn't been far behind.

Sadie growled and rolled over.

"Time to get up. School today." Sadie was in the afternoon session for kindergarten, but Renee still wanted her to maintain a regular schedule.

Those were the magic words. Sadie popped up. "When do we go?"

"I told you. Not until after lunch. Get up now and I'll make you waffles for breakfast. You'll have time to play and watch TV. Then, after lunch, I'll take you to school."

"That's soooo long."

Renee smiled. "Not as long as you think. Get moving. I'll start the waffles."

She headed to the kitchen to make some much-needed coffee and figure out how to wake Declan and get him working without treating him like Sadie. Oh, God. What if he slept naked? Declan was totally the type of guy to sleep naked. She couldn't just let herself in his room to wake him then.

She was so caught up in her thoughts she didn't hear him in the kitchen. She should've noticed the water running, but she was more worried about seeing him naked. And then, there he was, standing at her sink, chugging a glass of water. Naked.

His bare back was to her, muscles rippling as he drank. Her gaze followed down to see that he wasn't in fact naked, but he was standing in her kitchen wearing nothing but boxers.

She shook herself. "What are you doing?"

He turned slowly and held up the glass. With a sleepy smile, he said, "Getting a drink."

She inhaled deeply. "I meant, why are you standing in your *underwear*?"

His brow furrowed beneath his dark, sleep-tousled hair. "Because I just woke up?"

"I have a five-year-old little girl. She should not see you in your boxers."

"You said she had school today."

Renee blinked, surprised he would remember. "She doesn't go until afternoon."

"Okay."

She threw up her hands. "New rule. No walking around in your underwear. You must be fully clothed."

She crossed her arms and waited for him to make his way back to his room.

Instead, he stepped closer, shortening the distance between them by half. She checked her instincts to back away.

"What's the matter? Afraid you won't be able to control yourself?" He waved a hand in front of his bare, muscled chest.

She couldn't help but follow the movement but quickly covered with an eye roll. "Fuck you."

He sucked in a sharp breath, and his blue eyes grew comically wide. "Better watch it, Rennie, or I'll tell Sadie what a potty mouth you have."

"Don't call me that."

"It's a term of endearment."

"I hate it."

"I know." He chuckled and turned around toward his bedroom.

She absolutely did not watch his ass as he left. Instead, she busied herself making coffee and a batch of waffles for breakfast.

"I got the window company information from my brother last night. I also picked up my tools from my mom's house, so we can start on whatever project you want," he called from behind his nearly closed bedroom door.

"Okay."

The door opened as she cracked eggs into the bowl. He was still bare-chested, and she focused on whisking the eggs into the flour as he pulled on his T-shirt.

"I'm going to call the company in a bit to get a price. It'll probably take a couple of weeks to get the windows. What's the next thing you want to work on?"

She blew out a heavy breath. "Let's get a price first and then I can see."

He walked across the room and refilled his glass. Leaning on the counter beside her, he said, "We can start with something simple like painting rooms, assuming you don't want to do any altering of the space."

"Won't the walls get messed up when you rip the windows out?"

"Not if you know what you're doing. I shouldn't have to do anything more than some touch-ups around the new window."

"Well, then, I suggest you come up with a plan for Sadie's room since you made promises to her."

"And I'll keep them. Like I said, it's just paint. So if she wants silly polka dots now and in two years she decides she's over it and wants the entire room puke green, it's a couple coats of paint." He gulped his water.

He seemed really defensive and Renee had no idea what she'd done to put him there, but all she could think was that in two years, she'd be trying to figure out how to get that work done again because surely Declan would have moved on.

"Okay. Besides the paint and brushes, what do you need? Do I have to clear out the room?" She suddenly had images of trying to figure out where Sadie could sleep while her room was torn apart. She opened the waffle maker and poured the batter.

"She doesn't have much in there. I can probably move it all to the middle of the room and cover it."

"She's supposed to be at Graham's this weekend, so maybe we can do it then?" Although they hadn't talked specifics of when he would work, she didn't generally think he'd give up his weekends.

"Sounds good. It'll be a nice surprise when she gets back."

"You're okay with working through your weekend?"

"It won't take the whole weekend and she's a kid. It's not like we can tell her she can't play with her toys or sleep in her bed."

She started at his words. *We*. As if they made decisions together for her little girl. It had been so long since she'd been a part of a *we* that she didn't know how to react to hearing him talk like that.

"Thanks," she said quietly. For a guy who was all about making sure he had a good time, he was turning out to be far more thoughtful than she considered. "Waffles will be ready in a few minutes. You want some eggs, too?"

"I'll eat whatever you make. I'm gonna call the window company." He moved into the dining room and sat at the table.

She cracked a few eggs into a bowl and added a splash of milk. After removing the first waffles, she poured the next batch. From the other room, she heard Declan on the phone.

"Hey, Lindsay, just the woman I was hoping to speak to.

39

Ronan Doyle referred me to you. I'm looking to get a price on some windows." He paused, then chuckled. "Yeah, sorry to let you know, my brother is definitely no longer single. Yeah. Sure."

The man flirted with everyone. Some things never changed. She shook her head and scrambled the eggs. A moment later, she heard Sadie.

"What do you think? Is this the best first day of school outfit?" Renee leaned over, thinking Sadie was asking her, but she twirled in front of Declan.

"Sadie. Declan is on the phone. Leave him alone."

Declan shot her a look and said to the phone, "Lindsay, can you hold on a minute? I have a kindergartner who needs some first-day-of-school fashion advice." Another chuckle. Then he looked seriously at Sadie. "That, my lady, is a beautiful dress. But the real question is, can you run and climb in it? It's a nice day and you might want to play on the playground with all your new friends."

Her daughter considered his comments seriously. "Good point." Then she took off running.

Declan returned to his call. "Sorry about that, Lindsay. Let me get you those measurements."

Renee tuned out the rest of the conversation and finished making breakfast. When Declan hung up, Sadie asked his opinion on her next outfit. They both deemed it the best choice. Renee shook her head. "Breakfast is ready."

Sadie came running in. "I'll have three waffles."

"You won't eat three waffles."

"Yes, I will. I'm starving."

"How about you start with one and have some eggs? I promise there will be more if you're still hungry."

Sadie leaned close up on tiptoe and tugged Renee's

shirt. Renee bent over to listen to her daughter's whisper. "Declan eats a lot. He's big. He ate like ten pieces of pizza."

Renee bit back a laugh. "I promise there will be enough. And if we run out, I can make more."

She handed Sadie her plate as Declan came into the room.

"Never a good sign when two women are whispering together. You're either talking about me or planning to take over the world."

Renee smiled and handed him a plate. She waited until Sadie was in the dining room. "She was worried you might eat all the waffles. They're her favorite. *You ate like ten pieces of pizza*," she mimicked.

"Taken down by a five-year-old."

"Thank you for indulging her by the way. You didn't have to do that."

He gave her a confused look.

"Interrupting your call to talk clothes?" she clarified.

"It took two seconds and it made her happy." He shrugged and walked away. He sat at the table and chatted with Sadie.

She grabbed her plate and joined them. Sadie chattered about school and asked questions, as if either she or Declan remembered a whole lot of what kindergarten had been like. Declan distracted her by showing her paint samples so she could choose a color. It took far too long, but she settled on a bright blue.

Then Sadie began telling him all about a story she made up about a superhero. He listened intently, and Renee wondered how long it would take before Declan grew tired of this kind of interaction.

CHAPTER
Five

Declan got the email with the window prices and called Lindsay back to see if they could shave any more money off the bottom line. He was on the phone when Renee came back from taking Sadie to school. Her eyes were teary and her nose pink. She'd been crying.

What the hell?

Lindsay spoke in his ear. "I'm not supposed to do this, but I can get you a slightly better discount. Like another ten percent. Any more and the boss will notice."

He smiled even though he looked worriedly at Renee. "That would be great, Lindsay. Thanks. I really appreciate it."

He disconnected and followed Renee into the kitchen. "What's wrong?"

"Nothing," she said and inhaled a shaky breath.

"You've obviously been crying."

She gave him a watery smile. "I'm not as tough as I look. I took Sadie to preschool, no problem, so I didn't think anything of the first day of kindergarten. But she let go of my hand, waved goodbye, and went into school. It just hit me hard how big she's getting."

Declan paused, unsure of what to do. He wasn't afraid of a woman's tears, but he knew enough not to assume the next step. "Are you okay?"

She waved him off. "I'm fine. I should be thrilled that she was excited to go. Some kids fell apart and cried for their mom. That would've made it harder." She blew out a breath. "I'm fine."

"If you say so. I got you an extra ten percent off the windows. As soon as you're ready, we can order them. It'll take a few weeks for them to come in."

She reached into her back pocket and pulled out a slim wallet. "Here's my credit card. Go ahead and order them."

He waved the card. "Bahamas, here I come."

She laughed, which was what he was going for.

"Good luck with that. You'll be lucky if that'll get you a week in the Dells." She stood at the sink and washed the few dishes that were there.

"Do you have work, or do you want to spend some time going over the rest of the house and what you want to do?"

"Can we get through most of it before I have to pick up Sadie?"

"Probably. Let's start with the easy part. What do you want to get done? If you didn't have to worry about money. Let's rank the projects."

"I don't know. That's why you're here, remember?"

"You might not know what needs to get done, but I'm sure there are things you want to do." He paused. "Like the kitchen."

"The kitchen is fine. It's functional."

He smiled. "But you hate it. Even if you can't afford to go all out, we might be able to improve it."

"The cabinets are crap, as is the counter—what there is of it. This is a decent-sized room, but there's no counter space."

"Since it's just you and Sadie, you're not planning on putting a bigger table in here?"

She looked at the small round table and shrugged. "It seats four. We use the dining room most of the time. So this is fine."

"Hold on." He went to his room and grabbed a notebook. He sat at the table and started a rough sketch.

"You're wasting your time. I priced a new kitchen. It's way out of my budget until I find a regular full-time job."

He held up a hand and continued scribbling. Now that he'd been in the house a couple of days, he could understand why Renee bought it. It felt like a home. Just a rundown, beat-up home. Sliding the paper on the table he said, "What do you think about this?"

She looked at his sketch. "I don't understand."

He pointed at the cabinets. "We rip it all out and rearrange everything. The only thing I'm not totally comfortable with is moving plumbing. So if your ex—"

"Nope," she said. "Not only can I not count on him for anything, I wouldn't even ask."

"Okay. Then we have to leave the sink where it is, but we can still do the rest."

"Even with discounting your labor, I don't think I can afford all these cabinets."

"Maybe this weekend, you can go with me to look at some reclaimed cabinets. If we can find a full set, or at least a set that's close enough, I can make it work."

"Reclaimed?"

"Used. Perfectly good cabinets taken out of someone's kitchen when they remodeled."

"That's a thing?"

"Yep." He stood. "Stick with me. I'll show you the ropes."

She stared at the simple line drawing. "You think you can get this done?"

"I know I can. Now let's go see what else this house needs besides tearing out the god-awful wallpaper in the living room and dining room."

She stood and chuckled, all signs of her tears gone.

RENEE'S DAY HAD BEEN MORE JAM-PACKED THAN SHE'D planned. With Sadie starting school, her plan had been to take on additional jobs while searching for a full-time position. Spending the day with Declan was not part of the schedule, but at least she felt like they'd made progress. They had ideas and much to her surprise, Declan was more resourceful than she'd given him credit for.

After school, Sadie talked nonstop on the way home and kept going right through dinner. You'd have thought she'd been in school for a week instead of two and a half hours. Renee felt bad for Declan because Sadie really wanted his attention. Renee told him he could go do his own thing, but he insisted he didn't have anything better to do.

They ate dinner together and she and Sadie sat at the table and colored together while Declan relaxed on the couch, drinking a beer while watching some game on TV.

"What are you drawing?" Renee asked Sadie.

"Super Sadie. My teacher said we get story time every day. If I write my story, she said I can read it."

Renee bit her tongue right before she blurted that Sadie didn't know how to read.

"She said we're gonna learn our letters but I already know them. I wanna read."

"You've already started. You can read your name."

"And yours." To prove it, her daughter carefully wrote m-o-m on the page.

"Do I get to be in your story?"

Sadie squinted. "I don't know. Do superheroes have mommies?"

"Everyone has a mommy."

"Declan, do you have a mom?"

"Of course I do. Her name is Ann. And she's like a superhero, just like your mom."

Sadie's eyes got big. She lowered her voice, "You're a superhero?"

Renee smiled. "Not like you're thinking. Declan means most moms do a lot of the same things that superheroes do, like take care of you and make sure you're safe."

Her nose crinkled.

"Sorry to disappoint you. I'm just a regular mom."

Sadie returned to her picture of Super Sadie and carefully colored it in. She gave herself a purple outfit and a yellow cape. Declan walked by with his empty bottle and paused to look at Sadie's picture.

"What are your superpowers?"

"I haven't decided. But I think I wanna fly. That would be fun."

"Flying is pretty awesome. But I think I'd want to be super speedy. Imagine all the things you could do if you could run really fast. I'd zoom everywhere."

"Flying is fast," Sadie added with the irritation of a five-year-old who wanted to be right.

Renee interrupted, "They're both cool. Now go see what you want to have for a snack and then you can watch one show before bed."

"Can I have cookies?"

"Yes, you can."

Sadie ran off to the kitchen, and Renee straightened everything on the table before opening her laptop. Then she froze and looked at Declan, who was studying Sadie's drawing. "Sorry. I offered her the TV and didn't think about your game."

"It's fine. I was just passing time." He set the paper back down. "You want a beer?"

She almost answered no automatically, but then she reconsidered. "Sure. Thanks."

Declan followed Sadie into the kitchen and Renee could hear them continue their conversation about superpowers. She enjoyed hearing the noise in her usually quiet house. She opened her laptop to get some work done while Sadie watched whatever cartoon she'd put on.

When Declan and Sadie came back through, her daughter gave her a sly look as Declan set a beer next to Renee. Sadie rushed by, cookies clasped in her hand. "Hold on."

Sadie paused but didn't turn.

"How many cookies do you have?"

"Three. Just like always."

Declan smiled.

"And how many did you already eat?"

"See? I told you she'd know," Sadie said as she turned toward Declan. Then she whispered, "She knows everything." She reached out to hand Renee a cookie.

"You're right, Sadie. I should've listened." To Renee, he said, "It was my fault. We snuck one in the kitchen."

She looked at Sadie. "Being sneaky is not good. You shouldn't keep secrets from me. But since you tried to teach Declan a lesson, you can keep the extra cookie."

"Thanks, Mom." Running off, she called, "Come on, Declan. You gotta see the princess."

"I'm coming."

"Don't make me the bad guy with my kid, Declan. I've had enough of that."

"Whoa." He raised his hands in defense. "I wasn't trying to do that. We were just having fun. It's not like I snuck a whole package in her pocket. I'm sorry."

Renee knew she came off harsher than necessary. Sometimes Declan's fun personality was too much of a reminder of her ex, but Declan didn't deserve that. "You're fine. Don't make a habit of it."

She grabbed her beer and her laptop and sat on the couch. Sadie sat on the floor with her three cookies stacked on the table in front of her. Declan sat on the opposite side of the couch. For the next thirty minutes, Sadie kept a running commentary of all the characters so Declan could fully understand the show.

Renee tuned out the show, sipped her beer, and worked on another spreadsheet. She missed forensic accounting. The puzzle, the secrets—she missed unraveling all of them. Until recently, she hadn't realized how much. She switched gears and checked some job boards, making note to apply to a couple of places when Sadie was at school and she could give it her full attention.

When the show was over, Sadie turned with hands pressed together. "Another one? Please?"

"No. You have school tomorrow. Go get your jammies on, brush your teeth, and pick out a book. I'll be there in five minutes." She always said five, knowing it would take

Sadie more like ten to complete the tasks. It would be much faster if Renee took over, but she was trying to give her daughter some independence. Even though it crushed her own controlling nature.

Since she had a few minutes, she scrolled back to the dating sites she checked out the other day. It was time to get back out there. But she didn't know where to start. She glanced at Declan who was already flipping through different streaming services.

"You date a lot, right?" she asked. If she had a live-in expert, she might as well get some advice.

"Depends on what you mean by a lot, but by your standards, probably."

"By my standards?"

"No offense, but you're a divorced, single mom. Ty said you haven't had a boyfriend since Graham. He didn't think you'd dated at all."

"Single mom with unreliable ex. Anyway, which sites are the best for dating these days?"

"Again, depends on your purpose. Are you looking to date..." He glanced around. "Or to *date*?" he asked while executing a hip thrust.

"Hadn't given it much thought." *Liar.* Her libido had been doing plenty of thinking and if she recharged her vibrator too many more times, she'd be due for a replacement.

"A lot creeps online. Dudes who lie. Catfish. You might be better off just going to a bar."

"Seriously? That's your advice?"

"That's where I find most of my dates. You'd get some. You got this whole milf thing going for you." He waved a hand over her.

"Do not call me that."

"Why not? It's true."

"Milf is barely a step down from cougar and I'm not that old."

He took a pull on his beer. "Uh-uh. Milf is just another way of noticing a hottie. Just so happens she has a kid. But you're right that like a cougar, a milf can get all the D she wants because it's well-known strings-free. She doesn't want to get tied down with entanglements because the kid comes first."

"You're telling me that by virtue of having a child, it's a free pass to get laid whenever I want?"

He choked on his next sip of beer. "You're not that dense, Rennie. You've always had it goin' on. You just need to act on it. Any man with half a brain would want to tap that."

Her face flushed. She should not be having a conversation like this with Declan of all people.

"Well, I'm not sure I agree with you, but thank you. And on that note, it's time for me to go read a chapter of *Matilda* to my child."

She closed her laptop, set it on the table, and went to Sadie's room feeling pretty good. A compliment from Declan shouldn't count. It wasn't all that different than her brother telling her she was beautiful, but it had been a long time since any man looked at her like a woman, instead of like a mom and it was...nice.

Of course, now that she mentioned it to Declan, Tyler was bound to have a comment about her dating life. Maybe this weekend while Sadie was with Graham she'd go out for a few drinks and check out the dating pool.

She could at least dip her toes in the water.

CHAPTER
Six

Declan spent the rest of the week scrubbing and peeling wallpaper. It was tedious, but once he had all of it down in the living room, it was like he couldn't stop. The satisfaction of a bare wall made him continue. He continued right into the dining room.

He tried to be quiet, using earbuds instead of blasting a radio since Renee tended to work at the dining room table. He paused. Was his bedroom her office? It wasn't set up like one, but he couldn't help but think he'd taken her workspace.

Tugging out an earbud, he asked, "Is my room your office?"

She looked at him and blinked a couple of times as if processing his question. "No. It was Tyler's room when he was here."

"But it would be your office if you didn't have mooches like us."

She lifted a shoulder. "I hadn't thought about it. And I wouldn't call you a mooch. You've done more work in the past few days than I have in months."

"If you want to move in there, I can take the bed up to the attic or the basement."

"Don't be ridiculous. Those aren't living spaces."

He chuckled. "It won't be any different than Ronan's attic. Really not a big deal."

"I'm fine working at the table. Besides, I'm hoping it'll only be for a while longer. If I get a full-time job, I won't be doing this." She waved a hand over the papers and laptop she had in front of her.

"What about Sadie?" he asked. The look she shot him made him want to pull the words back.

"What about her?"

"She's only in school a couple of hours a day."

"And she'll be in daycare. Like millions of other kids. It doesn't make me a bad mom."

Ah, fuck. Now he stepped in it. "I didn't mean it like that. It's just..." He wasn't even sure what he was trying to say. "I see you guys together all the time. It seems like it would be hard."

"She's in school all day next year, so it's just this one that will be hard. Assuming I can even find anything full-time that will make it worth paying for daycare."

"I get it. My mom had a bunch of us. She always did hair in the basement. People came to her and she didn't have to pay a babysitter. I doubt she could've afforded one."

"But you have older brothers who could've watched you."

"They were too busy getting in trouble. So me and Nessa hung out a lot." He turned back to the wall, sprayed the solution, and scrubbed. "What time does Sadie go to her dad's today?"

"Whenever he comes to pick her up. It's supposed to be

before dinner, but if he's on a job or has something better to do, he's late. Why?"

"I figured I'd prep her room tonight so tomorrow, I can hit it hard and have it done before she comes back on Sunday. It's warm enough out that we can probably leave the windows open to air it out."

"Sounds good. Let me know what you need me to do and I'll get it done."

Renee returned to her numbers and Declan turned his music back up while he peeled away more ugly paper. Sadie came home and followed him around asking questions and wanting to help. Since he didn't think a five-year-old should touch the chemicals, he let her scrub ineffectively at a section of paper without solution on it.

"You have any fun plans with your dad this weekend?"

"I dunno. I wanna stay and help paint my room."

"I appreciate the offer, but painting a wall isn't nearly as much fun as painting a picture. Speaking of pictures. Do you have one of Super Sadie I can borrow?" He ripped at a piece of wallpaper and it came off in a huge chunk.

"Are you gonna hang it in your room?"

"I just want to show it to someone." He'd already asked Gavin to come over to paint one wall for Sadie. He thought it would be a good surprise.

Sadie ran off and came back with three pages. Drawing herself as a superhero had become a favorite pastime for the kid.

"Which one is your favorite?" he asked as he snapped photos of all three to send to Gavin. That turned out to be the right question because she launched into telling him stories about each picture. He was able to listen to her while pulling at wallpaper.

"Sadie, honey, Dad's going to be here soon. Do you have

your bag packed?" Renee came into the dining room, looked at the destruction, and cringed.

"I was talking to Declan, telling him about Super Sadie."

"Go get your bag. Don't forget to pack your toothbrush."

"What about *Matilda*?"

"You can bring the book if you want, but maybe Daddy has something else he wants to read."

"Nuh-uh. He only has baby books at his house."

"Picture books are not baby books. They still have great stories."

Sadie sighed and Declan stifled a laugh because even with her back turned to him, he knew she was rolling her eyes. She trudged out of the room toward her bedroom.

"You got your hands full with her. Attitude at five. Good luck at fifteen."

"Tell me about it." She tugged at a corner of ripped wall-paper. "After Sadie leaves, I'm going out with a couple friends. I assume you can fend for yourself with leftovers in the fridge. I already packed up a bunch of Sadie's room and moved the smaller things to my room so it's out of your way."

"I told you I'd get to it tonight."

"I know. But you're busy in here, so I got started."

He turned to look at her. She was fidgety. Almost nervous. "Something going on?"

She inhaled deeply and then huffed it out. "My friend Linda wants to go to a bar or club or something."

"Already gave up on the apps?"

"I barely started there."

"Shoot me a text if you decide to bring some dude back here. I'll make myself scarce."

She snickered. "Not likely to happen."

Not likely, but possible. For some reason, that didn't sit

well with him. Renee had had a tough time. He remembered when she and Graham first got serious. He and Tyler both knew Graham wasn't good enough for Renee, but they never said anything. He wondered if it would've made a difference.

"If you change your mind, seriously call. I don't want to hear any of that."

The doorbell rang.

"Daddy!" Sadie screeched as she tore through the house, backpack bouncing.

"Do not open that door," Renee called.

Sadie froze with her hand on the doorknob. "Who is it?"

"It's me."

Sadie shot a look over her shoulder as if to say See? She opened the door and Graham came in.

He scooped Sadie up and kissed her cheek. "Whoa. What's going on here?"

"Declan is working on the house so it's not so ugly," Sadie answered.

"Sadie," Renee warned.

"It's what you said. The house is good but ugly." She curled a lip as she looked at the walls. Then she turned to Declan. "It's still ugly."

"Sadie." Renee's voice was sharp.

"That's okay. It's supposed to be ugly now. It'll look better once I paint it."

"He's gonna paint my room when I'm with you," Sadie said to Graham.

Declan nodded to him. "Graham."

"Hey. It's been a while."

Like they'd ever been friends? Rather than comment, Declan just nodded again.

"Ready to go?" Graham asked.

"Wait!" Sadie yelled. "I need Larry."

Graham set her down so she could get her lion from her room. Declan still couldn't get over a kid naming her lion Larry.

Graham put his hands on his hips. "I can't believe you bought this shithole, Renee. What were you thinking?"

"I was thinking that I want my daughter to have a house with her own yard. A home."

"This looks stable to you? The place is torn apart, you have some stranger working here—"

Renee flicked up a hand to stop him. "First, Declan is not a stranger. I've known him most of my life—way longer than I've known you—and he's been in Sadie's life since birth."

"The house is not a shithole," Declan said quietly. "It's well built. It just needs some love."

"This has nothing to do with you. Stay out of it."

Declan put down the scraper and took a step toward Graham. Renee stepped between them. Although she was tall, Declan could still glare at Graham over her head.

"I don't need your opinion, Graham. It has no bearing on anything in my life. Why don't you go wait in the car and I'll send Sadie out?"

"Sadie deserves better than this." He waved a hand over the ripped walls. But then he turned and left.

"What the fuck, Renee? Why do you let him talk to you like that?" Declan asked.

Her shoulders sagged and she turned around. "There's nothing I can say to change who he is or what he says. I'm trying really hard to not let it affect me anymore."

"I got Larry. You made my room all messy, Mom. Where's Dad?"

"He's waiting in the car. You want me to walk you out?"

"Nope." She came closer and Renee squatted for a hug.

"Have fun with Dad. I'll see you on Sunday."

Sadie let go of Renee and then wrapped her arms around Declan's legs. "Want me to fly you to the car like Super Sadie?"

"Yeah." She jumped up and down and Declan scooped her up and put her on his shoulder.

Renee raced ahead of them and held the door open for them to fit through. He set Sadie down near the car. She climbed in on her own and buckled herself into her car seat. Declan said nothing, but he couldn't help but send another glare Graham's way.

LATER THAT NIGHT, RENEE STUMBLED UP HER FRONT STEPS. She was buzzed, maybe a little drunk. But what else did she have? The bar was a total bust. As she slid her key into the lock, she realized there was loud music coming from inside her house. What the hell? Was Declan having a party?

She pushed through the door and the living room was dark. So was the kitchen. The light in Sadie's room was on, so she headed there.

The smell of paint assaulted her as she entered the room. Declan's back was to her and he sang along with the radio, totally off-key, and unaware she was there. She started to laugh.

"Don't give up construction. You'll never make it as a singer."

He spun quickly at the sound of her voice, splattering

paint with the movement. Luckily, he'd covered Sadie's bed with a plastic tarp.

He reached over and lowered the radio. "You shouldn't sneak up on me like that."

"If the music wasn't so loud, you would've heard me come in." She looked at the walls. He must've been working the whole time she was gone. "It's really white," she said narrowing her eyes.

"It's primer. The color will go on tomorrow." He squinted at her. "Are you drunk?"

She held up her index and thumb close. "A little."

"Had a good night, then?"

"Hell, no. Your bar idea. Bad."

"What are you talking about?"

"One guy wanted to dance. His hands immediately landed on my ass uninvited. Another guy bought me a drink, and then wanted to meet in the bathroom so I could repay the favor."

"What kind of dive did you go to?"

"My friend picked it out. I should've stayed here. Could've helped you."

"I didn't need help. There's pizza in the kitchen if you're hungry."

"You ordered food? I told you there were leftovers in the fridge."

"Yeah, but I'd have to reheat something or eat it cold. Pizza is handed to me hot."

"Can I help with something?"

"Uh, no. Why don't you go have some water?"

She waved him off. "I'm fine."

Declan rolled the wall around the window. Renee watched, mesmerized by the rhythmic movement and sound.

"So is this what you want to do like for a career?

"Paint?"

"Construction. Paint. Whatever."

He shrugged. "It's what I know. Like they say, it's in my blood. My dad, my brothers. They all did construction at least for a while."

"But do you like it?"

"Most of the time."

"Then why don't you have a job?"

"Jeez, Rennie. Judgey?"

"I'm just asking. You obviously know what you're doing, so you're not an idiot who can't keep a job. Ty always makes it sound like you can't be bothered to work a regular job. I'm just wondering why." At this point, she was also wondering where her filter went.

"I never liked the idea of being tied down. I like my freedom. So I go wherever. Do whatever."

Renee couldn't help but think it sounded lonely. But he was also the same Declan she'd always known. Whenever Declan was around, everyone could count on having a good time. "It's late. Why don't you stop for the night and come watch some TV or something?"

"I am done. Let me clean this up and take a shower."

"You go take a shower and I'll clean up."

"Uh..."

"I'm buzzed, but I can handle cleaning some brushes and a roller." She shooed him. "Go."

She waited for him to leave, picked up the brushes and roller, and carried them to the kitchen sink. Running the water, she waited for it to get hot and then squeezed the brushes under the flow. The cool paint ran thick through her fingers. She knew the minute Declan started the shower because she lost some pressure.

Her mind wandered to Declan shirtless, in his boxers. He was a damn fine-looking guy. For as long as she'd known him, his dark hair was carelessly styled, as if he showered, shook off water like a dog, and then ran his fingers through it. So often, it flopped over his forehead and she wanted to push it back.

But it was the scruffy beard that got to her. It took away his boyishness. The charm was still there in his blue eyes and his grin, but now he was all man.

She shook her head. She could not think about her brother's best friend as anything other than that. She must've had more alcohol than she'd thought because while she could objectively see that Declan was good-looking, she never thought about him like that.

But tonight, as his muscles flexed while painting and he sang terribly, she thought about him standing up for her with Graham. For the first time in a long time, she had someone in her corner.

He might not have been the best choice because he definitely looked like he was about to hit Graham, but she'd been on her own for so long, anything was better than nothing.

She scrubbed at the brushes and roller and then set them to dry. The bar scene wasn't for her. She could accept that. She never liked it all that much when she was younger. Maybe she just needed to get out in the world more. With Sadie in school, she could go work in a coffee shop or something. Be around other people. She couldn't meet someone if she wasn't available to meet them, right?

And Declan assured her she had it going on. She snickered. Weird way to pay a compliment, but she'd take it.

Having Declan around was definitely good for her ego. The water in the bathroom shut off, so she grabbed a couple beers from the fridge and went to the living room. She plopped on the couch, turned on the TV, and waited for Declan.

He came in a few minutes later wearing basketball shorts and a T-shirt. She pointed to the beer on the table. "Grabbed you a drink."

"Thanks." He sat next to her and she handed him the remote. "You can pick."

"I don't care what we watch." She took a pull on her beer.

"You don't have to keep me company, you know. If there's something you'd rather do..."

She sighed. "I'm not keeping you company. You're keeping me company. I hate the weekends when Sadie's not here. The house is so quiet."

"So that's the deal with dating all of a sudden." He started scrolling through streaming services to look for something to watch.

"No. Yeah. Maybe. I mean, I am lonely, and having someone to date might be nice. But it's also time, you know? I've been divorced a long time. At least it feels long because as soon as we split, we were over even though it wasn't official."

"Are you saying you haven't dated *at all* since Graham?"

She sighed. "There were a couple of really lame dates."

"You haven't gotten laid in like two years?" He sputtered and his voice was obnoxiously loud.

She huffed again. "There were also a couple of less-than-stellar hook-ups. I decided my vibrator was a better use of my time."

Declan choked on his beer and then laughed. "I like this new Renee."

"What's new? This is who I've always been."

"Maybe. But you never let me see it. You always look at me like I'm your annoying little brother. Someone like that would never mention her vibrator."

"Point taken. I guess this is the first time I'm seeing you as a friend instead of Tyler's friend." She took another drink. "Thanks for all the help around here. It means a lot to me."

"We're doing each other a favor. I have a real bed to sleep in. I can hone my skills as a handyman. And I get to play with my favorite girl." He winked.

Renee blushed.

"I knew Sadie was cool, but hanging out with her this much makes me realize how awesome she is."

Yes. His favorite girl. Sadie. Her daughter. *Shut the fuck up, you stupid hormones.*

"She likes having you around, too. The work you're putting in is going to make this a real home for her. I can't top that by cooking you some meals."

"Hey. This is already a home because you're here. Kids don't remember ugly walls or bad water pressure. Not really. She'll remember having dinner with you and telling you about Super Sadie."

"How the hell do you know so much about kids?"

"Because I am one, right?"

It was her turn to snort. "Start the show already, you weirdo."

They watched some superhero show Declan picked out, and Renee didn't care because for a change, she wasn't lonely.

CHAPTER
Seven

Declan was up early Saturday morning. Not only was he determined to get Sadie's room done before she got back home, but he also knew Gavin would be there soon to work on the mural. He hoped it would be an awesome surprise for Sadie and Renee. He started a pot of coffee, surprised Renee wasn't already up and working. It seemed like she was always working.

He took his cup and went to Sadie's room to paint the base coat on the mural wall. With any luck, it would be dry by the time Gavin was ready to start. Once he got the bright blue paint on that wall, he went to refill his cup and see if Renee was awake. He didn't want to turn on the radio if she was sleeping in, but the silence was killing him.

She was sitting at the dining room table tapping away on her computer. She practically jumped when he walked by. "What are you doing up?"

"Painting. I told you I'd get Sadie's room done."

"Yeah, but it's really early."

"I know, lazy. I've already had a cup of coffee." He waved his mug at her. "How'd you think the coffee appeared?"

She shook her head. "I honestly didn't give it any thought. Weird. But thanks." She took a sip from her cup. "You need some help painting?"

"Nope. I got it. My brother Gavin is on his way to help."

"You don't need to recruit your family. I'm here and can help. It's not like painting takes some special skill."

He whistled as he poured his coffee. "Better not let Gavin hear you say that. As an artist, he might take offense."

"You know what I mean. Obviously, an artist has skills. Rolling paint on a wall is something anyone can do."

"Well, we got it covered either way. Continue with your boring numbers."

He hoped his nonchalant attitude wouldn't raise any flags. It would be hard to surprise her with a mural if she was in the room. On his way back to the bedroom, the doorbell rang, so he went to answer it. "It should be Gavin," he called, hoping to keep Renee where she was.

He swung the door open and said quietly, "Sadie's at her dad's but Renee is here, so don't mention the mural."

"Got it." Gavin handed Declan a bag of supplies.

Gavin paused and took a few steps toward the dining room. "Hey," he said. "I'm Gavin."

She turned and stood. "Nice to meet you. I'm Renee. I told Declan I'd help him paint, but he insisted he do it on his own." She shot Declan a look. "Thanks for helping him."

"No problem. I like painting."

"Declan mentioned you're an artist. Is paint your medium?"

"Sometimes."

"Come on," Declan said.

Gavin offered a little wave. "Just wanted to introduce myself."

"See you later."

Declan took the supplies to the bedroom and then stuck his head back out the door. "Hey, is the radio going to bother you?"

"Only if you put on crap," she yelled back.

He smiled and closed the door. Gavin was already sketching with a pencil on the wall. In addition to the pictures of Super Sadie Declan also sent a couple of Sadie, so Gavin would know what to work toward. His brother already had pages sketched out and worked to copy them to the wall. Although the lines showed a human shape, he had no idea how Gavin would make it look like Sadie.

It took a lot of concentration to not watch Gavin and paint the other walls instead. Watching his brother create a piece of art was fascinating. He turned on the music but kept it to a normal level. "Music okay with you?" he asked.

Gavin nodded without turning around. "It's fine."

They worked in silence for a bit. Then Gavin asked, "So how are you really doing?"

"Fine."

"I don't need the bullshit answer you give Brendan and Ronan. You don't have a job and you're homeless."

Hearing that stung. "I've been that way on and off for years. It's nothing new. And I have a place to live. This is a good gig. I work on Renee's house, and I live for free."

"But it's not long-term." He suddenly turned around. "Unless...You and Renee?"

"Nah. It's not like that. We're friends."

"You're not the kind of guy who's *just friends* with anyone that hot."

"Don't know what to tell you. We are." He shrugged. But Gavin was right. He'd never been friends with a woman who he also wasn't sleeping with, at least occasionally.

"What I was getting at, though, was how you're doing with all the shit about Dad."

"What's there to do? He's dead."

Gavin leaned against the plastic-covered dresser. "But you'd thought he ran off."

"I was wrong. Or so Cahill says anyway."

"You don't believe him?"

"I believe him, but I get where Ronan is coming from. For Alan Cahill to make some dying declaration to let us know Dad is dead but not give us any information about what happened or where his body is...it's shitty."

"He and Brendan are working to find the answers, but having those answers won't change how you feel, will it?"

Declan set the roller down. "No. I'm pissed off. Getting answers won't change that, but there's nothing I can do about it. I spent most of my life thinking Dad didn't want us. That he ditched us to have freedom. So be it. But now..."

Gavin nodded. "Your whole worldview has shifted."

Declan didn't respond. Gavin often said things that made little sense to him. But this time, something rang true.

"You've been running for more than a decade, little brother. We all see it."

"I'm just like him. Is that what you're saying?"

"Not like him. He didn't leave, remember?"

"I thought he did. So, what? I've been trying to be like him?"

Gavin shook his head. "No. More like an effort to *not* be like him. No way to let anyone down if you don't let them in."

Damn. He knew Gavin was right. He'd never voiced the decision to remain free, but he guessed he wasn't as complex a person as he'd thought. He turned to roll the next section of wall. Out of the corner of his eye, he saw Gavin pick up his pencils.

"You obviously don't want to talk about it, so I'll drop it," he started, "but what now? Now that you know he didn't run, that your view of a man, husband, and father is different than you'd imagined, how do you picture your life?"

I don't have a fucking clue. He couldn't say it out loud. It made him feel even more like a loser. But it was the reason he'd decided to move in here, so he could figure his shit out. Having his brother point out all of his flaws wasn't helping.

By THE TIME LUNCH HIT, RENEE WAS FEELING PRETTY GOOD. The music Declan played was loud enough to be background sound for her, but quiet enough that she wasn't distracted. She's managed to wrap up all of her work so tomorrow, she could have a full day off. In celebration, she popped open a beer and knocked on the bedroom door to see if Declan and Gavin wanted lunch.

The door opened a couple of inches, and Declan peeked out.

"Would you guys like a sandwich? Maybe some beer?"

"Sounds good."

"Why are you acting so weird? Open the door."

"Nope." He shifted, gripping the door tighter as if she'd try to push her way in. "It's a surprise."

"So help me God, Declan, if I come in there and you've painted polka dots or crazy stripes all over, I'm gonna kill you."

He gave her a broad smile, his eyes light with excitement. "It's a good surprise. Trust me."

"I don't."

Without releasing the door, he put a hand to his chest. "Hurtful, Rennie."

Then he slammed the door in her face.

"What kind of sandwiches?"

"Whatever you got is good with us," he answered from behind the closed door.

She went to the kitchen to make sandwiches, all the way reminding herself, as Declan had, that it was just paint. It was no big deal, no matter how hideous he might've made it.

After making lunch for both guys and herself, she set everything on the dining room table and called for Declan.

She knew when he opened the door because the music got louder. A few moments later they joined her.

"Is it safe for me to leave the door open or are you going to try to peek?" Declan asked.

"I'm not a child. While I don't like surprises, I can wait." She pointed at the sandwiches.

Gavin sat and said, "Thanks."

They each popped open their beers. "Is there anything I can do to help in Sadie's room? My work for the day is done, so I've got the rest of today and tomorrow to accomplish something on the house."

"Being sneaky by offering help isn't getting you in Sadie's room faster."

"I'm not being sneaky. I'm offering to work."

He looked around the dining room. "You can pick up where I stopped in here getting the wallpaper off."

She forced a smile. "Sounds tedious, but I'll be thrilled once this room is painted instead."

"When we're done eating, I'll show you what to do."

She studied Gavin. Seeing the two of them together, she could tell they were brothers, but if she'd seen Gavin on the street, she wouldn't have picked him out to be a Doyle. His face was a little rounder than Declan's. He was built similarly, and he had a full beard instead of Declan's trim scruffy one. But the eyes proved they were family. She wasn't sure what it was. The color? Sure. But it was like there was always a hint of amusement in them.

"So how did Declan rope you into helping him with my daughter's bedroom?"

"He asked. I wasn't busy. And I'm a better painter than he is."

Declan shoved his brother's arm. "I'm painting way faster than you are."

"Speed isn't everything."

"Whatever."

The rest of their short lunch was spent chatting and joking about inconsequential things. Renee had forgotten how much fun it was to have other people around to talk to. She spent so much time alone, it was easy to slip into a solitary lifestyle—not including her daughter, of course. But real adult conversation? With swearing and inappropriate jokes? Hardly ever happened in her life these days. By the time they finished eating, her face hurt from smiling so much.

Gavin disappeared into the bedroom, but Declan stayed behind to give her a tutorial on removing wallpaper.

She clapped her hands. "Okay. Let's do this."

"It's tedious but not difficult. Spray the solution on. Use a generous amount. Let it soak in for a bit. Then use this scrubber to score marks into the paper. It doesn't look like much but the edges are sharp. Then use the flat edge here to scrape away."

He demonstrated all the steps on a small section of the wall.

"Seems simple enough. Thanks for the explanation." She took the supplies from him. "And you can leave the door open so I can hear the music, too. I promise to announce myself if I get close to the room."

"Okay." He stepped away and then added, "It looks good on you."

"What?"

"The smile. You don't do that too much, and you should."

"Thanks, I guess."

"I'm going to finish painting. Yell if you need anything."

Renee focused on spraying and scrubbing and scraping. She'd watched Declan take off huge chunks of paper when he was doing it earlier in the week, but she had a miserable pile of beige scraps. She wondered if the paper had originally been beige or if it was just age. The texture was weird, and she was happy to see it go. If only it'd go faster. She tried using more solution, then less. Then more but leaving it on longer. It seemed like if she could just get the right combination, she could peel away a sheet of paper.

When the doorbell rang, it caught her off guard. She wasn't expecting anyone. She picked up her beer and drank as she headed through the living room. She opened the door to find Sadie and Graham standing there.

"Mommy!" Sadie threw her arms wide and crashed into her.

Renee automatically returned the embrace with her free hand. She shot Graham a look. "Sweetie, go into the kitchen, please. Declan is working on your room and I don't want you in there yet."

"Can I have a cookie?"

"Did you eat lunch?"

"Yeah."

"Fine." Once Sadie ran through the house, she turned on Graham. "What the hell are you doing here? You're supposed to have her until tomorrow after dinner."

"I know. But she said she missed you and wanted to come home."

"So what? Be a fucking parent, Graham."

"What? Are you saying you don't want our daughter to be at home? You're too busy drinking on a Saturday afternoon to care for her?"

"First, it's my Saturday. Second, I always—and we both know I mean *always*—take care of my daughter. This is bullshit."

"I'm sorry. I didn't know what else to do with her. She was bored at my place and said she wanted to be with you." He paused and ran a hand over his light brown hair. "And I know this isn't the best timing, but I can't take her next weekend."

"What?"

"I can't take her."

"Why the hell not? You agreed to switch weekends with me because it's Mariah's wedding. I won't be here."

"I figured you could ask your mom or Tyler to babysit."

"Are you fucking kidding me right now? I hardly ever ask you to take my weekend and I do it for you all the time." She flung an arm out behind her. "Case in point."

"Don't be a bitch, Renee. You know I don't have family to step in to help."

She held up a hand to stop the conversation before she

SHANNYN SCHROEDER

totally lost her shit. "You know what? Whatever. But plan to have her for your regular weekend—for the whole weekend."

"Thanks."

She couldn't even muster a response. She just closed the door in his face. Some days she had a hard time remembering what she ever saw in him. After taking a deep breath and draining her beer, she turned to the kitchen.

Sadie sat at the table munching a cookie. "I told Daddy you were gonna be mad."

"I'm not mad."

"Yeah, you are." She furrowed her brow and said, "You look like this."

Renee knew Sadie's expression was spot on, so she forced her face to smooth out. "Well, I'm not mad at you. Why did you tell Daddy you wanted to come home?"

Sadie's mouth slipped open, but she said nothing for a minute. "I said I was excited to come home because Declan promised to paint my room. I wanted to help."

Renee crossed her arms. "So you didn't tell Daddy you were bored and wanted to be with me?"

"Weeeelll, his house is boring, but I didn't say it cuz you said it's not nice to say stuff like that. But I didn't say I wanted to be with you. I don't think."

"Okay, baby."

"Is my room done? I wanna see."

"Declan is still working on it and I don't think he's going to let us in. He said it's a surprise."

That word acted like a fire under her kid. "In coming!" Renee yelled as she chased Sadie down the hall to her room. Sadie stopped to pound on the door.

As he did before, Declan opened it a crack. His eyes

72

widened to see Sadie standing there. "Sadie, my lady, what are you doing here?"

"I wanna see my room! Mom said it's a surprise."

"It is. Right now, no girls allowed."

The look of utter shock on her daughter's face made Renee laugh.

"But it's my room and I'm a girl."

"You and your mom can come in when we're done."

"Come on, Sadie. We don't need those stinky boys to have fun. Let's go put your stuff in my room because I think you're gonna have to sleep in there tonight. And then we'll bake some cupcakes."

"Yay! With blue frosting?"

"Maybe."

Sadie ran off again to grab her overnight bag.

Declan was still standing in the doorway. "I thought she was at Graham's until tomorrow."

"Yeah, she was supposed to be. Welcome to my world." She crossed her arms. "I really don't want to talk about Graham right now. Or maybe ever."

"Save us some blue cupcakes," he said with a smile.

"Only if you're lucky."

Once again, he closed the door on her, this time laughing as he did. Renee went to the kitchen to wait for Sadie and texted her mom to see if she could watch Sadie for Mariah's wedding. Graham had always been unreliable, but this one took the cake. He knew she was in the bridal party. It wasn't just any social engagement for her.

She'd tried hard to preserve any relationship Sadie would have with him, but he was making it difficult.

As Sadie bounced into the room, Renee tucked away all those thoughts and focused on enjoying the time with her daughter.

CHAPTER
Eight

Declan had the walls done, both coats and was finishing up the trim around the windows when Gavin said, "I think this is it. What do you think?"

He'd been watching his brother paint the mural of Super Sadie all day, so he knew what to expect, but seeing it completed was nothing short of amazing. The portrait was no caricature. It was so realistic, he could almost hear Sadie's laugh. Super Sadie wore purple and her yellow cape fluttered behind her. Her hair flowed with it. The mural was alive with movement. "Dude. I guess you really are talented."

"Shut up, fucker. Is this what you're looking for?"

He clapped his brother on the shoulder. "She's gonna love it."

"Hey, guys," Renee called from the hall. "Dinner will be here in about ten minutes."

Declan peeked out the door. "Sounds good. Send Sadie in."

Renee crossed her arms again. "Does that mean I can finally see what you've been doing in there?"

"It's a surprise for Sadie."

Renee rolled her eyes. "Sadie, Declan has something to show you."

Sadie zoomed around the corner and hopped up and down in front of the door. "Is it done?"

"Yep." Declan eased the door open a little more to let Sadie in.

"Seriously?" Renee said.

"Give us two minutes."

Sadie walked into the room and inspected the walls, nodding her head in approval, as if she were appraising the space. Her curls bounced with each movement. Then she turned to where Gavin stood in front of the mural. He stepped aside. Her jaw dropped, and her eyes opened so wide they practically filled her face. Then she squealed in such a high pitch that both Declan and Gavin cringed. Of course, the sound also summoned her mother.

Renee burst through the door, and Sadie ran at her, jumping into her arms. "Look, Mommy! It's me!"

She pointed at the wall and Renee stepped closer, her eyes matching her daughter's. Sadie slipped down her body and moved right in front of the picture. Striking the same pose as Super Sadie, with legs wide and fists on her hips, she said, "See?"

"I see, baby." Renee looked at Declan with tears in her eyes. "This is amazing." She turned to Gavin. "I can't afford to pay you for this, and it's way more than helping your brother paint a wall. This is stuff you get commissioned for."

Gavin waved her off. "I don't do these kinds of commissions. And as for payment," he added, pointing at Sadie

SHANNYN SCHROEDER

who was ogling the bigger version of herself, "that right there covers it."

"Thank you." Renee wrapped her arms around his brother.

Declan felt a stab of jealousy, which made zero sense. "Hey, it was my idea, and he gets the hug?"

She pulled away and smiled at him. "He did the work. But you can have a hug, too, if it'll make you feel better."

Declan spread his arms comically wide, but Renee was all straight-faced. As he wrapped her in his arms, the scent of her shampoo curled into him, making him want to inhale deeper.

She whispered, "I can never repay you for what you're doing here. You are making her feel like the most important little girl in the world."

"In my life, she is." He rubbed her back because she sounded like she might start crying. He couldn't remember if he and Renee had ever hugged before. They must've, for as long as they'd known each other. But this didn't feel like he was hugging his best friend's sister. It was...different.

The doorbell rang and Renee jolted from his arms. "That's dinner. Go wash up so we can eat."

She dodged making eye contact as she turned to Sadie. "You can admire yourself later. Go wash your hands."

After they left, Declan moved through the room, gathering the supplies to clean them up.

Gavin cleared his throat. "I thought you said nothing was going on between you two."

"It's not."

"Then what was that?" he said, circling his arm where Declan and Renee had hugged.

"She was thanking me for doing the work."

Gavin responded with a raised eyebrow.

"Look, I don't have the whole story, but I think she's had a shitty time of it since her divorce. Graham was always a tool, but it seems worse. He was supposed to have Sadie all weekend, but she's back already. That should tell you something."

"That you've been cockblocked by a kindergartener?"

"I told you, Renee and I are friends. We've known each other forever."

"Looks to me like things are changing in these close quarters."

"You don't know what you're talking about."

"If you say so." They gathered the brushes and rollers and packed up Gavin's stuff.

The whole time, Declan considered his brother's words. He'd been living with Renee for only a couple weeks. They talked and joked, but their relationship had always been that way. Maybe he needed to go out and have some fun away from the house. Have a few drinks, hook up with a woman for the night. It would set him straight and he wouldn't have any different thoughts about Renee.

"You want to go out tonight?"

"Haven't you spent enough time with me today?"

"I'm thinking about going out for a few drinks, having some fun."

They carried the brushes to the kitchen sink to clean up. Renee and Sadie were already at the dining room table.

"You can toss those in the sink. I can wash them after dinner," Renee said.

"It's okay. I got this." He ran the water and looked at Gavin. "You in?"

"Why not? It's been a while since we hung out."

"Cool. Go eat. This isn't a two-man job." While he scrubbed brushes and rollers, he thought about where they could go. Somewhere with cheap booze and fun women. That's exactly what he needed.

LATE SUNDAY MORNING, RENEE WAS DOING HER BEST NOT TO be totally bitchy, but she was failing miserably. After a long ass night of sharing her bed with Sadie who rolled and kicked and slept sideways, Renee was exhausted. At least the paint smell was clear and Sadie could move back into her own room tonight.

Declan went out last night and never came back. That shouldn't have irritated her, but it did. She wasn't even sure why. She didn't expect him to work weekends, and he had in order to get Sadie's room done. But since he hadn't come home—back—this wasn't his *home*, she was trying to return Sadie's room to order. Because she was so tired, the furniture felt even heavier than normal.

Just before lunch, as she started to drag the dresser to its new home on the wall adjacent to Super Sadie, she heard the front door open and Sadie greet Declan.

"Hey, Sadie, my lady. How's it going?"

Sadie said something suspiciously quiet, which meant she didn't want Renee to hear. Renee inhaled deeply and closed her eyes for a brief moment. Then she continued to shift the dresser.

"Hey," Declan said from the doorway. "I told you I'd move this back."

He hurried over and bear-hugged the dresser to move it.

"I didn't know when you were coming back. You obviously found someplace else to spend the night." She hated the bitchy sound of her words. She huffed. "Sorry. I'm just tired. I have to get this back in order because having Sadie in my bed for another night might kill me."

"That sweet little thing?"

"She kicks. A lot."

"You could've moved to my room."

"I figured you'd be in your room at some point." *Still sounding bitchy, Renee.* Maybe she should take a nap.

Her tone didn't bother Declan, though. He smiled over his shoulder and said, "I don't mind sharing. And I would never kick you."

"Thanks for the offer, but I'm trying to be more discerning with who I share my bed with."

"Ouch, Rennie. Why do you insist on hurting me?"

He was so overdramatic that she couldn't help but laugh.

"Go take a nap. I'll finish this up."

"It's fine. If we work together, it'll go faster. I'm not trying to eat up your whole weekend. I really appreciate you getting this done as fast as you did. It's not your fault Graham is a shitty father who would rather do anything than hang out with his kid."

"So he just dumped her off?"

"Yep."

"What if you weren't home? You could've pretended, right?"

"I suppose. But then he'd call and offer to meet up with me." She shook her head. "Every time he does it, he plays it off like Sadie is so unhappy at his house and she begs to come home. He knows I won't refuse her."

"Maybe you should."

They each grabbed a side of the bed and slid it back into place.

"It would just cause a fight and I'm done with that shit with him. I can't muster up any more fucks to give. I wanted to have a baby—which he was quick to point out throughout our marriage—so I don't care if she's here. I hate the uncertainty. I can't make plans or dates because he's so unpredictable." She straightened the blankets and fluffed the pillows as she talked.

"If you have plans for tonight, I'm here. I can babysit."

She smiled. "Thanks for the offer, but something tells me that having you babysit on a school night might not be a wise choice. You're a rule breaker."

"I can follow rules."

She barked out a laugh. "I'm not saying you're a bad guy because you're not. And I totally trust you with my daughter. But fun is more important to you than anything, and I imagine that I'd come home and Sadie would be hopped up on caffeine and sugar at midnight watching a horror movie."

Her example was specific because that was exactly what happened when they were kids. She was supposed to keep an eye on Declan and Tyler. They weren't as young as Sadie but no one trusted them to be left alone. They pretended to be asleep, and when she went to her room, they broke out snacks and movies. They stayed up all night and she got yelled at.

He didn't miss a beat and knew exactly what she was referring to. "I told you that was Tyler's idea. But it was a good time. We didn't care how much trouble we got into. It was worth it."

He gave her the grin that she was sure had gotten far too many people into trouble with him. "Sometimes, breaking the rules is worth it."

"And some of us can't afford to do that, no matter how fun it might seem."

"You can't be serious all the time either."

"I'm not." Was she? She and Sadie had fun. Maybe it was controlled, scheduled fun but still fun.

"Whatever you say, babe."

"Don't call me babe."

"It's just a term. Like dude. Didn't mean anything by it. Plus, it wasn't Rennie."

"Ugh." Maybe she should go take a nap. Her irritation was growing by the minute and he didn't deserve to be on the receiving end of her wrath. It was Graham who caused Sadie to be in her bed last night not Declan. "I think you're right. I'm going to lay down."

"I'll hang with Sadie."

"You don't have to. I'll have her put in a movie and sit on the couch with me." The tension in her shoulders eased. "I'm sorry. I'm being bitchy and you don't deserve it. Life is just...a lot right now."

"It's all good."

"Did you and Gavin have a good time last night?"

"Sure. Until the boyfriend of the woman Gavin was hitting on showed up. They were ready to brawl, so I had to drag my brother from the bar. We went back to his place and finished a bottle of whiskey."

"Oh." She'd assumed he picked up a woman. "Doesn't sound like a whole lot of fun."

"It was good to hang out with Gavin. We talked a lot about family stuff. You know, my dad and all. But yeah, not the wild party you were probably imagining." As he talked, he folded the last couple of tarps and laid them in the corner.

"You do have a reputation."

"Says who? Tyler?"

"Where else would I get my information?"

He stopped what he was doing with the tarps and crossed his arms. "A year ago, sure. But like you said, life right now is a lot. Part of the reason I'm here is because I need to figure things out."

Again, she felt like shit for the way she'd been thinking about him and the assumptions she kept making. "Take all the time you need. We're not going anywhere."

She headed toward the door. "Besides, this house needs a lot of work."

She heard his laughter all the way down the hall. "Sadie, pick out a movie. I'm gonna lay down for a bit."

"Yay." Sadie curled up behind Renee's legs on the couch and Renee closed her eyes. She needed to find better balance and relying on Declan for too much wasn't a smart move, no matter how good he was.

CHAPTER
Nine

Declan finished putting Sadie's room to rights and considered the rest of his day. He had nothing planned, and since last night was a bust, he wasn't going to try again. Besides, he'd been having fun hanging out here with Renee. He'd never been much of a homebody. He liked to go out and be with people, but maybe he was getting old because sitting on the couch, having a couple beers, and watching TV with Renee the other night had been pretty perfect.

He took the tarps from Sadie's room. When he got to the living room where he planned to drop them off in preparation for painting there, Sadie held a finger to her lips to tell him to be quiet. She sat behind Renee's legs and Renee was sound asleep.

"You want to go out to play?"

Sadie's eyes lit up, but then she frowned. "Mom said watch a movie. I can't go outside by myself."

"You won't be by yourself. I'll be there."

She jolted and then slowed her movements to climb off the couch. "Sure Mom won't get mad?"

"Yeah. Don't worry about it. Let's go have some fun."

Sadie carefully picked up the remote and paused her movie. Then she took Declan's hand like it was the most natural movement in the world.

"You should grab your jacket just in case."

She pulled her jacket from the hook near the front door and slid her arms in. Declan led the way out the back door. He hadn't looked at the yard yet, and he didn't know what he was expecting, but this was kind of sad. He clapped his hands. "Okay. What do you want to play?"

"I dunno."

"What do you usually do out here?"

"Nothing. I don't play here. There's nothing to do."

"Where do you usually play?"

"Mom takes me to the park."

Declan stared at her for a moment and debated. Had he just been scammed into going to a park? "Do you know where the park is?"

She shrugged and smiled. "We pass the green house and then the yard with the big dog. He jumps at us and barks real loud."

"Okay. Let's leave a note for your mom and then we'll try to find it."

They went inside and he left a note on the table by the remote and used his phone to try to find the closest park. Once they were down the front steps, he turned right.

Sadie tugged his hand. "This way."

He glanced at his phone, but she seemed sure, so he let her lead the way. At each corner, she paused and looked thoughtfully in each direction.

"You don't have any idea where we're going do you?"

"I thought so, but..." Her face screwed up tight, and he was afraid she was going to start crying.

"Hey, it's okay. We're on an adventure. Let's explore. There's nothing that says we have to go to the same park. Maybe we'll find something better."

She relaxed and took his hand again.

"What did you do with your dad this weekend?"

"Nothing."

"Come on. You must've done something."

"We had a snack and watched a movie. He doesn't have good books for story time at his house."

"Why don't you bring the book you read with your mom?"

"I did that one time but..." She looked up at him with wide eyes and lowered her voice. "Daddy's not as good as Mom at reading the stories. He just says the words. No voices or anything."

"Did you ask him to do voices?"

"No. But I never ask Mom." She tugged his hand again. "Look!"

He followed her pointed finger. They found a school playground. It wasn't a park but it would do. "Is that your school?"

"Nuh-uh."

They crossed the street. "What do you want to play on?"

"Can you teach me to do the monkey bars?"

"I don't know."

"You can't do them either?"

He stretched his arms above his head. "I used to be able to, but I haven't in a long time."

He reached up, took a bar, keeping his knees bent so his feet wouldn't drag, and swung down the line. Like riding a bike.

Sadie hopped up and down. "Like that. I wanna do it."

"Come here." He lifted her so she could grab a bar. Then

he paused and thought about how to explain the movement. "Now you want to swing your body like a monkey and reach for the next bar."

"I'll fall."

"I've got you." He kept his hands on her hips and helped her swing. "Reach!"

She hung there, stuck between the two bars. "Now what?"

"Doing monkey bars is about momentum."

"Huh?"

"You have to keep moving. If you stop, that's when you lose your grip."

Her eyes widened in fear.

"I'm still here. You're not going anywhere." He sighed. "Let go a second."

He set her back on the ground. "Watch me again."

This time he talked through how he swung and kept momentum. He dropped down at the end. "Got it?"

Her eyes were wide, but she said, "Maybe."

He lifted her again and held her as she swung. They went down the line and back. On the third trip, she told him to let go. Declan didn't like the idea, but he did.

On the third rung, she slipped and hit the ground. He braced for tears, but Sadie stood, her face pinched in anger. She looked so much like Renee that he almost laughed.

"I want to try again."

"Go ahead." He lifted her, figuring they would work on getting started another day.

Another day? While he'd known Sadie her whole life, he wasn't a regular part of it. He was right now, but this wasn't supposed to be a forever thing. He shook his head. Sadie had made it down the line and was dangling from the last rung.

"Now what?" she yelled.

"Let go. Drop to your feet, but keep your knees bent a little."

She dropped. As soon as her feet hit the ground, she fell back on her ass. He leaned over her and held out a hand to help her up.

"You did a great job. I'm impressed. You mastered the monkey bars in one day." He yanked her up.

"Not really. I can't get up by myself and I fell."

"Falling is part of learning. Ready to head back home? I don't want your mom to worry."

"I want a snack. I can't wait to tell Mom about the monkey bars."

They walked back to the house with Sadie chattering the entire way. Declan just smiled and agreed with whatever she said. She didn't seem to be looking for input.

RENEE JOLTED AWAKE WHEN THE FRONT DOOR OPENED. FOR A moment she was disoriented as she realized Sadie's movie was paused and she wasn't sitting by her on the couch. Then she saw the note from Declan at the same time Sadie ran into the room.

"We went on an adventure!"

"Did you now?" Renee asked, rubbing her face to fully awaken.

Sadie climbed up onto her lap. "Declan wanted to go to the park, but I couldn't remember the way and he said it was an adventure. Then we found a park and he taught me how to swing on the monkey bars. And I did it all the way. I fell once, but then I tried again like you always tell me to. Declan says I mastered it but I don't know how to get up yet, so I need more practice."

Renee blinked at the vomit of information. How long had she been asleep? "It sounds like you had a lot of fun with Declan. Go wash your hands and you can have a snack."

She ran off to the bathroom and Renee looked at Declan who stood there with his hands in the front pocket of his jeans. "You didn't have to take her to the park."

"We went to the yard, but your yard sucks. There's nothing to do out there."

"No, I mean, you didn't have to do anything with her. She would've been fine hanging out here watching her movie."

"I know. But you were really tired."

"She's not your responsibility. You should be out doing your own thing, having fun."

"Who says I didn't have fun? Sadie is a great conversationalist. I hardly had to do anything."

Renee laughed. "She is a talker." She stood and stretched, her neck feeling tight from sleeping in a weird position on the couch. "Are you going to be here for dinner?"

"Depends. What are you making?"

She rolled her eyes as she considered what she had on hand. "I'm thinking the ever-popular chicken nuggets for your friend Sadie, but I can do some stir fry or pasta for us."

"I was kidding. You could totally feed me chicken nuggets and I'd be good."

"Well, I'm not, so pick. Pasta or stir fry?"

"Whatever sounds good to you."

She went to the kitchen to start dinner. Since it had

been a busy weekend with a lot of upheaval, Renee let Sadie sit in the living room and watch some TV while they ate. She and Declan sat on the couch with their stir fry. It was one of Renee's go-to meals since it only required dirtying one pan.

"Mmm. This is really good," Declan said.

"Are you sure? I could always toss in some more nuggets."

"Chicken nuggets are better," Sadie chimed in.

"I don't know, Sadie. Your mom's a really good cook. Have you even tried this?"

"Nuh-uh." She wrinkled her nose as she did every time Renee offered her something different.

"Come on. Today is all about adventures, remember? We wandered around, tried a new park...you should try some new food."

Sadie huffed but turned around, opened her mouth, and closed her eyes. Renee sat in total shock. This man was the child whisperer.

He stabbed some meat and vegetables and put them in Sadie's mouth. Sadie chewed without opening her eyes. Renee half expected her to spit it out but she didn't.

Once she swallowed, Declan asked, "It's good, right?"

"It's okay. Nuggets are still better."

"But maybe next time, you can have a little stir fry with your nuggets."

Sadie bit into a nugget and squinted her eyes as she chewed thoughtfully. "Maybe."

Renee smiled and shook her head. To Declan, she mouthed *thank you*.

He leaned back on the couch. "I told you, Rennie, women find me irresistible."

She had no doubt.

As Declan helped her clear the dishes, he said, "So I've been thinking about your yard."

"What about it?" she asked as she filled the sink.

"It sucks."

"You told me earlier."

He stepped closer and lowered his voice. "I think we should build Sadie something out there. Swings or monkey bars. Something."

"That's sweet of you, but I can't consider that until at least the spring. There are too many other things that need to happen around here first."

"It's free labor."

"You can't build an entire playset on your own. Plus there's the cost of materials." She turned to face him. Placing a hand on his chest, she added, "I appreciate it. I really do. But I have to be realistic about what I can do."

"Okay." He turned away and instead of leaving the room, he picked up a towel and started drying dishes.

"You don't have to."

"I know." They didn't say anything else.

After cleaning up from dinner, Renee gave Sadie a quick bath and had her lay out her clothes for school. Renee settled back on the couch to read more of the book she needed to finish for book club. It was a good historical romance about two people who didn't want to get married but whose families were pressuring them. So they hatched a plan to marry each other in name only so they could each live their own lives. Renee was woefully behind because she'd been so busy with the house, and book club was Tuesday night.

"Five more minutes, Sadie. Then it's brushing teeth time."

"Okay."

Renee rolled her neck again to ease some of the tension.

"Are you okay?" Declan asked.

"Yeah, why?"

"You keep twisting your neck and I'm hearing some weird pops."

"Ha-ha. I slept funny on the couch. My muscles are a little tight."

"I knew that was gonna happen. That's why I told you to go to bed."

"It's normally not a big deal. I think I was just super tired."

He set his beer on the table and said, "Come here." He patted the cushion between his legs.

She huffed.

"Get your mind out of the gutter. Back to me and I'll rub the kinks out of your neck."

"I'm fine."

"No, you're not. Come on."

She sighed. A neck massage sounded great. "Fine."

As she shifted over, she told Sadie to go brush her teeth. She set her ereader on the table beside his beer and sat stiffly in front of Declan.

When his hands grasped her shoulders, she sucked in a breath.

"Problem?"

"No," she answered quietly.

Declan's fingers dug into the sore muscles of her neck and shoulder. "You're tight."

"That's what he said," she said with a chuckle.

He laughed behind her, his breath brushing across her neck. "Good one."

His thumbs press up the back of her neck, causing her to groan. It immediately relaxed her. Her head lolled forward as he worked some kind of magic. Then he hit some point in her shoulder and all she could do was moan, "Oh, God."

"That's what she said," he responded.

It was supposed to be light banter between friends, but with his breath coasting along her skin, it didn't *feel* friendly. She released a long, slow breath. This was getting out of hand. Between the steamy scenes of her book and not having been touched by a man in far too long, her libido was getting away from her. She should stop this. She *needed* to stop this.

But it still felt so damn good.

"Okay, Mommy. All brushed."

Renee stiffened again. She blinked and slid carefully away from Declan. "All right. Let's go read." She stood and took Sadie's hand. As she headed out of the room, she looked over her shoulder, and said, "Thanks."

"Any time." He winked and picked up his beer.

She had no idea how to read him. Her imagination was not doing her any favors. Declan would not be flirting with her. They were friends. They'd known each other most of their lives. He was her brother's best friend. Her *younger* brother. There. That thought was enough to douse her hormones.

She just needed to keep reminding herself.

CHAPTER
Ten

Declan took a long swig of beer. He should kiss Sadie for interrupting his impromptu massage. He didn't know what was going on. He'd been friends with plenty of women over the years. He knew how to be platonic. *And this was Renee.* He shook his head and set his bottle back on the table.

He picked up her ereader and swiped the screen. He started reading and two pages in, he was engrossed. He didn't know what the hell the story was about, but he knew when a couple was circling each other when they were hot and bothered. Lady Whoever she was had spent the better part of the first page checking out this Duke dude. When he asked her to dance, though, she got all snarky. Sure sign she was into him.

After a glare from her aunt, however, the lady conceded. No matter how stiff she tried to be, she liked being in his arms.

"What are you doing?"

Renee's voice startled him and he nearly dropped the ereader. "Hey. Sadie asleep?"

"She will be in a minute. What are you doing with my ereader?" She reached out as if to take it from him.

He lifted a shoulder. "It was sitting here and I wanted to see what you were reading."

"My book club book."

"Your book club reads porn?"

"It is *not* porn." Now she did snatch it back. "It's historical romance."

"And the difference is?"

"This is a story with complex characters who learn to fall in love with each other. It's not just about sex. It's not a pool boy coming to service the pipes."

He snickered. "But they do get it on, don't they?"

"I suppose they will. Could you imagine spending your life with someone and *not* having sex? I didn't think so." She huffed and plopped back onto the corner in the opposite corner, as far from him as possible.

"I was just teasing. It's really good. Tell me about it."

"No."

She pulled her feet up on the cushion and swiped the screen.

"I want to know. I didn't know what was going on, but Lady What's-Her-Face was playing games with the duke. She's got the hots for him but doesn't want him to know."

She looked over at him with an arched brow. "How much of this did you read?"

"I don't know. It was good. Explain it to me."

"Seriously? You're not asking just so you can make fun of it?"

"No. I want to know what Lady Whatever has against the duke."

She paused a minute and stared at him, probably waiting to see if he was joking. "Fine."

Putting the ereader on the couch between them, she launched into an explanation that was so detailed, he felt as though he'd read the book himself.

"They had a tentative deal to get married to gain freedom from their families, but they couldn't agree on terms."

"What terms?"

"He wants an heir. And she doesn't."

"I thought you said they were gonna have sex."

"I'm assuming they will, but she doesn't want to have a child that she'll be saddled with while he gallivants around living his life. Defeats the purpose of her gaining freedom, you know?"

"How are they going to fix that? If they're set up as the couple, they have to get together, right? Otherwise, the reader will be pissed."

Renee chuckled. "Read a lot of romance, do you?"

He grinned. "I don't have to read it. I live it."

She snorted and rolled her eyes again. "Yes, they'll get together. That's the whole point of the story. To be able to watch them fall in love."

He pushed the reader toward her. "Okay. So read."

"You want me to read to you?"

"Sure. Why not?"

Again with the staring. He wasn't being *that* weird, was he?

She picked up the reader again and began to read. He sat back and nursed his beer as she read the story. Sadie was right; she was really good at this. He closed his eyes and it was almost like watching a movie. Except Renee didn't do different voices.

"Alone in the study, he touched her cheek with his bare hand. Scandal be damned. He wanted her as his wife and he would get her one way or another. Her breath hitched as her bosom rose. Her tongue darted out and wet her lower lip."

Renee stopped. Declan's eyes popped open and watched Renee stretch.

"Why the hell'd you stop?"

"Because you looked like you were sleeping and I'm going to go to bed."

"I wasn't sleeping and you can't just stop there."

"Why not?"

"They were about to get it on!"

"Lower your voice. Sadie's asleep. And no, they weren't. This is historical. They don't rush to sex. Sometimes it doesn't even happen until *after* the marriage of convenience."

"Not this time, babe. My boy the duke is not waiting that long."

"Maybe not. But I'm still going to bed." She stood and cleaned up the table where Sadie had been snacking.

"Can I at least take the book and read it?"

"No. I read before bed."

"You're going to read without me?"

"What are you, six?" Her eyes were wide. "Give me your phone."

"Why?" he asked, as he pulled it from his pocket.

She tapped away on his phone. "Download the app. I'll send you a copy of the book and you can read it yourself."

He put in his passcode and she took the phone back. A few more taps and then she returned it. "Enjoy."

"Hey, if I read it, does it mean I get to join your book club?"

She laughed as she walked away. "Yeah, sure. You're

gonna want to spend your Tuesday night with a bunch of married or divorced women like me."

"You'd be surprised," he mumbled. She had no idea how much he liked hanging out with her.

He finished his beer and settled back on the couch to read the book. He scrolled through until he found the spot where Renee stopped reading. The story grabbed him again and he tore through the pages until he found the proof of what he'd known was coming. "They are so horny for each other."

He jumped off the couch to go laugh at Renee because he was right. He opened his mouth to yell for her but then remembered Sadie was sleeping. Slowing his pace, he crept up to Renee's bedroom door and raised a hand to knock, but he heard a quiet buzzing followed by a low moan.

Oh, shit. He knew what those sounds meant. With a smile, he had the brief thought of knocking anyway, just to interrupt her. But then he had a flash in his mind of Renee writhing in pleasure and he wasn't sure he could handle seeing it in the flesh.

Quietly backing away from the door, he headed to the opposite side of the house. He retreated to his room to continue reading the book and forget about what he'd just heard.

But as he read about the lady and the duke, he kept hearing Renee's moans while his hands were on her, and that didn't bode well for him.

RENEE WOKE THE FOLLOWING MORNING, A LITTLE SLEEPY BUT refreshed. She had a bagel in the toaster for Sadie and was enjoying her first cup of coffee in the quiet of the morning. At least until Declan came into the room.

"Morning," he said as he reached around her for a coffee cup.

"Hey."

"Sleep well?" he asked as he poured.

"Yes. Much better than having my daughter kick me all night."

"I bet." He added sugar to his cup and smiled at her over the rim as he drank.

The toaster popped and she buttered the bagel for Sadie. "Sadie, breakfast!"

"I kept reading last night after you went to bed."

"Yeah? Have I turned you into a romance reader?"

"Maybe. It was pretty hot. I called it."

"You called what, exactly?"

"I told you they were getting—"

"Hi, Declan," Sadie said as she came into the room.

"Morning, Sadie."

Renee handed Sadie her bagel wrapped in paper towel, and she took off to the dining room table. "You were saying?"

"The book was totally horny and you know it."

She smiled. "I never said it wasn't."

"But you didn't want to keep reading to me last night because it was hot and you didn't want me to know you get turned on. Because it is like porn. But better."

"What?"

He stepped closer, looked over her shoulder to spot Sadie, and in a quiet voice, said, "I came to gloat last night. I was about to knock on your door, and I heard you."

She swallowed hard. "Do you think you're going to embarrass me by saying that?"

"Hell, no." He leaned closer and whispered in her ear, "It was hot."

Then he stepped back, picked up his cup, and walked away toward the dining room.

What the fuck was that? She had no idea how to respond. She'd assumed he was being like her annoying brother and then he pulled that out? She cleared her throat. "You want something for breakfast?" she called from the kitchen.

"Nope. I'm good with coffee."

She puttered around the kitchen for a few minutes as she gathered her thoughts. He was still teasing her. That's what it had to be. When he figured he wouldn't be able to embarrass her, he was simply trying a new tactic. She topped off her cup and went to join them.

"When is book club?" Declan asked as soon as she sat.

"Tomorrow night. Why?"

"I was serious when I asked if I could join. I'll finish the book tonight."

"It's not a place to pick up women."

"Rennie. There is more to me than...that."

She chuckled at his pause because Sadie was at the table.

"What's it mean to pick up women?" Sadie asked.

It was Declan's turn to laugh.

Renee looked at her daughter. "It means to find someone to date."

"If Declan wants someone to date, why don't you date him, Mommy?"

Declan froze with his coffee mug halfway to his mouth. Renee blinked a few times. Sadie's gaze jumped back and forth between them.

"Declan and I are friends."

"You can't date your friend?"

Ah, shit. "Well, you could, but you have to like that person in a different way. Declan doesn't like me like that."

"Why not?" Sadie asked.

Declan shot Renee a look with his head angled. "I think what your mom means is that sometimes, even when you like someone enough to want to date them, you decide not to because being their friend is more important."

"Hm." Sadie took a bite of her bagel.

Renee stared at Declan. Did he just say he'd want to date her? That put a whole new spin on what he'd said in the kitchen. No. She couldn't go there. This was crazy.

"But why can't you date and still be friends?"

"Because sometimes grown-up relationships are complicated. Like you know Dad and I are friends, but we weren't good at being married."

Declan snorted. Renee glared at him, then she continued, "And even if you really like someone, dating them can make things super complicated."

Sadie turned to Declan. "Complicated is bad?"

He looked at Renee and held her gaze before answering. "Sometimes. But not always."

"I don't get it," Sadie responded. "People who like each other should just date."

Renee smiled. She never knew what to say to her kid when she asked difficult questions like this. No kid wanted to hear, "One day you'll understand," but that was exactly what Renee wanted to say.

"I agree, little lady," Declan said. Then he rose with his cup. "You have a good day at school."

"It's not school until after lunch," Sadie said with a side of sarcasm.

"I know. But I'm going out for a bit."

In the kitchen, he rinsed his cup. Sadie finished her bagel and took off to play, so Renee opened her laptop and started her daily search for a full-time job. After being at home with Sadie for years, she'd decided to be particular about the jobs she looked at. She wanted a good-paying job, but not one that would eat up all of her time. What she really wanted was to find some sort of work-life balance. It had been sorely lacking for as long as she had her laptop staring at her every moment of every day.

Declan came in with the coffee pot and topped off her cup.

"Doing something interesting today?"

"My brother Ronan needs an extra pair of hands on a job."

"Oh. You need a ride?"

"Nah. I'm good."

"It's no problem." She reached out and touched his arm as he turned to walk away with the coffeepot. "If you need some money, I can pay you. I have money set aside for the work. You haven't given me a price or anything. I don't know how to navigate this part."

"I'm fine. I'm doing him a favor and in exchange, he's going to get me some leftover material. It's all good. I'll be back this afternoon. And I should have the rest of this wallpaper down by the end of the week, so think about what color you want these rooms to be."

"What do you want for dinner?"

"I'm good with whatever you make."

"You always say that. Liver and onions?"

"Why do moms always go there?"

"Because that's punishment for pretty much everyone."

"Yeah, but we both know you don't want to punish me.

You like me too much." He winked, picked up his toolbelt, and headed out the door.

"Yeah, I do," she murmured to herself. And it wasn't necessarily a good thing.

CHAPTER
Eleven

Tuesday afternoon, Renee cleaned the living room as best she could. There wasn't much she could do about the half-peeled, ratty walls, but her friends all knew she was having work done. She also could've told them to have their meeting at someone else's house and she would skip, but she really needed her adult time. It was why she hosted every month. That way, she never had to rely on Graham to take care of Sadie. She just had everyone come over after Sadie was in bed.

Declan had missed dinner. He texted to say he was working late with Ronan. She felt bad about that, like he was taking on other jobs because she hadn't paid him. After everyone left tonight, she planned to address it again. He'd blown off her offer of cash yesterday morning, so that had to change.

She'd just finished washing the dishes from Sadie's dinner and was working on making a cheese plate and appetizers for book club when her phone rang. She slid the cheese plate into the fridge and answered the phone. "Hey, Mariah. How's the bride-to-be?"

"Frazzled, but okay."

"Anything I can do to help?"

"Wedding stuff is mostly handled. I'm here working on the table assignments for dinner and I noticed you don't have a plus-one."

Renee rolled her eyes. "You know I'm not dating anyone."

"Well, that's kind of why I'm calling."

Renee could almost hear the cringe in her friend's voice. "Spit it out."

"Graham is coming as Tina's plus-one," Mariah blurted.

Renee's jaw slipped open and she froze in anger. She closed her eyes and inhaled slowly and deeply. *That mother fucker.*

"Renee?"

She released the breath. "I'm here. It's fine. I give zero fucks about who he's dating."

Mariah cackled. "I'm so happy to hear that. I mean, I didn't think you were hung up on him or anything, but you know..."

"I'm pissed. Not because he's Tina's date but because he'd already agreed to take Sadie next weekend and he backed out. The weasel didn't even tell me why."

"Douche."

"Yeah, that's par for the course for him. He doesn't deserve any more of my energy."

"If it'll make you feel better, I'll sit him at the table with my Uncle Stan and Aunt Eileen, who've been married for forty years and hate each other. And my cousin Emily will be there to hit on him. She's almost sixty and just divorced her fourth husband."

Renee couldn't help but laugh. "You're a good friend."

"I know. I can probably come up with a hot guy to be your date. You can make Graham jealous."

Renee snorted. "Why the hell would I want to make him jealous? That implies I'd want him back. No, thank you."

"Maybe jealous isn't the right word. Regretful? He should know how bad he screwed up."

"And having a hot guy on my arm would do that how?"

"To remind Graham of how hot you are. That other guys are totally into you."

Renee laughed again. If only it were true. "I'm fine going solo. But thanks for the offer."

"Let me know if you change your mind. See you Friday for the rehearsal, or do you need to miss because you have Sadie?"

"I'll be there. My mom will stay the weekend. Thanks for the heads up about Graham. I can get all my anger out before Saturday, so maybe I won't feel the need to punch him."

"If the desire doesn't fade, I'm sure we can find a dark corner for you to catch him in."

"You're terrible. You shouldn't encourage my violent tendencies toward my ex."

"We've all been there."

"See you Friday." They said goodbye and Renee went back to prepping for book club.

An hour later, Sadie was in bed and all four of her book club friends had arrived. They started in the kitchen, snacking and drinking, and catching up on gossip. Sadie was less likely to hear her say anything about Graham from the kitchen.

Renee had just told them about her conversation with Mariah and then picked up a quesadilla to snack on.

"What an asshole," Lisa said.

Renee nodded. The best part about book club was hanging out with people who understood and were supportive.

Julie refilled Renee's glass with more margarita mix. "I'm with Mariah. You need to bring a hot-as-fuck date and rub it in Graham's face. Let him be jealous of your date because he's missing out on—"

"Stop," Renee cut her off. "What am I supposed to do? Hire a gigolo?"

Lisa snorted. "Who the hell uses that word? What are you, eighty?"

Renee threw a tortilla chip at her. "Sorry I don't know all the hip, new language. I'm not on SnapTok or any of those new-fangled thingies." She'd made her voice sound like a senior citizen and they all laughed. They stood there for over an hour talking about their lives and not even getting around to the book.

Kim poured the last of the margarita into her glass and said, "Uh-oh. I think we're out."

"That can't be," Renee said. "We haven't had that much." But the empty bottle sat on the counter mocking her.

"I can do a liquor store run," Zenia offered. "I haven't had a drop."

Renee eyes her suspiciously. "Why not?"

Zenia smiled and lowered her eyes. "I might be pregnant."

Everyone squealed and rushed to hug and congratulate her.

"It's not definite yet, but the home test was positive."

Renee held up crossed fingers. "They're pretty accurate."

Zenia had been trying to get pregnant for over six months.

"Thanks, everyone. I'm more than happy to run to the store even if I can't partake."

They didn't want Zenia to leave, and Renee remembered Declan. "Hold on. I'll text Declan and see if he can make a stop on his way."

Julie's eyebrows shot up.

"Just stop. He's Tyler's friend. He's the one doing the work." She waved her hand at the walls in the dining room. She sent a text and then said, "Let's go sit down and finally start talking about the book."

A moment later, Declan responded.

> I'll bring the booze if you'll let me talk about the book.

She laughed and everyone turned to look at her, so she read the text aloud.

"Bring it," Lisa said. "If he thinks he can hang with us, come on." She raised her hands and danced her way to the living room.

Kim followed, but said, "Does he know what we read?"

Renee cleared her throat. "Yeah, he picked up my ereader the other night and started to read it. He said he was going to finish it on his own."

"An enlightened man," Julie said. "Can't wait to meet him."

They settled in the living room and Renee let Declan know her friends invited him to hang out. He responded with a winky emoji.

Every book club started the same, with someone giving a summary in case one of them didn't quite get through the book. It rarely happened when they did genre fiction, but they did it every time so no one would feel left out. It was Zenia's turn for the recap and she took a lot longer than usual because she wanted to make sure she hit every emotional moment between Malcolm and Cecile.

By the time she wrapped up, the front door opened and Declan came in. He had a toolbelt slung over his shoulder and a gallon of margarita mix in his hand.

"Hello, ladies. Where do you want this?"

Lisa and Julie outright ogled him. Then Lisa said, "He's like your very own cabana boy, plying you with alcohol."

Declan snickered. "I live to serve."

Renee stood. "I'll take it. I assume everyone wants another round?"

He leaned on the back of the chair where she'd been sitting. Lisa tilted her head toward him and gave her wild eyes. Renee mouthed, "What?"

"Have I missed the book talk?"

"We barely started," Renee answered. "Zenia gave us a blow-by-blow summary instead of a quick recap. There's still some food in the kitchen if you want some."

"I think I'm going to take a quick shower. I'm a little ripe from work."

"Okay. Thanks for the booze."

He disappeared toward his room and Lisa jumped up and followed her to the kitchen.

"What is wrong with you?" Renee asked.

"Dude. He's hot. Take him to the wedding."

"What? No." She poured margarita mix into the blender and dumped in some ice.

"Why the hell not?"

"Because he's my brother's best friend. He's my friend. I can't ask him to pretend to be my date." To end the conversation, she turned the blender on.

Lisa shook her head and went back to the others. Renee finished blending and filled glasses for everyone. Hopefully,

Lisa wouldn't mention her hare-brained idea to the rest of the group. She didn't need that kind of peer pressure.

DECLAN TOOK A FAST SHOWER SO HE COULD DROP IN ON BOOK club. It made no fucking sense and he knew it. He didn't belong with a group of women discussing a romance novel, but he liked hanging out with Renee. He grabbed a beer from the fridge, loaded a plate with the appetizers the women hadn't eaten, and went to the living room.

As he sat, the one with the blond ponytail said, "Did you actually read the book?"

"Yes. Well, Renee gave me the summary of the first half of the book, so when I got my copy, I skimmed. But I read the rest. Do you want to give me a quiz?"

She narrowed her eyes and puckered her lips. "No, I guess I believe you. I'm Lisa." Then she pointed to the other women. "This is Kim, Julie, and Zenia."

"Thanks for letting me join. I've never done book club before. How's it work?"

Renee smiled. "There are no rules. We pretty much just talk about what we liked and what we didn't."

"Cool." He almost launched into all the things he liked but then figured he should wait his turn as the newbie and see how things played out.

"You want to start?" Renee asked.

"Sure." He wiped his hand on his sweatpants. "I thought the relationship was pretty realistic. I don't get the pretending to be a couple part. They were obviously attracted to each other. Why fake it?"

"Because if they admit they want each other, first, we wouldn't have a story. But more importantly, they would be giving in to the societal and familial expectations that they've worked so hard to avoid," Julie said.

"I get dodging family expectations. I never thought about it when it came to relationships, though." He nodded. It made sense. "But even when they both knew they wanted each other, there were a lot of games. I'm not into games."

"Really?" Renee said. "Tyler has told me some stories. Juggling different girls for each night of the week."

He shook his head at Renee. "Sure, when I was like twenty. I haven't done that for years. And I always—*always*—made it clear to every woman I was with that I was not exclusive. No games."

She opened her mouth like she wanted to argue. Instead, she licked her lips and took a sip of her drink.

"What was your favorite part?" he asked her. He barely resisted winking at her as he thought about how she'd gotten herself off after reading to him.

"I love how Cecile refused to back down on her dreams. If he wanted an heir, he had to compromise and not run off. She wasn't about to let him have his cake and eat it too. She'd be his wife in name only and he could have his freedom, but if he wanted a family, he was damn sure going to be part of it."

"It's not much of a compromise for the right woman."

Their gazes locked and he felt trapped in some kind of game with her that he didn't know the rules for.

"Whew. Is it hot in here?" Lisa asked. "Watching the two of you is almost as bad as Malcolm and Cecile."

Renee looked at her friend, so Declan's gaze followed. The woman was fanning herself.

"We're talking about the characters. Obviously, Declan

saw exactly what the author wants us all to see: that for the right person, for real love, we're willing to change our lives."

"Yeah, right," Lisa responded smiling.

For the next hour or so, they pulled the book apart and talked about favorite scenes and lines. Julie taught him how to highlight text on his phone so he could mark passages and quotes so he wouldn't have to try to remember. The whole time, he avoided direct eye contact with Renee.

It was almost eleven when they wrapped up. Declan stood and piled up plates to take to the kitchen.

Lisa handed him her empty plate. "So, are you doing anything interesting this weekend, Declan?"

God, he hoped she was just being friendly. He really didn't want to shoot down one of Renee's friends, but he had zero interest. "Just working around here."

"Hmm." She looked around him to where Renee was putting away food in the kitchen. "Before you got here, Renee was telling us about why Graham—you know about Graham, right?"

"Her asshole ex-husband? Yeah, I know Graham."

She smiled again and it was both approving and a little wicked. "Renee told us he's coming to her friend's wedding this weekend with one of the other bridesmaids. We've been trying to convince her to show up with a hot date that would let Graham know she's so over him."

Declan glanced over his shoulder. "She is over him."

"We know that. But we're not sure he does."

"Okay." The thought of Graham trying to worm his way back into Renee's life irritated him in a way it shouldn't.

"You know any hot, single, young guys who might be able to dote on her for a night or so?"

"You want me to find her a date? She'll never go for that. In fact, she might cause me bodily harm for suggesting it."

"Oh, you sweet boy," she said.

"Fuck," Zenia said. "She wants you to go with Renee."

"Me?"

"You, what?" Renee asked from behind him.

Lisa leaned back in her chair with a smirk on her face.

"Oh, Lord." Renee touched his shoulder. "Forget anything they suggested. They're half-drunk full of bad ideas."

He grinned at her. "Some of us are all about the bad ideas."

Lisa let out a whoop and Renee glared at her again.

Declan was smart enough to know not to say anything because Renee was clearly irritated by her friends. He cleaned up the rest of the dishes and glasses in the living room and took them to the kitchen while Renee said goodbye to her friends.

He filled the sink to wash the dishes and wondered what Renee had told her friends about him. They were full of jokes and innuendos. He had the first stack of dishes washed when Rene came in.

"You didn't have to do the dishes."

"I'm here. They were dirty."

"Thank you." She picked up a towel and started drying. "About what Lisa said..."

"You mean about being your date to the wedding?"

"Yeah. I'm not expecting you to do anything like that."

"So Graham canceled on Sadie so he could go to the wedding that he knew you were already going to?"

"Yep. He's the date of one of the other bridesmaids."

The dude was such an asshole. "I'm in."

"What?"

"I'll be your date."

"Don't be ridiculous. I'm not asking you to give up

another weekend—this time for people you don't even know." She stacked the dishes to put in the cabinet.

"I know you. What's one night for a friend?"

"It's not one night. The wedding is in Galena, so I'm heading there Friday afternoon and I won't be back until Sunday."

"Okay."

"Stop."

"I don't have any plans other than working on the house. Part of me really wants to piss off Graham. He's an asshole. Plus, it's a wedding so easy to get laid. Bridesmaids are always looking to hook up." He set the last glass in the drainer.

"I'm a bridesmaid and I will not be looking for anything."

"I didn't realize you're in the bridal party. That adds to Graham's douchey-ness. So if I go, who has the hotter date?"

Renee laughed. "Are you asking me to rate your hotness against a woman's?"

"Yeah. I already know I have a hotter date than Graham does. I want to make sure he knows he's beat on all fronts."

Renee shook her head. "I appreciate it. I really do, but you should enjoy your weekend. You've been working here and now with your brother. I don't need you to do more."

He didn't know how to explain to her that he wanted to do this. He liked being around her. He felt better about himself and his life when she was around. Even with the jokes she made, he never felt like a loser. His family didn't mean to make him feel that way, but he did. They all had their shit together. Renee was more like them than he was, but he was different with her.

They worked in silence to finish cleaning up, and for the first time since he came here, things felt tense or awkward. "Book club was a lot of fun. Thanks for letting me join."

"I think my friends had fun, too. It's not too often a man reads romance and doesn't make fun of it."

"Do you always read romance?"

"No, but we do read more of that than other genres. Sometimes we do a thriller or a mystery, and there are a few occasions when we do some literary fiction. I don't like those months. People are always miserable and dying in those books. Life sucks enough. I want a happy ending."

"Makes sense. Now that I've been to one meeting, does that mean I can join whenever?"

"I guess if you really want to. Don't you have friends to hang out with?"

"Not ones that read. At least I don't think they do."

"I'll let you know when we're meeting again. We still have to pick the next book."

"Cool." The kitchen was back to normal and it was time for bed.

Renee nodded and said, "Good night."

As she skirted around him to get to her room, he reached out and grabbed her wrist. In a quiet voice, he said, "I'd like to take you to the wedding. Let me be there for you."

She looked at his hand on her wrist and then at his face. "I'll think about it."

Then she slid from his grasp.

"Good night, Rennie."

"Still hate it," she called without looking back as she walked away.

CHAPTER
Twelve

The next morning, Declan was back at Ronan's house for another day of work. While he told Renee that Ronan needed help on a job, it wasn't the whole truth. He volunteered to do some more work on Ronan's house to get the office together now that he and Chloe lived together. He knew Ronan would throw him some cash, and it would probably be enough to buy the parts he'd need to put together a playset for Sadie in the yard.

He both loved and hated working at Ronan's. He loved not having someone stand over him to make sure he wasn't fucking things up. But he hated the total silence. It left him with too much time with his thoughts. He considered everything he'd believed about his father and how wrong he'd been. Part of him couldn't wrap his head around why his family never talked about it. Especially Ronan. If he had such a deep belief that their dad didn't run off, why didn't he tell Declan?

Everyone treated him like he was a total fuck up who would never grow up. The news about his father dying twenty years ago was a wake-up call for him. He'd intentionally lived his life free of most strings and responsibilities. By design, he made sure he would never be in a position to let people down the way his father had. Knowing that his father hadn't chosen to let them down was a blow to everything.

He wasn't looking to jump into having all the responsibilities he'd avoided his whole life, but he was starting to reconsider his options. It was time to make actual decisions instead of reacting to everything.

Asking Ronan for work to be able to build Sadie an awesome playground in her backyard was his first step. No one needed him to do this. He wanted to.

At least as much as he wanted to be Renee's date for the wedding. When they were younger, he and Ty had been protective of Renee, even though she was older and could absolutely take care of herself. Living in her house and hanging out with her had brought those protective urges back.

But it was more than that. He wasn't sure what to do with that, either.

Ronan came in as he was nailing in the last piece of trim.

Declan shot him a grin. "Check it out. Done on time, just like I promised."

Ronan nodded and looked around. "You do good work. You sure you don't want a job? I can get you on my crew."

"Fuck no. I don't know how you still work for Cahill. You think he had something to do with Dad's death, right?"

"Someone in that family knows something."

"Yet you keep working there."

"It's my best bet to gather intel. I don't care that Brendan wants to take over and be in charge of figuring things out. I've come this far, so I'm going to keep digging."

Declan leaned against the wall. "Has digging gotten you anywhere?"

"Not recently. But Danny hasn't been back to work. He's been settling his dad's estate. When he comes back, something's bound to pop. He blames Brendan for his dad's heart attack. He hasn't spoken to me, so for all I know, he might fire me."

"It's a lot of game-playing. What do you and Brendan think you're gonna find?"

"Answers. If we can't find out where Dad's body is, we should at least know what happened to him."

"Who are you kidding? You want to make someone pay."

"If I can, sure." As he spoke, he walked the perimeter of the room, inspecting Declan's work. "I have a deck job this weekend. If you want some more work, it's yours. And you can have whatever leftovers there are."

Declan opened his mouth to jump at the chance and then remembered the wedding. "I can't."

"I thought you needed the money for something."

"I need the money to build a swing set for Sadie in the backyard. She has nothing back there but a patch of sad grass."

"Then this job'll be perfect. There'll probably be some extra 4 by 4s you can snag."

"I have plans this weekend."

"What plans could you have that you can't do some other time?"

Declan scrubbed a hand over his face and debated telling Ronan. "Renee is standing up in a wedding in Galena and I'm going as her date."

He left out the part where she hadn't agreed to that. He figured she'd give in.

"I thought you were just friends."

"We are. But her ex is going with one of the other bridesmaids and I offered to go."

"Sounds complicated."

"Not really. We're friends. We like to hang out. And if I'm there, her ex won't be a total asshole to her."

"That's still more complicated than anything you've had going on in your life in...probably ever."

Declan shrugged. "This is Renee."

He didn't know why he felt that was enough of an explanation, but it was. Ronan could understand. Declan didn't need to detail his relationship with Renee. He wouldn't even know how to explain it.

"I'll see what I can scrape up from the job. You never know. Sometimes, extra material is ordered. The customer has no idea."

"That's not very ethical." Declan almost choked on the words. Since when did he care about ethics?

"For a regular paying customer, I would never do that. This is one of Cahill's *favors*. Cash job to get or repay a favor. I don't care if I cheat one of these dirtbags."

"Fair enough. I appreciate it. Sadie's gonna love it."

"Don't get too caught up over there. It's not really your life."

"I'm fine." He didn't need warnings about not getting too attached. This wasn't some random chick and her kid. It was Renee and Sadie and they'd been in his life forever. He saw no reason for that to change.

He gathered up his tools. "I'm gonna head home unless you need something else."

"This is good." Ronan reached into his pocket and

pulled out cash. Pressing the money into Declan's hand, he added, "I'm impressed with your work. When you finally settle into what you want to do long-term, let me know. I'm here to help."

"Thanks, man." The problem was, that he still had no clue what he wanted. He did know that bartending and jobs like that no longer held any appeal. He enjoyed working with his hands. Maybe being a carpenter like his dad and brother wasn't such a bad thing.

"Hey, you want to stay and order pizza or something?"

"Sure." He pulled out his phone to text Renee to let her know he wouldn't be back for dinner.

"Texting your woman?"

"Not my woman." Although the words didn't burn in his throat the way they normally would've. "I'm letting Renee know not to count me in for dinner."

Ronan huffed a laugh. "Just friends, huh? I'm your brother and you've never been that considerate."

Declan shrugged. "Turning over a new leaf."

In the past few months, that was exactly what it felt like. For the first time, he felt like he was coming into his own, becoming his own man.

RENEE POURED HERSELF A GLASS OF WINE TO HAVE WITH HER peanut butter and jelly sandwich. It was a sad dinner, but with Sadie eating with Graham and Declan not coming home for dinner, she hadn't felt like cooking. The house was too quiet again as she stared at the mostly peeled-off wallpaper in the dining room. She'd been alone in her house plenty while Sadie was with Graham. She didn't know why she was feeling lonely now.

But she did. She'd gotten used to adult companionship with Declan around. It wasn't a wise choice, and she recognized that. It was even worse that she was considering taking him to the wedding this weekend. With him there, she'd be able to laugh despite Graham's presence, but she couldn't deny there was something else simmering between them, and she couldn't let it continue.

She tossed the remainder of her sandwich and refilled her glass. While she didn't have regrets about putting Sadie first, part of her wished she could be like other women who demanded free time and went on dates. If she at least had a job she enjoyed instead of something she got through to pay the bills, she would feel more fulfilled. It was like being twenty all over again instead of a thirty-three-year-old adult.

Rebuilding your life sucked.

While doing another job search, she got a text from Graham saying he was bringing Sadie home. She looked at the clock. He was on time. It shouldn't surprise her. He was almost always on time to bring Sadie home; he preferred being late when he was supposed to pick her up.

More old resentments bubbled up and she swallowed them down. She finished the application she'd started for a job for a small neighborhood bank. She wasn't sure they could afford to pay what she was worth, but it might be a start.

When the knock on the front door came, she had just hit submit on the application. She opened the door to see Graham carrying Sadie. She was passed out on his shoulder.

"You let her fall asleep in the car?"

"What was I supposed to do?"

"Keep her awake?" She reached for her daughter, but Graham waved her off. He handed her Sadie's backpack for school.

He walked through the house and into Sadie's bedroom. Renee waited by the door. She'd take off Sadie's shoes after he left.

Graham came back in a minute. "Sadie's been talking about the mural in her room. She really loves it."

"I know. Declan's brother painted it for her." Renee stood with her arms crossed at the open door waiting for him to leave.

He stepped closer. "Look, I'm sure you know about me and Tina."

Renee's hand flew up. "I don't want to talk about this. I don't care who you date. What bothers me is that you didn't have the guts to tell me that was why you were backing out of taking Sadie this weekend."

"I was going to, but you were mad and I didn't want you to feel bad on top of it."

"Why the hell would I feel bad? I don't care who you date."

"It's just...I didn't want to rub it in your face that I moved on and had a date when you don't."

She had no idea if it was just all his bullshit or the wine that made her want to smack him, but she didn't. "Don't worry about me. I have a date for the wedding. Goodbye."

She pointed at the door and he shuffled through. She didn't wait for him to say goodbye or even look at her. She simply closed the door.

On autopilot, she went to Sadie's room and tucked her in. Then, she started to spiral over the fact that her mouth had gotten away from her. Why the fuck had she told Graham she had a date?

You know why, the little voice in her head mocked. *You want to go with Declan.*

But she shouldn't. Maybe she should find a different date. Someone more appropriate. Someone *not* Declan. She sighed again as she took another swig of wine. The problem was she didn't know anyone else. Trying to get in touch with one of her few hook-ups was an even worse idea. Maybe she should call Lisa and Jen. They might know someone.

But that would put her on a blind date for a wedding. This wasn't like her. She planned and scheduled everything. She predicted possible pitfalls before making a move. Why hadn't she considered a date for the wedding?

"Because I don't need a man for validation," she said aloud to no one. She straightened up the living room, piddling around while drinking her wine to waste enough time that she wouldn't feel like an old lady for going to bed so early.

Finally, she gave up, refilled her wine glass again, and flopped back on her bed. She didn't crawl under the covers, and her feet were still on the floor. But she lay there, allowing the wine to do its thing and relax her.

She didn't know how long she was lying there when she heard the front door open. Declan was home. She thought about reaching for her wine, but couldn't muster the energy. What she needed to do was find the courage to talk to Declan about being her date.

But it could wait until tomorrow.

"Hey, you okay?" Declan's voice startled her.

"Yeah."

"But you're in bed. At eight-thirty."

"I'm not really in bed. I'm thinking. And I'm an old lady."

"You're not old. What's going on?"

So maybe it wouldn't wait until tomorrow. At least if she got it over with now, she could die from embarrassment in the comfort of her own bed. She forced herself upright.

"Graham dropped Sadie off after their dinner tonight. He said he hadn't told me about Tina because he didn't want to make me feel bad." She took a deep breath and swallowed hard. "You know, because I'm so pitiful that I don't have a date."

"The fucker said that?"

"Not in those exact words." She reached for her glass of wine and gulped. "But he pissed me off, so I told him I have a date."

She didn't turn to look at Declan. Didn't want to see the look on his face. But then he was so quiet, and she didn't know what to think, so she glanced over her shoulder. He looked shocked.

"Do you?" he finally asked.

She shook her head. She heard him release a breath. Then he bounced on the bed next to her.

"Sure, you do. I said I'd go with you."

She flopped back and tossed her arm over her eyes. "But I shouldn't need you to. I'm pitiful."

"You're not pitiful. And I want to go. It'll be fun."

"That's nice of you to say. Thanks." She moved her arm and stared at the ceiling.

Declan lay down next to her. His hand brushed against hers. From the corner of her eye, she saw that he was looking at the ceiling. In profile, he didn't seem as young as she usually thought of him.

She returned to her own study of the ceiling. They lay in silence for a few minutes.

In a quiet voice, Declan said, "I offered to go with you because I like being with you."

Her heart thumped and tears clawed at her throat. "I don't know what to do with that," she forced out.

"Nothing to do. We're just gonna have a good time at the wedding. And make your ex-husband realize you are way happier without him."

She huffed a sad laugh. "The thing is, I am happier without him. It just doesn't look like it to everyone else."

"I see it." He sat up, the movement causing their hands to brush again. "You look happier now than I can remember in recent years. If others can't see it, they're blind."

He stood and she felt his eyes on her. "I'm going to shower. You want to watch some TV or something?"

"Sure. I'll be out in a bit."

Her gaze tracked him out of her room. She needed a few moments to wrangle these odd new feelings that were swarming about Declan. With every conversation and interaction they had, he was less and less of her little brother's annoying but fun friend and more of a man she enjoyed being with.

She didn't think she could handle that level of complication in her life.

CHAPTER
Thirteen

Declan stretched out on his bed and opened the reading app on his phone. Ebooks were the best invention. Maybe not ever—there *was* beer and porn. But it was pretty damn cool. If Tyler ever knew what he was reading, he'd never hear the end of it. This way, he could read and let his friends think he was watching porn on his phone.

He settled against the pillows and returned to the book he'd started after Renee's book club meeting. He'd discovered the author not only had a shit ton more books, but she'd written a series. The duke he'd read about with Renee had a younger brother. Declan didn't understand all of the lingo. Nick, the duke's brother, kept calling himself the spare. Declan assumed it was like being the red-headed step-child.

He was also a fuckboy.

Declan could get behind that. Nick had just met the chick he was gonna fall for. Not that Nick was aware. They sniped at each other every time they were in the same room. She was all prim and proper and he kept making fun of her.

But deep down, he admired her because she was smart and didn't put up with anyone's bullshit.

Declan knew a few women like that. He was caught up in the banter the characters used to hide how horny they were for each other. He was so focused on his phone, he didn't notice Renee standing in the doorway until she knocked on the open door.

"Hey," she said, glancing at the black TV screen.

"What's up?" he asked, dropping his phone on his bare chest.

She blinked a couple of times and then huffed out a breath. "I don't want this to sound rude, but I can't figure out a different way to ask."

"What? You wanna know how I fend off all the women who are after this awesome physique?"

Her cheeks flushed and she shook her head. "Do you have a suit to wear to the wedding?"

He smiled. "I'm getting one."

"Let me know what it costs. You shouldn't be on the hook for a suit you don't need."

He chuckled. "You can save your pennies. I'm borrowing a suit from Gavin."

She tried to hide the relief on her face, but asked, "You sure?"

"Yep."

"Okay. Thanks." She turned away and paused again. "The TV does work. You don't need to stare at a blank screen."

"I'm reading." He held up his phone. "No TV needed. Did you know the author from book club has a whole series?"

"Uh, yeah. How do you know that?"

He waved the phone at her. "What do you think I'm reading?"

"Oh! Is it good?"

"So good. Have a seat." He patted the mattress beside him. "I'll catch you up."

She eyed the bed.

He swung his arm around. "It's not like there's other furniture. I promise I won't bite."

When she still hesitated, he added, "It's about the younger brother."

"Nick?"

Declan nodded and patted the mattress again.

The lure of the book was too much. Renee crossed the room and sat on the bed. Declan tugged at her to get her to lay back. When she was settled—albeit stiffly—he asked, "You wanna read?"

She shook her head. "No, you go ahead."

"Okay." He kind of wanted her to read. He liked the sound of her voice when she fell into a story. He gave her a quick rundown of what he'd read, knowing his summary was nowhere near as good as the one she'd given him when he'd asked about the first book.

Before he picked up the phone again, he asked, "What's the deal with Nick calling himself the spare?"

"Oh, uh. The first-born son of a family is the heir. He'll inherit all of the land and responsibilities for the family. The second son is the spare—you know, in case something happens to the real heir."

Declan let that sit for a minute. He wondered if Ronan had felt like the spare. Of course, Brendan wasn't in charge of the whole family, even though he liked to think so.

"Spares are fun because they're usually the rakes. No

one takes them seriously because they don't ever want the responsibility that their big brother has."

Declan felt that. Not being taken seriously was tough. Sure, he'd set himself up for it, but...

"And then things change. Usually because of a woman. He falls hard and has to prove that he's a different man. That she can trust him and rely on him." She laughed. "I love watching them fall." As she spoke, she turned so she was on her side, one hand tucked under her cheek.

"I think you're getting a little too much pleasure out of it."

She poked his arm. "Just read."

He read the story, enjoying the characters. It was the first time he could remember reading something that didn't have a huge action plot to keep him interested. This was all about the people. He read for almost an hour and things were heated between Nick and Sophia. Nick had already decided he wanted to have her, but she was still fighting everything. They'd had two near kisses which was frustrating for everyone, even Declan.

He looked down and Renee's eyes were closed. A wavy lock of her reddish hair lay across her cheek. He turned to his side and studied her face. She was relaxed and peaceful in a way he didn't get to see her during the day. She was always worried about something. He reached out and swept the hair back from her cheek, rubbing the silky strands between his fingers.

Fuck, now he was starting to sound like the characters from the book. This wasn't how he approached women. Her eyes opened.

"Why'd you stop?"

"You fell asleep."

"No, I didn't. I was listening. It was like watching a movie."

"Sure it was. And the screen was the back of your eyelids."

"Of course," she said with a smile. "But I was listening. Nick's hand brushed Sophia's and they both got that shock of awareness, and then she rushed off. He followed and had her cornered, thinking about how much he wanted to taste her."

Her voice was low, just above a whisper. They were in their own little cocoon. And when she looked at him, all soft and sleepy, but spoke about being tasted, Declan lost his mind. He leaned forward and brushed his lips against hers.

When she didn't recoil in abject disgust, he held her hip with one hand and kissed her like Nick wanted to kiss Sophia. He tasted Renee and enjoyed every second.

Her fingers stroked his pecs and he rolled closer, his dick getting hard. She moaned a little and then froze.

Her eyes popped open and she gave his chest a little shove as she pulled away. She was at the edge of the bed and the movement caused her to lose her balance. She practically rolled off the mattress.

His grip on her hip was the only thing anchoring her, and she jolted back but then sat up. With her fingers on her lips, she asked, "What was that?"

"Sweetheart, if you can't recognize a hot-as-fuck kiss, someone's been doing you wrong."

"This isn't funny. We can't do this."

He sighed and sat up. Loose, relaxed Renee was gone, and the practical version was back. "Sorry. I didn't mean to take advantage of you or do something you weren't into."

Her eyes widened. "It's not that. Obviously, you weren't alone in the kiss. I mean, we... can't."

"If you're into it as much as I am, why not?"

"Because you're Declan."

He was sure his look showed his confusion.

"You live here. And you're my brother's friend. It's..."

"Still hot."

She smiled and gave his shoulder a nudge. "We're friends. Doing anything else is asking for trouble."

"A little trouble can be fun."

"As a parent, I need to avoid trouble. Sadie comes first and I don't want her to get hurt."

"I would *never* do anything to hurt Sadie."

Renee sighed and got off the bed. "I know you wouldn't intentionally. But she's young. She doesn't understand complicated relationships. I don't want her to get confused."

The conversation they'd had when Sadie told them to date reverberated in his head. He was a complication she didn't think was worth putting up with. She didn't trust him to not fuck up her life.

Maybe he and Nick had more in common than he'd thought.

"I get it. I'm not relationship material, and that's what you want. I'm not looking to be her father."

"It's not that. I don't want to screw up our friendship." She looked at him for a minute, and he was pretty sure she wanted to crawl back into bed with him, but she wouldn't let herself. "Good night. Thanks for the story."

"Anytime." And he meant it. Renee might not think he was good enough for a relationship, but he'd take what he could get because he felt good when she was around.

When she left the room, she closed the door behind her,

and he closed his fist around his dick, seeking release while he thought of her soft curves and deep moans.

RENEE SPENT THE NEXT FEW NIGHTS SLEEPING RESTLESSLY. She and Declan had continued reading together at night, but in the safety of the living room. It was wonderful and awful all at once. They laughed and joked and discussed the characters and plot like she would with any friend, but now there was an undercurrent of tension, much like she enjoyed reading about between characters. When she was living it, though, not so much fun.

The wedding was looming and she couldn't stop thinking about kissing Declan. While she never would've made the first move, the fact that he had made her head spin. She thought the attraction she felt was one-sided, a manifestation of her own fantasies because her love life was sad.

But that kiss was anything but pitiful. And now she was supposed to spend a whole weekend with him. Away from home. Away from all the responsibilities and stress. And he was supposed to be her *date*.

They would be expected to dance together and she didn't know how she could be in his arms without letting another kiss happen.

So what if it did?

The thought came so quickly, that she blushed. It would be bad. Like bad, bad. It couldn't end well. She would lose a friend, as would Sadie. It might cause problems between

Declan and Tyler. And she'd be back to square one with trying to get things done on her house.

For the last two days, Declan had shown no signs of the kiss they shared having an effect on him. Maybe it was as one-sided as she'd thought. But every now and then, while he was scraping the wallpaper from the dining room wall, she'd catch him looking at her. But she couldn't quite decipher what the look meant.

Late Friday morning, her mom arrived to spend the weekend with Sadie. When she walked in, Sadie ran to her for a hug.

"Grandma! We're gonna have so much fun while Mom's gone. We're gonna have a spa day!"

"I can't wait," she said as Sadie pulled her through the house. She stopped in the dining room. "What's going on here?"

"Hey, Geri," Declan called from on top of the step stool he was on trying to remove the last few stubborn strips of wallpaper. He climbed down and gave her a huge hug. "It's been a while."

"Too long. You should come around more often. What are you doing here?"

"Mom, I told you Declan is helping me get some stuff done on the house." Renee double-checked her purse to make sure she'd packed her phone charger and the makeup she'd need for the wedding. Then she glanced at Declan. "Are you packed?"

"Yep."

"You two should head out now. Go have a nice lunch at one of those cute little restaurants and check into your room. Then you can rest up before facing—"

"Okay," Renee blurted. Her mom was not great at censoring what she said about Graham, and Sadie didn't need to hear people talking shit about her dad. Even if it was warranted. "You sure you can get Sadie to school on time?"

"Yes. And I'll even remember to pick her up. Go. Have fun." She leaned closer to Declan and added with a wink, "But not too much."

Renee followed Declan toward his room. "Are you sure you don't want me to see if someone can bring you tomorrow?"

"Yes, Renee. I'm fine with coming with you now. Are you trying to get rid of me?"

"No. But this evening, I have the rehearsal for the wedding and I don't know how long it'll take, so you'll be on your own."

"No big deal. I have Nick and Sophia to keep me company."

"You're going to read without me?"

"Think of it as an incentive to hurry back." He grabbed a duffel bag and a garment bag. "Just kidding. I wouldn't read without you. They're about to fuck and I absolutely want you to be there when it happens."

His voice was low and husky. She swallowed hard. There was more of that tension she'd been trapped in. It was gonna be a long weekend.

"Come on. Geri says I get to have lunch with you all alone. No chicken nuggets today."

After a round of goodbyes, they were settled in her car and heading to the highway.

Renee drove in silence all the way to the highway. It was about a two-and-a-half-hour drive to Galena. That gave her plenty of time to stress and freak out. This was such a bad idea. After that kiss, how was she going to spend the weekend with him?

133

What if it happened again?

Did she want it to?

Hell, yes, she did. But she'd learned a long time ago that just because she wanted something didn't mean she should get it. She had a lot more to consider now—all the reasons she listed for Declan. Plus the ones she didn't.

Like how would Ty react to her dating his best friend?

Declan had said nothing about dating. It was a kiss. One that promised more, but still just a kiss.

And there was the fact that she was older than him. People would look at them funny. Her damn book club friends called him a cabana boy. As if she was a cougar. She winced at the thought.

"Everything okay?"

Declan's question pulled her from her overwhelming thoughts. "Yeah. Just a lot going on in my head right now."

"Anything I can help with?"

She swallowed, thinking again of how good that kiss was. "No. I'm stressed about the wedding."

"Because of Graham?"

"A little. We've managed to remain civil when we see each other, but we only see each other when we're dropping off or picking up Sadie. We're not assholes in front of her."

"I've never seen you be an asshole."

"I get plenty bitchy towards him. I can't help it. He pushes my every last button." She released a pent-up breath. "I think this is the first time I've seen him outside of Sadie time."

"Are you saying you won't be able to control the bitch?"

She shrugged. "Depends on whether he goes out of his way to annoy me. And that's not fair to Mariah. It's her day. The last thing she needs is two divorced people airing their shit for public consumption."

"Then maybe he should've thought of that before deciding to go to your friend's wedding."

She shook her head. "That's just it. He doesn't think about those things. He does what he wants." He always had.

"Well, I can be your buffer for the weekend. Whenever he's around, I'll pull you away. I'm a great distraction."

She couldn't help but smile. "Thanks again for doing this."

"It's not like it's a hardship to be with you. Come on." He tapped her thigh. "We're gonna have a good weekend."

He turned on the radio and began to sing along in an obnoxious voice. For most of the rest of the drive, Declan's lightheartedness eased the tension she'd been carrying and they did have fun. As they neared the bed and breakfast, she had another awful thought. Graham and his date were probably staying at the same place.

"How about lunch before we check in?"

"Sounds good. I'm starved."

"You should've said something. We could've stopped earlier."

"It's fine."

"What do you think you want?"

"I've never been to Galena."

"Neither have I." She pulled over on a side street and picked up her phone. She Googled restaurants. "There's a Cajun bar and grill, Mexican, Italian—"

"We live in Chicago and can get Mexican and Italian all the time."

"How about a Brewpub? They do tastings and tours and they have food. Might be fun."

"If you're good with that, sure."

She hit the directions to get them to the brewery. When

they got there, they discovered they had plenty of time before the tour, so they decided to eat first.

Once they placed their order, Renee said, "Thank you again for doing this. Just having you here is making everything seem a lot better."

"No problem. You're plying me with alcohol now, there's probably an open bar tomorrow. Plus music, so I can convince you to dance with me. What's not to love?"

"It's still a wedding with no one you know."

"Sometimes that's the best kind of party."

The server delivered their beers. "So how are things with your family?"

"What do you mean?"

"You haven't mentioned anything about them, even though you were working with your brother earlier this week."

"Ronan is fine. He's getting really serious with Chloe. Nessa's been laying low for a while, so she might be hiding some new guy. You saw Gavin when he painted the mural." He shrugged.

"How are they all taking the news about your dad?" As soon as the words slipped out, she clamped her jaw shut. "If you don't want to talk about it, that's okay. It's just that you listen to me talk all the time and you never say anything about your life or family."

CHAPTER
Fourteen

Declan stared at his beer for a minute and rubbed his thumb down the condensation on the side of the glass. In truth, he hadn't talked to anyone about his family or his dad since he and Ty had gone out for drinks when he first moved in with Renee. And it had been weighing on him.

Renee reached across the table and wrapped her fingers around his hand. "I'm sorry I asked. I'm not trying to pry."

"Yeah, you are. But it's okay. I was trying to figure out what to say." He inhaled deeply. Renee was removed from the entire situation, so maybe unburdening himself to her would help. "So here's the deal. I'm going to tell you some stuff, but you can't tell anyone, okay?"

Her eyebrows curled in and created a deep crease on her forehead. "Intriguing."

"We let everyone believe we just decided to declare Dad dead because it's been twenty years. The truth is, we got some confirmation that he's dead."

"From who?"

He took a drink of his beer, a local brew that went down

smooth, and considered where to actually start. "My oldest brothers, Ronan and Brendan have each been trying to investigate what happened back then. Brendan works for the FBI and Ronan works for the same construction company my dad worked for. They were sure Alan Cahill, the owner, knew something about our dad. They'd been close, almost friends. Then they figured he had something to do with our dad disappearing."

"Wait a minute. You mean Alan Cahill the former mayor who just died?"

"Yep."

"No way."

"Way."

"What? Why?"

He shrugged again. "They're still searching for answers. They were on to something, and then the old man died."

"Then how did you find out your dad was dead?"

"The old fucker wrote us a letter that was delivered after his death. It basically said to stop looking for answers. Dad was dead, so we should move on."

"But no information about how he died or where he is? That's shitty."

"That's what convinced my brothers to keep digging."

The server delivered their food and they tasted everything. Declan waited for Renee to react to what he'd said, other than to offer sympathetic words.

"How do you feel about everything?"

He took another bite of his burger and thought while he chewed. "I've been trying to figure that out. I mean, he's dead. No amount of information is going to change that."

"Might give you some peace, though?"

"I don't know. In some ways, the information has given me less peace. I assumed all this time he took off. Like having all of us kids was too much. I was okay with that." He dragged a couple of fries through ketchup and popped them in his mouth.

Renee swallowed a bite of chicken wrap and stared at him suspiciously. "Are you sure about that?"

"Yeah."

"I'm just saying that for as long as I've known you, you don't take anything seriously. Your version of Daddy issues?"

He groaned. "Please don't say shit like that. It sounds really bad."

She laughed and it was loud enough to draw the attention of the few other customers. She covered her mouth, but her eyes were bright with humor. "Sorry," she mumbled as her laughter subsided.

"You sound real sorry." He finished off his last bite and thought about what she said. He'd heard it from his siblings before, but somehow having her say it made it a little more obvious. "Except for the way you phrased it, you're not totally wrong. I was telling Ty that Dad's death was making me re-evaluate my life. I've avoided a lot of things because of him and now I'm thinking it wasn't necessarily the best choice for me."

"Well, I'm here any time you want to talk or bounce ideas around." She wiped her hands on her napkin and waved the server over for the check. "We have to go get in line for the tour."

"We don't have to if you're not interested."

She smiled. "It might be fun."

They stood and he held out his arm. "Lead the way."

THE BREWERY TOUR WAS SHORT, BUT THEY ENJOYED THE samples of beer. Instead of going back to the car, they decided to wander through the downtown streets for a bit. Galena was a quaint little town. Renee was having so much fun with Declan that she didn't want to hurry to the bed and breakfast. Unfortunately, her bridesmaid duties called. Her phone pinged with a text from Mariah.

> You haven't checked in. Are you close?

> In town, just had lunch with Declan. Touring downtown. Hanging out.

> I can't wait to meet him. Bring him to dinner tonight.

Renee stopped walking.

"Problem?" Declan asked.

"Uh. No. Mariah is inviting you to come to dinner tonight. The rehearsal dinner."

"Okay."

"I'll tell her no. You don't have to suffer through that."

He wrapped his fingers around her wrist. The calluses on his hand scraped deliciously along her sensitive skin. "If you prefer I don't go, that's cool. I can totally watch TV in the room. But don't tell her no because you think you're imposing. I'll go with you."

She bit her lower lip. "You sure?"

"Yeah. Tell her I can't wait."

She smiled and shook her head. He had no desire to

meet her friends, but he was so good at playing along. He's in. Thanks for asking him. See you soon.

They walked back to the car so they could get settled in their room before Renee had to go to rehearsal. She parked in the lot and when she went to grab her bag, Declan already had both in his hand. She grabbed their garment bags.

At the front desk, she gave the clerk her name. She checked her in, handed her two keys, and said, "One King no smoking. Room six is right down the hall that way."

"Uh, no. It's supposed to be a double."

The woman squinted at the computer and said, "No. You're registered for a King."

Renee huffed. "I *was* registered for a King. Then I called and asked to switch. I spoke with a younger guy. I can't remember his name. He said I could switch no problem. In fact, he said he'd make the change in a jiffy."

The woman's face drooped. "I'm so sorry. That would be my nephew, Jeremy. He didn't make the change. And we're all booked. I don't have another room to offer you."

Declan stepped closer. "Don't worry about it. We'll be fine."

Renee spun to glare at him, but he took her by the arm and led her away. He'd shifted the bags, so he carried them in one hand, allowing him to pull her.

"What are you doing?"

"Are you really going to cause a scene over this?"

"No."

"You look like you're ready to. It's not a big deal. A King bed is huge. You can make a pillow barrier if you don't trust yourself to sleep next to me."

She yanked away from him. "Very funny."

He led the way down the hall to their room. "We're

adults. If we can't stay in the same bed without controlling ourselves, we have some issues."

Of course, he was right. But they hadn't done a good job of controlling themselves the other night in his bed. They had made out in a way she hadn't done in years. "I do not have issues."

She stepped in front of him and unlocked the door. Inside, she went to the closet and hung up their garment bags.

Declan set their duffels on the chair next to the TV. Then he spun and threw himself on the bed. Patting the spot next to him, he said, "Come on. Give it a spin."

"I'm fine."

He sat up. "If being in the same bed is that much of a problem, I can sleep on the floor. I'm not trying to make you uncomfortable."

"I'm fine. And it would be ridiculous for you to sleep on the floor. I'm irritated Jeremy didn't do his job. That's all." That and she couldn't help but wonder if Declan was going to wear those low-slung gray sweatpants to bed. The ones that allowed her to clearly see his hard-on.

"The upside is that we get to be cuddle buddies. Do you want to be the big spoon or the little spoon?"

"Stop it. There will be no spooning. Friends don't spoon."

"Some friends might."

She couldn't help but laugh again. This man was hard to resist. "I'm going to take a quick shower to get ready for rehearsal. You need to use the bathroom first?"

"I'm good." He wiggled his eyebrows. "Unless you want company."

"No thanks. We already talked about how that's not a good idea."

"Your loss." He picked up the remote and turned on the TV.

After the kiss the other night, she had no doubt it was her loss.

She took a quick shower and pulled her hair back up into a ponytail. Mariah had said the rehearsal was casual, and dinner was at a family-style restaurant, so she didn't need to fuss too much. But she didn't want to look like a schlub either, so she chose a shimmery black tank top to pair with her favorite jeans and killer heels.

She stepped from the bathroom and Declan was lying in bed, eyes closed, one arm under his head and the other across his abdomen. Totally relaxed. She rarely felt that kind of peace.

"Why are you staring at me?" he murmured.

"Trying to decide if I should let you nap or wake you up."

"How much time do we have?"

She checked her phone. "About thirty minutes."

"Then we've got fifteen for a power nap. Come join me." Again, he patted the mattress.

"I just got dressed."

He popped one eye open. "I promise not to wrinkle you."

She hesitated and he held up a hand reaching for her. Rather than take his hand, she climbed into the bed and laid down on her back. A power nap did sound pretty good, especially if she had to play nice with Graham tonight. She didn't know if he was going to be at the rehearsal, but since Mariah invited Declan, she assumed Graham had been invited too.

She set an alarm for fifteen minutes and closed her eyes.

Thirty seconds later, Declan rolled to his side, wrapped an arm around her hip, and pulled her close.

"Relax."

So she did. Even though she shouldn't be relaxed in his arms. Even though she knew it was a mistake. Maybe for this weekend, she could enjoy herself. Live her life like Declan led his.

When her alarm went off, Renee startled awake and discovered they were in full spoon mode. Declan had his whole body curled around hers. And it felt far better than she wanted it to.

"Declan."

"I know." He shifted to sit up. He looked down at her with a flirty grin and said, "So you like to be the little spoon."

She shoved his chest. "I was asleep, so I don't think I got a vote." But he wasn't wrong. She thoroughly enjoyed being in his arms.

"I prefer to be the big spoon so we fit well."

She rolled her eyes. "Go get ready. We need to go in a few minutes."

"Do I need to dress up?"

"Nope. Casual all around. I don't know what they have planned other than rehearsal at the chapel and family-style dinner. Some of the bridal party are talking about going out after, but we can cut out."

"We can play it by ear." He disappeared into the bathroom and she climbed out of bed.

She slipped her heels on and touched up her makeup. When the bathroom door opened, she turned. Declan let out a long, low whistle and she blushed. He'd changed into a button-down, navy shirt, a shade darker than his eyes, but wore the same black jeans he'd had on before. She preferred him in a T-shirt because he had some damn fine arms.

"Maybe coming back here right after dinner is a good idea." His gaze traveled up and down her body.

"Why?" she asked.

"So I can see what you have under those sexy clothes."

Her heart rabbited in her chest. Was he seriously suggesting they sleep together? "That's not happening."

"Why not? It'll be a whole lot of fun."

"We talked about this the other night."

"You said you needed to avoid complications because of Sadie." He looked around exaggeratedly. "No Sadie here."

"I'm still her mom."

"Not this weekend. You're just Renee, hot bridesmaid, having a great time."

She opened her mouth to argue, but then his words sank in. Could they throw caution out the window for the weekend? No, it would definitely come back to bite her in the ass come Monday.

Declan raised his eyebrows. "Your silence tells me you're interested, and you're trying to talk yourself out of it."

Damn it. He was right. "No. I'm cataloging all the ways it would be a bad idea."

"And I bet I can counter all of them. But I don't want to make you late, so we can argue later."

He stepped close and put his arm around her shoulder. He even smelled good. It might not be much of an argument if he kept this up.

That thought should've worried her more.

CHAPTER
Fifteen

Declan sat through the boring rehearsal ceremony, even though Renee had told him he could go ahead to the restaurant and hang out at the bar. Graham was sitting across the aisle from him staring at the bridal party at the front of the chapel.

Declan assumed Graham was looking at his date. What was her name? Tina? But since Renee was standing next to her, Graham could've been ogling Renee. She looked fucking hot in that tank and those heels. He wondered if she dressed to remind Graham of what he lost or if she wanted to make him jealous. Renee didn't strike him as the kind of woman who played that game. The jealousy part.

He could totally see her rubbing her sexiness in his face to make him regret what he lost. He scrolled around on his phone, tempted to read, but he liked his reading time with Renee. It wouldn't be fair to go on without her, but he didn't have the attention span to read two books at the same time.

Luckily, the rehearsal didn't last too long. His lunch had worn off long ago and he was starving again. Renee came down the aisle toward him and he stood.

So did Graham. He tugged at the sleeves of his shirt and then at his collar. He was more uncomfortable than Declan was.

"Renee," Graham said with a nod.

"Hi," she answered with zero inflection or emotion in her voice.

With a tilt of his head and a raised eyebrow, Graham continued, "Really? Declan is your date? Are you that desperate?"

"What?" Declan said, his hand automatically fisting.

Renee stepped in between them. "First of all, Graham, who I date is none of your business. Second, Declan is a thoughtful, caring man who can rock my world with a kiss. So, no. I'm not desperate. Haven't been since our divorce."

Declan couldn't stop the chuckle. She'd warned him she could be bitchy, but damn. Not that Graham didn't deserve it.

Graham looked past Renee to Declan. "I didn't mean to offend you. But you are younger than she is and let's face it, she only knows you because you're Tyler's friend."

"And you only know Tina, and everyone else here, because they're my friends. What's your point?" Renee asked. "And you really, *really* don't want to talk about age differences."

There had to be a story behind that comment. Declan wondered. Tina didn't look super young or anything.

She turned to face Declan. "Ready to go to dinner?"

"Sure." Although he'd been prepared to defend her or run interference with Graham for her, he loved watching her take care of herself. He appreciated a woman who didn't need to be rescued.

Over her shoulder, she said to Graham, "Please do not sit with us during dinner."

Declan held her hand as they left the chapel. Renee's back was straight and the line of her shoulders was stiff with tension. Outside, he tugged her back so she crashed into him. Lowering his mouth to her ear. "That was fucking hot."

"Watching me yell at my ex?"

"Watching you tear him apart. That alone made my night." He brushed his lips over her earlobe. "At least till later. I'm sure you can top that."

She laughed and he felt her soften. He hated Graham had that effect on her.

"Let's go to dinner. I'm starving."

"You still eat like a teenager. It's not fair." She turned toward the car without a comment about later. She also didn't respond when he took her hand again.

At the restaurant, they had one long table to seat the entire bridal party and their dates. The bride and groom made some quick speeches to thank everyone for being part of their wedding. Then, finally, the food arrived.

As requested, Graham sat at the other end of the table, but he sat across from them. Declan felt the constant staring. If Graham wanted a show, Declan could give him one. He made a point of touching Renee in small ways that gave the impression of intimacy. He knew her well enough already to know what she would like. Nothing over the top.

But tucking a stray lock that fell from her ponytail back behind her ear? Yeah, that earned him a small smile. As the salad plates were being cleared, he picked up her hand and kissed her knuckles. When she looked at him with one eyebrow raised, he simply returned her gaze and added a grin as he thought about getting her naked.

He knew she'd be able to read the look.

She leaned closer and whispered, "Are you flirting

because you think you're getting me naked tonight, or are you just trying to irritate Graham?"

"I'm definitely getting you naked. I can't stop thinking about it. But irritating the fuck out of Graham is an excellent bonus."

Laughter burst out, and she slapped a hand over her mouth as people around them turned. "You're terrible."

"Yeah, but you like me anyway."

"I do," she said with another of those soft, genuine smiles he'd come to want from her.

The rest of dinner went off without a hitch. He talked to the people on his side and across from him, fielding the usual questions he'd expect when dating someone. It was easier though with Renee since he had known her most of his life. There was no stumbling over information. Except when the woman across from him asked how long they'd been together. They hadn't talked about what to tell anyone. He'd figured he'd be arm candy to strangers and a buffer between her and Graham. He hadn't given their status any thought.

Renee patted his thigh. "It's still pretty new."

He interlocked his fingers with hers. "But in some ways, it doesn't feel new. I guess that's a perk of starting off as friends."

She let him hold her hand, and it was like their own little secret. This wasn't about irritating Graham. It was about whatever they had simmering between them and her coming to terms with acting on it.

The bride stood and clinked her fork on her glass to get everyone's attention. "I know tomorrow is a busy day, but we have some fun planned for us tonight. We're going as a group to a bar down the street to do karaoke."

Renee groaned.

Mariah pointed at Renee. "Don't even think about slipping out of here. We haven't had a karaoke night in years. You owe me."

"You sing?" he asked.

"Not very well. And usually drunk."

"It'll be fun!" Mariah said. "Let's go."

RENEE REALLY WANTED TO PINCH HER FRIEND, BUT SINCE IT was Mariah's wedding, she'd let this slide. They hadn't sung karaoke since before she had Sadie. But that was because she was a bad singer. Hence the reason for her to be drunk when Mariah insisted on singing.

Everyone stood and pushed their chairs back under the table. Some slammed back the rest of whatever drink they had in front of them. Unfortunately, her glass was already empty.

"We'll get drinks at the bar."

"I hate singing."

"Just wait until everyone has had a few more drinks and no one will remember what you sound like. They'll all be buzzed and talking and won't pay attention to you."

"I still won't like it."

He took her hand again. He seemed to want to touch her in any way she'd let him. Even the small ways. And she liked it.

They were a good-sized group, about twenty people, all walking down the street en masse. Renee slowed her pace so they could be at the back of the pack. While she knew the bridesmaids, she didn't really know anyone else, and she was tired of small talk.

"Everything okay?"

"Yeah. I don't like big crowds." She nodded toward the group in front of them. They waited at the curb as the first people entered the bar.

Tina came up to them—thankfully without Graham. "Can we talk a minute?"

"Sure. What's up?"

"You want me to—" Declan pointed over his shoulder.

"Wait by the door. I'll be right there."

Tina waited for him to step away and continued, "I figured since you and Graham divorced a long time ago, dating him was okay."

"It is."

"We haven't been dating long, but..."

"What is it, Tina?"

"I'm not sure he's over you."

Renee laughed. "He was over me long before the divorce."

"Are you sure?"

"Yes. And even if he's got some silly idea in his head about wanting me back, it's never going to happen. I'm always going to be tied to him because of Sadie, but that's all. Maybe one day, I'll be able to be friends with him, but most days, it's an effort to remain civil. So he's all yours."

Tina smiled. "Given how much he's talked about you since this morning, I'm not sure I want him either. I wasn't planning on asking him to come with me, but he kind of weaseled the invite."

Renee rolled her eyes and shook her head. "That *was* probably about me, but not in the way you think. He was supposed to take care of Sadie all weekend for me. This way, he didn't have to."

"I still think he's hung up on you."

"Not my problem. Let's go get a drink."

"Sounds good. I'm glad you're not upset."

"No worries at all."

At the front of the bar, Declan held the door open for Tina and when Renee moved to enter, he put his arm around her. "What was that all about?"

"Absolutely nothing important. I need a drink."

"Beer? Wine? Margarita?"

"A shot is the best way for me to make up to the stage, but since I want to be able to function tomorrow, let's go with beer."

"I'll get the beer. You get us a spot." He stepped away and added, "Away from Graham. Every time I see his smug face, I want to punch him."

Renee pointed at him. "No punching. This is Mariah's wedding."

"As long as he keeps his mouth shut, I'm good."

Renee went to the back room to find the rest of the party. On stage, Mariah's and Kent's moms were singing some song she'd never heard. This was gonna be a long night if Mariah expected them all to sing. Maybe she should just choose something to get it over with and then leave. She grabbed a small two-seater table and waited for Declan.

Before she even got to sip her beer, Mariah was demanding all of the bridesmaids come to the stage to sing with her. Renee hung her head but stood. At least in a group, no one would know how bad she sounded.

Declan arrived as she was leaving the table. She took the bottle from him and took a quick gulp. "Be right back."

Once on stage, Mariah handed all of them a microphone. "I trust you all know this one."

The opening notes let Renee know it was "Girls Just Wanna Have Fun," which was, in fact, a fun song. The four of them sang and laughed.

Renee saw Declan standing next to their table, smiling at her.

When the song ended, she stepped from the stage and Graham stood as she passed. "You looked good up there, Renee."

"Thanks." She didn't stop to talk. She went straight back to Declan, who was still smiling at her.

"You're nowhere near as bad as you made yourself out to be."

"I'm a horrible singer. But since Mariah dragged me up there, I can return the favor when it's my turn." She was already planning what song to sing. "But first, I need to call Sadie to say good night and then get some more alcohol in my system."

As she raised the bottle to her lips, he wrapped his fingers around her wrist. "Don't overdo it. I'll be sad if you pass out before I can get you naked."

Her cheeks warmed again and she was glad the bar was dim. "I won't get pass-out drunk. I promise. I have to stand up in the wedding tomorrow."

Plus, she really wanted to know what Declan had been thinking about all day. She wanted to experience whatever he had planned for her.

Declan ordered another round for them while she stepped outside to call Sadie.

"Hello, Renee. Everything is fine."

"I know, Mom. I'm just calling to say good night to Sadie."

"One second."

Renee heard some rustling on the line and then Sadie's cheery voice said, "Hi, Mom."

"Hi, baby. I'm calling to say good night. Got your pajamas on?"

"Uh..."

"I know Grandma's gonna let you stay up past your bedtime, but at least get ready, okay?"

"Okay. Are you having fun?"

"A little bit."

"Can I say good night to Declan?"

"I came outside the restaurant to call. He's inside, but I'll let him know you asked."

"If Declan's there, you gotta have fun."

Renee smiled. "I will. I'll call you tomorrow. Big hug and kiss." She made a smacking noise into the phone.

Then her mom came back on. "How're things going?"

"Good. We're doing karaoke now with the rest of the bridal party."

"And Graham?"

"Still an ass." She thought about how mad Declan got on her behalf. "But it's not bothering me much. Don't let Sadie stay up too late."

"Of course not."

Renee rolled her eyes. "Talk to you tomorrow."

Back inside, she had another beer and decided it was time to sing. She grabbed Mariah and told her they would sing Lizzo's "Good as Hell." It had been the song they sang many times the year before she had Sadie. Mariah had a hard breakup and the song became an anthem of sorts for them. Because who the fuck needed to be wasting their time over a man who didn't really love them?

Mariah held up a hand before the music started. "Just

over six years ago, I was in a horrible relationship and my pal Renee helped me bounce back from it. This is a song we rocked every time we were together until I felt ready to get back into life. If she hadn't done that for me, I wouldn't have met Kent to be here today."

Mariah wrapped her arms around Renee's neck and planted a sloppy kiss on her cheek. "That's what friends are for."

The music started and for once, Renee didn't care how she sounded. She was back in her car and in Mariah's living room dancing around singing full volume to make her friend feel better. When they were finished, she received a standing ovation—probably more for their enthusiasm than ability, but she didn't care. It was fun.

CHAPTER
Sixteen

Declan was mesmerized by Renee on stage. They hadn't done anything more than kiss once, but he was falling for her in a way he didn't think was possible for him to fall for a woman. He found joy in her happiness, which was weird. With other women, it was about feeling good physically in the moment, but with Renee, all the moments felt good. But if he said that to her, she wouldn't believe him. Like most people, she didn't take him seriously. He was a good-time guy, and it had always been enough.

She made him want more.

As she made her way back to the table, she was strutting. She'd always been confident, but she was owning her space and it was a fucking turn-on. When she neared, he pulled her close and kissed her hard, not caring who stared.

With one hand on her ass, he held her tight to his body and stroked his tongue against hers until she moaned. Yeah, she couldn't deny this.

She pulled back slightly but didn't step out of his arms. "What was that for?"

"Good singer or not, that was hot."

Her smile was crooked and she ducked her face away from him. He stepped back and sat down. While she'd been gone, he ordered her another beer. He pushed the bottle toward her.

"We can probably escape after this one." She took a drink.

"Do you want to escape so you don't have to sing again, or are you looking forward to being back in the room alone with me?"

"Both."

He smiled. At least she was honest. She wasn't trying to pretend they weren't attracted to each other.

She scooted her chair closer to him and leaned closer to him to talk quietly. "I want to see what you have planned for us. I want to feel your hands all over me. To feed this attraction. But it's only the weekend."

He turned his head to look into her eyes.

"This weekend, I'm fun Renee who sings on stage and drinks a little too much and throws caution to the wind—within reason. You can do what you want to me this weekend, but when we get back to Chicago, we go back to being friends."

He licked his lips and considered her words. If he pushed for anything more right now, he wouldn't get to have her at all. If he agreed, he had the weekend to show her what they could be. "Whatever you want."

She initiated the kiss this time and he fell into her taste. He hoped a couple of days would be enough because he wasn't sure how he'd handle not being able to touch her again.

"Let's go back to our room and check out the king-size bed."

"What do you think I am? I think you should romance me some more," he said with a grin.

"I'll romance you plenty when we're naked."

He didn't need to be told twice. He grabbed her hand and pulled her through the bar and straight out to the street, where he held out his free hand. "Keys?"

She just looked at him.

"You've had more to drink than I did. You needed the liquid courage to get on stage."

"I'm fine to drive, but if it'll make you feel better, here." She dug into her purse and handed him the keys.

At the car, he opened the door for her and waited for her to get settled. As he walked around to the driver's side he considered how much she'd had to drink. He got in and adjusted the seat and mirrors. "How drunk are you?"

"Not at all." She paused. "Buzzed, but no more than I am on book club night."

"You sure?"

"You ask that a lot. Do I strike you as the kind of woman who says things she doesn't mean?"

He started the engine and pulled away from the curb. "No. I never want to assume anything and overstep."

"Aw, Declan, are you worried you're taking advantage of me?"

He slid her a look at her patronizing tone.

She leaned across to get close to him, stretching her seatbelt. She slid a hand along the inside of his thigh. "I am not drunk. I am in full control of my senses. I am making the conscious choice to get naked and fuck you."

She stroked him through his jeans and then slipped back to her seat. "It might not be the wisest choice I've ever made, but I doubt I'll regret it."

"That's all I needed to know." He whipped into a

parking spot at the bed and breakfast. "What time do you have to be ready for the wedding tomorrow?"

"I'm meeting Mariah and the other girls after lunch to get our hair done, but then I'll finish getting ready in our room. Ceremony starts at five. Why?"

"I don't want to be the cause of you not making it on time because I kept you up too late, but that's plenty of time to work with." He took the key from the ignition. "Maybe."

She grinned. "I like the way you think."

They walked to their room like civilized people, not groping and climbing all over each other, even though the thought had crossed his mind. The sexual tension had them practically speed-walking as if they didn't want to waste any time. When they got to the door, he pressed close to her while she unlocked it. He skimmed his hands over her hips and brushed a kiss on the curve of her neck.

She shivered under his touch as she popped the door open. He held her pressed against his body until they were clear of the door and he kicked it closed. Only then did he release her and she turned to face him.

She ran her hands up his chest and then wrapped her arms around his neck. "I had a good time tonight. I'm glad you came with."

"It's about to get a whole lot better." He began walking her backward toward the bed.

"Really? Is that a guarantee?" she asked with a grin.

"Definitely."

"Pretty sure of yourself. What if I'm a hard-to-please woman? I've been told I can be difficult." She pinned him with challenge in her eyes.

He pushed her back onto the bed. "One, you just spent part of your night with your asshole ex giving you a hard time. That's pretty fucking easy to top." He unsnapped her jeans. "Two, I don't believe you're all that difficult. I had you moaning from a kiss." He slid his hands beneath the waistband and tugged the denim over her hips. "And three, I've got all night to make this happen."

She wore simple black underwear, not particularly sexy, but seeing her with her jeans around her ankles as he peeled them from her body, he was so fucking turned on he wasn't sure how long he'd last. She sat up and took off the tank top as he yanked the jeans all the way off.

"Problem?" she asked.

He realized he was staring. Holy fuck. Renee Kane was nearly naked and waiting for him. He took a deep breath. "Not at all. I was enjoying the view of a sexy as fuck woman."

"No flattery needed. I'm already in bed and wearing far less than you are. Planning on joining me anytime soon?" She scooted back toward the pillows.

He unbuttoned his shirt and watched her move. "Anything off limits?"

"Like what?" she asked suspiciously. "Wait. Shit. Please tell me you have a condom. That's off limits."

He tossed his shirt onto the pile of clothes on the floor and bent to reach into his duffle. He grabbed his condoms and set them on the nightstand. "Always prepared."

Shucking his jeans, he said, "I was asking about more specifics. Like how to do feel about oral?"

"Giving or receiving?"

"Both." He climbed on the bed, covering her with his body. He kissed her neck while waiting for an answer.

"I'm good with either, but it's been so long since I've been on the receiving end, I can't recall how good it might be."

He laughed against her collarbone. "Setting the bar kind of low for me, Rennie."

"Don't do that."

He sucked her nipple through her bra. "Huh?"

She arched toward him. "Don't call me Rennie. But do that some more."

He chuckled and gave the other nipple the same attention. He slid a hand under her to unclasp the bra so he could feel her skin. She rose up enough for him to discard the bra.

Before he had the chance to go back to her breasts, she held his face and brought his mouth to hers. She kissed him deeply and fiercely, like she did most things. He pressed against her, twisting his hips so she could feel what she did to him.

Wrapping her legs around him, she thrust up. Then she shoved at the waistband of his underwear. "Get rid of these."

"In a minute." She looked so disappointed, that he almost laughed. "First I have to leap over the low bar you set."

His meaning registered and she let her legs slide from his hips, and she lay back. With a wave of her hand, she said, "By all means."

He trailed wet, open-mouth kisses down her abdomen and across the line of her underwear, the smell of her arousal making him harder than he thought possible. She raised her hips for him to take her underwear off. He tossed them aside and shouldered her thighs wider. Her smooth skin slicked against his shoulder as he gripped under her legs and around her hips to anchor her in place.

He would show her he was not the kind of man to leave her wanting or in need, so got comfortable to be here as long as necessary. He started slow, nuzzling his nose in her scent, tracing her edges with the tip of his tongue. She immediately started wiggling. He tightened his grip.

He followed with long, wet kisses, taking in her taste. He thrust his tongue inside her and she bucked, causing his nose to bump her clit. So she did it again, chasing the thrust of his tongue. So he gave her what she wanted. Circling her clit until she moaned. Then he flicked it with his tongue.

She grabbed his hair, pressing him close. He worked her over, alternating the tip of his tongue with broad strokes of the flat of his tongue allowing her taste to coat him. When she began writhing and trembling, he sucked her clit between his lips and pressed his tongue on the magical little button.

Then he pushed two fingers deep into her and pumped. Her body vibrated as she took over the rhythm and pace, using his mouth and his hand to find her release.

She remained quiet, just a low, long moan, and whispered, "Oh, God."

Her thighs trembled around him until he felt every part of her being go taut. Her legs became vice-like and her grip on his head tightened to the point of pain. Lustful, pleasurable pain. And then a final, barely audible, "Fuck."

Her pussy pulsed against his fingers and his dick begged to sink into her wet heat. Slowly, she came down. Her fingers relaxed first, allowing him to move his head. Her legs slid off his shoulders.

Placing one last kiss on her glistening skin caused her hips to jump in reflex. He pulled his fingers from her and kissed his way back up her body. She looked at him with blissed-out, glazey eyes.

"Still with me?"

"Uh-huh."

"Good. 'Cuz I'm not done with you yet." He reached for a condom and slid it on.

He poised himself at her entrance and lowered himself to kiss her as he slid in. She pushed her hips up to meet him, taking him deep.

"Hey, Declan?"

"Hmm?" he said, concentrating on not being a two-pump chump.

She pulled him close and whispered in his ear, "You flew so high over that bar, it's no longer in sight."

He smiled as he kissed her again before driving into her. His release was building but he wasn't ready to be done.

Grabbing her hips, he rolled to put her on top. She froze. At first, he thought he'd startled her with the movement, but she suddenly looked uncomfortable.

"This okay?"

RENEE STARED DOWN AT DECLAN, HIS INTENSE BLUE EYES roamed her face. She braced her hands on his muscular chest. "Yeah, of course," she lied.

It had never bothered her to be on top before. Sometimes she even preferred it. But that was with Graham. Even with some random dude, it probably wouldn't bother her. But she didn't want Declan to see all of her this way. Her flabby parts, the stretch marks that would surely be more visible as she sat up in the light.

She moved slowly over him, trying not to bounce too much. He reached up and cupped her breasts, rolling her nipples between his thumbs and fingers. It felt so good, her head lolled back a little.

"I see you like that as much as I do. Come here." He tugged her forward to suck on her. His beard added a unique sensation.

His mouth drove her toward the edge again and she picked up her pace, bouncing on his dick as he thrust up and into her. It was like she couldn't get enough of him. Her nipples became so sensitive, she needed a break.

She sat back up, his hands never leaving her breasts. She rolled her hips to try to find just the right spot.

Then Declan slipped a hand between them where their bodies joined. His thumb pressed her clit, sending shocks through her body. She gripped his wrist to hold him in place while she rocked back and forth. He continued his upward thrusts.

The movement was awkwardly mesmerizing. Her mind was blinding white. Every nerve sizzled and waves rushed through her. As she pulsed around Declan, he drove up hard and fast. Flashes of light sparked behind her closed eyes until he growled his release with both hands gripping her hips. Fingers pressed tight on her flesh, pushing down on his hard length. His dick filled her in the best possible way as her body continued to pull and pulse and milk him.

Finally, they both sighed and she slid down on top of him, hot and sweaty and sticky. And so spent that she didn't care.

Her whole body hummed in pleasure as she lay on top of Declan. His heart thundered under her cheek, but his hands were gentle on her back. As her body came down, she began to feel awkward. What was she supposed to do now?

Roll off him and say, "Thanks for the lay?"

This wasn't some stranger she was screwing for the night. This was Declan. Her wedding date. The same guy she was driving home with on Sunday.

Fuck.

She knew this was a bad idea.

Oblivious to her wild thoughts, his fingers caressed up her back and into her hair. He tugged to get her to look at him. "Hey."

She lifted her head and rested her chin on her hand on top of his chest. "Yeah?"

"That was incredible. But now I'm hungry again. Think we can DoorDash something in this town?"

She smiled. Even though he'd just given her an amazing orgasm and she was sprawled on top of him naked, he was still the same Declan. "I'm sure we can."

She pushed up and looked for her purse to get her phone. While rummaging through the things on the floor, she slipped Declan's shirt on so she wasn't parading around naked. She got her phone and scrolled. "Not a lot of options, but here you go."

She handed him the phone. "Order what you want. I'm going to shower."

"You want anything?"

"Maybe just some fries."

Before heading to the bathroom, she grabbed her sleep shorts and T-shirt from her bag. She didn't close the door all the way so steam could escape the small room. She took in her appearance in the mirror. She looked like she had just gotten laid. It felt fabulous. Beard burn marred her chest and her nipples perked up at the thought of Declan's mouth on her.

While the water warmed, she emptied her bladder and

then laid the small mat in front of the tub. She stepped under the hot spray and wet her hair.

A minute later, Declan came in. "Can I join you?"

"Don't you have food coming?"

"I've got at least twenty minutes." He pulled the curtain aside. "Plus, we'll save water this way."

She had the bar of soap in her hand, but he took it from her. "Let me."

He lathered the soap and then ran his hands all over her body, turning her on again. Once she was rinsed, he slid a hand between her legs and stroked gently.

She sighed. "I don't have a condom in the bathroom."

"Don't need one," he said as he kissed her neck.

She was slick and turned on in moments. She reached for him and stroked in the same rhythm he used on her. They held onto each other and rode the waves of pleasure. Working each other over in near silence, their heavy breathing was the only sound competing with the streaming water.

He came second after she did, and for a long moment, they continued to stand under the hot spray, clinging to each other.

Finally, he stepped back and swatted her ass. "Outta the way. I gotta clean up before my food gets here."

She turned toward the water once more to rinse away all evidence of what they'd done before stepping from the tub and wrapping a towel around herself. She quickly dressed and went to check her phone for a notification about the food. Sure enough, the driver was less than two minutes away.

She slipped on a pair of socks and walked back to the lobby to grab the food. As soon as she smelled it, her stomach growled. Dinner had obviously worn off. She should've ordered more than fries.

Back in the room, Declan stepped out of the bathroom wearing those well-worn gray sweatpants that barely held onto his hips. His hair was a wet mess and dripped water onto his shoulders and chest.

His wide smile caught her attention. "Like what you see?"

"What straight woman wouldn't? You're a good-looking guy standing half-naked in my bedroom." Plus, there was the fact he'd given her two phenomenal orgasms that replayed so vividly in her brain she could still feel the aftershocks.

He laughed.

"What?"

Lifting a shoulder, he said, "I don't know. I was making a joke and you're so serious all the time. I expected a smartass comment and you give a real answer. Takes some getting used to."

He reached for the bag. "You okay eating on the bed?"

"As long as you don't slop food everywhere." She climbed on the bed and sat cross-legged.

He ripped open the bag. "I know you said you just wanted fries, but I thought you might be hungrier, so I got you a kiddie burger."

"Oh my god. Thank you. I thought I was good, but as soon as I smelled the food, my stomach let me know how empty it was."

He handed her the small burger and a bag of fries. Then he sat next to her. They devoured the food and cleaned up.

Then, she started to feel awkward again. Spending the night with someone wasn't something she did.

"Are you gonna stay awake long enough to read?"

There was no way she was going to fall asleep right now. Even with a full belly and being sexually satiated. She was buzzing from the good time. "I think I can handle that."

She propped the pillows up against the headboard and slid under the covers. After she set her alarm for the morning, she grabbed her ereader and handed it to him.

"You want me to read?"

"Yeah. I like the sound of your voice." He climbed under the covers with her and slid an arm around her shoulders, pulling her closer.

This was different than how they'd been reading. They'd stayed a safe distance from each other on the couch. Having sex changed things, even small ones like this. She couldn't even try to lie to herself about that.

But she'd said they could have the weekend. Monday was going to be painful. She already saw it.

For now, though, she pushed it from her mind and enjoyed the feeling of his chest against her cheek as she lay on him and let his voice lull her.

CHAPTER
Seventeen

Declan lay awake after Renee had fallen asleep in his arms. He contemplated how to treat what would surely be an awkward morning for them.

However, when the sun streamed through the window and he rolled over to pull her close, he found he was alone. He sat up, scrubbed a hand over his face, and checked the time on his phone. She'd said she was getting her hair done or some shit, but it was only nine.

He got out of bed and took a shower. Maybe she left because she had regrets. He hoped the fuck not. That would make for an even more awkward weekend and a long drive home.

Plus, he wasn't ready to walk away from what they'd started. When he got out of the shower, he heard noise in the bedroom. Renee must've returned, so he wrapped a towel around his waist and went out. "Hey."

"Hi." She turned and flashed him a bright smile. "I thought you'd still be sleeping. I went out and grabbed some breakfast and coffee."

He froze for a minute, completely unsure of how to respond. He'd been so sure he was going to have to argue with her about how good last night was and how it wasn't a mistake that seeing her happy caught him off guard.

"You okay?" she asked.

"Yeah. I was wondering where you'd gone."

She held up a bag. "Breakfast. I figured we both worked up an appetite last night. Even with the midnight snack."

"Honestly, I thought you slipped out because you were having regrets." He stepped closer and wrapped an arm around her waist. "I've never been so glad to be wrong."

He lowered his mouth and kissed her. The faint taste of coffee mixed with mint, but underneath, Renee's uniqueness. And he wanted more.

Her fingers gripped his shoulder, flexed, and then pressed him back. "Let's eat."

"What time do you have your hair thing?"

"After lunch, which I'm supposed to eat with them."

"Then I have plenty of time."

Her smile was soft and warm. "We do. That's why I brought breakfast back here. We can fuel up and then burn it off before lunch."

She stepped out of his embrace, but took his hand and led him to the small table by the window. She pulled wrapped sandwiches from the bag, and the smell had his stomach growling.

She smirked. "See? You're hungry."

Since he couldn't argue, he took a sandwich from her, held the edge of his towel, and sat down. She sat across from him and stretched out her legs until her feet rested on his lap. It was such a comfortable move, it caught him off guard. Why had he thought this morning would be awkward? They were good together.

He took a huge bite of the sandwich and gave himself a moment to thoroughly enjoy the flavors before asking, "What's the schedule for today?

"I need to have lunch with the girls. We're going to get our hair done together. Then I'll be back here for a little bit to get dressed and do my makeup. Thankfully, Mariah's not doing a whole bunch of pictures before the wedding. The photographer is just doing shots of her. I have to be at the hall at four. The ceremony is in one room and then we move down the hall for the reception."

"So you don't need me until it's time for the wedding?"

"The day is yours."

It wasn't like he was looking forward to spending time at a wedding with a bunch of strangers but hanging out in a town where he didn't know anyone wasn't much better. They finished eating and cleaned up.

"You want to go for a walk or something? It looks like a great morning," he asked.

She looked a little puzzled. Flicking a thumb over her shoulder, she said, "I thought we had plans."

"It's not even ten."

Pulling him close, she repeated what he'd said last night, "Then we have plenty of time."

She tugged the towel off his waist and his dick immediately took attention. She stroked him a couple of times, pulling a moan from him. Then she lowered herself to her knees and took him in her mouth.

"Fuck," he whispered.

She licked down the length of him and sucked on the head. When she released him from her mouth, she looked up at him with a wide grin. "Still want to go for a walk?"

"Fuck no." He gently gripped her head and moved her back to his throbbing dick.

She went back to sucking and stroking him. Her free hand slid up his chest and toyed with his nipple before coasting back down and massaging his balls.

His grip on her hair tightened and he flexed his hips. In his head, he recalled the recipes for mixed drinks he created as a bartender because he would not embarrass himself by coming too quickly.

Renee squeezed him gently and moaned deep in her throat. He felt the vibrations all the way up his spine. He thrust into her mouth twice and then pulled away. "I want to be inside you. Now."

He yanked her up and pushed her on the bed.

She huffed a laugh as she yanked off her shirt and pushed down her jeans. "In a rush?"

"Fuck yeah, I am." He sheathed himself in a condom. Lowering himself to kiss her, he stroked her and found her already wet. "You like having my cock in your mouth?"

"If I didn't, I wouldn't have done it." She wrapped her legs around his hips and pulled him close.

He guided himself to her entrance and rubbed her with his head. When he bumped her clit, her hips jumped. He sank into her, covering her body with his, so he was on top of her, skin to skin. He thrust slowly, drawing out pleasure for both of them. When he pushed deeply into her, he rotated his hips a bit to rub her clit. He wanted her as off balance as he was.

They moved together and he knew he couldn't hold out much longer. Reaching between them, he used his thumb to circle her clit. She threw her head back and he felt her muscles constrict and pull him deeper. Her thighs trembled on his hips.

He buried his face in her neck, pumped a few more

times, and followed her over. They lay silently, except for their rapid breaths. He inhaled her scent and considered that he would never get enough of it.

When his heart rate returned to almost normal, he rolled off her and disposed of the condom. Then he flopped back next to her.

"I've really missed having great sex," she said.

"Glad to be of service." He turned to his side and toyed with her hair. The sun highlighted the reddish-brown strands as they slipped through his fingers. "I'm glad we're doing this weekend together."

"So am I."

"What about after this weekend?" He knew he shouldn't have brought it up, but he figured in the post-orgasmic moment, she might agree to more.

She turned to face him and levered herself up on her elbow. "We talked about this. Us having a relationship would be messy. I have enough messy relationships to last a lifetime."

"Why do you assume it has to be messy?"

"Because you're my brother's friend. You live in my house and are my contractor." She hesitated. "And really, I'm not sure either of us is ready for any kind of commitment."

It was the last one that meant the most to her and stung the most for him.

"It's not that I don't think you're capable," she added. "But even you said part of living with me is so you can figure out your life. You might figure out you're meant to live a nomad life and travel the country in an old RV. That would never be me. You might want someone who doesn't come with a ready-made family."

"I'll never not love Sadie."

She smiled at him and stroked the line of hair on his chest. "I know. It's one of the many reasons you're an awesome guy who will make a woman incredibly happy."

Why can't it be you? He wanted to ask but feared the answer. He wasn't good enough. Not yet.

"I don't suppose you'd be willing to wait for me?" he joked.

"Sure, dude. I'll put my life on hold and pine away for you like we're in a novel."

"Pining is good."

She laughed and sat up with a sigh. "I should probably shower and get ready. I don't want to go to lunch smelling like sex."

"I thought the goal was to make them all jealous."

"That was never the plan. I don't need to make Graham jealous. I don't want him to want me, and jealousy would imply that." She walked toward the bathroom. "Make him regret his life choices? That would be okay. But I could not care less what anyone thinks about my relationship status."

He watched her walk away and began plotting how to get her to give them a real chance.

RENEE SAT AT LUNCH WITH THE BRIDAL PARTY AND THEY chatted about the singing and drinking at karaoke the night before.

Mariah pointed at her. "You cut out early."

"Not that early. I sang twice." Then she smiled a grin

that she'd been trying to hide since she left the room. "It's not my fault I got a better offer."

Mariah cackled. "I bet it was a better offer. Declan is hot. When the hell did that happen? When you mentioned a plus-one, I thought you were bringing a friend."

"He is a friend."

"Who is obviously offering some damn good benefits. You're practically glowing."

Tina nudged her shoulder. "You are looking good. Whatever you have going on, keep it up. I'm pretty sure it's driving Graham crazy."

The smile fell from her face. "I'm not trying to make him anything. Really. There is zero possibility of a second chance romance here."

"Oh. I didn't mean it like that. I believe you. I'm not sure he does, but that's on him."

The whole thing felt too familiar to Renee. "So I guess you aren't in it for the long haul, huh?" She slapped a hand over her mouth. From between her fingers, she added, "Sorry. That is none of my business."

Tina chuckled. "You're fine. Unless something changes pretty quick, no, I won't be around much longer. I'm really starting to think he's with me to try to make you jealous. We're all too old for those games."

"Thanks. I appreciate it. I don't think he's dating you to make me jealous. I think he wants to prove he's moved on, and I'm fine with that."

Tina lifted her Bloody Mary. "To all the men who aren't assholes. May they make you laugh and come in equal measure."

The whole table burst into laughter and conversation turned to advice for Mariah about how to keep the spice going in her marriage.

As a group, they went to the salon and took turns getting their hair and nails done. It was a nice, relaxing afternoon. When they finished, Mariah was a whirlwind of excitement as she and her sister were off to meet their mom to get ready and take pictures. She yelled at all of them that they had less than two hours to finish getting beautiful and get to the hall.

They all gave their assurances they would be on time. Renee felt light and happy. Of course, the champagne they'd shared while at the salon played a part in that. But the rest had been hanging with friends, even if they weren't close. This weekend had been a blessing—a break she didn't even know she needed so badly.

As she walked down the hall to her room, she vowed to make some more time to relax and do things for herself. Tyler or her mom would babysit for her. She entered the room and was met with silence. Declan must've decided to go out and find something to do.

She looked around the room. Other than watching TV, there was nothing to do here. She pulled her dress from the wardrobe and took it with her to the bathroom to finish getting ready. After sending a text to Declan to remind him what time the ceremony started, she applied her makeup. She never spent a lot of time on makeup, but for the wedding, knowing she'd have to smile for a gazillion pictures, she put in a little extra effort.

Still not a lot of makeup though. She didn't need it rubbing off on Declan's borrowed suit. The thought brought images of being in his arms, dancing. And more. Suppressing a shudder, she stepped into the dress, glad Mariah had kept it simple.

The navy blue dress had a sweetheart neckline and little off-the-shoulder straps. It flared a little at the waist and swirled around her knees. It was the cutest bridesmaid dress she could remember ever seeing. That included the ones her friends had worn at her wedding.

The door opened as she put in her earrings. She stepped out of the bathroom. "Hey. Did you find something fun to do?"

He stood staring at her. His eyes went a little dark. "Just wandered around a while."

"We have less than an hour to get to the ceremony, so you should probably start getting ready."

He stepped closer. "It only takes me a few minutes to change my clothes."

Wrapping an arm around her hip, he tugged her close. He nuzzled her neck and then kissed her. "You smell so fucking good."

She tensed and tried to step back. "We cannot do this. I'm dressed and you need to get ready."

"You said I had an hour."

"*Less* than an hour."

He kissed her neck. "Ten minutes to get to the hotel. Ten minutes to change. That gives me at least twenty minutes to make you come."

"No!" She gripped his shoulders. "I'm ready. I don't have time to change and if you mess up my hair, Mariah will kill you."

He shifted to look into her eyes. "So, as long as I stick to the schedule, and I don't mess up your hair or dress, I can do what I want?"

"I didn't say that."

His hand skated up her thigh. "But you want to."

"We don't have time."

"We do. Let me prove it."

"We can't be late."

"I promise you will be on time, looking hotter than the bride." He stroked her through her panties.

Her eyes fluttered closed. This man was going to be the death of her. She didn't respond. There was nothing to say. Whenever he touched her, she melted and couldn't think straight. He had her hot and ready and she was already breathing heavy.

"Come here and sit down." He led her to the chair by the window.

"I can't wrinkle this dress."

"Sweetheart, if I make you come while you're standing, you'll fall over and mess yourself up. Trust me."

As she lowered to the seat, he lifted her dress so it flowed behind her and over the arms of the chair.

"Now lift up a second so I can take off your underwear."

She did as she was told.

He tsked at her. "Already wet. You might want to get a fresh pair." He inhaled deeply before tossing them aside.

She closed her legs and pressed her thighs together.

"Uh-uh. That's for me." He slid her dress a little higher, careful not to wrinkle it, and disappeared between her legs.

He didn't toy around but dove right in, sucking and licking. One arm scooped behind her ass and scooted her forward. Without missing a beat, he thrust fingers inside her and began pumping to the rhythm his tongue kept. She tried not to move, afraid of messing up her hair and the dress, but he felt so fucking good.

She slapped a hand on top of his head and held him as she shifted to keep his mouth where she wanted it. He suddenly switched his movements rapidly alternating between flicking her clit and sucking hard on it.

"Oh, god. Don't stop. Please."

He chuckled and she felt the puff of air against her wet

skin as an added sensation. She no longer cared if the dress was wrinkled. She thrust her hips up and rode the fuck out of his face until she was shuddering and shaking, sparks of light flashing behind her eyelids, and unable to speak coherently.

When he was done, every muscle in her body was loose. He'd been right. There was no way she'd still be upright if she'd been standing when he did that.

He popped out from under her skirt and looked at the bedside clock. "By my count, I still have about ten minutes."

"Oh god. I can't do more of that. I won't be able to walk down the aisle."

"Don't worry. It's my turn. Stand up."

Even though she wasn't sure her legs would hold her, she did what he asked. He spun her to face the mirror over the desk in the corner. Skimming his fingers across her collarbones, he whispered against her neck, "You're so beautiful I can't control myself. Every time I look at you, I want you again."

Her eyes drifted closed as he spoke.

"Bend over and hold onto the desk. I need to be inside you, but if I lay you down, everyone will know I fucked you right before the wedding."

She leaned forward, keeping her eyes on his as he dropped his jeans and kicked them to the side. He lifted her skirt and flipped it over her back. With both hands, he grasped her ass cheeks. "Oh, fuck," he said reverently.

As he massaged her cheeks, her eyes fluttered closed again. Everything he did felt so good, but it was almost over-whelming. Almost.

His hands left her body and she heard him tear the condom wrapper. She reopened her eyes and watched him in the mirror as he entered her. With a grin, she said,

"Better hurry. We're on a schedule. I'd hate to cut you off before you finish."

He smacked her ass as he thrust deeper. A rotation of his hips had her eyes rolling back in her head. How did he know how to get to her every time?

He began pumping into her and after a few strokes, he lost his restraint. He pounded into her, flesh slapping. Every time they connected, she came a little closer to the brink and it was like he knew it. He reached around and pinched her already sensitive clit.

It sent them both over again.

When she reopened her eyes, she caught him staring at her in the mirror. The look was filled with something other than lust, but she didn't know what to think. Her mind was foggy from sex.

He pulled out and said, "Don't move."

"Wha—"

"Stay." He pointed a finger at her.

"I'm not a dog."

Returned a second later with a washcloth. "I promised you would not only be on time but that you wouldn't be a mess."

He gently cleaned her up.

The action was so kind and thoughtful, that Renee didn't know what to do with the swell of emotion bubbling up in her.

"Okay." He tossed the washcloth into the bathroom. "Now go get some fresh underwear while I get dressed."

"Yes, sir."

"You don't want to start, or we'll never make it out of this room."

She shivered a little but stepped away from him. True to his word, he was ready in less than ten minutes. She freshened her makeup and they were out the door with five minutes to spare. They walked to the hall holding hands like a real couple.

Renee chose not to think about the ramifications of that. Right now, she was too happy to care.

CHAPTER
Eighteen

Declan barely paid attention to the ceremony since he didn't know either party. He sat near the back and his eyes were glued to Renee. She was beautiful walking down the aisle. Her smile was radiant, and he liked to believe he played a part in that. He snapped a picture to send to Sadie later. She should know how pretty her mom is.

He'd thought that at the reception, he would be able to sit with Renee, but she was at the head table for dinner. When she found out, she apologized profusely. He assured her it was fine. He never had problems making friends.

Until he found his table. What the hell was Mariah thinking putting him and Graham at the same table?

Graham was already sitting when he found the table, so Declan chose a seat across from him, deciding that having to look at him was better than having to talk to him. Luckily, he'd already grabbed a beer and a backup from the bar. He'd been to enough weddings to know the bar usually closed during dinner.

Hopefully, the two bottles would be enough. He sat and looked at the woman to his right. "I'm Declan."

"Sarah. Flying solo tonight?"

"Nope. My date is in the bridal party."

"So is mine," she said with a smile. "I guess now we know how Mariah did her seating chart."

At least that made sense. "Have you known Mariah long?"

"Yeah. My husband is the best man. He and Kent have known each other since college. I was there was Kent and Mariah met. How about you?"

"I just met Mariah. I'm here with Renee, one of the bridesmaids."

Her eyes widened and she darted a glance across the table to Graham.

He swallowed a chuckle. "Yep. That is her ex-husband. I'm sure he's known Mariah for years since she and Renee are friends."

"Have you and Renee been together long?"

"Nope. It's really new."

Her eyebrows shot up. "And she invited you to a wedding?"

"I've known Renee since we were kids. So even though this is new, our friendship isn't."

"Oh," she crooned. "You're dating your friend. It's like a novel."

He took a swig of beer. If he'd learned nothing else from Renee, it was how to talk about books. "I can do you one better. Her brother is my best friend."

"Get out." She grabbed his forearm. "You're making this up."

"Nope. Tyler and I have been friends since elementary school and Renee could barely tolerate either of us."

"That is so cool."

Someone began clinking a glass and the speeches started, putting an end to the conversation. Declan tuned out most of this. It wasn't likely he'd ever see these people again. Instead, he watched Renee.

Every now and then, she'd glance over and smile at him. He swore every time it happened, Graham took a drink. While the last speech was wrapping up, dinner arrived. While they ate, Sarah chatted about the ceremony and Mariah and Kent.

The woman on the other side of him listened to Sarah without ever introducing herself. He finished eating and excused himself. He walked around a bit and got some fresh air while he waited for Renee to be released from her duties. When the music started, he headed back toward the room, and his phone buzzed with a text from Renee.

Where are you?

In the hall. On my way back.

Come to the dance floor.

He didn't need to be told twice. He couldn't wait to have her in his arms again. She stood at the edge of the dance floor looking out across the tables when he spotted her. The bride and groom were finishing up their dance. Renee crossed the floor to meet him.

"Can I get you a drink or something?" he asked.

"No. I want to dance."

"Don't you have to do the bridal party thing and dance with whoever your partner was?"

She took his hand. "Lucky for you, Mariah's not that old-fashioned."

The next song was another slow one, which made Declan happy because he really wanted to touch her. He slid an arm around her waist and tugged her close. She was comfortable in his embrace, wrapping her arm around his shoulder.

As they swayed, he asked, "Did you have a good time?"

"Yeah. How about you?"

"I was stuck at a table with Graham, but I was smart enough to take a seat across from him."

"I'm so sorry. I had no idea it was going to be this bad. Tina keeps telling me she thinks he's still hung up on me." She shook her head slightly.

"He'd be stupid not to be."

"We don't belong together and he's gotta know that."

"He might, but he realizes what a catch you are, and who the hell wouldn't want that in his life?" He was talking as much about himself as Graham at this point.

"That's very nice of you to say. You're not so bad yourself."

They moved to the music in silence then. He only had tomorrow to convince her that they could continue what they started here. He considered his words, but then the music changed to something upbeat, and she stepped back.

"Let's see your moves."

He smiled. "Did you forget I have a sister? She's always grabbing me to dance with her at parties."

As she moved her hips to the rhythm, he closed in again, allowing his body to brush hers.

With a smile, she said, "I hope you don't dance with your sister like this."

"Don't be dirty."

She spun around, thrusting her ass into him. "Who are you kidding? You like me dirty."

185

Fuck yeah, he did.

For the next few hours, they drank, talked, and danced. They meshed with each other in ways he never would've considered.

It was one of the best nights of Declan's life.

WHILE WATCHING HER FRIEND GET MARRIED AND ENJOY THE happiest day of her life was fun, Renee knew she wouldn't have had nearly as good a time if Declan hadn't been there. She hadn't thought he'd dance with her all night, but he did —to the fast songs as well as the slow ones.

And when they cut out of the party, he took her back to the room and they had slow, luxurious sex. Being with Declan made her feel young and free again.

Which, in the light of day, was a stark reminder of why they couldn't be together. She wasn't young or free. Her number one priority was Sadie. She had to be because Graham would never put their daughter first. So, she bolstered herself to get her shit together and say goodbye to this fabulous weekend. It was time to get back to reality.

As she climbed out of bed, trying not to disturb Declan, she took stock of how sore her body was. Every muscle ached in one way or another, but it was a satisfying ache. She sighed quietly. So what if she'd have to wait a few more years to feel this way.

Then again, maybe not. Maybe she should put in some effort to get out in the world and date. She wasn't old crone or hag age. Hadn't Declan told her repeatedly that she was sexy enough to get whatever man she wanted? Maybe she should make an attempt.

She moved silently around the room, gathering discarded clothes. Picking up the wedding dress, images swamped her of Declan going down on her and then taking her from behind. Her whole body flushed with the memory. If nothing else, this weekend gave her plenty for her spank bank.

She tossed dirty clothes in her bag and pulled out something clean to wear and put the rest in Declan's bag. As she turned toward the bathroom to shower and get ready, he stirred.

"Come back to bed."

"I'm going to shower and get dressed. You can sleep a little bit longer, but we have to hit the road soon."

"I wasn't talking about sleep." The sleepy grin on his face melted her a little.

"As much fun as I've been having, my body needs a break."

He sat up. With one eye squinted, he asked, "Was I rough last night?"

She chuckled. "Wow. That's not much of an endorsement of my performance if you can't even remember last night. But no, you were the opposite of rough. You did, however, manage to stretch and use muscles I'd forgotten I had."

"I bet a hot shower will fix you up. Then we can go again."

"Then we can head home."

"You're no fun." He flopped back on the pillows.

"I get told that pretty often." She went to the bathroom and started the water. While it heated, she brushed her teeth and studied her reflection. There were no outward signs of how she'd spent her weekend, but she saw the difference in her eyes and her smile.

The hot water eased her muscles and she closed her eyes to relax. The bathroom door opened, startling her. Then she heard Declan peeing. A sudden fear that he would do this when they got home hit her.

"What are you doing?"

"Taking a piss. Kind of thought that was obvious."

"Well, yeah, but..."

"But what?" He tugged the curtain aside a little. "I had my mouth and my dick all over your body the past two days, but hearing me piss is too much?"

She felt ridiculous. "No. But it's a level of comfort I didn't think we had. We spent two nights together."

"Sweetheart, we've been living together."

"It's not the same."

He cocked his head to the side.

"It's not."

He sighed. "If we're gonna argue about this, I'm coming in."

"I'm not trying to argue." She shifted over a little to let him get wet, but he caught her hip and pulled her into his arms.

"We have been living together for weeks." He kissed her neck. "We eat meals together. We read together after Sadie goes to bed." He nibbled on her earlobe, causing her to shiver despite the warm water. "And we spent the weekend fucking."

"That's my point. The weekend is separate from everything else. When we get home, are you going to pee in front of me?"

"If you want me to."

She hung her head and bit back a smile. "You know what I mean."

He touched her chin and lifted her face. "I don't know where we go from here, but I've had a great time this weekend. You have, too. Why does the weekend have to be separate?"

"For the exact reasons you gave for why it was weird to come in and pee."

His face squinched in confusion.

"We're friends. We live together. We hang out. We're *not* a couple."

"But we could be."

"No, we can't. Couples don't start with living together and then fucking."

The water started to cool. She shifted out of his embrace. "You finish up before we have no hot water. I'll finish packing."

She escaped as quickly as possible. What the hell was he thinking? That all of a sudden, they were going to be a couple? They'd agreed that this weekend was about letting off some steam. Exploring the attraction. That was it.

CHAPTER
Nineteen

Renee was running scared. Declan knew it because he'd spent a good chunk of his life avoiding anything that was hard. And he understood pursuing a relationship with Renee would be complicated. Not nearly as complicated as she thought it would be, but he let her go and finished showering.

He was drying off when she leaned next to the open door—pointedly not looking at him—and said, "I'm going to run down the street to the little candy shop we saw and get something for Sadie."

Wrapping a towel around his hips, he moved to the door to stand in front of her. "Give me a minute and I'll go with you."

"You don't have to—"

"I want to. You said I had the weekend with you and I'm going to take full advantage of every moment."

She shot him a look like she would give Sadie when the little girl found a loophole for some directive Renee had given. But she didn't argue.

He dressed in the clothes she'd left out for him and ran

his fingers through his hair. "Should we put the bags in the car, or do that when we get back?"

He watched the debate run across her face. Leaving the bags meant they'd have to come back to the bedroom. Take them now, and there was no turning back.

"Might as well load up now."

He hoisted both bags, even though she reached for hers. That might not have been the decision either of them wanted, but he had to respect her ability to stick to her guns. He nodded for her to go first through the door. She grabbed the garment bags like she had when they arrived. She must've hung up Gavin's suit because he sure as hell hadn't. All he'd been thinking about was getting her naked again.

He followed her out the door and down the hall. While she stopped at the front desk to check out, he kept going to the car. He set the bags on the ground and leaned against the back of the car. She joined him a moment later and unlocked the car.

"Let's leave the car and walk," he said.

She glanced at him as she closed the door.

"Are we in a hurry?"

She half-shrugged. "Not a hurry, but I miss being at home with Sadie. I've never been away from her this long."

He took her hand and tugged her away. "You both need space. It's how you grow."

She froze and looked at him as if he'd grown an extra head.

He pulled her to keep moving. "I've done a lot of self-growth. I learn things."

"It just doesn't sound like the Declan I know."

"That's good. It means there are things about me you still need to learn."

He shifted his hand to interlock their fingers as they strolled down the street. She didn't argue but seemed like she wanted to. "What's your plan for this week?"

"I need to buckle down on the job hunt. I'm sorely out of practice with that, too. Just like everything else."

"You hide it well."

"Hide what?"

They reached the candy shop and he pulled the door open. Whispering in her ear, he said, "Being out of practice. You had no problems the last two nights."

Her cheeks grew pink, as he knew they would.

"What does my friend Sadie like?"

"She's five. Anything made of sugar is a hit."

They strolled down opposite sides of the bins of candy. Declan didn't normally snack on candy, but he paused when he saw a bin of Pop Rocks. In an instant, he was Sadie's age and standing in the convenience store with his dad, begging him to buy a few packages. His dad let him pick out 3 envelopes. Declan had been thrilled. In their family, they usually could only get something if there was enough for everyone, and with seven kids, it was special.

As they walked home, his dad had told him it was their little secret. He detoured and took Declan to a park where they shared the Pop Rocks. The look on his father's face had made him howl with laughter and still pulled a grin from him today.

He reached into the bin and pulled out a few packages.

"Pop Rocks? Really?"

"They're awesome."

"They're weird. Fizzing and popping. Tickling your tongue and tonsils." She gripped her stomach. "And there was one time Tyler dared me to drink a can of pop with a package. He thought it would make my stomach explode."

"Your brother's sadistic."

"Lucky for him, I didn't explode, but my stomach was so upset. I couldn't even think about candy for months."

"I guess I'll have to change your perception of Pop Rocks." He grabbed a few more packages. "Find something for Sadie?"

I got some fudge and some gummy bears."

He walked the aisles, checking out the candy. In the last section, he found a tall canister of mermaid lollipops sitting on the shelf. He pulled out a blue one and then noticed they weren't all mermaids. Some were sea animals like dolphins and whales, so he chose a collection.

When he brought his bounty to the counter, Renee took one look and said, "I never noticed you had such a sweet tooth."

"The Pop Rocks are for us. The lollipops are for Sadie."

"She does not need that much candy."

"But they're cool. There are mermaids and dolphins and even a shark."

She shook her head and rolled her eyes. "When she's bouncing off the walls, I'm sending her to hang out with you."

"No problem." He meant it, too. He never got tired of Sadie.

They paid for their purchases and headed back outside. Renee looked up at the sky and smiled. "It's a beautiful day."

"Let's walk and enjoy it. Maybe grab an early lunch."

She took a breath as if she were readying her argument, but then she angled her head. "Okay."

He thought he'd have to convince her, but her agreement meant she wanted more alone time with him as much as he wanted with her. "Tell me more about the job hunt."

"There's not much to tell. I'd like to get my foot in the door somewhere part-time so that next year, when Sadie's in school all day, I can transition to full-time."

"Is it hard to find a job being an accountant?"

"Forensic accounting is in demand, or so I'm told. I used to work at a law firm. I dug through clients' financials to find irregularities."

"Like what?"

"Usually fraud of some kind. Some government work. The law firm I worked for dealt mostly in family law, so I was always working divorce cases. Divorce is never pretty, but when they called me in, you know it was downright ugly."

"Wow. I never knew you did that."

"Why would you? We've only been on the outskirts of each other's lives. When we'd see each other, it was mostly small talk."

"But Ty never mentioned it either."

"I didn't talk about my job much. It was depressing. Walking away from it to stay at home with Sadie was an easy call. But there are parts of it I've been missing."

They'd reached the end of the busy part of Main Street and turned a corner where they saw a park. They headed there, and Declan took her hand again.

"What parts?"

"I'm not sure I can explain it. It's kind of like putting together a puzzle backward. You don't have any idea what the whole picture is, you just have these pieces. But once you start snapping the pieces together, a picture forms. I miss figuring out the puzzle."

He led them to a bench and they sat. "Where can you do the puzzle part without the depressing shit?"

"Lots of placing are hiring. Most forensic firms want

full-time. I've been doing some consulting on an as-needed basis, but I'm stuck in a weird position no one ever tells stay-at-home moms. I have too much experience to go be a first-year, low-level employee. But at the same time, I've been out of the field for five years."

"What difference does that make? It's not like you forgot how to do your job, right?"

"I'm a risk. Because I've got multiple degrees and certifications, I'm too expensive to take a chance on because the field has changed in the last five years."

"It's shitty that you get penalized for staying at home."

"It's life. I'm more than okay with the choices I've made. It's time for a new chapter."

He slid his arm around her shoulders. "New chapters seem to be the thing this year."

"And what's your new chapter?"

"Still working on it. But so far, this is good." He hoped she got his meaning.

"Everything is an experience to learn from. Including this weekend."

He withheld his sigh. Chipping away at her resolve was going to be harder than he thought. Maybe she was right and they should chalk this weekend up to part of their new chapters and turn the page.

"I'm starving," she suddenly said. "You suggested lunch and now my stomach is telling me it's a good idea."

"You want to drive and stop on the way home or eat here?"

"Here's probably best. Otherwise, we'll have to get off the highway to detour through random small towns."

"Okay. Let's go find some food." He stood and held out his hand.

She hesitated and then took it. They were both uncertain about so much in their lives, but he would take any small win.

AFTER A FILLING LUNCH OF BURGERS AND FRIES AND A fabulous chocolate shake that Declan had talked her into, they were finally hitting the road. They walked back to her car and set the candy on the back seat. She turned on the map app on her phone and directed it to home. The sun was high in the sky, so they would be home well before dinner.

Moments after getting on the highway, Declan reached into the back seat. He ripped open a packet of Pop Rocks and spilled some in his mouth. She curled her lip.

"How can you not like these? It's a whole fun experience."

"It feels weird. They sizzle and it kind of tickles but kind of burns."

"I think we need an experiment."

"Like what?"

"Get off at the next exit. I need your full attention for this."

She sighed, but let him dictate the exit. Even with a silly detour, they'd be home for dinner. She got to the bottom of the off-ramp and said, "Where to?"

He glanced up and down the road and shrugged. "Take a right."

They drove for a few minutes and then he told her to take another right. It was an old dirt road. The kind she would never turn down alone.

"Pull over here." He directed her to an alcove that others had obviously used as a turnaround spot on the small road.

"Have you been here before?"

"No. Why would you ask that?"

"You're sitting over there giving me directions like you have a plan."

"Oh, I have a plan. I'm just lucky I found a good spot." He shoved the gear lever to put the car in park. "I want you to see how much fun these can be."

"Seriously? I got off the highway and parked in serial killer lane here so you can force-feed me some candy? Fine. Let's get this over with and you'll see that I still don't like these." She unbuckled and twisted to face him. Closing her eyes, she opened her mouth, stuck out her tongue, and waited for the sugary assault.

He shook the little envelope and sprinkles hit her tongue. As she pulled her tongue back, his joined hers. The movement startled her and she opened her eyes, but his hand at the base of her skull, guiding her into a deeper kiss had her reclosing her eyes and absorbing all of the sensations.

The rocks began to explode. His tongue slicking against hers cut down on the fizziness, but she began to tingle all over for a completely different reason.

He pulled back and rested his forehead against hers. "See? Good stuff."

"We're not supposed to do this anymore."

"It's still the weekend."

Hell, yeah it was. She grabbed his shoulders and pulled him back for another kiss. The sugary sweetness still clung to them but the lust was always simmering. His hand skated down the front of her shirt, easily finding her nipple. He tugged and squeezed, causing her to moan into his mouth.

He trailed wet kisses down her throat, and she threw her head back giving him better access.

"Maybe we should've done a late check-out," she said breathlessly.

"You were too busy pretending you didn't still want this." He reached between her legs and stroked her through her jeans, applying enough pressure to make her hips writhe.

"Fuck. We can't do this. We're in my car."

He glanced around. "I've done it in worse places."

Sitting back in his seat, he flicked the lever, moved the seat back, and reclined it. He unzipped his jeans and pulled out his hard dick. "Climb on."

"It's broad daylight."

"On Serial Killer Avenue, remember? We'll make it quick. I promise." He rolled on a condom.

Even as she undid her jeans and tried to figure out how to get them off, she said, "I'm too old to be doing this."

"Never too old for a good time, babe."

As she struggled to pull her legs out, he reached over and continued to stroke her, making her wet while losing her ability to focus. She sat back and let him play with her. Her eyes rolled back, jeans forgotten for the moment.

"God, I love watching you." He brought his mouth to her breast and sucked her nipple through her shirt.

She arched into him, seeking everything. She rode his hand until she trembled. Her underwear was soaked and his hand was trapped between her thighs.

"Now that you got yours, get your sweet ass over here."

She finally shoved one leg out of her jeans and climbed over the center console. Straddling him, still a little tangled in her clothes, she let him guide himself into her. She sank onto him. "God, you feel so good."

She was still pulsating from her orgasm, but she wanted more. She rocked her hips, grinding her pelvis low, sending more shockwaves through her. Declan fumbled to push her shirt and bra up and latched onto her nipple again as he thrust upward.

He switched back and forth between her nipples as she rocked, rubbing her clit against him, getting close all over again. Then he gripped her hips and pulled her nearly all the way off him before slamming her back down. It was powerful but not painful. She braced a hand against the roof and let him take over bouncing her on his dick.

He felt so good, but her orgasm was just out of reach and she wanted to scream. As if sensing her frustration, he said, "Don't worry, sweetheart, I know what you need."

Reaching between them, he pressed his thumb on her clit while still managing to thrust her up. Two thrusts and she saw stars. She squeezed around him and jerked as every nerve became wired and sensitive. He brought her close and kissed her as they rode out her orgasm. Then he continued pumping to get his own release.

She collapsed against his shoulder and breathed in his scent. He was going to make walking away from this hard, and it was starting to piss her off. "You tricked me," she mumbled against his neck.

"I only prompted you to do what you wanted. I got you to give yourself permission to be a little bit selfish. Plus, I needed you to see that Pop Rocks are good."

She laughed but forced herself away from him and back to her side of the car. She used a napkin to clean up and untwisted her clothes. "That was one hell of a way to wrap up the weekend, I'll give you that."

He grunted and stepped out of the car to take off the condom, wrap it up, and fix his pants. By the time he sat down again, she was dressed and was studying her face in the mirror, pulling her hair up into a ponytail.

He sat down and buckled up.

"Ready?" she asked.

"Whenever you are."

She pulled out of their little hiding spot and re-engaged her GPS. By the time she got on the highway, the realization hit her. Her weekend was officially coming to a close, and she didn't want to be as conflicted as she was. She'd known that doing anything with Declan beyond friendship would be a mistake, but she almost couldn't help herself.

In the moment, it felt right and so fucking amazing. But now, she was having regrets. She had about two hours to make sure they were going to be okay. That they could go back to being friends.

About a half hour into the drive, Declan turned the radio down a little. He'd been engrossed in whatever he had on his phone. With the lower volume of the music, he looked at her and said, "You totally downplayed your job."

"What?" She hit the button to turn the radio off completely.

"You made it sound like a forensic accountant looks at numbers on a spreadsheet and that's all."

"That is kind of what we do."

"Forensic accountants are the ones who put away Bernie Madoff. You mentioned you could work for the government, and I figured you meant the IRS, but you could work for the FBI or CIA. You could be a badass spy."

"The FBI is out for me. Even if I made it through the application process, I'd have to do their training course at Quantico for five weeks."

"And?"

"Quantico is in Virginia. I live in Chicago. I can't leave Sadie for five weeks."

"But you've thought about it."

"I looked into it as part of my job search. But immediately ruled it out. Plus, private sector always pays better."

"But being a spy is cooler."

She laughed. Not only was his comment funny, but the conversation made her believe they'd be okay. "I don't think any accountant considers themselves a spy, no matter who they work for."

"Why are you looking up forensic accounting anyway? Thinking about a career switch?"

"Hell, no. I could never sit in front of a computer and look at numbers all day. I like to work with my hands. And be around people."

She nodded. It made sense. "I can't imagine you working in an office. Or wearing a suit every day."

"Are you saying I don't look good in a suit?"

"You look great in a suit. I just can't imagine you doing it every day." She drummed her fingers on the steering wheel. "You still didn't tell me why you were looking up my job."

"I want to understand what you do. It's a big part of who you are and you want to spend more time doing it."

She had no words. No guy she'd ever dated just decided to learn more about her career. They'd assumed she played with boring numbers all day. Even Graham had never really understood what she did—even when she was working on a particularly hard case and tried to explain it to him. He mostly tuned her out.

She knew her job wasn't interesting to most people. She was fine with that, but Declan made her feel interesting.

"You got awful quiet. Did I say something wrong?"

"I just realized that you're the first person—except for

maybe my mom—who cared enough about my career to want to learn more about it."

He leaned over and toyed with her hair. "I like learning about you. I want to know what makes you tick."

"Why?" she whispered.

"Because whether you want to admit it or not, this thing between us isn't over."

She swallowed hard and stared at the road ahead. Yeah, he was definitely *not* going to make this easy for her.

CHAPTER

Twenty

While Renee drove the rest of the way, Declan read to her from their book. By the time they reached home, they only had a couple of chapters left. As soon as the car was parked, Sadie came running out of the house yelling for her mom.

Declan grabbed the bags from the back and let Renee have the fun of giving Sadie the candy she'd bought. Sadie talked a mile a minute, wanting to know all about the wedding. When they got to the door, Geri held it open so he could pass.

"Have a good weekend?" she asked.

"Yeah, it was fun. How about yours?"

"I had a great time with Sadie. Did you by chance punch her father in the face?"

Declan chuckled as he set the bags down in the living room. "Sorry to disappoint you. I was on my best behavior."

"Since it was a wedding, I guess I'll have to let it pass."

Renee and Sadie came through the door. Sadie ran up and looked at Geri. "Declan got me special mermaid suckers. Want one?"

"No, thanks," Geri said. "You save them for yourself. But thank you for asking."

Renee cleared her throat, and Sadie shot her an impatient glance. She looked so much like her mother, Declan smiled.

Sadie wrapped her arms around his legs. "Thank you for the candy."

He placed his hand on her head, her soft curls tickling his palm. "Any time, sweetheart."

"Can we have pizza for dinner?"

Renee groaned. "Is Declan the one you should be asking?"

"He likes pizza."

Declan chuckled. "I don't think she's asking me permission as much as trying to get me on her side."

"Smart girl," Geri said. "Wear Mom down with an ally."

Renee rolled her eyes. "That's fine. I don't feel like cooking anyway." Grabbing her bag, she turned toward her room. "I'm going to unpack. Mom, are you staying for dinner?"

"No. I'm going to head home."

Renee dropped her bag and gave her mom a hug. "Thanks for staying with Sadie."

"Never a problem. Let me grab my things from your room."

Declan took his bag to his room and dropped it on the bed. When he unzipped it, he realized the bag only held the clean clothes they'd brought and not worn. He pulled Renee's clothes out and did his best not to notice the pink, lacy underwear as he stacked it in a pile to return to her.

When he got to her room, he knocked on the doorframe. "These are yours."

She looked over her shoulder. "Sorry. When I was

packing up this morning, I figured it made more sense to put all the dirty clothes together, so I shoved them all in my bag. I forgot to tell you."

He set her clean clothes on the bed. "Want to give me my dirty stuff?"

"I was going to throw in a load. Except your suit. I'll drop that at the dry cleaner tomorrow when I take in my dress."

"I can handle my own stuff."

"I'm going there anyway. And you only had the suit because you were doing me a favor."

He sighed. "I think we're past the favor shit, don't you think? I went with you because I wanted to."

Sadie came running in at that moment, effectively cutting off any rebuttal Renee had. She jumped up on Renee's bed.

"Did you have a good time with Grandma?" Renee asked.

"Yeah. We painted our nails." She held up her little hands to show off blue nail polish that was already chipping away. "And we read *Matilda*, but she's not as good as you."

"Your mom is a really good reader, right?"

"Yeah. Are you a good reader?" Sadie asked.

"I'm not as good as your mom."

"Yeah, he is," Renee added. "I'm not sure if he can do voices though."

She tossed all their dirty clothes into a basket, and Declan took it from her. "I'll throw these in. Hang out with your kid."

He started the laundry and then sat in his room, drawing up the design for the jungle gym he was planning for Sadie. He should've probably told Renee about his plan, but she would tell him it would have to wait. He had the resources to make it happen now—with his brothers' help—so there was no reason for Sadie to have to wait.

Renee yelled when the pizza arrived and the three of them sat around the table eating and talking. It was like having a second family. Growing up with Tyler and Renee had been like this. He'd forgotten what it felt like. But Geri had always welcomed him to hang out at their house, eat meals, spend the night, whatever.

After dinner, he finished his sketch for the yard and estimated the materials he still needed to get that he didn't have from Ronan. He snapped a picture and sent it to Ronan to get his input.

> That's a lot of playground for one kid.

Declan smiled.

> Yeah, but she'll be the envy of the neighborhood.

> Got me there. It would've been awesome to have this as a kid.

> Can you check the estimate I have for price? I want to make sure I'm in the ballpark.

> I have some more stuff for you that'll knock it down a little.

> Are you still available this weekend? Sadie is supposed to be with her dad and I want to surprise her.

> You're really involved with this kid.

> She's practically family.

> You better remember this when I start having kids.

> Something you want to tell me?

> Not yet. But when you find the right person, you know.

Declan wasn't sure he'd ever know. He'd never given thought to a permanent relationship. Wanting more from a person didn't occur to him. Until now. He liked how he felt with Renee and Sadie.

> Does Saturday work?

> Only if we start early. None of that starting after lunch shit.

> I don't do that. At least not anymore. I'll be ready.

> I'll be there at 7.

> Thanks, man.

> No problem.

He had everything lined up. Sadie would be ecstatic. She'd be swinging like a monkey on her own in no time. And with any luck, Sadie's happiness would keep Renee from being mad at him.

He went to the kitchen to get something to drink and Sadie came in.

"Good night," she said.

He squatted to get a hug. Once her arms were wrapped around his neck, he stood, letting her body swing from him. She squealed in delight, so he walked like that to her bedroom, and Renee followed.

"Can you read to me?" she asked as he plopped her on the bed.

"Uh..."

She looked at her mom. "You said he's a good reader."

"He is," Renee said, climbing to get off the bed. She held out a book to him.

"You know, Sadie, your mom really missed you this weekend, so how about you let her read tonight and I'll do a different night this week."

"Promise?"

"Promise." He kissed her on the head and said good night again.

He went to the kitchen to grab the can of pop he took from the fridge and went back to the living room. He heard Renee's quiet voice reading. He couldn't make out the words, but it was a soothing sound regardless. When she came to the living room, he held up his phone. "Ready for our story time?"

"What?"

"We have the last couple of chapters of Nick's book."

"Do you think that's a good idea?"

"Why not?"

"Because reading together is how this—" she waved a hand between them— "started."

"And before this weekend, we managed to read together right here on the couch without anything happening."

"I don't know."

"Come on. I want to see how it ends. What sense does it

make for us to go to separate rooms to read the same thing? Look. I'll sit all the way in this corner and you can sit over there. I won't be able to touch you."

"Fine." She crossed the room and sat in the opposite corner, pulling her feet up in front of her.

"I guess I'm reading tonight?"

"You have it out."

He opened the book and picked up where they left off. Nick was groveling and trying to convince Sophia that she belonged with him. He forced his voice to remain calm, even though the storyline was hitting a little too close to home. These two people were so clearly right for each other, but the emotions were wild, and Sophia couldn't see that she could trust him. Declan began to wonder how the author would pull this off.

Renee released a wide yawn.

"You want to stop?"

"No. We gotta be close to the end."

He continued, and the book ended with Sophia dragging Nick off to bed. Renee sighed. Or maybe it was another yawn.

"That was so good."

"Yeah, it was."

"I'm going to bed. Back to regular routines tomorrow."

Declan rose. "Think about me when you drift off."

"I'll be thinking about Nick." She smirked.

"You keep telling yourself that. We both know I'm better than a fictional character."

"Says who? I have an incredible imagination."

"Let me know when you need another demonstration."

She huffed. "This is not conducive to being just friends. Please don't make this hard."

"That's what he said."

She laughed, as he'd wanted her to.

"I don't want things to be weird between us. I think we can have more of what we had this weekend. But I can respect you not wanting to pursue it."

"Thank you."

"Doesn't mean I won't make the occasional joke, though."

"I can probably live with that."

He hoped he could.

RENEE COULD HARDLY BELIEVE IT, BUT DECLAN WAS TRUE TO his word. He worked on her house during the day—current job: painting the bathroom—and they continued to hang out in the evenings after Sadie went to bed. Some nights they read together, and other nights they watched TV. But he didn't try to convince her to have sex. He didn't attempt to touch her or kiss her.

And yet...there was something about the way he looked at her. When their eyes met across the table while listening to Sadie tell them about her day. Or when things were heating up between the characters they read about. The look told her he still wanted her. Wanted them to be more than a weekend.

But she was conflicted. Nothing had changed about her arguments for why it was a bad idea. The more she thought about it, the more she was worried about the upcoming weekend. Sadie would be with Graham and Renee wouldn't have the buffer of her five-year-old to save her. Maybe she should make plans to get out of the house and keep busy.

Keep her mind off her libido and desire to be naked with Declan again.

The feelings would fade.

They'd spent the last five days in this friendship pattern and it felt like she had it handled. But now it was Friday and Graham was on his way over to pick up Sadie, so they would be alone. They hadn't really been alone since they'd gotten back from the wedding, so this would kind of be a test.

At five-thirty Graham was at the door and Sadie was jumping up and down, excited to hang out with her father. Renee opened the door. "Hi."

"Daddy!" Sadie scooted around Renee's legs.

Graham scooped her up and kissed her cheek. "Ready to go?"

"Yep."

Renee leaned forward and kissed Sadie's head. "Have fun." Looking at Graham, she added, "See you Sunday."

He nodded but didn't say anything else. Renee went back in and straightened up the kitchen. Declan came from the bathroom carrying a paintbrush and roller. "Bathroom is done. Want to check it out?"

"I'm sure it looks good." She took the paint supplies from him and began cleaning them in the sink. "Got plans for tonight?"

"Not really. Why?"

"Just wondering if you're going to be around for dinner."

"Let's go out."

"Out?"

"Yeah, you know, grab some burgers and beers."

She thought about it as she scrubbed the brush. Friends went out to dinner together. It might be good to get out of the house. "Sure. Got a place in mind?"

He leaned against the counter and shrugged. "We can find someplace. Maybe we can find a karaoke night."

"Hell no."

"Come on. You were good."

"I wasn't and I'm not about to embarrass myself again. Food and drinks. That's all." She squeezed the brush out and set it on the edge of the sink.

"Whatever you say, boss. I'm going to go clean up. Is it okay if I use your bathroom?"

"Of course."

He disappeared to shower and she finished the paint cleanup. While he was gone, she looked at the other bathroom. It looked good. The light bluish-gray paint brightened the room, which wasn't a difficult task considering it had been a murky green color. However, now that the walls looked good, the age of the vanity and medicine cabinet was painfully obvious. Maybe she'd look into replacing them.

It seemed like every small project grew in scope no matter what.

While Declan was getting ready, she went to her room and changed her clothes. Nothing fancy—this wasn't a date —but she didn't want to be a slob either.

When Declan came out, his hair was damp and probably finger-combed, messy on top and falling a little on his forehead. He wore jeans and a T-shirt, so he wasn't looking at this like a date. They were on the same page.

"Ready?" he asked.

"Yeah. I'm hungry. Hope you have someplace good in mind."

"Why don't you pick?"

"I never go out. I don't know what's good."

He huffed. "Fine. Let's go."

She grabbed her keys, but he held out his hand. She looked at his outstretched hand.

"It makes sense for me to drive since I'm choosing."

"Fine." She set the keys in his palm. His fingers curled around them, brushing along her hand. Tingles of awareness shimmied up her arm, but she shoved the feelings down.

Declan smiled and turned to the front door. He held it open for her. On the way to the restaurant, they chatted about Sadie and projects on the house. When he pulled into the parking lot, she laughed. "You've got to be kidding. A country bar?"

"Trust me. They have the best burgers. Plus, you might enjoy the music."

She halfway rolled her eyes. This was what she got for telling him to pick. She couldn't complain now.

Inside, the music was loud but not obnoxious. She followed Declan to a table near the back. A table near a dance floor. He couldn't possibly think...No. They were friends having a drink and burgers. No dancing. Definitely no slow dancing. The last thing she needed was to be in his arms.

When their burgers arrived, she jumped in. After two bites, he asked, "So what do you think?"

"I think this is one of the best burgers I've ever had." She pointed to the dance floor. "The entertainment's not bad, either."

A group started a line dance. They were fun to watch, even though they were a little messy. They were enjoying themselves, and that's what made it fun.

"We should give it a try."

"I don't know how to do that." She took another bite of her burger.

He said nothing else but dug into his own food. "Are you doing anything tomorrow?"

"No plans. Job hunt. Work. Nothing exciting."

"You should take the day off. Go out and do something fun. You're always working."

"I do what I need to do."

"You should take a spa day or something."

She barked out a laugh. "Do you know me? I've never done a spa day in my life."

"All the more reason to."

She eyed him suspiciously. "Are you trying to get rid of me?"

As she had the thought, her brain scrambled. A spa day wouldn't last into the night, so he wasn't planning a party or an overnight guest. What was he up to?

"No. Why would I want to get rid of you?"

He got dodgy after that. Renee's mom sense was on high alert. He was up to something. Declan focused on his burger and waved the server over for another round of beers.

"What's your plan for the weekend?

"I'm gonna work on my to-do list for the house."

"I told you before that I don't expect you to work weekends. You should go have fun."

"I'm going to." He grinned.

After a swig of beer, she set her bottle down. "I don't like surprises."

"Noted."

"I'm serious, Declan. Don't do some crazy bullshit and think I'm going to be cool with it."

He sat back in his chair, took a drink of his beer, and sighed. "You should trust me more. I surprised you with an awesome mural in Sadie's room, right? What do you think I'm going to do?"

He was right, of course, and it made her feel like an ass for accusing him, but she didn't like not knowing what was going on.

As if sensing her discomfort, he leaned forward again and grabbed her hand. "I promise I'm not going to mess with the house. At all. I just have a side project I'm working on."

She wanted to feel relieved, but he was right—she didn't quite trust him.

"Come on. Let's go dance."

"Nuh-uh."

He rose, still holding her hand, and yanked her from her chair. He pulled her to the dance floor and they joined a line dance mid-stride. She did her best to follow along, but she made a mess of it. Declan's rhythm was way better than hers, but he didn't care. By the end of the song, they were laughing.

The music switched and a slow song came on. She turned to go back to the table, but he tugged her back into his arms.

"Afraid of a little dance with me?"

Yes, the voice in her head screamed. "Of course not." And she allowed him to pull her closer. She had no idea what the song was about. Her thoughts were consumed by the feel of his arms around her, the press of his palm against her lower back, the rise and fall of his chest against hers.

Fuck. She was in too deep. This was such a mess. But rather than pull away, she simply closed her eyes and swayed to the music.

CHAPTER
Twenty-One

Declan had accomplished the near-impossible: Renee in his arms again. This past week had been nothing short of torture. Every time he looked at her, he wanted to grab her and kiss her. But he couldn't.

He'd promised he wouldn't.

But it didn't mean he didn't want to. He understood her hesitation, but they were good together. And right now, things felt pretty perfect.

When she didn't pull away, he did his best not to cheer.

He enjoyed feeling her pressed against him as he considered his next move.

The song ended, and she slipped away from his body. He continued to hold her hand.

"That was fun. Thanks for the dance," she said before pulling away.

He followed her back to the table and ordered them another round. When they sat, he said, "I wish you wouldn't pull away from me."

"You know why."

"I'm not sure I do. We like each other. We get along. We have amazing sex. When we're together, we can spend hours talking or just sitting silently. How many people have you had that with? I know for me, the answer is zero."

Their drinks arrived, but he wasn't really thirsty. Renee, on the other hand, chugged about half her beer.

Then she sighed as she set her bottle down. "Why can't we have all that without the sex? We had it before we spent the weekend together. I just want to go back to that."

"I don't want to." If he was being honest, he wasn't sure he could.

She shook her head.

"You don't have to decide anything right now. Let's just enjoy the night. Want to dance again?"

She looked past him to the people on the dance floor. "I would."

They danced for a few more songs and stopped in between for drinks. While he switched to water, Renee continued with another beer. More dancing and more drinking on her behalf until he finally called it quits. She was more than buzzed, and he hated the possibility that she was drinking that much because of him.

He paid the tab and she said, "I don't want to go home yet."

"Babe, you're drunk."

"I'm not drunk. You told me to have fun. I'm having fun."

"But you won't have fun tomorrow. You'll be hungover."

"Pssh. I don't have Sadie for the weekend. I can sleep it off." She stood and wobbled toward him. "Wanna sleep it off with me?"

Sure. *Now* she makes the offer. If he'd thought that was on the table, they would've been out of here hours ago.

"We'll see," he said, knowing full well that he'd be tucking her in alone.

He led her to the car with an arm wrapped around her shoulders partially to keep her steady, partially because he wanted to hold on to her as long as he could. She was quiet on the drive home and he thought she'd fallen asleep, but as soon as he'd parked the car, she huffed.

"What?"

"As much as I love my life—and I really do—I kind of didn't want tonight to end. If last weekend taught me nothing else, it was that I need to have more time for me to be Renee." She opened the car door and stepped out.

He met her and put his arm around her again. "I'm here any time you need a break."

"I know. That's part of why I can't be with you."

"What?" He unlocked the front door.

"You're all about having fun. I get that. I'm even a little envious. But you've seen my life. Most of it isn't fun. I can't take off whenever I want. I can't stay out late and party. I can't just decide to *not* come home. But you can." She kicked off her shoes and wove her way through the living room to the kitchen.

"Are you saying we can't be together because I'm irresponsible?"

She poured herself a glass of water. "It's not that you're irresponsible. It's that you don't have any responsibilities. And that's okay. It's your choice. Just like I made my choices to take on the responsibilities I have. I didn't have to buy a house. Certainly not this one. But I wanted to even though I knew it would be hard. I'm looking for a full-time job even though it'll be hard to not be with Sadie all day."

Nothing she said was wrong. She wasn't even criticizing him, but it still stung. "I don't understand your logic. I'm happy to take on some of your burden. That's what you do when you're with someone."

"I don't want you to take on my burdens. And neither do you. Not really."

"Then what do you want?"

"I'm not even sure. I need someone who gets it, and I don't think you do."

"Because I don't have a house and kid?"

"Or a regular job or a car payment or an apartment. You live a no-strings life, and I can't comprehend that."

"So we can't be together because I'm too different and we don't understand each other." He stepped closer and looked directly into her eyes. "I understand you better than most people in your life. I think you're scared. We have something pretty good here and you don't know how to handle it. You're used to doing it all on your own and the thought of letting some of your control slip freaks you the fuck out."

She jerked back a little as if surprised he would call her out.

"But know this. I'm not going anywhere. You will be able to count on me. And you only have to loosen the control you feel comfortable with." He kissed her temple and stepped away. "I'm going to prove to you that we work."

He went to his bedroom vowing to himself to figure out a way to show her that they deserved a chance.

HOLY CRAP WHAT WAS THAT NOISE? RENEE SAT UP IN BED, checked the time, and flopped back. While it was later than her usual wake-up time, it was only eight, and without Sadie in the house, she thought maybe she imagined the noise. She closed her eyes again and allowed herself to enjoy being in bed.

But there it was again. Someone was yelling. And power tools? She sat up and her head thumped a little. Next to her phone on the nightstand was a glass of water and a couple Ibuprofen with a note from Declan.

This should help.

She hadn't had that much to drink last night, had she?

After taking the pills and drinking the water, she thought back over her evening. She'd had a great time with Declan, dancing and talking. Then she vaguely remembered asking him if he wanted to join her to sleep it off. Shit. That had launched them into a longer conversation about why they needed to remain just friends.

He wasn't buying into it though. She hoped her reasoning wasn't going to drive him away anyway. The whole point was to be able to keep him in her life as a friend. She kicked off her covers and stumbled to the bathroom for a shower. Once she was dressed, she decided to investigate the noise. She couldn't imagine one of her neighbors was doing some kind of work that would be that loud.

Which meant Declan had started whatever his project was.

Damn it. He'd promised he wasn't going to mess with the house. She went through the living room and into the kitchen but saw no sign of him. Then she heard another yell. It wasn't like a fearful scream but more of a command or barked order. She looked out the window and saw

Declan in the backyard with two other guys building something.

She was going to kill him. But first, she was going to enjoy a cup of coffee. The caffeine might be enough to stave off homicidal thoughts.

She poured a cup and watched them work. She couldn't tell what they were building but after watching, she realized the guys with him had to be his brothers. They looked similar even though the one was hugely muscular.

That had to be Ronan. He was the one barking orders. The sounds of a saw and drill filled the air. She had no idea how long they'd been at this, but whatever they were building on the ground seemed pretty big. Once her coffee was finished, she headed outside.

As she neared, Ronan noticed her first and tilted his chin in her direction. Declan turned around.

"Hey, you're awake. Feeling okay?"

"I'm fine. What's going on here?" she asked, waving a hand in the general direction of the lumber spread on her lawn.

"We're building a playset for Sadie."

She closed her eyes and tried not to blow a gasket. When she reopened them, she spoke calmly. "We talked about this. I can't afford an extra project. This isn't a necessity. Good windows are."

"Your windows are coming in a week or two. And this isn't costing you anything. Ronan got me extra materials from jobs."

She eyed the lumber. "All of this was free?"

"Mostly. But I did some work on his house to pay for the rest."

She hung her head. She felt like a loser. "God, Declan. This is not your job."

He came closer and grabbed her upper arms. "I'm doing this because I want to. I want Sadie to have an awesome backyard."

When he gave her such an earnest look, she couldn't stay mad at him. "I suppose your brothers are working for free, too?"

"Hell yeah. That's what family is for. Speaking of which, Tyler will be here later to help."

"Jeez. Now I'm gonna owe Ty, too? Are you trying to kill me?"

"Shit. You know Ty will work for food."

He slid an arm around her shoulders and turned with her. He pointed across the yard. "See where Ronan is standing? That's going to be monkey bars. Then, where you see Brendan, that's going to be the swings. On the other side of the monkey bars, I'm going to add a slide."

"How big is this thing going to be?"

"Pretty big, but we want her to be able to grow into it. It would suck to have something for a little kid and not be able to use it later."

"I don't know what to say."

"How about—Declan, you're amazing and I bow to your greatness."

"Now you sound like Ty." She nudged him with her elbow. "Thank you."

"No problem. I better get back to it before Ronan gets mad."

She followed him where the others were putting wood together. "What can I do?"

Ronan looked up from where he held a circular saw and a length of wood balanced against his leg. "Unless you can use power tools, nothing."

That seemed a little harsh.

The saw whirred and he zipped through the wood, dropping a smaller piece on the ground. When he set the saw down, she stepped closer. "I'm Renee. Thank you for doing this. I don't know how Declan got you here, but I'm willing to help or try to pay you something."

"He got me here because he's my brother. You can scrap up when we're done. Till then, you'll just get in the way."

She stepped back and turned around. Brendan met her. "Sorry my brother comes across as a dick. He doesn't mean anything by it. He's not good at using his words."

Renee cracked a smile at that. "Thank you for what you're doing here."

Brendan waved in the direction of the house. "Go about your business. We got this."

"Are you sure? I don't feel right about leaving you all here to do work when you don't even know me."

"You must matter to Declan, or he wouldn't ask, so that's it."

She nodded, unsure of what else to say. If roles were reversed, would she do the same for Declan? Yes, she would, even if they had never slept together. They'd known each other for too many years to not have some connection.

Since she couldn't help them build, she would do what she could. She'd run to the store and get some beer and plan to make them a good lunch.

Once she got back from the grocery store, she hauled in the food and beer and loaded the fridge. Then she got to work. She made a batch of cookies. Desserts weren't really her thing, but cookies were easy. Then she seasoned the chicken and steaks she got for the grill. She wouldn't be using the grill too much longer as the weather got colder, so she liked the idea of using it for Declan and his family.

She didn't know what time they would break for lunch,

so she went outside to ask. As she walked out the back door, she couldn't believe what she found. The three men were raising a structure and attaching it to another. If Declan hadn't told her what they were building, she might've been confused, but she could envision what he planned. The monkey bars were up and they were attaching the section where he would hang swings.

It was a pretty massive project, but she had to admit it was going to be amazing. She took a deep breath and waited for what she thought would be a good time to interrupt.

"Hey, I got some food to grill for lunch. When do you guys think you'll take a break?"

"Food?" Declan asked. "We'll stop whenever it's ready."

She checked the time. "About a half hour?"

"Sounds good. Thanks."

She started the grill and went back inside to check her cookies. She pulled them out of the oven and set them to cool. Then she stood by the window and watched the guys work. It was a thing of beauty to watch men build something from nothing. A few minutes later, Declan jogged toward the house.

"Hey," he called from the door.

"Problem?"

"I don't think so. Ronan's girlfriend Chloe is coming over. You got enough food for her to eat too?"

"Of course."

"That's what I figured, but Ronan was ready to have her bring food for both of them. He doesn't want to impose."

"Impose? The man is like eight feet up in the air bolting things together for my daughter, who he doesn't even know. I think I can spare some chicken and steak."

"Steak? Going all out to impress my family?" He wiggled his eyebrows.

"To thank your family? Yes."

He came closer, snatched a cookie from the rack, and jumped back before she could swat at him. He scooted around her, leaving a wide berth as he went to the fridge. "And you got more beer? It's like heaven."

"The bar is pretty low there."

"Whatever." He loaded three bottles in his arms and reached for another cookie.

This time, she did smack his hand.

He just laughed and said, "Yell when lunch is ready."

Once he cleared the door, she heard him yell, "We got steak, chicken, and beer."

She shook her head and went back to preparing the meal.

CHAPTER
Twenty~Two

Declan handed each brother a bottle and went back to drilling the holes needed for the swings.

"Renee seems nice," Brendan said.

"She is."

"Gavin said he thought something was happening with her," Ronan added.

"Gavin should keep his mouth shut."

"So it's true."

Declan looked at Ronan. "Not sure."

Brendan chuckled. "Not a good sign."

He twisted the eyelet into place. "We're attracted to each other and we spent last weekend together at a wedding, but she wants to stay just friends."

"With benefits?" Brendan asked.

"Nope."

"Shame."

"Tell me about it."

"Why?" Ronan asked.

"Why what?"

"If she fucked you and then called it quits, there has to be a reason."

"She was upfront and said we could have the weekend. I figured I could convince her for more, but she's not sure. She's afraid of fucking things up. Ty's my best friend and we have a lot of shared time." He took a swig of his beer. "Then there's Sadie."

"Kids change things," Brendan said. "Especially for a mom."

"I would never mess with Sadie. I love her."

A truck pulled up out front and Tyler hopped out.

"Don't mention anything to Ty. No need to get him pissed off over nothing."

Brendan narrowed his eyes. "Are you sure it's nothing?"

"It's more for me. Or at least it could be. But she's not ready." He waited until Tyler was at the edge of the house. "About time you showed up, lazy ass. Just in time for lunch, of course."

"I had work." He took Declan's hand and pulled him in for a pat on the back. Looking at the swing set, he said, "Sadie is gonna love this."

"Yeah, she is. She'll have the monkey bars mastered in no time."

"Where do you need me?" Ty asked.

Ronan moved his ladder over to the other side. "Declan and Brendan are working on swings, but you can help me with the slide."

"Sure."

Declan returned to Brendan's side and worked on the swing hardware.

"What are you gonna do about it?" Brendan asked quietly.

"About what?"

"Renee."

"Not sure exactly. I'm gonna figure out a way to show how it's a good idea."

Brendan laughed. "You're a good idea?"

"Fuck you." The comment held no venom. He knew his family saw exactly what Renee did: an irresponsible kid. "Anything on your investigation?"

"Not exactly." Brendan's eyes darkened. "We keep asking people about Alan Cahill, but he was so revered that most people have nothing bad to say. Even the ones who hated him have nothing to say because they never got close enough to learn anything of value. It's just speculation, which is all I've had for years."

"Let me know if I can do anything."

"Brendan's too busy trying to do it all himself. God forbid he ask for help," Ronan called from the top of the slide.

"You're one to talk," Brendan shot back.

"Look, all I'm saying is Danny Cahill hasn't come back to the company, and he hasn't fired me yet. Now's the time to poke around."

"If you poke around, your ass will get fired."

Tyler watched the two of them go back and forth, and then asked, "Poke around for what?"

He looked at his best friend. "Remember what I told you about Alan Cahill? They're still investigating." He pointed at Ronan. "He wants to dig around Cahill's company because it was Alan's before his son took over. But Mr. FBI over here," he pointed at Brendan, "doesn't want Ronan doing anything else."

He looked at his brothers. "And these two don't realize

they had to work together to get as far as they have. So much for the older siblings being wiser."

Tyler held the plastic slide in place while Ronan bolted it in, mumbling something about him being a smartass. A little while later, the smell of food from the grill hit them, and Declan's stomach growled.

"Hey, guys," Renee called from the door. "Food's almost ready."

"Thank God," Declan said. "I'm starving."

Ronan climbed down. "Good timing. Nothing will fall over if we take a break."

"Fall over? It's nearly done," Declan said, stepping back to admire their handiwork.

They went inside together and took turns in the bathroom to wash up. Of course, his brothers felt the need to check his work in the bathroom and then moved through the house to see what else he'd done. He'd expected to be on the receiving end of some teasing, but surprisingly, they complimented his work.

"Offer still stands," Ronan said as they sat at the dining room table. "I can bring you on my crew."

"You think I want to work with you? Shit, maybe if we didn't share a last name." In truth, he had given it some thought. He could work for his brother, but he wasn't sure that was the kind of work he wanted to keep doing. He liked working with his hands. He guessed he got that from their dad.

But he didn't think he could work for the family that might've played a role in his death. The doorbell rang, and Declan got up to answer it since Renee was busy in the kitchen. Chloe stood on the porch.

"Hey, good to see you," he said.

"This feels weird. Why did Ronan tell me to come here to eat lunch? I don't know this person."

Declan laughed. "You'll like Renee. And as far as Ronan telling you to come here, his original plan was to go out to lunch with you or have you pick something up. He wants to hang out with you since you're working tonight." He pulled her through the living room. "What can I tell you? The man loves you."

"Yeah, I do." Ronan stood and kissed Chloe.

It was good to see his brother, who normally grunted at people, express actual emotions publicly. There might be hope for him yet. Declan left them to help Renee in the kitchen.

"What can I do?"

She spun in a circle, waving her arms around tons of food. "Take something to the table?"

He stepped closer and touched her arm. "Slow down. This doesn't need to be a production. They don't care."

"But they're doing so much work—for *free*."

"First, don't let them fool you. It's not really free. They'll call in this favor from me when they need help. It's how our family works. Second, you got them beer, and that would've been enough."

She continued to stare at him.

"Take a breath."

For a change, she listened. When she released it, she seemed calmer.

"I'll grab the platter of meat. You grab the salads." He turned with the plate that held a mountain of chicken and steak. When he reached the doorway, he said, "Hey, Ty. Go grab beers for everyone."

"Since when do you tell me what to do?" he asked, even as he stood to head to the kitchen.

"Don't be an ass to our guests," Renee said behind him.

"Ty is not a guest."

"I was talking to my brother."

Declan made a face at his friend as they passed. They set the food on the table and everyone started complimenting Renee on the food. He shot her a smile as she took a seat next to him.

They all passed food around so everyone could pile up their plates. After a few minutes of silence as they ate, the questions started.

Chloe looked at Renee. "This is delicious."

"Thanks."

"So, what do you do besides make an awesome meal?"

"I'm a forensic accountant."

"Really? Like for the IRS and you go after tax evaders?"

"No. Well, I could, I guess if I wanted to work for the IRS. But before having Sadie, I mostly did divorces."

"Oh. You hunted down all the money the douchey husbands were trying to hide."

Renee chuckled. "More or less."

"Why does it gotta be the husband? Maybe the wife was hiding assets," Ty said.

Both women gave him the same look—one that called him stupid without using the words.

"I don't want to go back to that, though, so I'm looking into other options now that Sadie's in school. How about you?"

"Believe it or not, I have an accounting degree, but I hated every minute of it. I manage a bar."

"Soon to be bar owner," Ronan said.

Chloe's face lit up. "Hopefully. I'm trying hard not to jinx it."

"How about you, Brendan? Declan said you work for the FBI?"

His brother nodded. He'd been following the conversation but had yet to speak. "Forensic accounting, huh?"

Renee nodded.

"So, you're good at looking for fraud, hidden money, payoffs. Schemes like that?"

"I'm a little rusty, but in theory, yes."

"If I got some old political campaign records, could you look for discrepancies?"

"No," Declan said.

"I'm not asking you."

Renee looked between the two of them.

"This has something to do with Dad, so you leave her out of it."

"What? She'd be looking at numbers. Public record. Probably."

"Drop it," Ronan said, and Brendan clamped his jaw in irritation.

Luckily, Chloe came in for the save, and conversation turned to the work he'd done on the house, and Ty was impressed. "I knew sending you here was a good idea."

"You just wanted me off your couch."

Ty laughed. "Well, it was more my roommate, but this worked out."

Renee smiled at Declan. "Yeah, it has." Turning to Ty, she added, "He's already saved me so much. Not just in labor, either. For the first time since moving in, this is starting to feel doable."

"I wish I could say the same," Chloe said.

Ronan grunted, so Declan explained. "Ronan's house has been under construction since he bought it. And now Chloe is living with him."

"My bedroom and bathroom are done."

Chloe patted his hand. "And Declan did a great job on the kitchen. The living room is just about finished, too. I love everything, but I'm not used to living in construction, you know?"

Renee's forehead crinkled. "I hadn't thought about that. For me, it's an inconvenience, but I can still live my life. Although, when we get around to the kitchen, I might change my attitude."

"I think you're all nuts. No way would I want to buy something to have to work when I get home from work," Ty said.

"What about you, Brendan?" Renee asked. "Are you an own-a-house person or a rent-forever person?"

Brendan took a drink of his beer. "I'm living in a condo now, so it's kind of halfway. I own, but it doesn't need work. One day, when I'm ready for a family, I'd like a house. I want to live in a neighborhood like where we grew up."

"That's why I'm here. I really wanted Sadie to have a place that was ours, you know?"

"Yeah. Kids need a backyard and to be able to run around through the neighborhood."

Declan was a little uncomfortable with the way Brendan and Renee were getting along. It was like they clicked, and a spike of jealousy speared him.

"Speaking of kids, we should probably head out and finish in the yard."

Ronan stood with his plate.

Renee held out her hands. "Please, leave it all. I'll clean up."

"You sure?" Ronan asked.

"I'll help," Chloe volunteered.

Ronan shrugged, gave Chloe a kiss, and said, "See me before you leave."

"Of course."

They all made their way to the door. Declan had the urge to kiss Renee the way Ronan had kissed Chloe, and it irked him not to be able to. As he walked by, he said, "Thanks for lunch. It was really good."

"You're welcome. Let me know if you need anything out there."

He held her gaze for a moment, willing her to want what he wanted, and then he followed his brothers outside.

ONCE THE GUYS WERE GONE, RENEE SAID TO CHLOE, "YOU don't have to stay to clean up. I can handle it."

"I don't mind. You fed me. It's only fair that I help clean up."

"Thanks. I appreciate it." She loaded her arms with dishes and walked to the kitchen. Chloe held almost twice as much.

When Renee's eyes widened, Chloe said, "I spent a lot of years waitressing."

"That explains it." She began wrapping the leftovers into smaller packages so the Doyles could take them home. Once that was done, she filled the sink to wash dishes. It gave her reason to stand at the window and watch the progress outside.

"They are a sight, aren't they?" Chloe asked by her side.

"Hmm?"

"The Doyle boys. They are nice to look at."

"Oh. I was watching—"

Chloe held up a hand. "It's all right. You don't need to explain to me. I grew up across the street from them. As long as you're not ogling Ronan, we're all good."

Renee smiled. "I have no idea how I'm going to pay them back for this."

"You won't have to. That's not what this is." Chloe turned to look at her. "Regardless of whatever is going on between you and Declan," she gave Renee a knowing look, "he talked to Ronan about doing this for Sadie. They all have a soft spot when it comes to kids. Well, maybe not Brendan, but Declan is twice as soft. I heard him talking to Ronan about your daughter. He really loves her."

"She loves him, too." As hard as it was for her to accept, she might have to let this be a gift. She nodded and focused on washing dishes.

"I have to admit that I had an ulterior motive for volunteering to clean."

Renee set a rinsed dish on the rack. "What's that?"

"As I mentioned, I'm trying to buy The Black Rose, the bar I manage. I've worked there for years, and the owners are friends with my parents. My parents are backing me to get a business loan, but as I'm digging into the books, something is off, but I can't figure out what. Is there any chance you might be willing to look it over?"

"Sure. What are you thinking?"

"I really don't know. The Byrnes are old, but still very on their game. It's not an obvious error in accounting. There are some things I can't quite add up. And let me be clear, I could be totally wrong. I'd just like a fresh set of eyes on it if possible."

"Sure. Send me the files, and I'll take a look."

"I have some I can email, but the Byrnes have been old school for a long time."

"Oh, God. Not another ledger person." Renee didn't even try to keep the whine from her voice.

"If you don't want to—"

"No. I mean, yes, I'll look. I'm longing for the days I can stick with my computer. I've got a couple of bookkeeping clients who send me a physical book and it's just...ugh."

"I get it. I can't imagine having to log everything in a book. I've been doing the daily stuff online, but I've only been doing it for about a year."

"Before you leave, I'll give you my email and you can drop the rest off whenever. If I'm not here, Declan usually is."

"Thanks."

They finished washing and drying the dishes, and then Chloe had to head to work. From the kitchen, she watched Chloe say goodbye to Ronan, and Renee was struck by how much she missed that simple act. Having someone to kiss goodbye or hello. When her kitchen was back to rights, she went outside to help clean up—at least that's what she assumed Ronan meant when he said "scrap up."

But when she got to the yard where they were building, there wasn't much laying around. "What do you need me to do?"

Tyler walked by carrying a few chunks of wood. "I think they're done. I'm going to grab us beers."

She stepped closer to the playset. "This is amazing. Thank you."

Ronan nodded and walked past her carrying a ladder.

"Hey, you told me to clean up."

"Your brother got it all," he called over his shoulder.

Declan stood next to her.

"Does your brother not like me or something?"

"What do you mean?"

"He doesn't talk to me. He mostly grunts."

Declan laughed. "That's Ronan. He's not much of a talker."

Brendan stood by the swings, tugging at the chains. "But Declan more than makes up for Ronan being quiet. It's like he took all the talking genes."

"Fuck you," Declan called. Then he reached for Renee's hand. "Come on. Take it for a spin."

He led her to the swing and she sat down.

"Wait a minute," she said. "Am I your guinea pig to see if this'll hold? If I swing too high, am I going to go crashing to the ground?"

"That better not be the fucking case," Ronan said, returning from his truck. "I taught him better than that."

"It's done right." He grabbed the back of the swing and then pushed her high enough to duck under her and come out in front.

A small squeak escaped because she hadn't expected him to do that. But once she was going, she didn't want to stop. The fall air was crisp and cool and the breeze swung her ponytail around. She extended her legs on the way up and pumped them to keep going.

"So it passes?" Declan asked.

"More than. Sadie is gonna love it." She let go of the swing and jumped from a decent height like she had as a kid. However, she misjudged the distance and crashed directly into Declan.

He wrapped his arms around her and took the impact of her body, but her momentum took them both to the ground.

"Oh my God. I'm so sorry. Are you all right?" She pushed up and looked down at him.

He laughed loudly. "If you wanted to be on top, you just had to say so."

She swatted at him, got up, and held out a hand to help him up.

"Dude. Are you fucking my sister?" Tyler asked, as he stood a few feet away holding bottles of beer.

"Uh..." he looked at Renee, clearly at a loss.

"Who I sleep with is none of your business."

"It is if he's my best friend."

"We did. And now we're not. So don't worry about it." Declan didn't look happy about her announcement, but she wasn't going to lie or be embarrassed. She snatched a beer from Tyler's hand and took a drink. Everyone around her fell silent.

Brendan came up behind Declan and cupped a hand on his shoulder. "Better watch out for her. She's tough." To Renee, he nodded. "It was nice to meet you, but I have to head out."

Ronan took a beer from Tyler, who still hadn't recovered from Renee's announcement.

"Ronan, is there anything else I can help you pack up?"

"No, I got it."

"I have leftovers from lunch packed up for you guys. Shoot. I didn't give Brendan his."

"I'll take his share," Ronan said.

"Will you get it to him?"

"Nope. His loss."

She smiled and shook her head. "I'll be right back."

While she was in the kitchen getting the food, she saw Ty and Declan in a serious conversation. She hadn't thought about what to say to Tyler. That wasn't true. She hadn't planned on telling him at all because it *wasn't* any of his business. But there was something about the way he accused Declan, as if he'd done something wrong.

They were both consenting adults and her love life was none of her brother's business.

Fuck. Love life? No. Sex life. That was currently being locked back down.

She stared out the window at the guys and the playset they'd built for her daughter. Her heart thumped like it didn't have enough room to beat.

She definitely had to step back and control whatever the hell this was.

CHAPTER
Twenty-Three

"I can't believe you fucked my sister," Tyler said again. "I didn't ask you to stay here to take advantage of her."

Declan barely suppressed the chuckle. "Do you honestly think *anyone* could take advantage of Renee?"

"She's just getting her life back. She doesn't need another dude to screw it up."

"I would never screw anything up for her. Besides, she ended it. It was a weekend. She made it clear she doesn't want more."

Tyler's stare burned into him. "What the fuck?" he ground out.

Declan looked up. "What?"

"Did you fucking fall in *love* with my sister?"

Declan couldn't tell if it was disgust or horror tinging his friend's words. He lifted a shoulder. "I care about her. And without going into detail, we're good together."

"She's not ready for anything, and if she was, she'd be looking for something serious. Someone who'd stick."

Declan took a swig of beer, swallowing down his anger. "So I'm not good enough for her?" He nodded.

"I love you, man. But she's my sister and she's been through enough shit with Graham."

"Do not compare me to him."

Tyler huffed. "I know you're not like him. But you've never done any relationship. She needs someone stable who will put in the work. You run at the hint of commitment."

"People change."

Tyler opened his mouth again, but Renee came back with containers of food and handed them to Ronan. Declan grabbed the last of the power tools and carried them to Ronan's truck. They said their goodbyes and he took off.

When he came back to Tyler and Renee, they were talking quietly, so he took a wide curve around them. But he caught her muttering, "I don't need you to police me."

Declan smirked. He almost felt sorry for Ty. With his beer in hand, he walked over the grass to make sure they didn't miss anything.

"What are you doing?" Renee asked.

He looked up to see Tyler was gone. "Ty leave?"

"Yeah."

"Is he really pissed?"

"No. He's worried. As if I can't take care of myself. I used to take care of him."

"He thinks I'm going to mess you up."

Her gaze held his for a minute before breaking away. But in that moment, he saw that she cared, too. They had more than great sex.

Pointing at the ground, she asked, "So what are you doing?"

"Making sure we didn't drop screws or pieces of wood

that Sadie can get hurt on." He resumed his slow walk across the yard, scanning for small bits of danger.

She stepped next to him, head down.

"What happened between you and Graham?"

"I don't want to talk about it."

"Tyler compared me to him in a not-so-subtle way."

She shook her head. "Don't listen to him."

He paused and touched her arm. When she looked up, she heaved a sigh.

"When Graham and I met, we were young. He was a lot of fun. Even when we first got married and started building a life, it was light and fun. But when I mentioned buying a house, he kept saying we had time. There was no rush to dive into having a mortgage."

Declan resumed his study of the ground as she talked.

"Looking back now, I can clearly see how Graham was only invested in us in the way it made him feel. When I got pregnant with Sadie, at first, he was shocked. We hadn't been trying. I was thrilled. I figured my happiness would spill over. To a certain extent, it did."

"I'm not gonna like where this goes, am I?"

"He's not a monster if that's what you're thinking. He loves Sadie. But he never changed. Having a kid is supposed to change you, right? I mean, there's this whole other human who's completely dependent on you. You can't come first anymore. It was never like that for Graham. For a long time, I thought it was because he was the dad. She didn't grow inside him, didn't bond with her the way I did.

"But he was still living his life. He missed having fun. I was dragging him down because I was so serious. Because I wanted him to step up and be a father."

"Doesn't seem like too much to ask for."

"It obviously was. So, now he gets to be exactly what he

always wanted: to be the fun weekend dad. No real respon-sibilities. He can take her out for fun, feed her crap, and never have to worry about the hard stuff."

Declan took in everything she'd said. "And since I have no responsibilities, you and Ty think I'm the same."

The words burned in his mouth. Yes, he'd chosen to live his life without responsibilities, but he would never abandon his kid. Ty's comment about sticking hit him.

This time, she touched his arm to make him stop. When he looked at her, she said, "I don't think you're like Graham. When you're with Sadie..." She shook her head and looked at the playset. "I know you love her. I know you wouldn't hurt her. Neither would Graham. But being a parent is more than just loving a kid."

"What does that mean for us?"

"There can't be an us. I don't know how to even begin navigating a relationship as a single mom. I don't want Sadie thinking she can count on someone who might disap-pear from her life."

"I won't."

"Being Uncle Tyler's friend and being Mommy's boyfriend are two different things."

"Yeah. Boyfriends come and go. I'm already more than that." He took her hand. "I don't know anything about being a father. Hell, I barely had one. But for the first time in my life, the idea of responsibility doesn't scare me. Having you rely on me actually feels good. Knowing I can do something for you to make your life easier, gives me a sense of purpose I've never had."

"I'm glad I can count on you. But it'll get old. You've been here for like a month. Having a family is a long-haul adventure."

"Maybe I'm ready for an adventure."

"I don't think I can risk it."

"What can I do to prove to you that I'm worth the risk?"

"It's not you—"

He dropped her hand. "Fuck no. Do not finish that sentence. We're both better than that."

He stepped back and returned to his search on the ground. "Do you plan on being alone until Sadie is grown?"

"I don't know."

"You deserve better."

"I don't have a plan. I just got to the point that I can even think about dating."

"Yeah. I got that. Online profiles, right? They get a chance, but I don't."

"No, they don't. Deciding to go on a date is for me. Just me. Renee. The woman. Not the mom. Sadie doesn't meet them. They don't get a piece of her."

Suddenly it clicked. She wasn't afraid of Sadie learning to depend on him. She feared for the loss Sadie would feel. He knew better than most what that loss felt like. He also knew there was nothing he could say to convince her he would never do that to Sadie. Or her.

Even if he could prove it to her, should he? Did he really want to? In his own head, he needed to figure out what he wanted. He wasn't sure if he was pushing this to make a point or if he really wanted to be with her.

Instead of continuing to argue, he simply said, "I get it."

But at the same time, his words from last night thundered in his head. *I'm not going anywhere.* He didn't think he could stay here and watch her start a new life with someone else.

They finished their search of the grass in silence. They found nothing. He should've known that Ronan wouldn't be sloppy. Not in a kid's yard. But he had to be sure for Sadie.

He gathered the last few tools that were sitting out and brought them in the house.

As he washed his hands in the kitchen sink, Renee asked, "You want to order in something for dinner?"

"I'm good. I'm going to hang with my sister. Nessa's been nagging me to go out. You can enjoy some quiet."

"Are we okay?" she asked.

"Yeah."

Her eyes said she didn't believe him.

He inhaled deeply. "I would love to see where this leads. But I understand why you can't. I've never given you reason to think I'm the kind of guy who would step up. Sadie's more important than my desire to be with you. But understand I would never let anything happen to your little girl."

She gave him a tight smile and a nod. "Have fun with your sister."

"Enjoy your night. Do something for you."

He texted Nessa and took a quick shower. She responded with a thumbs up and a link to a bar to meet at. Getting away from the house and being alone with Renee was probably the best decision he'd made all weekend.

RENEE OPENED A BOTTLE OF WINE AND TEXTED HER BOOK club friends to see if anyone wanted to come over to hang out. While she waited to see if anyone was free, she sat at the dining room table and scrolled through a few job boards, desperately trying to tune out Declan getting ready to go out. The tension between them was killing her. He was acting like everything was okay, but she didn't believe him.

She knew sleeping together was a mistake.

But she didn't regret it. Wasn't that some stupid shit?

She took another swig of wine. He came from his bedroom wearing jeans and a long-sleeve shirt. A gray Henley. It was like torture. If he pushed the sleeves up, she might start drooling.

This was why sleeping with him was a mistake.

Yet, the fond (oh, so fond!) memories of their weekend were why she couldn't regret it. He cleared his throat and she realized she was staring at his forearms.

"Problem?"

"Nope." She smiled over the rim of her glass. "Just be warned that romance readers you might run into will have thoughts about that shirt."

He ran a slow hand down his torso. "Based on the look on your face, I'm guessing those would be good thoughts?"

"Oh, yeah. The only thing that might get a stronger reaction might be those gray sweatpants you have."

Then he had the nerve to lean on the door frame. Someone had been doing research.

"Huh. So if I want to get laid, I know what to wear."

She nodded. "Yup."

He stepped behind her, lowered himself, and said in a low voice, "Then I guess you know what I'll be wearing when I come home."

She swallowed hard. "I was talking about other women you might meet while you're out."

"Are you saying you're immune? Cuz you're the only one I'm looking to sleep with."

She sucked in a sharp breath. "Declan—"

He straightened and she knew if she looked over her shoulder, she'd be staring at his crotch.

"Yeah, I know. But if you don't want the truth from me, you shouldn't start."

He was right, but she'd been hoping to get back to normal with him. She twisted in her seat. "I wasn't trying to flirt. I don't like the tension and unease between us."

"No unease, here, babe. But you know what will break the tension. Just tell me when."

"You're relentless."

"Persistent. I like to get my own way. Comes from being the youngest boy in the family. We're a little spoiled."

"Have fun tonight."

"You should, too." He reached over her and closed the laptop. "Do something other than work."

"I texted my book club to see if anyone wanted to come over. I was passing time."

"You can come with me and Nessa if you want. But be warned that she picked the bar we're meeting at."

"I don't need to crash your night out. I'm fine on my own."

"I know you're fine. You have a night off. You should be able to have something more than fine."

Her phone buzzed in quick succession. One after another, her friends let her know they were busy. Nothing like not being able to make last-minute plans to convince Declan she didn't need help.

"Come with me."

She rose, putting space between them. "I don't need a chaperone or a babysitter. I can enjoy myself here."

"But Nessa and I are more fun."

She had never met his sister, but if she was anything like Declan, she would be fun. "I'm not even dressed to go out."

"You look good to me."

She glanced down at her ratty jeans and worn-thin T-shirt.

"But I can wait if you want to change."

Something about the small smile that played on his face made her want to agree. "Are you sure Nessa won't mind?"

"We come from a family with seven kids. We're used to extra people popping up. Why would she care?" He pulled his phone out. "But I'll text her to make sure."

He thumbed a message quickly. "Go change. She'll say it's fine."

Before Renee even had a chance to put her wine glass away, his phone beeped.

"See? It's fine. Her exact words are *hell yeah, bring her*."

"All right. Give me five minutes." As she rounded the table to walk past him, she said, "Are you sure it's okay?"

He reached over and tugged her closer by the waistband of her jeans. "I like spending time with you. Especially when you let yourself be Renee, the woman. I have a particular fondness for her."

Damn this man. He kept making it hard for her to remember why they couldn't continue to sleep together. She pulled away and tried to give herself all the reasons why she shouldn't go out with Declan and his sister. But having Nessa there wouldn't be like going dancing last night. It would be like hanging out with a group of friends.

And if she were being totally honest with herself, with the exception of the hangover this morning, last night was a ton of fun.

She needed to be herself more. She deserved that.

In her room, she grabbed fresh jeans and her old college sweatshirt. Nothing sexy. She let her hair down, realized it was too wild, and scooped it back up into a neat ponytail. A quick swipe of mascara and lip gloss and she was good. Set for a night out with friends.

Except her plan was foiled when she walked into the living room and Declan looked up from his phone. His gaze traveled all the way up her body like he had x-ray vision. He stopped at her face and the heat in his eyes was undeniable.

"You know advertising you're a smart chick is sexy as fuck, right?"

"I wasn't trying to advertise anything. I chose something comfy and unsexy. I'm trying not to lead you on or give you any ideas."

"Babe. I don't need help with ideas. They're always there." He picked up her car keys. "Let's go."

She wanted to argue about his need to drive considering he didn't have a car. But she liked not having to be in charge of anything for a change. "I can drive."

"I know where we're going."

"I mean, if you want to drink, I can drive home."

"I'll make sure we get back safely."

Something about his assurance whittled its way deep into her chest. She didn't want him to see how it affected her, so she gave him a quick nod and walked out the front door.

CHAPTER
Twenty~Four

What the fuck was he thinking? He just told himself spending time away from Renee was the smart move. Then he invited her to go out with him and Nessa.

He planned to go out without her, but when she stared at him all thirsty and flirty, how could he not flirt back? No matter what she said, Renee was as into him as he was into her.

In that moment, he had a couple of realizations. One, she was scared. And two, he wanted Renee more than he wanted things to be easy. He just had to prove to her he was worth the risk. He had no idea what that should look like, how to make it happen, or even if it was the right move. But he wanted it. Wanted her.

He followed her to the car, and they drove to the bar Nessa suggested. When he parked and came around the other side of the car, he reached for Renee's hand. She took his hesitantly.

"What are we doing?"

"Going out for dinner and drinks with my little sister. Be warned. Nessa is an acquired taste."

She tugged his hand. "You know I mean this."

"I thought I was pretty clear. I know you're worried about Sadie. For now, Sadie doesn't have to know anything. This can just be for us. Once you're sure about me, then we can figure the rest out." He pulled her close. "We're not done with this. I know you feel it, too."

She paused and stared at him. "You want to carry on a secret affair with me?"

"Not secret from everyone. Unless that's what you want. Just from Sadie."

"She's a smart kid."

"I'm pretty sure I can fool a five-year-old."

"That would mean no kissing and touching when she's around. No flirty comments."

"I can control myself. Can you?"

"I'm a mom. My whole life is built on self-control."

"Then we have nothing to worry about." He smiled and pulled her toward the bar, afraid that if given the chance, she'd come up with more excuses. Right now, he'd won. He planned to keep it that way.

Inside the bar, a band was setting up in one corner. He hoped Nessa hadn't chosen a place with a metal band playing. He couldn't imagine Renee sitting through that. He scanned the bar and walked toward the back to see if Nessa was there.

Of course, she wasn't. He should've known; his sister was always late. "Let's grab a table."

He moved to the farthest section from the band just in case. Then he texted Nessa to let her know. They sat at a high-top table and a server came by and set menus down.

"Can I get you something to start?"

"Wine?" he asked Renee.

She shook her head. "I'll stick with a beer."

"Make it three. My sister will be here soon." The server left and he glanced at the menu. "I'm not real hungry. You fed us a huge lunch."

"You were working all day. I've seen you eat, and given the size of your brothers, I didn't want to risk not having enough food."

"You cooked like you were feeding my entire family. It wasn't even half of us."

"I don't know how I can ever thank you and your brothers for that."

"Seeing Sadie having fun in her own yard is all I'm hoping for." He glanced down at the menu again. "Want to get some appetizers to share?"

"Sure. Whatever you want."

He looked up at her. "What I want isn't on the menu."

She bit her lip and ducked her head, her cheeks growing pink. But she glanced up from under her lashes. So fucking hot.

A moment later, someone crashed into his shoulder. Nessa.

"What's up?" she screamed in his ear.

"Hey." He rolled his eyes. "Nessa, this is Renee. Renee, my charming sister."

"Fuck you. I *am* charming. What's with the sarcasm?" Turning to Renee, she said, "Tyler's sister, right?"

Renee nodded.

"I like Tyler. When he's not acting like he's too cool for everyone. Is he coming tonight?"

"Not that I know of," Renee said, looking at him.

"Uh-uh." He stood and shifted over a chair to let Nessa

have his. "I already ordered you a beer. Renee and I plan to have some appetizers."

"Sounds good. Let's get a crap ton and share."

The server stopped by, set three bottles of beer down, and took their order. Nessa ordered a full ton of food.

"Did you not eat today?"

She shot him a dirty look. "Didn't Mom ever tell you it's rude to question a woman's eating habits?"

"You're not a woman. You're my sister."

Renee snorted. "She's right. Don't be a dick."

He was beginning to question his sanity for putting his sister at the same table with a woman he wanted to sleep with.

"I wasn't trying to be a dick. It's a lot of food." Pointing to the other side of the bar, he asked, "Do you know what kind of band is playing?"

"Nope."

He wasn't sure he believed her.

Nessa took a drink of beer and studied Renee. "So, Renee, are you using my brother for his tools or his body?"

Renee paused with her beer at her lips.

"What the fuck," he muttered.

Renee set her bottle down. "Your brother and I have an agreement. He's living rent-free in my house in exchange for doing some work I need done. I don't think that qualifies as using him."

"Ah, so it's his body," she said with a wink.

Renee's mouth lifted in a half-smile. "Again, if we have an understanding and we both benefit, does it count as using?"

Nessa barked out a laugh. "I like her."

Renee took a drink.

Declan leaned over. "I'm sorry my sister is being a bitch. It normally takes a few beers for that to start."

"I'm not being a bitch. I'm testing the waters. It's my duty as your sister. If she couldn't handle a little poking from just me, how the hell would she handle being around all of us?"

"So this is a test?" Renee asked. "Respectable."

He stared at her. "What?"

She shrugged. "I get it. If Ty was with some woman I wasn't sure about, I'd want to poke around, too. What if he got in deep and she was bad for him?"

"Women are too fucking weird."

Nessa shoved his shoulder. "Are you kidding? I've seen you stalk my boyfriends to check them out."

"Not since you were a kid."

"What do you do for a living, Nessa?" Renee asked.

"I'm a bartender mostly. Still figuring out what I want to be when I grow up. Kind of like this one." She bumped his shoulder again.

He clenched his jaw. It shouldn't irk him that everyone —including his family—thought he was a loser who had no plan for his life. He still didn't have much of a plan, but he was getting there. And it wasn't like he'd been a bum who never worked.

"I'm skilled labor."

"Bartending is a skill," she said.

He snorted. The server delivered their food. All of the plates barely fit on the small square table.

"What do you do, Renee?"

"I'm an accountant."

"Ouch. That sounds boring."

"Watch it, Nessie," he warned.

"Don't call me that." Turning to Renee, she said, "When

I was in middle school, he used to call me Nessie, like the Loch Ness Monster."

"You're terrible," Renee said. "And what is it about you and messing with names?" She looked at Nessa. "When he wants to get under my skin, he calls me Rennie."

Nessa smacked his arm. "You're the worst."

"Anyway," Renee cut it. "My job can be boring. But when I'm working as a forensic accountant, it's more interesting. It's like digging through a puzzle to find the missing pieces."

Nessa bit into a hot wing and said, "Dude, you're in trouble. She's too smart for you."

Renee excused herself to go to the bathroom.

As soon as she was gone, he said, "What's wrong with you?"

"What?" Nessa asked, sauce all over her fingers.

"Are you trying to scare her off?"

"No. I'm having fun. It's what we do." She looked genuinely confused.

He took a deep breath and then finished his beer. He waved their server over to order another round.

"Oh my god. You *like* her like her."

"Why else would I be with her? Although right now, she might question why I would expose her to you if I like her."

"No, I mean like you're into her deep. I thought you guys were just having some fun. A little fling with the lonely housewife kind of thing."

"This is getting worse."

"You know what I mean. You're gone for her. I had no idea." She smacked his arm again. "Why didn't you tell me?"

"I wasn't sure I could convince her we should try for more than a quick weekend. I do really like her, but it's complicated because of Sadie."

"That makes it complicated for her."

"Me, too. I wouldn't want Sadie to get hurt. She already has an asshole for a dad. Not that she knows it yet. But one day she will. I don't want her to think of me like that." Saying his fears out loud to his sister didn't feel good.

Their fresh beers were delivered and he took a long drink.

"So don't fuck it up. Decide if Renee is the real thing for you and if not, cut her loose. If she is, go all in. I don't think there's another way with a mom. That's why we never knew our mom had anyone." Nessa grabbed another wing and bit into it.

Renee returned and took her seat. Looking at the new bottle of beer, she said, "I'm not sure I'm ready for another."

She picked up a slider, added ketchup to the burger, and bit in. "Did I pass?"

"Fuck yeah, you did," Nessa said. "You'll keep him on his toes." She leaned across the table toward Renee. "In case you didn't know, the Doyles are a handful."

Renee laughed and he enjoyed the look on her face so much it didn't even bother him that he was the butt of his sister's jokes.

The rest of dinner, they talked about nothing and everything. Renee talked about her job before she had Sadie and how much it skewed her view of marriage and divorce. Nessa kept them in stitches telling stories about the bar and all the bad dates she'd witnessed.

The band started playing and it turned out they were some kind of cover band, but they didn't seem to have a theme or genre. They were all over the place playing everything from the Stones to Brittany Spears. But he didn't care because he was able to sit next to Renee and watch her unwind.

She looked as relaxed as she had at the wedding, which was not how she appeared most days. He wondered if there was a way for her have more time like this. When the food was gone, Declan suggested one more round.

Renee yawned. "I don't think I'm up for staying out late again. I can call a car and leave mine for you."

"Hell, no," he said. "We can leave."

"Aww," Nessa said.

"You can stay and hang out with your sister. I don't want to ruin your night. I should've stayed at home. I just didn't think I was going to be this tired."

"I'll take you home."

Renee opened her mouth to argue again, but Nessa cut her off. "Dude. He wants to be with you. When you've got a guy willing to walk out on a fun night of drinking to be with you, take it."

Renee smiled. "Fine. If you're sure."

"I am."

"Nessa, it was nice to meet you. I think I've met like half your family now, but I don't know if I'll remember all their names."

"I'm easy to remember because I'm the most fun."

"Or maybe it's because you're the only girl," he said.

Nessa rolled her eyes.

"You're good?" he asked.

"Yeah. I'll head out, too. This music isn't doing it for me."

They stood and Nessa threw her arms around him. Quietly, she said, "I like her. Hope you don't fuck it up."

"Real inspiring. Thanks."

He took Renee's hand as they walked to the car.

RENEE TRIED TO IGNORE THE WARM FLUSH SHE FELT EVERY time Declan touched her. It was just some innocent hand-holding, but her body acted like it was more.

"Thanks for inviting me out."

"I like spending time with you." He unlocked the car.

"You're okay to drive?"

"Yes. I'm fine." He opened her door and she got in. When he got behind the wheel, he asked, "So Nessa didn't totally scare you off?"

"I like her. She's a lot of fun. She might've been right in saying she's the most fun sibling."

Declan sucked in a sharp breath. "But not more fun than me."

"I don't know. She was pretty funny."

"Take it back." He reached over and pinched her thigh. It wasn't hard, but it was enough to make her squirm. It was definitely flirty.

Her head was spinning and it wasn't from the beer she drank. She had no idea what she was doing with Declan. Giving herself a weekend with him had made sense. Declan was not a settling-down kind of guy. He'd been clear about not wanting to be a father. But she shouldn't be thinking about settling down either. She'd already survived one marriage and wasn't looking for another.

How did other single moms do this? She had no idea how to have a life separate from her daughter.

"Everything okay?" Declan asked with a hand on her thigh.

He did that a lot. Casual touches. She must've been starved for physical contact because she wanted to keep his hand there always.

"Yeah. I'm just thinking."

"About?"

"This. Us." She huffed. "I'm probably making this more complicated than it needs to be. "But this is new. Dating or whatever when I have Sadie."

"We take it at your pace. Don't overthink it."

He was right. She was overthinking. But she'd spent years in a relationship that required her to overthink. She sighed again and stared out the window as Declan drove them home. Home. She wouldn't have any other guy she was dating living in her home.

They could probably keep it a secret from Sadie. It wasn't like Sadie knew anything about dating or sex. She was five. And she knew Declan and liked him, so she was safe. It wasn't like Renee was introducing some stranger into their lives.

When Declan parked, she had convinced herself to do what she wanted. It was easier than usual to talk herself into doing something.

She opened her door to get out and he was already on her side of the car.

"So what did you come up with?" he asked.

"What do you mean?"

He took her hand again as they headed to the front door. "I could almost hear the conversation you were having with yourself about us."

"Oh."

"Well?"

"I think I want to keep doing this. I'm having fun and the sex...whew."

He chuckled as he opened the door.

"But Sadie can't know. That part is too complicated. Neither of us is looking for something serious and I won't have Sadie getting confused about the people in her life."

He bit the corner of his lip and nodded. "Okay."

"Yeah?"

He locked the door and reached for her. "Yeah. Does that mean I can fuck you again? Because I've been dying to get you naked."

She smiled. "Yes, please."

"Very polite." He kissed her with his hands on her hips, anchoring her to him. He began walking her across the room. "Let's see what we can do about that."

He turned them toward her room, but she stopped. She suddenly realized this would be the first time she had sex in this house. Her house. But going to her bed felt weird. Serious. "Let's go to your room."

He dipped his lips to hers again. "Wherever you want."

She turned and pulled him through the dark house, only the moon lighting their path. She really hoped Sadie didn't leave any toys on the floor. Stepping on a Lego might ruin the mood.

In his bedroom, Declan pulled her to him again and kissed her. "You sure about this?" he asked against her lips.

"Yeah."

"Because it'll kill me if we start this again and then you tell me I can't have you."

"I'm not that special Declan. If this ends between us, you'll survive." In the back of her head, the word *if* echoed. Shouldn't it have been *when*? Because this wasn't supposed to be serious.

His response was a low rumble against her neck. He licked and nuzzled her and she had a hard time catching her breath. He pulled her shirt up and his fingers grazed over her abdomen and up to her breasts.

She pulled away. "Too many clothes."

Pulling her shirt over her head, she walked backward toward the bed. She kicked off her shoes and shimmied out of her pants. "What are you waiting for?"

He smiled. "I like watching you strip for me. Plus, I don't need to be naked for what I'm starting with."

His gaze raked over her body and she shivered. He nudged her onto the bed and stroked her thighs. His heated gaze stayed on her while he peeled her underwear away.

RENEE OPENED HER EYES AND SQUINTED AT THE SUNLIGHT streaming through the window. The glow wasn't too bright, so it was still early. She glanced over her shoulder at Declan who snored quietly. He slept on his side, his hand possessively on her hip. Nothing about this felt casual. Having sex with him in her house. Spending the night in his bed.

But Sadie wasn't home. That was the deal they made. But was that practical? At best, she had two weekends a month free. Realistically, it was usually one weekend. And if Graham caught a whiff of her having a good time, he'd probably find more excuses to not take his weekends.

She sighed. She couldn't get used to this. That's all it meant. She could enjoy her time with Declan until he came to his senses and realized a ready-made family was too much. It was sweet that he'd said he was going to prove to her he wasn't going anywhere. But he didn't know what that actually meant.

Shifting quietly, she slipped out from under his hand. Step one of not getting too attached would be not spending the night with him. She stood and gathered her clothes from the floor and went back to her room. It was a little after seven, so she debated going back to bed. She had things to do, but sleeping in sounded so good. She pulled on a sleepshirt and crawled under her covers. The cool sheets reminded her of the warmth she left in the other room. But it was for the best.

At least that was what she told herself.

CHAPTER
Twenty-Five

Declan stretched and reached for Renee, only to be met with empty space. He sat up and listened. Maybe she ran to the bathroom. But he heard nothing. He climbed out of bed and pulled on his underwear. Her clothes were gone from the floor. No sign of her in the kitchen or at the dining room table. He continued through the house until he was at her bedroom.

Sure enough, she was asleep in her own bed. She'd fallen asleep in his arms last night, so he had no idea when she left. Or why.

As much as he wanted to crawl back under the covers with her, she hadn't invited him here. And if he knew anything about Renee, it was that she needed to make that call. So he turned around and went back to the kitchen to start a pot of coffee. While it brewed, he checked the bathroom. He had to do some touch-ups, but then it would be done.

Today would be a good day to check out reclaimed cabinets. Sadie was supposed to be with Graham until dinner, and although the windows would be in soon, he could start on the kitchen. Even if she wanted to wait on ripping things out, they could store the cabinets in the garage until they were ready.

He grabbed his clothes and used Renee's bathroom to shower and get ready. As he was tugging on his pants, Renee knocked.

"Almost done?"

Opening the door, he said, "All yours."

His gaze raked over her. She wore a long T-shirt and he wanted to see if she had on anything underneath. "Sleep well?"

She blushed. "Yeah." Brushing past him, she said, "Excuse me. I gotta pee, and I don't need an audience."

He left her to do her business. In the kitchen, he poured them both a cup of coffee. When she came in, and went to the pot, he handed her the ready cup.

"Thank you."

He leaned against the counter, trying to remain casual. "Want to tell me why you snuck out of my bed?"

She rolled her eyes. "I didn't exactly sneak. I woke up. After thinking about it, I decided staying in your bed wasn't a great idea. What if Sadie came home early? How would I explain that?"

Bullshit. The word almost slipped from his lips.

She bit her lower lip. "Spending the night together feels like more than fun. I don't think that's where we are."

"We? Or you?" He took a step closer to her. "Because I'm telling you, I'm ready for whatever you want, Rennie."

She snorted. "We talked about this. Sadie can't know about us."

"Yet."

Her eyes narrowed at the word. He looked around exaggeratedly. "And no Sadie. You left because you're scared."

"Yeah, I am." She set her cup on the counter. "I don't know if I'm ready for anything beyond fun. And you have your life to figure out too. If we fuck this up, everyone gets hurt."

"I get that. But sleeping in my bed when Sadie isn't home can't hurt. I like having you in bed. In my arms." She looked so conflicted and he was afraid to keep pushing. He said he wouldn't. "Besides, it's harder to have wake-up morning sex if you're not there."

She smiled. "Maybe I don't like morning sex."

He recoiled playfully. "Who doesn't like morning sex? It's a great way to start your day. Loosens your muscles. Keeps you relaxed."

"Makes you sleepy and want to stay in bed..."

"That's not bad thing."

She rolled her eyes and shook her head.

"What do you think about going to check out some reclaimed cabinets today?"

"Today?"

"Graham has Sadie till dinnertime. You're usually busy during the week."

"But I'm not ready to start this project. I mean, you already have the windows to do, and the living room and dining room need to be painted." She looked around the kitchen.

"I'm not saying we have to start this. But we can look and see what's available. If, by chance, we find something that's perfect, we get them and store them in the garage. It'll give you an idea of what's possible."

"Okay. Let me get dressed. Want to go to breakfast first?"

"Sure." They parted and went to their respective rooms to finish getting ready.

RENEE DIDN'T KNOW WHAT SHE'D EXPECTED AFTER HER awkward conversation with Declan over coffee this morning, but it was like it never happened. They had a great time at breakfast, talking about so many different things. And he made shopping for cabinets fun. They didn't quite find what she'd need, but now she had some ideas. He was making her believe that a new-ish kitchen was possible.

Once they were back at home, she sat on the couch and checked job boards half-heartedly. Declan went back outside to check the playset one more time. As if something had changed since last night. He was so excited for Sadie to come home. She glanced at the time on her laptop. Knowing Graham, he'd be dropping Sadie off soon.

She went to the kitchen and washed the few dishes that were in the sink while she considered what she should make for dinner. She had some leftovers from lunch yesterday. That would probably be enough. From her spot at the sink, she could see Declan testing the chains on the swings and then hanging from the monkey bars. He was being so careful, worrying about whether her daughter would be safe. Her chest tightened at the sight.

All of a sudden, her feet were wet. Stepping back from the sink, she saw water trickling from the cabinet. She slapped her hand on the faucet to turn off the running water. "What the fuck?"

She opened the cabinet and found water streaming

from the pipe. A puddle filled the base of the cabinet and continued to drip onto the floor. She grabbed her towel from the counter and slapped it on the floor. Then she ran to the bathroom and grabbed a few more towels.

Just as she was mopping up the puddle, the doorbell rang. Taking a deep breath, she went to let Sadie in. When she opened the door, Sadie smiled and said, "Hi, Mom."

"Hey, baby. Go put your bag in your room."

Graham took a look at her and asked, "What's going on?"

"The pipe under the kitchen sink is leaking."

He shook his head. "I told you this place was a money pit."

"Seriously? That's all you can say?"

"What am I supposed to say?"

"You're a God damn plumber. You could offer to fix it."

He huffed. His blue eyes filled with scorn. "You wanted to be on your own, Renee." He stepped closer. "Is this you saying you need me?"

She stepped back. "No. I'll handle it."

He shook his head. "That's always your problem. You can never admit when you need help."

"I have no problem asking for help. You just reminded me of all the strings that come attached to your help. No thanks." She started to close the door, so he'd get the hint.

Sadie came back into the room. "Where's Declan?"

"He's out in the yard. He has a surprise for you."

"Yay!" she squealed and ran through the house.

Renee followed her, pausing to toss more towels on the puddle under the sink. Outside, Sadie was already testing out the swing.

"Mom! Declan made me a jungle gym!"

"I know. It's pretty cool isn't it?"

"It's the best!" she yelled as Declan pushed her higher on the swing.

As much as she wanted to stay and play with them, she had a mess in the kitchen. "Are you okay out here?" she asked Declan.

"Of course. We have to test out the monkey bars next."

"Thank you." She hoped he understood how much Sadie's happiness meant to her.

In the kitchen, she picked up the sopping towels and carried them to the washer. Then she added fresh towels to the floor. She reached under the sink, twisted the water shut off, and hoped it would be enough to stop it for now. She pulled all the items out from the cabinet and filled the counter and kitchen table.

As she looked at the new mess in her kitchen, Sadie came through the back door with Declan behind her. "Can we go back out and play after dinner?"

"You didn't eat dinner with Dad?" Her blood began to boil and she inhaled deeply. "Don't worry about it. I'll throw some chicken nuggets in the oven in a minute. Go to the bathroom and wash up. After dinner, it'll be too late to play, but you can play after breakfast tomorrow. Okay?"

"Yes." She took off through the house.

"What's going on here?" Declan asked.

"I was washing dishes and all of a sudden, my feet were wet." She kicked at the towels she had on the floor. "The pipe is leaking. And when Graham showed up, you think he would've said, 'Hey, let me take care of this simple little thing, you know, since I'm a fucking plumber.' But no, not that shithead. Not unless I was ready to ask *really* nice."

Her body vibrated with anger.

"Hey. It's okay." He stepped over the pile of towels and pulled her into a hug. She stiffened.

"Sadie isn't here and even is she was, this isn't sexual. I'm giving a friend a hug." His hand rubbed her back. "I got this."

She pulled away. "Don't worry about it. I'll call a plumber in the morning."

"I can figure it out. It's probably something simple. Go put the nuggets in for Sadie. I'll grab some tools."

As much as she didn't want to be relieved Declan was here and offering help, she was. His calm attitude eased everything inside her that had knotted up. "You sure?"

"If I can't figure it out, we'll call a plumber tomorrow."

His use of *we* had her heart tripping. It meant nothing, and she knew it, but she missed being part of a we, especially at times like this. "Thank you."

He disappeared to the basement where he had all the tools he'd brought. She put chicken in the oven for Sadie. While Declan crawled under the sink, she kept Sadie in the living room so she wouldn't bother him. A few minutes later, he stood in front of her with a wrench in his hand.

"I gotta run to the store to grab some supplies. Can I take your car?"

"Of course. If you write down what you need, I'll go get it."

"You stay. Feed Sadie. I'll be back soon."

She handed him her keys and credit card. He looked like he wanted to argue about taking her card, but she was not about to have him buy anything when she hadn't even paid him for any of the work he'd already done.

While he was gone, she let Sadie have a picnic on the living room floor and listened about what she'd done with Graham all weekend and how much she loved the playset in the yard. She wanted to have the monkey bars mastered by next week.

Renee smiled and shook her head. Her life had taken a hell of a turn since Declan showed up on her steps. She didn't know what she was doing. He was so involved here that it was making her nervous. None of this seemed like just some fun.

CHAPTER
Twenty-Six

As he strode through the store on a Sunday evening buying a new trap for under the sink as well as some extra fittings just in case he broke something, he had Ronan on the phone. "Can you believe that prick? He does this shit for a living and didn't so much as take a look at it."

Ronan grunted. "They're divorced."

"If she lived alone, sure. But Sadie lives there. Why would you want your kid to live in a house that had problems? I wouldn't expect him to come in and renovate everything, but damn it's a leak. She had a pile of wet towels sopping up the puddle."

"You need me to come over?"

"Thanks for the offer, but I think I got it. If I get stuck, I'll find a video online. I'm pretty sure it's just the trap. But if it's more, you got a plumber, right? She has no contacts, so she'll just Google shit like she did for the windows."

"I'll text you a number in case you need it."

"Thanks, man."

They disconnected and he paid for his purchases. He

couldn't wrap his head around having to call strangers to fix things in your house. He had memories of his dad fixing things and once he was gone, his brothers handled most repairs. For bigger things, there were guys from the neighborhood. They all relied on each other.

Renee didn't have that. Maybe once she was in her neighborhood longer, she might find that. She was still new to the area.

When he got back to the house, Renee was on the couch with her laptop open and Sadie was playing with dolls on the floor. He patted her head as he walked by and went to the kitchen. Sitting on the floor in front of the sink, he watched a video on his phone to see if there was anything he needed to be careful of.

Seemed pretty straightforward. He already pulled the old trap off and tossed it. He shifted so the top half of his body was under the sink. A moment later, he felt someone next to him.

"Can I help?" Sadie asked.

He hunched a little to see her. "It's kind of gross down here, but you know what would be a big help? Can you hold my flashlight so I can see what I'm doing?"

"Sure."

He crawled out and handed her the flashlight, which was bigger than her entire forearm. She gripped it with both hands, and he showed her where to point it. Hopefully, he wouldn't be blinded by it.

She did a duck walk to get closer and he felt her eyes on his every move. He got the trap in place but not tightened yet. He slid back out. "What do you think? Does it look good?"

He showed her the picture from his phone. She leaned under the sink and studied his work. "I think so."

"You want to help me tighten it?"

Her eyes lit up. "Yeah."

She laid on her back beside him and he helped her hold the wrench. Together they tightened the fitting.

"Sadie?" Renee called.

Sadie froze and her eyes got wide.

"Did you do something wrong?" he whispered.

"Mom told me not to bother you."

He smiled. "No problem then. You're not bothering me. You're helping."

"Sadie. I told you to leave Declan alone."

"You said don't bother him. I'm helping. Declan said it's okay."

"I've never had a better helper. Now, do you know the difference between your right hand and left hand?"

"Kinda. Sometimes I forget."

"Well, I'm going to teach you the cardinal rule for tightening and loosening things. It works for screws and jars and everything. Righty-tighty, lefty-loosey."

She giggled.

"That means when you want something to get tighter, turn it right. When you want it looser, turn it left." Together, they tightened the second fitting. "Okay. Let's test it."

The both shimmied out from under the sink. Renee stood with her arms crossed.

"How do we test it?"

"Turn the water on."

Her eyes got wide again. "But it'll make a mess."

"Not if we did our job right." He lifted a shoulder. "Ready?"

She made a worried face, and when he reached for the faucet, she squinted her eyes. Once the water was on, he closed his eyes. "I can't look. Go under and see if we're making a mess."

She crawled under the sink. "There's no water."

He turned off the faucet and joined her under the sink. "I think we did it."

They gave each other a high five. Renee was still staring at them.

"What?" he asked.

She turned her attention to Sadie. "When I tell you to leave Declan alone, I mean it. It's not his job to entertain you."

Sadie's smile disappeared and she mimicked Renee's angry face. "I was helping."

Declan waved his hands. "Hey, it's okay. She was curious. She asked if she could help."

"Not the point." Turning back to Sadie, she said, "It's bedtime. Go get ready."

Sadie stomped off without a word.

"I'm sorry if I overstepped again. I didn't know she wasn't supposed to be in here until you called her. She wanted to help."

"I appreciate you letting her help and do whatever. But she needs to listen to me."

She followed Sadie out of the room and Declan was at a loss for what just happened. Renee wasn't mad at him. He knew what that looked like. She wasn't herself. Her reaction didn't fit the situation. At least not from his perspective.

He cleaned up the mess, made sure the bottom of the cabinet was dry, and put Renee's stuff away.

Renee got Sadie into bed. Before she opened the book to read, she looked at Sadie. "I'm sorry I snapped at you."

Sadie's face was still puckered in anger.

"But when I tell you to leave someone alone, it's usually for a good reason. If Declan was doing something dangerous, you could've gotten hurt."

"Declan wouldn't let me get hurt."

"Not on purpose, no. But he's not a parent and he doesn't always see the dangerous stuff I do. And even if you were safe, you might've distracted him and he could've gotten hurt."

"That would be bad."

"Right. So next time, if you have questions, or want to help, we need to talk about it first. Sneaking off when I'm busy isn't okay."

"I'm sorry." She snuggled close to Renee, all signs of anger gone.

She read until Sadie was near sleep, gave her a kiss on her head, and left the room.

When she went back to the living room, Declan wasn't around. In the kitchen, she found that he'd put everything back under the sink. She walked to his room and knocked on the open door. He was stretched out on his bed, phone in hand.

He set his phone on his chest and looked at her.

"Got a minute?"

"Sure."

She was suddenly at a loss for what she wanted to say to him.

"What's up, Rennie?"

She rolled her eyes.

"Have a seat." He patted the mattress beside him.

Whereas a few weeks ago, she might not have thought anything of sitting on the bed next to him, everything now felt full of innuendo.

"Come on." He inched up so he was leaning against the headboard.

She joined him and sat near the edge, legs outstretched, but not close enough to touch him, regardless of how tempting it was. "I'm sorry I snapped at you."

"It's been a rough day."

"It wasn't though. Not most of the day. I don't know how I keep letting Graham and his shitty attitude affect me." She huffed. "But it's not all him, either."

She needed to explain how it almost hurt seeing him let Sadie help him. He wasn't her dad—didn't want to *be* her dad—but Sadie might start to view him that way. And although it hurt, she couldn't let that happen.

But she also didn't know how to say that without sounding like a supreme bitch.

"What is it?" he asked, touching her thigh.

"I love the way you are with Sadie. I wish her dad was more like that. Graham would never take the time to let her help like that."

"It wasn't a big deal. She's a kid. It's hard to control your curiosity. I'm sorry if it felt like I was undermining you."

"No. I know you weren't. I'm just—" She scrubbed a hand over her face. "Fuck. I don't know what I'm doing."

"Babe. You don't have to know everything." He slid an arm around her shoulders and pulled her to his chest.

She tried to pull away, but he held tighter.

"Sadie is sound asleep. We both know she sleeps like the dead and never gets up. Just be with me until you feel better."

"You're a bad influence."

"I've been told that before." They sat in silence for a few minutes. Then he asked, "Want to tell me what's really bothering you?"

She didn't move. Didn't want to look at him. "This weekend was great. I love my time with you when I can just be Renee. But that's not my whole life and I feel split. I want the fun with you, but since you live here, I don't know how to keep things separate."

"Why does it have to be?"

"I told you why."

"I'm here. Sadie is used to me being around. But she was also used to me just popping up. Kids are resilient."

She felt the underlying sentiment that he could disappear and pop up in her life like always and Sadie would be fine. He wasn't necessarily wrong. But she didn't know if she'd be fine.

After a few more breaths, Renee pulled away and sat up. This time, Declan let her go. "Want to watch TV or something?"

He pointed at the screen on the wall. "We can stay here and watch something. Or..." He lifted his phone. "We can read."

She chuckled. "I thought we agreed to keep the reading in the living room."

"You're afraid you can't control your horny self when we read sexy books." He grinned.

She couldn't help but make the comparison between his blue eyes full of humor and Graham's eyes. She sighed. "Fine. Read to me." She settled against the headboard.

He eyed the distance between them but didn't comment. She wouldn't go so far as to admit he was right because she absolutely could control herself. But he also made temptation a real, tangible thing for her. She settled in and listened to him read.

DECLAN WASN'T SURE HOW HIS LIFE MANAGED TO FLIP SO many times so quickly. Just when he thought he and Renee had a plan, she spun out. He'd spent the better part of the night trying to get her to relax and be with him. She wouldn't even kiss him good night before hustling from his room.

First thing in the morning, Sadie was rushing through breakfast so she could go outside and play. From where he was still lying on his bed, he heard her usual chatter with Renee. Sadie was excited, which was what he'd wanted when he came up with the idea for the yard. He climbed out of bed and tugged on a pair of sweatpants, not bothering with a shirt.

In the kitchen, Sadie bounced from her chair. "Wanna go outside and play on my monkey bars?"

"Sadie. Let Declan wake up."

"He's awake." She pointed at him as if Renee was blind.

"I mean, let him have some coffee and get dressed."

He looked over at Renee and smiled. "I'm dressed enough for a quick run around the yard." Turning to Sadie, he said, "Let me go to the bathroom and brush my teeth. I can drink my coffee outside."

"Yay!"

As he walked past Renee, he ran his thumb along his waistband, drawing her eye. She slowly licked her lips and he wasn't sure which of them was more tortured. He did his business in the bathroom and when he got back in the kitchen, the room was empty. Looking through the window, he saw Renee and Sadie swinging together. Although he couldn't hear what they were saying, the sounds of their voices carried. They were happy.

For the first time, he saw what she wanted him to see— they were a family by themselves. She'd keep him at a distance to make sure he couldn't disrupt what she was building with her daughter.

"Fuck me," he muttered to himself. He poured a cup of coffee and gulped the hot liquid. What was he doing here? He'd told Ty he was ready for something different. Was he really? Or was he talking out his ass like he usually did?

Setting his cup on the counter, he strode to the back door. When he slid it open, a cool fall breeze swept in and he decided that putting on a shirt would be a smart move. He retreated to his room and grabbed a shirt. He wasn't ready to walk away from what he had with Renee, but he didn't know if he was really ready to sign on for the whole thing.

What if he fucked things up for her like Graham did? Renee said she was worried about Sadie, but he was beginning to believe she was every bit as worried about herself.

Going to the yard, he yelled from the back steps, "Sadie, my lady, are you ready for some monkey bars?"

"Yes!" she screamed as she jumped off the swing. She raced over to the monkey bars and used the ladder to climb up. It was still just a little too tall for her. They'd been guessing how tall she was and what her reach was. She stood on the top step, gripping the side rails and looking up at the first bar.

As he walked by Renee, he said, "You can go to work if you want. I'll hang with her a while."

"Thanks."

He turned his attention to Sadie. "You might have to jump to grab the first one. But remember what I told you about momentum?"

"Kinda."

He grabbed her hips and said, "You're gonna do a little jump. Just enough so you can reach the bar." She looked unsure, so he added, "I'm right here. I won't let you fall."

She leaned and reached more than jumped and if he hadn't been holding her, she would've hit the ground. He hoisted her to the bar. "Let's start with the part you know how to do."

They spent the next half hour or so swinging back and forth on the monkey bars. Who the hell needed to go to the gym when you had a kid to play with?

When Sadie was tired of the monkey bars, he asked if it was okay for him to go back inside to work. She didn't care because she still had the slide and swings to play on. As he walked inside, he smiled. This was what he wanted for Sadie.

He poured himself another cup of coffee and went to the dining room to figure out a plan for painting. Renee was at the front door waving at someone. She turned and came back in carrying a pile of books and folders.

"You have clients drop things off at your house?" Even though she was an accountant—like the most boring job ever—it still didn't seem like a good idea for strangers to have her address. Not with Sadie right outside.

"No. That was Chloe."

"Chloe?"

"Yeah. When we were cleaning up on Saturday, she asked if I could look over the books for The Black Rose."

"What?" Every muscle tightened. *That mother fucker*.

Renee shrugged. "She said something was off about the books and she asked me to take a look. It's the least I could do after your brothers built the playset."

"No, it's not. I told them to leave you out of their bullshit."

"This has nothing to do with political campaigns. This is the bar she wants to buy. Not that either one should matter. I'm looking at numbers, not running around like a cop."

He clenched his jaw. He didn't believe it. He wouldn't put anything past his brothers. They were on a mission to find answers and they didn't care who got hurt. But to send his girlfriend? That was low, even for Ronan.

He also knew arguing with Renee wouldn't change anything. He needed to calm down and later today, he'd go see Ronan. He'd calmly tell him to stay the fuck away from Renee.

CHAPTER
Twenty-Seven

After spending a chunk of his day patching the living room and dining room to prep it for paint, his anger hadn't subsided. Renee hadn't said anything else as she worked on the books Chloe dropped off. He tried to convince himself his family hadn't totally ignored what he'd said, but it didn't work. Ronan and Brendan wouldn't drop it.

Once Renee had Sadie home from school, he asked to borrow her car. She didn't ask what he needed it for. Just handed him the keys. He drove straight to Ronan's house without thinking. He should've texted first to make sure his stupid brother would be there. But he wasn't thinking straight.

Luckily, Ronan's truck was parked on the street. Declan knocked on the front door even though he still had a key. He didn't want to walk in on Chloe naked. Ronan opened the door.

"Hey, I was just about to call you. Your windows are in. They called me by mistake. I can make some time tomorrow—"

"What the fuck is wrong with you?" Declan said.

"What?" Ronan opened the door wider to let Declan inside.

"I told you to leave Renee out of all the bullshit with Dad."

"First, Brendan was talking about that, not me. I haven't had any contact with Renee since we left on Saturday."

"Of course not. You sent your fucking girlfriend to do your dirty work." He paced the living room. It had less space now that there was actual furniture in the room.

"You better watch what comes from your mouth. I didn't *send* Chloe to do anything."

Just then, Chloe came downstairs. "Hey, Dec." She looked at Ronan. "Send me to do what?"

"This asshole thinks I sent you to have Renee work on the shit Brendan wanted done to look into the Cahills."

"Oh." She winced. Turning to Declan, she said, "Ronan didn't know I talked to Renee."

"What the fuck," Ronan grumbled.

She held up her hands. "But it's not about the Cahills at all. I swear. I was going over the books for The Black Rose and something felt off. I asked her to take a look. I don't want to buy the bar and then have the IRS coming after me."

Ronan crossed his arms over his chest. "If you think the Byrnes are shady, find a new bar to buy."

"It's not that. The Byrnes are old, not shady. At least I don't think so." She turned back to Declan. "I wouldn't ask Renee to get involved with the Cahills."

"My brothers would." His muscles were still tight and his gut burned.

Ronan crossed to Chloe, kissed her head, and said, "Give us a few."

"I'm heading to work anyway." She pointed a finger at them. "No fighting."

"No promises," Declan answered.

Once she was out of the room, Ronan sighed. "Look, I get why you're pissed. I'd be ready to kill someone too if I thought they put Chloe in danger. Hell, I was ready to kill Brendan when he involved Chloe. But there are two things you need to know."

Declan looked at his big brother.

"One, I wouldn't intentionally put someone in danger. And two—and this is the one you really need to get—your woman is gonna do whatever the fuck she wants and you won't be able to stop her."

He almost argued about Renee being his woman. While she was trying to keep them casual, she felt like she belonged to him. He scrubbed a hand over his face.

Ronan continued, "I told Chloe to stay out of it, but she wouldn't listen. It didn't hit home for her until Danny Cahill showed up at her apartment."

"He did what?"

"He did just enough to make her feel uncomfortable."

Declan watched as Ronan tensed.

"He knows something. His father must've told him. Or he was around when whatever happened to Dad went down. That's why Brendan and I are pushing this. But I wouldn't put anyone in danger. Danny Cahill has nothing to do with Chloe buying the Rose."

Declan felt a pinch better but not much. What else had his brothers been holding back? He rubbed the top of his head and then down the back to his neck.

"I don't get why you keep poking around the Cahills. Alan is dead. Even if he knew something, he took it to the grave."

Ronan shook his head. "How can you *not* want answers? You spent your whole life thinking Dad ran off because what? He didn't want us?"

Declan lifted his shoulders in agreement. That had been what he'd thought.

"I was older, so I knew better. He loved being a dad. He adored Mom. I wish I'd gotten my shit together and started looking for these answers a long time ago. They owe us at least that."

"But it's not gonna change anything. So you get answers about how he died. Great. He's still dead. I still don't have a dad."

"You're right. That part won't change. I guess we're hoping answers will make us feel better. And if the Cahills were behind it, we'll make them pay." He paused. "Now, do you want to order pizza and have a beer?"

Declan sighed. "Yeah, sure. What were you saying about windows when I got here?"

"The window company called me instead of you. Renee's windows are in. I can make some time later this week to pick them up to save her the delivery charge."

"Oh. Thanks. That'd be good." He pulled out his phone and texted Renee to let her know he was having dinner with Ronan.

"Checking in with the woman?"

Declan grunted.

"You were all about dishing it out when I got with Chloe. You should be able to take it."

"Whatever. I'm grabbing a beer." While he was in the kitchen, he heard Ronan calling the pizza place. After grabbing a couple of bottles of beer from the fridge, he stood back and admired his handiwork in the kitchen.

He'd built this and it was damn good. Ronan had had

his doubts, but Declan had proven himself. If he could do it here, there was no reason he couldn't prove himself to Renee, too.

With beer in hand he went back to the living room and sat on the couch. "This room is much homier with furniture. Makes people want to hang out."

"Maybe I don't want people to stay. Did you ever think of that?"

"Maybe most people, but you actually like me." He took a swig of beer.

"You sure?"

They sat for a couple of minutes while Ronan flipped through channels on the TV. "How'd the kid like her playset?"

"Sadie loves it. She spent all morning on it and went back out after school."

"What other work you doing over there besides windows?"

"Mostly cosmetic. Patching and painting. The kitchen needs a complete overhaul, but Renee doesn't think she can afford that right now." He wasn't interested in the game Ronan put on the TV. His mind was on Renee and what he needed to do. "How did you land a chick like Chloe?"

"What?"

"I mean, she's nice and the kind of girl who wants to settle down and that's not how anyone would describe you." He took another drink.

"Fuck if I know."

"How did you convince her you were worth it?"

"I'm a damn good catch." Ronan gave one of his rare smiles.

"Better watch it. You're starting to sound like me."

Ronan leaned forward and braced his beefy forearms on his knees. "I assume this is about Renee?"

"Yeah. She keeps saying we need to keep it casual. Just have fun. Which, yeah, I'm on board for that. But she's keeping me at a distance."

"Did she say why?"

"She says it's because of Sadie. She doesn't want her to get hurt if things don't work out. And I get that. But today, I saw them playing on the swings and it hit me that they're like their own little family. She doesn't want to take a chance on me messing that up."

"She's known you a long time. Your track record isn't great. The real question is, why *should* she give you a chance?"

Fuck if he knew. He just knew he wanted to be with Renee. He liked who he was when he was with her. But hearing those thoughts sounded selfish as hell.

"She's rebuilding her life. She's not going to take a chance on someone who isn't making her life better or easier, you know? Think about our mom. Dad was gone and she figured shit out on her own. Renee's the same."

"So what you're telling me is I'm fucked."

Ronan shrugged. "Maybe. I've never been a single mom. When you showed up here, I gave you a chance to do my kitchen, but in the back of my mind, all I thought was if you fucked it up or didn't follow through, I could fix it. That's not an option for her."

The reality of everything hit him hard. The doorbell rang and Ronan got up to get the pizza. Declan really wanted another beer, but he didn't want to get too drunk and not be able to drive Renee's car home. He grabbed a beer for Ronan and a can of pop for himself.

He had a lot to think about.

. . .

A COUPLE OF HOURS LATER, HE SAT IN RENEE'S CAR AND instead of going back to her house, he went to see his mom. Every time he walked up to his childhood home, a weird feeling came over him. The place held so many childhood memories; it should be happy. But he always felt like there was a gaping hole in his chest.

It was the reason he always chose to couch surf with friends rather than to move back home. This place was suffocating.

But he needed to figure his shit out and Ronan wasn't much help.

He parked and climbed the new stairs Ronan had built. Shoving open the front door, he saw the TV on, but the living room was empty. "Ma?" he called.

"Declan? What're you doing here?" she asked as she came from the kitchen carrying a cup of tea. "What's wrong?"

"Nothing. I figured you'd still be up and I wanted to talk."

She side-eyed him but sat in her chair. She muted the TV. "Come in and talk."

He plopped on the couch, uncharacteristically at a loss for words. And of course, his mom was no help.

"Why didn't you date after Dad?"

"As I told you all before, who said I didn't date?"

"But it was obviously nothing serious. You never brought anyone home or introduced us to a guy."

"Finding a man wasn't a priority. Making sure my children made it to adulthood was." She sipped her tea. "What's all this about?"

"You remember my friend, Ty, right?"

She smiled. "Of course. The two of you have always been thick as thieves."

"I've been doing work on his sister's house."

"She's the one with that adorable little girl, yeah?"

Surprised she knew about Sadie, he paused.

"Last time you brought Tyler here, he showed me a picture of his niece."

"Oh. Well, we've been kind of dating."

"Kind of?" She raised her eyebrows.

He rolled his eyes. "You know what I mean. She wants to keep it a secret from Sadie. She keeps saying we're having fun, but that's all it can be."

"And?"

"And I want more."

"What exactly do you want?"

"Her."

She set her cup on the table beside her chair. "She's cautious, as she should be. She can handle a broken heart. I'm sure she's handled it before. But no mother wants to see her child's heart broken."

"I wouldn't do anything to hurt Sadie. I told Renee that. No matter what happens, I'll still be in her life. Tyler's my best friend."

"But it wouldn't be the same, now would it? For her to get used to you being around all the time and then you go back to being her uncle's friend. For a little one who's already been through some upheaval, it's a lot. Her mother is trying to protect her. That's all we ever want to do." She settled back in her chair and picked up her tea again.

Declan ran a hand over his face. It was the same argument he'd had with Renee. "I was hoping you'd have answers."

"What answers are you looking for? You haven't asked a question."

"How do I make her believe this isn't just fun for me? That I'm not going anywhere."

"That part is easy. Show up. Be there for her and her daughter even when it's not easy. When it's inconvenient. When she pushes you away. You have to show her you're willing to sacrifice because that's what being a parent is."

Whoa. Parent? "Sadie has a father, as shitty as he might be, and he loves her."

She hefted a sigh. "Even if you're not making decisions and disciplining the child, you're there as her mother's partner. You might never be *dad*, but if you want to be in Renee's life, you can't pick and choose the easy path."

The look she shot him said it all.

He'd spent his life choosing the easy path.

"You know I love you, Declan. But since you were young, you've run from challenges. Pretended to be too dumb in school so pretty girls would help you with homework. Bounced from jobs as soon as there was mention of additional responsibilities. She doesn't have doesn't have that luxury."

"I know that."

"Instead of asking me what you should do, you need to ask yourself if you're ready to stop running."

One thing he'd always loved about his mom was that she never pulled punches. She was blunt and told you what you needed to hear even if you didn't like it. Here she was echoing pretty much everything Ronan had said.

"Well?" she prompted.

"I don't know. I really care about her and I adore Sadie. But you're right. I don't know what it means to choose not to take the easy way. I hang out with Sadie and play with her. I don't need to go out partying all the time. I love hanging out in the living room reading a book with Renee."

"That's still about the things you enjoy. What about the boring monotonous things? What about when Sadie is sick and Renee is out of sorts because she hasn't slept and has to work and there's vomit-filled laundry on the floor?"

He couldn't stop the face he made, because vomit. "I'd help her."

"That's what she's afraid of. That she'll come to rely on you."

"And then I'll fuck up."

"You might. But what you do after matters. If you're going to give up, leave her be."

"Thanks, Mom." He stood to leave.

"The door is always open. You have a place here."

He bent and kissed her cheek. He knew she was talking about more than him stopping by for advice. He could move back home if he needed to. But he didn't want to.

What he wanted, even after all of the warnings, was Renee.

CHAPTER
Twenty~Eight

Renee didn't know where Declan had taken off to, but she'd given up on him coming home to read or watch TV with her. She sighed and reminded herself this wasn't his home. Not really. She looked at the books Chloe dropped off. She'd pulled them out and gave them a once-over. Without having some idea of what Chloe thought was wrong, she'd have to give them real attention.

Tonight wasn't the night for that.

She poured herself a glass of wine and bought the next book for book club. She'd spent so much time reading with Declan that she was behind for book club. She had a little more than a week to get it read. It was enough time as long as Declan didn't distract her.

She decided to go sit in the yard since it was a gorgeous warm evening. There wouldn't be too many more days like this.

Sitting on the back porch, she considered grabbing one of the kitchen chairs. Furnishing her yard hadn't been a priority. She made a mental note to look around for some used patio furniture because she could get used to this.

Taking a deep breath full of fall air, she closed her eyes and leaned against the house.

She sipped from her glass and opened the book. She barely got a page in when the back door slid open, and Declan walked out.

"Hey," she said.

"What are you doing out here? I figured you'd be in bed."

"Not yet. It's beautiful out and I wanted to enjoy the warm weather."

He looked pointedly at her ereader. "Are you reading without me?"

"Not the book we're reading. Book club is next week, so I'm starting that."

"Without me? Just gonna not include me in book club?"

"I didn't think you were really interested in book club."

He plopped down beside her. "I don't want to intrude since it's your night with your friends, but I like it because you're there."

She ducked her head and smiled.

"So what's this one about?"

"I have no idea. I'm on page one."

He scooted closer, his arm around her, and kissed her cheek. "Cool. Get started."

His breath on her neck was distracting, so she forced her eyes back to the screen. She started reading and Declan put a hand on the ereader.

"Wait a minute. Where's the duke or earl or whatever?"

"No dukes this time. This one is contemporary not historical."

"So like now. With people like you and me."

"Yep."

"So they're gonna be banging early on."

She slid him a look. "Maybe. Maybe not." In her head, she scrambled to remember what the book was about. Sometimes what they chose bordered on erotica. "I guess we'll see."

"I missed you tonight," he murmured.

"Where'd you go?"

"I went to see Ronan and then my mom."

"Everything okay?"

"Yeah. Pretty good actually."

He laid a hand on her thigh, and she half-expected him to make a move. But he leaned against the house and closed his eyes as she began to read.

Declan's fingers traced random patterns on her leg. The rhythm of the movements along with the cool breeze and the wine she'd consumed made for one very relaxed Renee. She was very glad they were at the beginning of the book because chapter one reminded her why Zenia had chosen this book. It was gonna get steamy.

At the end of the chapter, she set the book aside.

"That's it?"

She turned to face him. "It's late."

"When's book club?" His voice was barely above a whisper.

"Next week." They were practically nose to nose and their quiet voices created a bubble of intimacy.

"Not a lot of time to read."

"It's not a long book."

"I don't want you to go inside yet."

"Why not?"

"Because then you'll go to your room and I'll be in my bed all alone."

"We can't spend the night out here."

"But we can make out for a little bit."

She raised a brow.

He grinned. "We're outside. Sadie's not here."

"What are you, king of the loophole?"

"When it works to my advantage. Come here."

He reached behind her, across her hip, and pulled her onto his lap so she was straddling him.

She had to admit that was impressive.

"You like that, huh?"

"Maybe."

"I got some other tricks I can show you, too." He tugged her hips closer so she was fully notched against him, the movement causing a zing of pleasure to shoot through her body.

Her breath caught. His right hand caressed her jaw and his fingers threaded through her hair before pulling her in for a kiss. As their lips met, gently, Declan's left hand cruised across her body: squeezing her hip, palming her ass, sliding up her shirt to pinch her nipple.

What started as a sweet kiss quickly morphed into a hot exploration. He had the power to take her from zero to needy in seconds. He pulled his mouth away to kiss her jaw, her ear. Then his hot mouth was her pulse point on her neck.

Her thighs tightened and she thrust her hips forward, seeking relief. His groan rumbled against her neck and a jolt of need rippled through her. She rocked a couple more times and then forced herself back.

Leaning her forehead against his, she whispered, "This is a bad idea. You keep luring me to break the rules."

"Rules are meant to be broken."

"Not when my kid's involved." She shifted to get off him, but he held tight.

His grin slipped and his face grew serious. "I'm gonna

say this again, and I need you to hear me. I will. Not. Hurt. Sadie."

God, she wanted to believe him. "I know you won't intend to. I can't take that chance."

"Yet."

When she tried to pull away again, he tugged her closer. "Just stay a little bit longer. Let me hold you."

At her look, he added, "It'll stay totally PG."

She slid off his lap and curled next to him, resting her head on his shoulder. His arm came around her shoulder and held her close.

They sat like that, cuddled together for a few minutes. Then she said, "You never talk about your dad. Why not?"

"Not much to say. He disappeared—died—when I was little."

"Do you remember him?"

"Yeah. As much as a little kid would."

"Tell me what you remember."

"Why?"

She looked up into his eyes. "You've been living here for more than a month. I've been leaning on you this whole time. You're dealing with this stuff with your dad. Even if you pretend it's not affecting you. Maybe if you think about some of the good times, you won't be so angry."

"I'm not angry."

"Yes, you are." She sighed, giving up, and lay her head back on his shoulder, because even if he wasn't going to open up, sitting like this with him felt really good.

Another few minutes passed. Renee closed her eyes and let the warmth of Declan's arms lull her.

"He was a do-er."

Renee opened her eyes but didn't move.

"Anytime something needed to be done, he was there."

He got quiet again. "One time, I wanted a race track for my cars and he spent a whole Sunday morning building me one out of scrap material he had laying around."

She imagined little Declan racing Hot Wheels with a man she would never get to meet.

"Mostly I remember he loved my mom. He was always touching her. Walk through the kitchen and kiss her cheek. Slide a hand around her waist while she was standing at the washer. They were always kissing. As a kid, I thought it was gross. Parents, you know?"

Renee chuckled.

"But even though it was gross, I still knew he *loved* her. Like he would do anything for her. She would look at something that needed to be done and before she could say anything or even think about doing it herself, he was there."

"Because he was a do-er."

"You're right about me being mad. I'm not now, but I was for a long time. I thought he left because of us. He loved my mom. I never thought he'd leave her. So when he was gone, I was just mad. If we knew he died, it would've been different."

Her heart broke for that little boy.

"I never wanted to be like him." His voice was thick as he spoke the last part.

She didn't stir, didn't look at him. She didn't want to break the spell.

"But now." He blew out a heavy breath. "The night he disappeared, he said he was doing a job for Alan Cahill. He'd been working lots of extra jobs because my mom was pregnant again."

"With Nessa?" She didn't think they were that far apart in age.

"No. There was going to be an eighth Doyle. My mom

miscarried after my dad disappeared. None of us knew. Mom just told us when all this came to light. Everything he did was for his family."

"He sounds like a good man."

"I'm finding that to be true. I have a whole life of ideas that are changing."

"Change can be good."

Renee sat up and stretched. "I need to get to bed."

"Party pooper."

"You're the one who stayed out late."

He stood and reached down for her hand. He tugged her up quickly, causing her to crash into him. It gave him another reason to wrap his arms around her.

"This was fun," she said.

"Fun for who? I have an unresolved hard-on and spilled my emotional guts like a pre-teen girl."

She laughed. "The hard-on is your fault for trying to bend the rules. But the second part? I like that you talked to me about your dad."

She kissed his cheek. "Good night."

When she turned and bent to grab her wine glass and ereader, he smacked her very fine ass. When she glared at him, he said, "Couldn't help myself."

"Hmm-mm. See you tomorrow."

After she went inside, he stayed on the porch for a bit. His brain was swirling with too many things. Coming back home and reading with Renee was supposed to give him a break. And for a little bit, it did.

Then she had to ask about his dad. As if Ronan and Mom hadn't given him enough to think about. But surprisingly, he did feel better.

He couldn't remember a time he thought about good times or happy memories when it came to his dad. Renee had been right. He had been angry. Now he didn't know how to feel.

Turning back to the house, he looked at it and considered everything he'd told his mom. He wanted this. Change was good. Now he just had to prove to Renee that change was good for her too.

CHAPTER
Twenty~Nine

For days after their make-out session on the porch, Declan was all business. Well, not *all* business. But he'd been painting the living room and hadn't tried to get in her pants once. Not that he was supposed to, but she'd expected him to. They'd fallen into a rhythm again of hanging out during the day and reading at night. And while they'd kissed, they remained fully clothed.

She busted her ass to work ahead on paying customers so she could finally dig into Chloe's books. Today was a perfect day because Declan had plans with Ty, so he wouldn't be there to distract her.

Renee had ledger books spread out all over her dining room table. Books stacked on open books. When she first started looking at the spreadsheets Chloe sent via email, she saw no red flags. But then she opened the old ledgers and knew something was off.

She tried to convince herself she was assuming there was something there because Chloe thought there was. But as she was getting Sadie ready for bed, the nagging feeling wouldn't go away. She didn't know what wasn't right, but her gut told her there was something hinky going on.

It was late when Declan came back. When she heard him come through the front door, she blinked and checked the time on her phone. Eleven. "Hey. Have a good time?"

"What's all this?" he asked.

"Chloe's books."

His face went stony for a second before he covered it. She didn't know what his problem was with her helping Chloe.

"You've been at this all day and night?"

"Kind of. Not nonstop. I just got into it after putting Sadie to bed and..." She waved her hands over the books. "There's something here. I know it."

His eyes hardened again.

"What's your problem? Chloe asked for a simple favor and since my kid got a brand-new yard, it's not too much to ask."

"It doesn't look simple." He huffed out a breath and scrubbed a hand over his face. "When I went over to Ronan's last week, it was to yell at him for getting Chloe to ask you to do this."

"What?" she practically screamed, and then lowered her voice so she didn't wake Sadie. "What is wrong with you?"

"There are things you don't know. I told you my brothers believe the Cahills know what happened to my dad and Alan might've had something to do with it."

"What does that have to do with the Black Rose?"

He looked at the books scattered on the table. "I was worried that this wasn't just about Chloe. She reassured me the bar has nothing to do with the Cahills but the owners of the bar and Cahill were friends. That's how my brothers gathered information. And then Ronan admitted Danny Cahill came after Chloe."

"Oh my God." She sank to a chair and tried to process everything. "When?"

"I don't know. I guess when Alan died. He didn't make any real threats, but he made her uncomfortable." He stepped closer and cradled her jaw. "I never want you to be in that position. Definitely not for my family."

Worry spiked in her at his words. Obviously, she would never put herself or Sadie in danger, but she was just looking at numbers. Then she remembered what Brendan had asked at lunch that day.

"Why did Brendan ask me about campaign contributions when he was here? Does that have something to do with this?" She swept her arm over the mess on the table.

"I think he's fishing. Trying to figure out what Cahill was doing. But as usual, Brendan doesn't tell anyone anything."

She stared at the piles, unsure of her next move.

Declan rubbed her back. "I wasn't trying to freak you out. I just want to make sure you're safe."

"I get it. Thanks."

He grabbed her hand. "Want to read or watch TV?"

"Reading sounds good if you'll do the reading. My eyes are tired from all the numbers."

"Go put on your jammies and meet me in my room."

She stood and shot him a look. "We agreed no funny business when Sadie is here."

"No funny business. I've been well-behaved. We can lay together and read. Talk nice to me and I'll massage your sore muscles since you've been hunched over these books all day."

Oh, man. A massage sounded heavenly. But she also knew where that would lead with Declan.

He swatted her butt. "Get your mind out of the gutter."

"Why? Yours doesn't want company?"

"I see how it is. You'll pay for that."

She slid away and headed to her room to change. "Yeah, sure. You don't scare me."

But in some ways, he did. He was making her life too easy, too much fun. What would it be like when he left? She shoved the idea from her head and slid into comfy sleep shorts and a tank top. It was starting to get chilly out, but she knew she would be plenty warm lying next to Declan.

With her ereader in hand, she stopped in the kitchen for a glass of water before heading to Declan's room. She heard the water running, so she had some time until he got out of the shower. Stretching out on his bed, she closed her eyes and numbers danced on the backs of her eyelids. It was like moving pieces of a jigsaw puzzle around. She just needed to find the right position.

Now she had extra pieces, thinking about the Cahills and campaign contributions. Just enough to leave nagging thoughts in the back of her mind.

"Did you fall asleep on me?" Declan asked.

She cracked open an eye just in time to see him drop his towel before stepping into a pair of shorts. "Just thinking."

But now numbers were the last thing on her mind.

"Ready to read?"

"Mm-hmm." She scooted over and turned to her side as he got on the bed.

He took the ereader from her but asked, "You want your massage first?"

"No massage needed."

"You sure?"

"Yeah." She curled up next to him and laid her head on his chest. It had quickly become one of her favorite places to be. Declan's voice washed over her and its calming effect caused her mind to completely shut down. She couldn't hold the thread of the story at all.

DECLAN WANTED TO KEEP READING—THE PLOT WAS IN A pivotal point—but Renee had fallen asleep. He set down the book and listened to her breathing. He wanted this all the time. But he needed to change his approach. Living here was the problem. Although his family often teased him about being jobless and homeless, they weren't completely wrong.

He had to become the man Renee needed. And that had to start with him leaving. He couldn't be sponging off her as a roommate. He knew he was pulling his weight, but he wasn't paying rent. Somehow, he didn't think she would take money from him. He needed to figure out how to be her equal.

If that was even possible.

Closing his eyes, he wrapped an arm around her shoulder and relaxed as he planned his next steps.

Suddenly, Renee shot up.

"What?" he asked.

She flicked up a hand to silence him and he thought she was in the middle of a dream. Like she was sleep-talking or something.

"I got it."

"Got what?"

"Money laundering."

"Babe, lay back down. You're not making sense."

She jumped off the bed. "No. The books. I'm not sure, but I think it's money laundering."

He pushed to sit up. "Dude. You're still not making any sense. You're tired. You fell asleep. I think you need to go to bed." *Even if it's not with me.*

But it was like he wasn't even in the room. She scooped up her hair and pulled it into a ponytail. "Just give me a little bit. I need to check."

And then she was gone. He sighed and got out of bed to follow her. Of course, she was hunched over the books on the table again. He stood in the doorway to the kitchen as she flipped books around, shoved one out of the way, grabbed another.

He sighed. He'd lost her. She was in her own world. He went back to his room, grabbed her glass of water, refilled it, and delivered it to the table. She muttered a thanks but didn't look up.

Declan went back to bed and made some plans. If he wanted to make Renee his, he needed to make changes.

AFTER A FITFUL NIGHT'S SLEEP, HE WENT TO THE KITCHEN TO make coffee. He glanced into the dining room to see Renee slumped over the books, sound asleep. She was gonna regret that. He checked the time. Sadie would be getting up soon. He scooped Renee up and carried her to bed. She barely stirred. She must've been truly exhausted.

Then he knocked on Sadie's door. When he didn't get an answer, he swung the door open. Sadie was curled up hugging Larry the Lion. He didn't know how Renee usually woke her up. Sadie just always seemed to be awake.

"Hey, Sadie. Time to get up." She didn't move, so he stepped up to the bed and touched her shoulder. "Sadie."

"Grr."

He chuckled. "Did you growl at me?"

"I don't wanna go to school."

"First, you love school. Second, school isn't for hours yet. If you get up now, I'll take you out to breakfast and then you can play in the yard."

She rubbed her eyes as she sat up. "Pancakes?"

"Whatever you want."

"Is Mom coming, too?"

"Mom's really tired. She stayed up too late working. I was thinking we could sneak out so she can sleep."

"Like a secret mission."

"Sure." He loved her imagination. "Get dressed and brush your teeth. I'm going to leave your mom a note so she doesn't worry."

He started the pot of coffee, assuming Renee wouldn't sleep too late because she never did. Then he scribbled a quick note and left it on her nightstand. By the time he got dressed, Sadie was ready to go.

They walked to the car and Sadie buckled herself in.

"Do I need to check that?" he asked, pointing to the car seat.

"No. I always do it myself. I'm not a baby."

She was so offended that he had to smother his smile. "I'm just being safe."

As he closed the door, he could've sworn she rolled her eyes at him.

He drove to Super Cup, the diner he'd gone to his whole childhood. Sadie climbed into the booth across from his and sat on her knees. "You need a booster thing?"

"No," she said, with a hint of question as she glanced up at him.

He had a feeling he was being played. "Is it one of your mom's rules?"

"Not a rule. She usually gets one, but I don't need it." She straightened up. "I'm big enough."

"Okay." He opened a menu and read to her from the kid's section. She still settled on pancakes.

The waitress came and took their order and for a moment, he sat looking at Sadie wondering what he was supposed to do next.

Luckily for him, the silence didn't last. Sadie filled their morning will tales from school. He learned about all of her classmates, the ones she liked and the ones she didn't (even though Mom said she shouldn't talk like that). Declan decided Sadie was in the right to not like Tristan.

She also taught him he needed to cut up her pancakes for her and keep his hand on the syrup as she poured because she would most definitely overdo it.

But all in all, it was a successful breakfast date.

Renee stretched and looked out the window. The sun was streaming bright. She glanced at the clock. Nine. Nine! She jumped out of bed. She didn't even remember getting in bed.

Then she saw the note. Declan's scribble told her coffee was ready and he and Sadie went out to breakfast so she could sleep in.

She wasn't sure how she felt about that. Her body loved being able to sleep because she was sore after working so late last night. But part of her felt like a slacker because she was supposed to be up with Sadie. Mom guilt was no joke.

But the other part was her fear of leaning on Declan. She'd thought she could count on Graham and look how that turned out. She loved hanging out with Declan and enjoyed that part of her life, but she wasn't sure she was ready for him to be in *all* parts of her life.

Not in that way. Yet.

Ever?

"Ugh," she said to the empty room. She needed coffee. Then she could attempt to untangle her thoughts.

She dressed and headed to the kitchen. Passing the dining room table, she had a flash of last night. Money laundering. It was there. She almost had it figured out. She itched to dive back in but moved away to get her coffee.

As she took her first sip, she saw Declan pull up. She stood at the front door and watched as he helped Sadie out of the car and she swatted his hand away until he handed her a takeout container. He closed the door and said something to Sadie as she came toward the house, totally focused on the container.

Renee's chest suddenly felt tight. Declan looked up and smiled at her. Her heart squeezed more. *Fuck*. How was she falling for him? She'd just gotten clear of an entire marriage. She was supposed to be out in the world meeting people, not falling in love again.

In love?

No. She was tired and her emotions were running a little wild. It felt good to see Sadie so happy. She opened the screen door. "Whatcha got there?"

Sadie looked up with a grin. "We brought you French toast."

"Thank you. Did you have a good time?"

"Declan took me to a new place. He didn't make me sit in a booster seat, and I was good. The pancakes were great. Can we go back? I think they were the best pancakes ever. Except for yours."

Renee took a deep breath and met Sadie on the steps to take the container from her. "I'm glad you had fun with Declan."

"Declan said we could play in the yard when we got back. I got hours till school."

"You do and you can."

Sadie raced past her to the backyard. All the way on this side of the house, Renee heard the sliding door bang and pop back open. She was going to have to remind Sadie again not to slam the door. She needed it to last until next year.

Declan studied her face. "Did you get enough sleep?"

"Yeah. Thank you. You didn't need to do that."

"I wanted to. And you were exhausted." He reached out and stroked her cheek. "How are you feeling?"

"I'm good. I've gotten by on far less sleep." She turned and went back through the house with her breakfast. "So where did you guys go?"

"Super Cup."

"That place is still open?"

"It's a staple of the neighborhood."

From the backyard, Sadie's voice echoed, "Declan! Come play."

He moved past Renee toward the back door.

"You don't need to play with her."

"I told her I would. It would be shitty to back out."

Renee huffed. "Maybe you can teach that one to Graham."

As soon as the words slipped out, she bit her lip. "Sorry.

You don't need to hear that. And you don't have to be Sadie's playmate."

"I like playing." He winked and headed out the door.

Standing over the kitchen sink, she ate her slightly cold French toast and watched Declan and Sadie play in the yard. She had no idea what game they were into, but they both looked like they were genuinely having fun. She finished her breakfast and decided to join them.

As unsure as she might be about the feelings she was having for Declan that she was *not* supposed to be having, she couldn't deny the smile he put on Sadie's face. It was both wonderful and worrisome. She'd always wanted to surround her daughter with as many loving people as possible, but she didn't know how Sadie would respond to having Declan blow into and out of her life.

CHAPTER
Thirty

Declan scooped Sadie up and she squealed an ear-splitting scream-laugh. He twirled her around a couple of times before setting her down. Renee crossed the lawn.

"What are you guys doing?"

"Declan's a monster. He's trying to catch me before I kill him." Sadie stood on the top of the slide holding a small branch.

"Teaching my kid to be violent?" she asked with a smile.

"Hey, I offered to play tag or hide-and-seek." He lowered his voice. "She's a little monster who came up with the violence all on her own."

Renee chuckled. "Yeah. That would be Uncle Ty."

"Don't you need to work?"

"There's always work, but part of the reason I work from home is so I don't have to miss out on time with Sadie."

A sudden jab in his ass had him jumping. He spun around and stared as Sadie ran off giggling.

"You're dead now, monster. I win."

He glanced at Renee. "Did you distract me so she could stab me?"

"Don't blame me because you couldn't outwit a five-year-old. That's on you."

"Come on, Mom. Swing with me." Sadie was on a swing and Renee sat on the one next to her. "Give me a push, Declan. I want to go higher than Mom."

"You got it." He went behind her and began pushing. Renee had already started swinging, so Sadie had to catch up.

They swung quietly for a few minutes, other than the occasional taunt from Sadie or Renee lobbed at the other, both arguing about who was going higher. As he gave Sadie another shove on her lower back, his only thought was that he could do this every day and not get tired of it.

His mom warned him about being ready to be here for the boring stuff, but it was only boring if you let it, right? There was nothing special about this morning, but he was able to let Renee sleep in—something she never did—and he hung out with Sadie. It was an everyday, normal experience, but it wasn't hard.

He felt a level of peace he couldn't remember having in his life. Being in Renee's house, being with Renee and Sadie made him feel balanced. He didn't see how that could be a bad thing. His thoughts returned to last night. He was sure now that he had to leave in order to be a partner to Renee. He needed to figure out his life.

He gave Sadie another push and his phone buzzed in his pocket. He took it out and saw a text from Ronan.

I've got your windows.

Damn. He'd forgotten Ronan said he could pick them up.

Cool. I'm at Renee's.

Be there within the hour.

"Problem?" Renee asked as she swung past him.

"Ronan has your windows. He'll be here soon to drop them off."

"If you need to go do something, you don't have to hang out here. We're good."

He winked at her. "I like hanging out with you."

She smiled at him as she swung by. He couldn't think of a time when a woman smiled at him like that. It wasn't the usual smile women gave him—flirty and fun. It was a smile that said she really liked him as a person.

"Hey, Sadie, my lady. I gotta go in and get ready for windows. How about one more big push?"

"Underdog!" she yelled.

He grabbed the swing on each side of her hips and they counted together. "One, two, three." He shoved her up high and ran under her. As he walked toward the back door, her happy squeal echoed through the yard.

Inside, he moved the furniture in Sadie's room away from the window. He'd wait until she was at school to do this one, but he'd get it done today. Then he went to the other rooms to move furniture for the windows he figured he could reasonably install today.

A horn sounded outside and he went out to meet Ronan. He didn't know if his brother had to get back to the job, so he didn't want to hold him up. He propped the front door open so they could bring the windows in.

Ronan already hefted the first window and was carrying it to the door. "Where you staging these?"

Declan pointed a thumb over his shoulder. "Just against the wall. I'll take them to the right room after we get them all in."

Ronan eased past him and he went to the truck to grab one. They worked in silence, passing each other with the double-hung windows. The last one was the picture window they had to carry together. Declan hadn't considered how the hell he was going to install it himself.

Once they had the windows lined up along the wall in the living room and down the hall, Declan grabbed a glass of water for each of them.

"Thanks for bringing these," Declan said as he handed a glass to Ronan.

"No problem. Want me to stay and help you get the picture installed?"

"Don't you have to get back to work?"

Ronan lifted a shoulder. "The company's been a shitshow for weeks. First it was a mess because of Cahill's death, but now Danny is half-assing it more than usual because he's pushing hard on his campaign."

"Campaign?"

"He's still running for alderman. More determined than ever to follow in his father's footsteps."

"What does that mean for your job?"

"Who the fuck knows?"

"I guess this is a bad time to ask about a job, then, huh?"

"I thought you didn't want to work for me."

"It's not about working for you. It's about me getting serious." He glanced over his shoulder toward the kitchen. "This thing with Renee feels real. But I need to step up my game and be a man who will be an equal partner. I know she's not going to give me a real chance if she even sees a hint of her ex's behavior. She doesn't need that shit again and she knows it."

Ronan drained his glass. "So you finally decided to grow up."

"Fuck you." He set his glass on the table. "It's time to move on."

RENEE STOOD IN THE KITCHEN AND OVERHEARD DECLAN AND his brother talking. *It's time to move on.*

Hearing him say it was like a punch to the gut. He was doing exactly what she'd expected but feared. She took a deep breath and refilled her coffee cup. Forcing a smile, she walked into the dining room. "Hey, Ronan. Thanks for delivering the windows."

"No problem." He smacked Declan's shoulder. "Let's get the picture window done."

"You sure?"

"It's a two-person job, and I don't think Renee can be the second person." He glanced past Declan to her and said, "No offense."

"None taken. I know nothing about windows and that sucker looks huge."

Declan turned around. "Will it bother you if we do this now?"

"I'll have Sadie play in her room till lunch. If the noise is too bad, I'll join her." A moment later the back door crashed open and Sadie raced into the room.

She pulled up short when she realized Declan wasn't alone.

"Sadie, honey, this is Ronan, Declan's brother."

Sadie turned around, eyes huge. "He's a giant," she gasped.

"Ronan helped Declan build your playset in the yard. You should thank him."

She spun back and stared at Ronan. "Thank you. It's awesome. I play on it every day. Declan is teaching me how to swing on the monkey bars, so when I'm at school, I can swing better than the stupid boys."

"Sadie."

Her shoulders dropped. She continued to address Ronan. "Sorry. I'm not supposed to call people stupid. Even when they are. But the boys are mean because I can't swing as good as them. Yet."

The corner of Ronan's mouth lifted. "Glad you're enjoying it."

"Sadie, go wash your hands and play in your room. Ronan and Declan are working here to put in the new windows."

"Can I watch?"

"No," she said at the same time Declan said, "Sure."

She tilted her head and shot a look at Declan. He shrugged.

"She's curious. What if we have the next generation of carpenters here? But," he added, turning his attention to Sadie, "you have to be safe. That means no coming close to the window."

"If you stay on the couch or the chair, you can watch," Renee said, knowing it would be a losing fight.

"Keep your jacket on or go grab a sweatshirt. It might get cold in here," Declan told her.

Sadie climbed up on the chair and curled up, eyes on the two men. Figuring they didn't need two sets of eyes on them, Renee went to work. She had paying jobs to do, but Chloe's books called to her. She was close to figuring something out and really wanted to dig back in.

But she would be the responsible person she's supposed to be and work on the spreadsheets that would pay for the windows being installed.

"Can I watch TV?" Sadie asked.

"Sure." Renee checked the time. If she focused, she should be able to finish this job, eat lunch with Sadie, and then use the afternoon for Chloe's books.

Of course, focus was not her friend because she was distracted by Declan and what she'd overheard. She fought for calm. He said he wanted them to be more than a good time, and as soon as she even considered it, he was leaving.

While she might be hurting a little, at least Sadie would be okay. Declan would just be like Uncle Ty, a man who breezed in and had fun and went back to his life. She would know she was loved and she had people she could count on. That was enough.

Renee wished she could convince herself to be satisfied with the same.

CHAPTER
Thirty-One

eclan didn't think he'd like working with his brother, but this was the second project they'd done together at Renee's house and for the first time, Ronan didn't make him feel like an idiot. While Ronan definitely had more construction experience and knowledge, he didn't treat Declan like his dumb little brother.

It was a nice change. They had the old picture window out quickly and Ronan volunteered to take it in his truck to dump it later. Then they insulated and with minimal cursing, got the new one in. The whole time, Sadie sat in the chair, legs hanging over the arm and stared at them. When he'd told her she could stay and watch, he'd been sure she'd get bored within a few minutes, but she didn't.

"Wow," she said as they balanced the new window in place and Ronan screwed it in.

Declan glanced over his shoulder. "Pretty cool, huh?"

"Uh-huh."

Renee had disappeared from the dining room table and

was banging around in the kitchen. Probably making chicken nuggets for Sadie.

"Were you serious about a job?" Ronan asked over the whine of the drill.

"Yeah."

"Sadie, go wash up for lunch," Renee called from the kitchen doorway.

"Aw. I wanna keep watching."

Declan looked at her. "We're pretty much done with this one. There's not much left to do." He'd already decided to wait until she was at school to cut and install the new trim.

Resigned, she hopped up and ran to the bathroom.

"Sandwiches good for you guys?" Renee asked.

Declan smiled at her. "That'd be great. Thanks."

"You do one window and you think you deserve food?" Ronan asked.

"She's offering. I'm not dumb enough to say no. And neither are you."

"Got me there."

Once the window was secured, they stood back and looked at it.

"Looks good," Declan said.

"You need help with the others?"

"Nah. They're all small double hungs. But I appreciate the offer."

"You still need a guy to do the capping?"

"You know it. I hate that shit. It's tedious and too easy to make it look messed up."

"I'll send you my guy's number. He works fast and relatively cheap."

"Thanks."

Ronan picked up his tools. "Walk me out to the truck. I want to run something by you."

Declan grabbed the plastic they'd taken off the window and balled it up as they walked to the door. Outside, he asked, "What's going on?"

After putting his tools in the cab of the truck, he said, "I'm thinking of starting my own company."

"Okay."

"With Brendan digging around the Cahills, I don't want to quit just yet, but if shit hits the fan, I'll be the first one out on my ass. I want to have a contingency. If you're serious about steady construction work, it'd be great if you can start running things while we build it up."

Whoa. Declan's heart thumped. Ronan wanted to start a company with him? "You mean, we'd be partners?"

"Yeah. Not equal since you don't have a pot to piss in and have no equity coming in. I'll front the business costs. You front the sweat equity to hustle jobs."

"I know how to hustle. You sure now is a good time for this? With Chloe trying to buy the bar?"

"Like you said, it's time to move on."

"I don't know shit about starting or running a business. Let me know what you need me to do."

"Come by later this week and we'll start mapping it out. I have plenty of connections, so we can start with those. Spread word that we're taking on jobs." He glanced back at the house. "How much more work you got here?"

Declan shrugged. "Painting and the windows. That's about it. The kitchen needs to be done at some point. But not now."

"You gonna make cabinets for her, too?"

"I don't know. Lumber costs money. We checked out some reclaimed cabinets."

"Custom are better."

"You should know." He nudged Ronan's shoulder. "We

should get back in. Renee made lunch and if we don't eat it, I'm gonna hear about it."

They turned back toward the house. "Thanks for having faith in me."

"You proved yourself on my house, and I see what you're doing here. You're good."

"Don't mention anything to Renee, though, okay? I want to have things in place first."

Ronan nodded.

As they walked to the front door, Declan began to wonder what it would be like to own a house like this, to come home and know it was his. Then his brain began to spiral. This was Renee's house. Could it be his too? She wouldn't want to move. Would she be able to see him as an equal if it was her house?

Being a serious adult was really fucking sucky. He didn't like all the questions and doubts. He missed the simplicity of being the slacker.

But then he walked through the door and Sadie's voice carried through the house as she talked a mile a minute and Renee was urging her to eat her nuggets.

Renee looked through the kitchen door and smiled at him. "Where'd you guys go? Lunch is ready."

That look and those sounds made him realize it didn't matter whose name was on the deed. This was home. And he'd do anything to keep it that way.

DECLAN AND RONAN WOLFED DOWN THEIR SANDWICHES quickly. Ronan thanked her for lunch.

"Thanks for helping Declan. Again. And let Chloe know I'm working on the books. I almost have it figured out."

He stiffened. "There's a problem?"

"Maybe. I don't want to get too into it until I figure out more. I just didn't want her to think it's sitting here untouched."

Declan huffed. "You've been practically snuggling with those books." He looked over at his brother. "Like slumped over the books in the middle of the night. The other night she even—"

Renee shot him a look, knowing exactly where he was going. Turning to Ronan, she finished, "While we were reading, I had a sudden realization about the books."

"Reading, huh? That's what we're calling it?"

Renee felt her cheeks flush.

"Mom reads a lot," Sadie chimed in.

Ronan chuckled. "I bet she does."

"Oh, God," she mumbled and went to the sink to wash dishes. She couldn't even look at these men right now.

Declan started laughing, and Sadie asked, "What's funny?"

"Nothing."

"Sadie, finish lunch. It's school time soon."

"But then I'll miss Declan putting in the windows."

"I'll save one for you for after school, okay?"

"Can I help?"

"Uh. I don't know about that. You can hand me tools, though."

"Cool."

"Eat," Renee repeated.

"I'm gonna head out," Ronan said. "Thanks again for lunch. I'll let Chloe know what you said."

Renee wiped her hands on a towel. "Thanks for the delivery and the help. The window looks really good."

"No problem. Family, you know?" He shrugged and headed out the door.

Renee didn't know what to do with that. These Doyles were certainly good at knocking her off balance. She wasn't family. But the fact that he'd show up for Declan (repeatedly) said a lot about the brothers. She felt a little bad Sadie didn't know that feeling. Ty might be a pain in her ass, but he was still her little brother.

Declan walked Ronan outside and she cleaned up from lunch. While Sadie got ready for school, Renee looked at the books stacked all over her dining room table. She considered how much she was enjoying the puzzle of these books. Sure, the danger Declan hinted at wasn't appealing, but finding answers was. She wondered what the market was for freelance forensic accountants.

She loved making her own hours and being here for Sadie, but after years of boring bookkeeping and tax forms, she was ready for a change.

"Huh," she said to herself. "I guess I'm ready to move on, too."

The thought and saying the words aloud settled her. Kind of like when she'd decided to file for divorce. It was scary but it felt right. And so did this.

She smiled as she rearranged the books on the table so she could dive in once she got back from dropping off Sadie. The answer was in the handwritten ledgers. That much she was sure of.

Declan came in the door. "Hey, what's the best order for me to do the windows in so I don't mess up your day?"

She glanced at the books. "Can you do the bedrooms and kitchen first? Save this for last? I want to dig back in."

"Mom! Come play with me!" Sadie yelled from her room.

Renee smiled. "Duty calls. You need anything?"

"Nope. I'm all good." The smile he gave her sent a tingle down her spine.

That tingle tap danced across her body when he put on his toolbelt. She'd always been a sucker for a man in a tool belt.

"Better watch it. You keep looking at me like that and these windows will be on hold while we *read* in my bedroom."

She felt her skin flush as he chuckled. "I'm going to play with my daughter now."

But as she walked to Sadie's room, the idea of a little afternoon *reading time* sounded really good. She'd missed being naked with Declan. And by the time she sat on Sadie's floor to play superheroes, she had a plan.

ONCE RENEE AND SADIE WERE GONE, DECLAN TURNED UP THE volume on the radio. Something about loud music made the work go faster. Renee's bedroom window as well as the bathrooms were all done. He had the dining room, Sadie's room, and his room left. His room. It was Renee's guest room. He had to keep reminding himself he wouldn't be here much longer.

But he'd be back. And next time, he wouldn't be in the guest room.

When Renee left to take Sadie to school, he decided to take a break from the windows and return to painting the dining room. He wanted it to look nicer for Renee since she spent so much time there working. It wasn't much of an office for her. She should turn the guest room into an office. How many people visited that she needed a guest room?

First Ty. Then him. Her parents lived locally. He'd ask her about it when she got back. He was getting ready to pour paint into the pan when Renee came back. "No errands today?" he yelled over the music.

She tapped the button on the speaker. "No errands."

"I was going to get these walls painted, but if you're going back to work, I'll do the other windows."

"Or..." she said with a smile, "we can go to your room and read."

"Read?" His brain glitched for a minute before her meaning hit him. "Now?"

"Unless you'd prefer to paint. I can respect your work ethic."

He set the paint bucket down with a thud. "All work and no play isn't healthy."

She snickered. "Don't I know it."

He undid his toolbelt while she watched, giving him the same horny look she had that morning. "I warned you that look was trouble."

"Are you gonna punish me now?"

"Fuck, yeah. In the best way." He stepped forward and she backed up, so he rushed her and scooped her up, tossing her over his shoulder.

"Declan! Put me down."

"You're not getting away this time." He slapped her ass and she squirmed against him.

In his room, he dropped her on the bed. He peeled off his t-shirt and crawled over her body as she scooted back on the mattress. "How much time do we have?" he asked against her torso as he breathed her in through her clothes.

"Two hours."

"Ugh. Maybe enough time."

He shoved her t-shirt up her body, his hands sliding along her ribs, followed by his mouth. Her legs scrambled around him and he realized she was kicking off her shoes. He unbuttoned her jeans and tugged them over her hips.

She raised her ass to get them off. He peeled them away and dropped them on the floor. She propped herself on an elbow and opened her mouth to say something, but he dove back at her, shouldering her thighs wide so he could put his mouth on her warm, wet pussy.

Fuck, he'd missed this. His tongue made a wide path up tasting all of her. Then he sucked on her clit, pulling a long, low moan from her. Wrapping his arms around the tops of her thighs, keeping her wide open to him, he feasted on every inch of her. He brought her to the edge, her hips following his very movement, her hands gripping his hair.

Then he pushed fingers inside of her stroking her inside and out until she screamed his name and curse words he'd never thought he'd hear from her. He lapped at her as her thighs twitched around him.

He nuzzled the crease where her thigh met her hip. Nipped at the fleshy part of her thigh. Listened to her heavy breathing.

"Get naked," she said. "I want to feel you."

"We'll get there. I'm not finished here yet."

"I'm pretty sure it was obvious how hard I just came."

"Yeah. And I want to see it again."

"Oh, I don't think—"

"Stop right there. If you can still think, I haven't met my objective." He started slow, knowing she would be sensitive.

He worked his way around her clit, suckling parts of her, stroking her gently with his fingers and tongue.

"Really, Declan. Come up here." She tapped his shoulder.

"Shh."

His breath against her made her jolt. So he did it again. Blowing gently. Lick. Nibble. Suck. Suck harder. Over and over.

Her breath was coming in short hard pants again. She was fighting it. "Let go, babe."

"I can't."

He looked up at her face. He moved up her body. Pressed a kiss to her lips while his hand still covered her pussy protectively. "I got you."

He went back down and started again. He pushed his tongue deep inside her, pressing his nose against her clit.

"Oh. God. Declan. I can't. I can't."

"Trust me."

He repeated everything again. Slow build. Licking and suckling. Thrusting and biting.

"Please," she begged.

His tongue and fingers became a flurry of movement. Both of her hands gripped his hair and held him through her spasms and screams. She finally came down and her limbs slid away.

He stood and wiped at his mouth and chin. As he unbuckled his pants, he remembered he was wearing his boots. There was no kicking them off quickly.

Fuck it. He shoved his pants and underwear down his thighs, grabbed a condom from the drawer.

"You doing okay?" he asked.

"I don't know. I've never felt like this." She gave him a soft, sweet, almost sleepy smile.

"You need a nap?"

Her smile widened. "I'm not that sleepy. Get your ass over here."

She beckoned him with a crook of her finger. He rolled on the condom and shoved his pants low enough to be able to climb back on the bed.

He covered Renee's body with his and slid into her. She wrapped her legs around him and they rocked slowly together until he came with her walls throbbing around him. Then they lay wrapped in each other for a long while, saying nothing, but feeling everything.

CHAPTER
Thirty-Two

Renee lay with Declan on top of her. They were sweaty and sticky and totally relaxed. His face was nestled in the crook of her neck, his breath fluttering over her skin.

"You doing okay?" he asked.

"Mmm-hmm. Don't know that I can move."

"Then I guess I did my job."

She felt his lips curve into a smile against her skin. She would definitely miss this when he moved on. But she knew now she was ready for more. He'd taught her it was okay to carve out time for herself. She took a deep breath.

"Uh-oh. I know that sound. You're about to shove me off you."

"Not that I wouldn't like to stay like this. You made me very sweaty and sticky. I think I need a shower."

"Is that an invitation?"

She laughed. "Are you serious? How do you have the energy?"

He rose on his forearm and brushed her hair away from her face. "I can't get enough of you."

She rolled her eyes even as she blushed. He pulled away and sat up. She giggled at the sight of him.

"What's so funny?"

"You didn't even take off your pants."

"I had more important things on my mind. Plus, my boots are a pain in the ass to take off."

"Points for expediency." She climbed off the bed and gathered her clothes. She left him sitting on his bed as she strode through the house to get to her bathroom. After starting the water to warm up, she put her hair in a high ponytail to keep it dry. Catching the sight of her face in the mirror, she had to admit she looked like she'd been well fucked.

She stepped under the warm spray of the water and closed her eyes. A minute later, Declan came into the bathroom. Her heart bumped a little harder.

"Can I come in?"

"As long as you don't hog all the hot water."

He stepped into the tub and pressed his body against her back. She turned in the circle of his arms. So much for her hair staying dry.

"I think we should pencil this into your schedule every day after dropping off Sadie." He lowered his mouth and kissed her.

She wrapped her arms around his neck. "I have to admit it was one of my better ideas."

Taking her loofah from the hook, she squirted some body wash on it and rubbed it gently across his shoulders and chest. Then down his torso. With her other hand, she used the bubbles and stroked his dick, which grew with the movement. It throbbed against her palm. She continued to stroke while washing his arms and reaching around to his back.

He closed his eyes and fisted his right hand. She stepped away from the spray so the water rinsed away the soap. His dick was fully hard again.

"Seems as though you have a bit of an issue here." She squeezed a little on the upward stroke. "What are we going to do about it?"

"I could bend you over and take you right here."

"Or..." She looked up at him and winked. Then she lowered to her knees and took him in her mouth.

He slapped his left hand against the tile wall and groaned when she took him deep. His right hand settled on the back of her head where her ponytail sat. She cradled his balls and ran her thumb gently between them while she created a rhythm with her mouth and tongue.

"Fuck, babe. Yes."

She didn't realize how much she enjoyed that encouragement. She increased her pace and took him deeper. His grip on her hair tightened and she felt all of his muscles flex.

Suddenly, he pulled her away, grabbed his cock, and directed his stream all over her chest.

She stood. "Really?"

With a cocky grin, he said, "Now I get to clean you up."

Just like she had, he took the loofah, squirted body wash on it, and began to clean her up. His movements were slow and sensual. Even if she hadn't already been turned on by giving him a blowjob, she'd be there now.

He spun her around to face the water. Using both hands, he rinsed her, paying special attention to her nipples, which were hard peaks begging for that attention. He rolled one between his thumb and forefinger while his other hand skated down her body.

The slow circles he made on her clit almost made her

knees buckle. He tightened an arm around her waist and she rested her head against his shoulder. He kissed her neck and bit her shoulder when she rocked her hips to follow his hand.

He pressed and pinched her clit while pinching her nipple and biting her shoulder. All three pain points skyrocketed her pleasure and she came hard, gripping the back of his neck to keep her balance. With his hand gently covering her pussy, he held her until her trembling stopped.

They stayed like that until the water ran cold. Renee knew if they kept this up, Declan was going to ruin her for other guys. Meeting on her schedule, in her timeframe without question, and putting her pleasure first would be tough to beat.

He was almost too good to be true. And that worried her.

BY THE TIME SHE WAS DRESSED AGAIN, RENEE WANTED A NAP, but then she would have no time to get back into Chloe's books. Declan went back to his room to get dressed, and she took a blow dryer to her hair to get it somewhat presentable.

She still had some time before picking up Sadie, so she went to Chloe's books. She just had to find the one little thread to pull, the one hint that she knew was lurking in the old ledgers. She opened up five different books and spread them across the table, opening each one to the first page.

Week by week, month by month, she slowly turned the pages and scanned the entries. She knew how men hid money from their wives. But money laundering was something she hadn't had to search for in a long time.

Taking a deep breath, she closed her eyes and took a step back. Declan's noise while he worked was a surprisingly good soundtrack for her thoughts.

On the backs of her eyelids, she saw numbers, but none of them made sense. She went back to the books. She didn't know why she had the idea that there was money laundering happening here. Maybe her imagination had run away. Lord knew she'd been bored with her current jobs. It was possible this was her subconscious giving her some adventure.

"How do criminals use a bar to money launder?"

"Is that a question for me?" Declan asked from the doorway.

"No. I'm thinking aloud. I don't know if I'm trying to convince myself there's something here or if there really is."

"Well?"

"Well, what?"

"How would you use a bar to launder money?"

"Phony invoices for services. Something inflated. That's the most common."

He pointed at the books. "So find the fake invoices." Then he disappeared back to work.

Could it be that simple? Using her index finger, she ran down pages in one of the older ledgers. Nothing. Nothing. Noth— She stopped and picked the book up for a closer look. A supplier invoice. She couldn't make out the whole name. A.C. something.

She dropped the book and began searching for others. The task would've been so much faster if everything was in a spreadsheet. Then again, having it handwritten helped with hiding money. Only the bottom line was officially used and seen. She scanned through three more books before her alarm went off to remind her to pick up Sadie. She scribbled dates and amounts on a list before heading out the door.

The pickup line was hectic as usual, but today it irritated Renee more because her mind was racing with possibilities for what was going on at The Black Rose. Sadie jumped in the car and began her running commentary on what happened during school. Once they got home, Sadie raced to find Declan.

"Homework," Renee called, even though she thought homework in kindergarten was dumb.

"Declan said I can watch him do another window."

Renee sighed. "Let's see how busy he is. I have work to do, so I can't sit with you."

"Declan's here."

"But if he's working, too, he can't pay attention to you."

"I wanna watch."

"Hmm-mmm. I think he's in your room."

Together they walked to Sadie's room. He had moved furniture and toys out of the way again, but he wasn't there. "He might be in my room."

Just as they stepped in the hall, Declan was walking toward them.

"Ready for work, Sadie, my lady?"

"Yes! Told you, Mom."

Renee bit her lip and inhaled deeply. "Are you sure she can hang with you? I'm in the middle of something."

"Of course she can hang with me. Best helper ever."

"I'm serious."

He looked her dead in the eye. "So am I."

The certainty he answered with made her insides flutter

again. Looking at Sadie, she said, "One hour. Then homework. Even if Declan's not done."

"Okay."

Declan skirted around her and took Sadie's hand. Sadie immediately launched into telling him about her day, just as she had in the car.

Renee let them get to work and she returned to her list and pile of books. With each passing page, she had the realization she was on to something. She wasn't quite sure what she was onto, but it was something. The hour she'd given Sadie passed quickly and Renee had a hard time pulling away to make her daughter do her homework before dinner.

Rather than move the piles on the dining room table, she called Sadie to the kitchen and had her pull out the coloring pages she had to do. It was simple tracing and coloring, so she didn't need help. Renee looked through the fridge to figure out a plan for dinner. She really needed to get better at meal planning. This last-minute scramble made her miserable.

"Did you have fun watching Declan?"

"Yeah. Did you know there's pink and yellow itchy stuff inside the walls?"

"The insulation?"

Sadie shrugged. "It keeps it warm."

"Yes, it does." Giving up on anything that would take effort, she said, "How about breakfast for dinner?"

"Yes!" Sadie said, executing a fist pump.

Renee chuckled and shook her head. To be so easily excited.

Declan finished up Sadie's room while Renee made sausage and eggs for Sadie. He got the trim re-installed and grabbed the vacuum cleaner.

As soon as he started vacuuming, Renee was in the doorway, yelling, "What are you doing?"

He turned off the vacuum. "Cleaning the mess so Sadie can have her room."

She stepped forward and put a hand on the vacuum. "This is the kind of thing you tell me to do."

"Why? Do you think I don't know how to vacuum?"

"I can't imagine you would struggle with it. But you're installing the windows. I can clean up."

"You were feeding Sadie. It's not a big deal."

"It is."

"Renee, it doesn't make you weak to let someone help."

"I'm not weak."

"I fucking know that," he said in a low growl. "And I'm not incompetent. So let me vacuum."

She pulled her hand away, but he reached out and grabbed it.

If he was going to make this work, he needed her to believe he could be a partner. "We help each other. That's the way things are supposed to work. Sometimes it's more on you; other times, it's more on me. It's just vacuuming."

"I know. But I've been doing it all on my own for a long time. Help always came with strings."

"No strings here, babe." He grinned. "But I will be

collecting payment at a later date. Like around one-thirty tomorrow."

She laughed, which was what he wanted. "Go do your work or play with Sadie. I'll be done in here soon."

She glanced at the door and then leaned in and kissed his cheek. It wasn't sexual, but it was definitely progress.

CHAPTER
Thirty~Three

Declan worked nonstop for days, pushing to get Renee's house as finished as he could get it. He still found time to read with Renee in the evenings, and they had a few afternoon quickies, but his focus was work.

Ronan wanted to get together tonight to talk about the new business. Declan had never been actually excited about work. But he was excited to start a business with his brother.

He finished cleaning up the brushes and roller from painting the dining room while Sadie colored at the kitchen table.

"What do you want for dinner tonight?" Renee asked.

"I'm going over to Ronan's. Sorry. I forgot to tell you."

Although she looked a little startled, she wasn't mad.

"Okay. Have fun."

Sadie sidled up to him and took his hand after he dried it on the towel. He looked down at her.

"Can we go for pancakes tomorrow?"

"Sadie!"

Sadie looked at Renee, wide-eyed and confused.

"You don't ask someone to take you out to eat."

"I ask you all the time." The poor kid was so confused.

"I'm your mom. Declan is—"

"A friend she can *always* talk to *and* ask for pancakes."

Renee practically growled. "You should wait to be invited. Unless you have money to buy breakfast, and then you can do the inviting."

Declan shot Renee a look, then squatted in front of Sadie. "Sadie, my lady, will you do me the honor of taking you for pancakes tomorrow morning?"

"Yes," she said with a huge grin. She skipped away toward her room.

"I'm trying to teach her some manners."

"She's five. She's got plenty of time to be stuck with that. And she doesn't need manners with me."

Renee gathered the crayons and papers Sadie left behind.

"I think the real problem is that you still worry about her counting on me."

She stiffened but didn't turn around.

He took her by the shoulders and forced her to face him. "I'm not going anywhere. Sadie can call me in ten years because some dumb kid broke her heart, and I'll go beat him up."

Renee rolled her eyes. "That's real responsible. Getting arrested for beating up a teenager."

"It'd be worth every minute in jail for Sadie to know she deserves better."

Renee sighed and leaned her forehead on his chest. He rubbed her back.

"Do you need anything before I head out?"

"No. Although you're gonna miss book club tonight."

"Damn. I forgot. I'll try to make it back for the good parts."

"And what, exactly, are the *good parts*?"

He leaned close and whispered, "The parts that make me imagine you naked underneath me."

He nipped her earlobe and stepped away before she could smack him.

After taking a quick shower, he got dressed and grabbed the notebook he'd been using for ideas for Renee's house. "I'm heading out."

Sadie was watching a cartoon. "Bye."

"Make sure you go to bed early so you'll be up for pancakes."

She rolled her brown eyes the same way Renee did. "I'm up before you all the time."

"Not *all* the time."

Renee turned from where she was still huddled over Chloe's books. "You can take my car."

"You sure? I can call an Uber."

"I'm not going anywhere." She pointed to the dish by the front door where she kept her keys. "If Chloe's there, tell her to give me a call. I think I have this figured out."

He fought the anger that wanted to bubble up. "I'm guessing that means you found something illegal."

"I think so. But there's nothing dangerous here. I promise."

The only reason her words calmed him was because he knew she would never do anything to put Sadie in harm's way.

He drove to Ronan's. It was still early, but Ronan was usually home by four. If they got things hammered out, he could make it back for book club. Not that he'd ever admit to Ronan that was the reason he wanted to get home.

Chloe opened the door just as he was about to knock.

"Oh, hey," she said.

"Before you run, Renee asked me to tell you to call her. She thinks she has your books figured out."

"Damn." Chloe's face fell. "Figured out means it's not all clean. I didn't imagine it. Fuck. How bad?"

Ronan was suddenly at her back. "What's going on?"

She looked over her shoulder at Ronan. "Renee found the problem in the Rose's books."

"I'm just the messenger. I don't know what she found. But one night she did randomly yell, 'Money laundering.' But she hasn't said more. Other than to assure me there's nothing dangerous."

"Thanks. I'll call her." She kissed Ronan and then went to her car.

Declan followed his brother into the house. They went to the kitchen. Ronan handed him a beer.

"I got a guy who's gonna help with the paperwork to incorporate us as a company. We need a name."

Declan twisted the cap off the bottle and shrugged.

"I was thinking Doyle Brothers Construction."

Wow. Declan hadn't considered a name. But a company—a business—with his name on it sounded really good.

"I'll drink to that."

They clinked bottles and then had a seat at the table.

"How are things with Renee?"

"I'm almost done with the work there. Windows are in. I just have to finish the painting. I should be done by this weekend."

"I meant with Renee. Not her house."

Declan sank back in his chair. "Good. She's still not sure I'm serious. I'm going to move back home. Take time to build my own life so that she can see I'm serious. That I can do it."

"You love her?"

His immediate gut response was fuck yeah, but he hadn't said it to Renee. Telling Ronan first felt weird. He didn't know what his expression said, but Ronan chuckled. "Yeah, I get it. Let's move on to business."

Declan slapped his notebook on the table and flipped to a blank page.

"For now, I think we'll run everything out of here. My garage is filled with tools. You have the code to access everything. When we grow and need more space, we'll look."

"Makes sense. Why spend money before we're making a profit."

"We need to figure out what kinds of jobs we want to take. What things you can handle. What you'll need me or other guys for."

"What other guys?" Declan asked.

"No one yet. But once we start taking on jobs, we'll need to man them."

Declan's shoulders tensed. He figured it would be the two of them working like they had on Renee's windows or Ronan's kitchen. Now he'd have to compete with other guys?

Ronan slid some printed pages across the table. "There are some classes offered at the community college. Construction management. I know school wasn't your thing, but this will give you the knowledge you need."

"What about you?"

"What about me? I've been doing this. Running a crew."

"Won't you be running the crew for our company?"

"Yeah, but so will you. Especially at the beginning." He took a long pull on his beer. "What did you think I was talking about building? We'll be big. Inside a year or two, we'll be handling huge projects. I want to be able to rival any company out there. Union or not."

Declan guzzled his beer, his throat suddenly dry. Could he do this?

"I know you've never done this. The classes will give you background. I'll fill in with the practical knowledge."

"I know fuck all about running a business."

"But you're a people person." He pointed a finger at Declan. "And the pretty face doesn't hurt. You're a salesman. But you'll be better than others because you actually understand the work. You won't be talking in hypotheticals."

"Fuck. I don't know what to say."

"Let's come up with a plan. Decide what we need to do now to get started and what can wait."

"Okay."

While Declan was gone, Renee made more notes in Chloe's books before putting Sadie to bed. She dumped some appetizers into the air fryer and considered cleaning the dining room table, but she didn't want to disrupt her process.

They never sat in the dining room anyway, and it wasn't like her friends would judge the mess.

Lisa and Julie arrived first carrying the margarita mix. Before she closed the door, she saw Zenia's car pull up, so she waited. Zenia approached the steps and the telltale bump had Renee doing a happy dance.

"You look so good! Congratulations!" She hugged Zenia tightly.

Zenia handed her a bag. "I got the chips and salsa, but be warned, I've been craving the super spicy stuff."

Renee led her inside where Lisa and Julie also gushed over the peanut-sized baby. Kim arrived by the time they'd poured their first drinks.

As she folded her sweater over the back of a dining room chair, she asked, "What's all this?"

"I'm going over some books for a friend who's planning to buy a bar."

"A bar? Which one?" Julie asked.

"The Black Rose?"

"I've been there," Kim said. "Nice neighborhood bar." She looked around at the other women. "You guys must've heard about it. That's where former Mayor Cahill keeled over."

They all nodded, except Renee, who hadn't known that.

"Who's the friend?" Zenia asked.

"Chloe. Declan's brother's girlfriend."

Lisa made a point of looking around. "Speaking of Declan, where is he?

"At his brother's house. He'll be back later."

"And how are things going there?"

Renee took a big drink from her glass. She'd known they'd ask about her relationship with Declan, but she hadn't formulated an answer. Finally, she settled on, "We're having fun."

"Fun, huh?" Zenia said. "But you're doing favors for the family."

Renee rolled her eyes. "His family build a huge jungle gym for Sadie in the backyard. It's the least I could do."

"And?" Julie prompted.

"And we're seeing where things go."

"Straight to the bedroom," Kim added.

They all cheered her on and clinked glasses. Renee laughed. She really loved these women. "This isn't a forever thing. Declan's ready to move on, I think. But it's been a great experience for me to get back into dating and relationships."

They all eyed her disbelievingly.

"Really. It's been great." She lowered her voice. "And I can't put the quality of sex into words. But Declan is figuring out his life. He doesn't need a ready-made family."

They nodded but Renee didn't think they believed her. Hell, she wasn't sure she believed it herself. They stuffed themselves on crappy food and caught up on one another's lives for an hour before even thinking about the book they were supposed to be discussing.

Taking snacks and drinks to the living room, they settled in to talk about the book. Just as Kim wrapped up the summary for those who hadn't finished reading (Lisa *and* Julie), the front door opened and Declan came in.

Silence filled the room as he entered.

"Damn. Did I miss all the good parts?"

"We just started," Renee answered.

"Good. I brought more margaritas. I know how you ladies like to go through bottles."

"Woo-hoo! Cabana boy for the win!" Kim yelled.

Declan stiffened for a second, almost imperceptibly. Renee got up and took the bottle from him. "I'll take this to the kitchen. Anyone need a refill?"

Kim and Julie both held up their glasses.

Declan followed her to the kitchen. "Help yourself to food."

"Thanks."

SHANNYN SCHROEDER

She stopped mid-pour. "You know Kim was joking, right? She didn't mean anything by it."

"Of course."

His face didn't look like he believed her. "Can I mix you a drink?"

"Margaritas aren't my thing. I'll have a beer."

She finished filling glasses. "You're coming, right?"

"Wouldn't miss it." He grabbed a plate and a beer and followed her back to the living room.

"Did you have a good time at Ronan's?"

"Uh, yeah. I'll tell you about it later."

Renee took a deep breath and tried to shake off the uneasiness of this whole interaction. She'd decided to enjoy more parts of her life, so that was what she was going to do. She would believe what she'd told the girls.

Her relationship with Declan was amazing and fun, but when it was over, she'd be fine.

346

CHAPTER
Thirty~Four

Declan enjoyed book club, but he couldn't shake loose the nagging feeling he'd had since he got home. Hearing Kim refer to him as a cabana boy shouldn't have irked him. She was teasing. He knew that.

But Renee hadn't corrected her.

That was the real problem. Shouldn't she have said something?

Anything?

He gathered plates and glasses while Renee said goodbye to her friends.

When she joined him in the kitchen, she said, "You don't have to clean up."

"I know."

"So," she started, leaning against the counter. "The girls suggested we let you pick the next book club book."

He froze. "What?"

"We take turns choosing the books we read, and they said if you're going to keep crashing book club, you might as well pick the next book."

His smile was huge. He probably looked ridiculous.

"But you have to choose fast, so we all have time to read it."

"Anything?"

"We obviously prefer romance, but we've read thrillers and mysteries. Just don't pick something boring."

"As if I could."

She took dishes out of his hand and loaded the dishwasher. "You might want to get to bed. Sadie's counting on pancakes in the morning."

"I remember. It's not that late."

"What happened at Ronan's? You said you'd tell me later."

He stopped and turned to her. He wanted to see her face when he told her. "We're starting a business together."

Her eyes popped wide. "What? Really?"

"Yeah. He's been thinking about it with everything that's been happening with the Cahills. He wants to build something big to rival a company like Cahill. I'm going to start building it up while he's still working there."

"Oh." Her face fell a little, but she tried to hide it.

"I'm going to finish the painting here. That's all that's left right now anyway. I won't leave you hanging. And when you're ready for the kitchen, I'll take care of it."

"No, no. I'm not worried about the house. Congrats. This is huge. I had no idea you wanted to run your own business."

"Neither did I. Not until I did the work here. Then when Ronan asked, it just felt right, you know?"

"That's awesome." She wrapped her arms around his neck and hugged him.

When she released him and moved to step away, he pressed her against the counter and kissed her. It wasn't long, but it was thorough.

She placed a hand on his chest. "I'm going to let you get away with that because this is a big deal. But you're not supposed to do that."

He rolled his eyes. One day soon, she wouldn't even consider this an issue. "Let's finish the dishes fast and you can help me pick out a book."

"Deal."

They worked together seamlessly. He liked all of this. He finally felt like he was making the right moves in life.

Renee was key.

FOR THE NEXT COUPLE OF WEEKS, RENEE'S LIFE FELT OFF. SHE and Chloe still hadn't met up, but Chloe was supposed to come over soon, while Declan and Sadie were at breakfast as they had been doing every Wednesday morning.

Renee had figured out as much as she could about the books. Maybe the unsettled feeling came from missing the hunt she'd found in those books.

Things with Declan were good. Kind of. They'd fallen somewhat into a routine. At least when he was around.

He'd been spending a lot more time with Ronan, which made sense. Getting a business off the ground was a lot of work. He'd been trying hard to juggle finishing the painting and minor things on her house while he was meeting with potential customers.

All of that meant their alone time—both naked and clothed—had diminished. And she missed it. Not just the sex—although that was pretty spectacular—but all the little things, too.

It felt like he was pulling away. Unfortunately, it was a phenomenon with which she was familiar.

She tried not to be hurt by it. She'd thought she'd prepared for it. Of course, it had been inevitable. She'd been telling herself that all along.

She struggled to come to terms with that and the fact that Declan was being true to his word. He was still doing all the jobs on the house he said he'd complete. And he hadn't missed a weekly breakfast with Sadie.

She'd tried to get Sadie to understand she shouldn't come to expect it. Not that a five-year-old could understand lowering her expectations. Maybe it could become a special mommy-daughter breakfast.

Renee laughed. As if that were any different than any other meal they shared.

The doorbell rang. When she opened the door, she was surprised to see Ronan and Brendan with Chloe. "Hey."

As she stepped through the door, Chloe said, "I hope you don't mind these two tagging along."

"Not at all. Come on in."

"Where's Declan?" Ronan asked as he closed the door.

"He took Sadie out to breakfast."

Ronan gave a short nod. Renee didn't know how to interpret that.

"I have everything on the table over here." She led them to the dining room table. "Can I get you all coffee?"

"That'd be great," Chloe said.

Brendan followed her. "I'll help."

"That's not necessary."

"You don't need to act as our waitress. You have two hands and so do I."

She filled three cups and Brendan doctored two of them with milk. She topped off her own cup.

He scooped up two mugs and she grabbed the other two. She couldn't help but feel like he wanted to say something else to her but changed his mind.

Once they were all settled around the table, Renee explained what she'd found.

"When I first started with the books, I worked backward and while nothing stood out as odd, I had a feeling like I was missing something. I considered I was imagining it based on you asking me to look."

"But?" Brendan asked.

"Money laundering. I don't have real proof. This purely circumstantial. But I know what it looks like."

"Fuck," Chloe muttered.

Ronan laid a hand on her thigh and squeezed.

"Here's the weird thing. It was pretty regular for years. Then it stopped. Except for two random entries this summer."

Chloe inhaled deeply. "How do you know it's money laundering?"

"On the surface, nothing is a red flag. But when you look at money in, money out, there are patterns. That's what caught my attention. The two entries this summer. While the bar tends to be busier during the summer, there are two entries where the income for the night was excessive. I could chalk it up to a party or advertising. Whatever.

"But it's the money out that's suspicious. There are entries for invoices to an A.C. something. I can't make out the name on the invoice in the ledger. You don't have it in your spreadsheet. The amount spent on the invoice to A.C. is about the same as the increase that was labeled income."

Ronan held up a hand. "You need to explain this to me like I'm Sadie. A bar has money coming in and going out every day."

Brendan cut him off. "She's saying someone has been using the Rose as a front. They put extra money in and then create a bogus invoice to get it out. No one knows where it really came from."

"Exactly."

"And you said they're all labeled A.C?" Brendan asked.

"Yep."

"Like Alan Cahill?"

Chloe, Ronan, and Brendan all stared at one another. Renee didn't know what to say. Then they all turned to her.

"I have no way of knowing what or who A.C. is. I have a list of all the entries." She slid books aside and pulled out her notepad.

"We can find something else for you to buy," Ronan said to Chloe.

"I want the Rose." Her eyes locked on Renee's. "What's the likelihood a bank would find this?"

She shrugged. "Little to none. I'm not sure I would've found it. I did because I was looking. Most banks are just checking the financials to make sure there's nothing wonky. And with the exception of this summer, it's been clean."

Brendan rubbed a hand over his jaw. "So it was dirty when Alan was in office. And when Danny decided to run, it started again. This is their election corruption."

"Whoa," Renee said. "I don't know that. There is zero proof. You'd have to cast a much wider net for that type of investigation."

"But it's a starting place."

Turning back to Chloe, she said, "I'm sorry I don't have better news. That said, I don't think this should be the reason for you to walk away. In general, most banks and investigations are only going to go back seven to ten years.

It's a gamble, but it might be worth taking. Only you can decide that."

"Thanks." Chloe stood and gathered the piles of books and notes Renee made.

The front door swung open and Sadie came barreling through. She skidded to a halt in front of Renee.

"What's the hurry?"

"Declan said I could play outside."

"It's a little cold out."

"I'm wearing my jacket. Bye!" she yelled as she sped through the house. A moment later, the back door slammed and bounced.

Renee growled. "She's gonna bust that door one day."

Declan came in and asked, "What's all this?"

"Chloe came to pick up her books. I explained what I found."

Chloe smiled. "Thank you again."

"I'll be glad to see that stuff go." Turning to Chloe, he added, "No offense. It just has a bad vibe."

Declan leaned over and kissed her cheek. "Breakfast might be a little cold."

"I told you not to bring me anything."

"And I know if you're not feeding Sadie, you won't eat."

He wasn't totally wrong.

"Aw..." Chloe said. "They're so cute."

"Yeah, yeah," Ronan said, and he shuttled her toward the door with a hand on her hip. "See you later, Dec."

"I'll be there this afternoon and we can go over bids."

After Ronan, Chloe, and Brendan left, Renee took their cups to the kitchen. "Bids already, huh? That's a good sign."

"Ronan has a lot of connections."

She leaned against the counter and crossed her arms. "Do you have a business card? I have connections, too. Lots of moms in the pickup line would love to have you come over and work on their houses."

"Nothing to worry about, babe." He curled his fingers in the waistband of her jeans and tugged her close. "You're the only mom I have my eyes on."

She melted a little against him even though she knew she shouldn't. The back door slid open.

"Coming?" Sadie asked.

Declan slowly released his grip. "On my way."

Sadie turned back to the yard.

"Do NOT slam the door."

Sadie inched the door closed with wide eyes. If sarcasm was an expression, it was the one her child wore at that moment.

Declan chuckled. "She's gonna be a handful."

"Gonna be?"

"Even more than she is now. I love it."

He truly sounded excited at the prospect of Sadie growing up and being bolder and snarkier.

Again, he wasn't wrong. As much as she dreaded it, Renee also looked forward to her daughter being fearless.

"So I shouldn't count on you for dinner tonight?" she asked as he neared the door to follow Sadie.

"Probably not. But I should be back early enough to read."

"Sounds good."

She watched him head to the yard to play with Sadie. This might not last, but she was going to enjoy every moment of it she could.

CHAPTER
Thirty-Five

Declan was feeling good about his life right now. He'd finished all the work on Renee's house. At least until she was ready for a new kitchen. And if he had his way, he'd build it all himself like he had for Ronan.

He was dog-ass tired from trying to get everything done for Renee and running around visiting prospective jobs for him and Ronan. Unfortunately, that meant he and Renee hadn't had as much time together. He'd even fallen asleep one night while they were reading.

Renee had spent days working on making Sadie's costume for Halloween. Sadie insisted on being Super Sadie like the mural Gavin had painted on her wall.

He just came in from the garage after organizing the extra materials they had for the house when Sadie came in from school.

"Guess what?" she asked.

"What?"

"You're supposed to guess."

"Can you give me a hint?"

"It's about Halloween."

"Mom finished your costume?"

"Yeah, but we're putting on a show at school. And I get to wear my costume."

"Awesome."

"Will you come? They said we can invite our families."

Right then, he felt like the Grinch with his heart growing three sizes. *Sadie considers me family.*

Renee trudged in carrying Sadie's backpack. "Your bag is your job to take care of, Sadie."

"Sorry. I was excited to invite Declan to my show."

Renee's eyes shot to his. She looked panicked.

"You know, Sadie, my lady, I would love to see your show, but I don't want to take your dad's ticket. He probably really wants to come."

"My teacher said I can invite everyone. Mom, Dad, Grandma, and you!"

"Then name the time and place, and I'm there."

"Mom knows." Then she took off to her room.

"Sorry about that," Renee said.

"What?"

"You don't have to come. It's silly little show. The room will be crowded. She won't know."

His heart deflated. "Do you not want me to come?"

"No. It's not that. I just..."

"If Sadie wants me there, I'll be there."

"You're busy trying to get your new company off the ground. This is going to be in the middle of your day."

"So I'll carve out the time. Let me know when."

Renee was already worked up, so now was probably not the best time to bring up moving out, but he felt the itch to keep the forward momentum. Staying here would make him feel like a sponge. And he knew Renee wouldn't take rent from him.

Neither would his mother, but she was Mom.

"As long as Sadie's busy, can we talk for a few minutes?"

"Sure," she said warily.

He took her hand. "You're right. Things are a bit hectic with all the running around. But things here are done."

She nodded.

"So..." His words disappeared as he looked into her beautiful face. "It's time for me to move out. I got you to the point where your home isn't as ugly, and I've got a plan."

"There's no rush, Declan. You can stay as long as you need to. I have the space."

"So does my mom. Plus, I think she's lonely without any of us at home. I'm going to move in there for a while until Ronan and I get things going."

"If you're sure."

"I am." He kissed her lips. "But thanks for everything."

"What are you thanking me for? I think I got the better end of the deal."

He laughed. She had no idea how much better his life was for having her in it. "What's the best way to tell Sadie?"

"I can tell her."

"No. I will. Should I tell her now?"

"The sooner the better. That way she has time to adjust. We're used to having you around."

"I won't be far." He kissed her again and went to talk to Sadie.

He found her in her room, practicing Super Sadie poses. She was such an amazing kid. He loved her. "Hey, can we talk?"

She stopped and narrowed her eyes, looking a whole lot like her mom.

"Come here," he said as he sat on the edge of her bed.

She hopped up next to him and stared expectantly.

Damn, this was gonna be hard. "You know how before I lived here, Uncle Ty did?"

"Yeah."

"And Uncle Ty moved out to his own place?"

"Yeah."

"Well, now that I did most of the work your mom needed done on the house, like the windows and the painting—"

"And my jungle gym!"

"Yep. It's time for me to move out."

"Why?"

"Because I was living here to help your mom."

"But I like having you here."

"I like being here."

"So stay." She leaned close and whispered, "Mom likes you being here way more than Uncle Ty."

Declan laughed. "I know. And I'll be back."

"To take me to breakfast?"

"Absolutely." And a whole lot more. But he couldn't say that yet.

"Will you still come to my Halloween show?"

"Wouldn't miss it."

"Where are you gonna live? Can I come visit you like I visit Uncle Ty?"

"I'm going to live with my mom for a little while. And you can come visit whenever your mom says it's okay. I bet my mom would love to meet you."

"Cool." She hopped off the bed. "I'm hungry."

"I'm sure your mom has a snack." It was funny. He didn't

have to think about it. He just knew part of Sadie's afternoon routine was to have a small snack after school. Renee was probably cutting up an apple now.

Weird. But it felt right.

TWO DAYS LATER, A TRUCK RENEE DIDN'T RECOGNIZE RUMBLED up to the house and Declan got out. When he came in, she asked, "What's that?"

"The first truck in Doyle Brothers Construction's fleet," he answered with a huge grin.

"Fleet, huh?"

"Everyone's gotta start somewhere. I'm manifesting that shit."

She chuckled. "What's your plan this afternoon? I thought you had job to do."

"I do. I figured I'd pack up and get my stuff out of your way. If you want, I can help you rearrange the bedroom so it can be a real office for you."

"I don't need an office. And you really are welcome to stay as long as you need." She wanted to ask him to stay, but that would feel too much like she needed him. And she'd promised herself a long time ago she would never *need* a man again.

"Thanks for the offer. But Ronan lives in the same neighborhood as my mom, so it'll be a little easier for us to get together."

"Okay. You need any help?" She knew he didn't. The man had arrived with one bag.

"Nah. Go back to whatever you got going on."

Renee tried to focus on work. She had a job interview later this week she wanted to do some more prep for. But knowing Declan was two rooms away packing up his things to leave gutted her.

She looked around the living room and dining room. The space had totally changed with the facelift Declan had given it. The warm yellow color made it new and fresh. And homey. He'd made some magic here.

He'd had the same effect on her life.

Since being with him, she felt even more capable. Ready to handle a new job. Maybe she'd tackle dating again. He'd made it seem a lot easier.

A little while later, Declan came back with his bag slung over his shoulder.

"I put the sheets in the wash."

"You didn't have to do that."

"Yeah, I did."

"I guess I'll see you around."

His brow wrinkled. "I'll see you tomorrow morning."

"Why?"

"I have my breakfast date with Sadie." His look made her feel dumb.

"Oh. I—"

He held up a hand. "Do me a favor and don't finish that statement. I promised her. This isn't finished. I have a lot going on with the new company, but I won't flake on her."

She took a breath to stop herself from arguing. "Okay."

She really wanted to believe he'd keep his promises to Sadie.

"Don't forget to send me the Halloween information."

"I'll do it right now." She pulled her phone out and began texting

As he passed her, he kissed the top of her head. "See you in the morning."

DECLAN THOUGHT WALKING OUT OF RENEE'S HOUSE WAS ONE of the toughest things he'd had to do. He knew she doubted he'd stick. He wanted to confront that. Push her up against the wall and show her that he wasn't going anywhere.

If he'd done that, he would've been tempted to stay. And they wouldn't be able to move forward as equal partners. He needed to prove he could stand on his own so she'd take him seriously.

But as hard as leaving yesterday was, coming back to pick up Sadie was harder. Waking up and knowing he couldn't stroll to the other side of the house to scoop her up and fly her around hit hard. When he got to the house, he rang the bell. He heard Sadie yelling through the house.

She swung the door open and Renee came running up behind her.

"I told you not to open the door. You didn't know who it was."

Sadie looked over her shoulder. "Yeah, I did. It's Declan."

Looking up at him, Renee added, "Declan has a key, so he shouldn't be ringing the doorbell."

"I didn't want to assume I should use the key. What if you were dancing around naked?"

Sadie giggled. "Mom doesn't do that."

"You're right. Go get your jacket. It's too cold for just a sweatshirt."

SHANNYN SCHROEDER

Renee stepped back so he could come inside. Her arms were crossed. It was the most damn awkward he'd ever been around her.

"Something wrong?"

"No." She looked up at him.

"Hey, I need your car seat for Sadie."

"You can take my car if you want."

"I promised Sadie she could ride in my new truck. It has a back seat so she'll be safe."

"If I didn't think you would keep her safe, she wouldn't going with you," she said with a smile.

It made him feel a little better.

Sadie came running back wearing her coat. "Ready!"

"If you unlock your car, I'll grab the seat."

She reached around and pressed the button for her car.

"Bye, Mom," Sadie yelled as she ran out toward his truck.

"Uh, I'll have her back soon."

Rene rolled her eyes. "No rush. I mean, extra time in a quiet house. Whatever will I do?"

His mind flipped through a few things they could do in a quiet house. "French toast today?"

"You don't need to bring me breakfast."

"I know."

He went out and transferred the car seat into his truck. On the way to Super Cup, Sadie filled the silence.

While they ate breakfast, Declan's mind wandered to thoughts of doing this long-term. He liked the idea of having this special time with Sadie. He didn't understand how Graham thought this was tough.

When he dropped Sadie off, he moved the car seat back, and as much as he wanted to go in and hang out with

Renee, he needed to get moving on his day. He had a full schedule of appointments for quotes. Then he was meeting Ronan to talk about business stuff.

He just hoped Renee would understand why he was doing this.

CHAPTER
Thirty-Six

The next couple of weeks in Renee's life were super quiet. She'd managed to get a couple of job interviews lined up, which was good because the silence of her house in the afternoons was starting to get on her nerves. Maybe she should get a dog.

Sadie would love a dog.

Graham never wanted a dog. He thought they were too much work. When Sadie was a baby, she agreed, but now? She'd like a friend to hang out with during the day.

But if she went back to work in an office all day, that might not be fair to the dog.

Instead of assessing why she thought her house was suddenly too quiet, she looked up some animal shelters.

But then she found herself hearing Declan's voice comment on the dogs she looked at. She couldn't stop the smile.

Fuck. She missed him. They'd talked via text most days. He was busy working with Ronan. Logically, she knew that, but part of her felt like he was quiet quitting, a slow ghost until she no longer noticed he wasn't around.

She made a point not to pressure him or ask him to come over. She was just glad he'd kept his breakfasts with Sadie. And she'd get to see him this afternoon at Sadie's Halloween show.

She sent another reminder text to both Declan and Graham about the show time.

Declan swore he'd make it.

Graham said he'd try.

Fucking men.

Outside, fat snowflakes started to fall. There wasn't supposed to be any real accumulation, but it sucked. Hopefully, it would warm up by tomorrow. There was nothing worse than trying to trick-or-treat in freezing weather. No one could see your costume because you had to wear a coat. Staying out and making multiple trips through the neighborhood wouldn't happen because you got too cold.

This was the first year Sadie would really get to have fun.

Renee got to the school early and snagged three chairs together off to the side. She debated the sense of that move, but she prayed Graham wouldn't make any of his usual snarky comments.

Folded paper programs were passed out. She snapped a picture and sent it to Graham in case he didn't make it. Kids from older grades piled in and sat on the floor in front of the stage.

When the kindergarteners filed onto the stage, taking their places on the risers, some pointed to kids she guessed were siblings.

Sadie might never have that. Chairs filled up and people began giving her sideways looks for saving two chairs.

When the lights dimmed, her heart sank. She was the only one who showed up for Sadie.

She tried not to get teary-eyed watching her baby perform with a big smile on her face. The songs were silly and the kids forgot words, but she loved every minute of it.

The lights came on and she stood to wave to Sadie. But Sadie was already waving wildly in the other direction. Renee turned around to see Declan blow a kiss to Sadie and duck back out the door.

He came.

He told Sadie he'd show up and he did.

Renee wiped a tear away. She reminded herself that him showing for Sadie was more important than how she felt. It didn't matter that she wanted him sitting beside her. It was okay he wasn't that person for her.

She'd get over it.

AFTER HER TWO QUIET WEEKS, THE PAYBACK WAS TWO DAYS OF total chaos. The weather was all over the place, and while Sadie had fun trick-or-treating, the sugar overload was getting on Renee's last nerve. Sadie had the day off school. Teachers knew what they were doing there, making it an in-service day.

So Renee had to keep Sadie entertained. She was distracted and totally botched one of her job interviews. To top it off, the back door kept sticking.

Of course that meant every time Sadie went in and out —which was like every four freaking minutes—she slammed it harder and harder to get it to close.

"Stop slamming the door," Renee called as Sadie grabbed a water bottle to take outside. Renee waited a second to hear the thump, but it didn't come. "Thank God she actually listened."

Renee turned her attention back to the job boards.

She'd been considering getting in touch with a headhunter to see if that would help. Maybe she should take a course or two to brush up on her skills.

The doorbell rang, which was her sign to put her computer away. Pizza had arrived. That meant food, bath, and then it would be wine time. She paid for the pizza and went to call Sadie in.

She saw why she hadn't heard the door slam. Sadie had left it open. "Pizza's here! Time to come in."

Sadie came running to the door. She grabbed the handle and yanked. The door didn't budge. "Mom. It won't close."

Fuck. She did not need this shit tonight. "Go wash up."

Sadie took off to the bathroom and she pulled the door. It wouldn't move for her either. Turning her body so she could put one hand on the handle and the other on the back of the door, she nudged it with her hip to apply pressure.

It squeaked and moved maybe a half-inch.

Renee took a deep breath.

She walked away from the door and poured a glass of wine. If she'd learned nothing else about having a run-down house, it was that she needed to step back when something went wrong. She took her glass into the dining room where Sadie was waiting.

Renee scrolled through videos on her phone to see if she could figure out what happened to the door and how to fix it.

An hour later, her frustration was growing. She had her measly spread of tools on the kitchen floor and she was on her fifth video showing her how to lever the edge of the sliding door up to adjust the rollers underneath.

She managed to smash her fingers at least five times and nothing had improved. She even thought about kicking it.

Sadie came up behind her with a wrench. "Try this one, Mom."

Renee huffed. "A wrench won't work for this. Please just go back and watch your movie."

"Declan lets me help."

Those were the last words she needed to hear. "Well, I'm not Declan and he's not here."

Sadie's eyes got wide at her sharp words. Renee immediately felt guilty. She blew out a breath. "I'm sorry I snapped at you. I'm frustrated. How about I make some popcorn and watch the movie with you?"

"You're gonna leave the door open?"

"I'll work on it more later. You know how sometimes when you're doing homework and it's hard and I tell you to take a break? This is the same."

"Okay. But for sure you'll fix it tonight?"

"I'm gonna try."

"But if you can't close the door a bad guy could come in."

"You don't have to worry about bad guys. You're safe."

They sat on the couch, snacking on popcorn, and watching cartoon superheroes. But Renee's brain was stuck like the door. She put on a serene smile for her daughter and got her into bed.

Then with her glass of wine, she went back to the kitchen. Again, she Googled how to fix the door. She took it step by step, pausing the video to follow the actions and to rub her hands to warm her numb fingers. For two more hours, she tried again and again. Finally, she did kick the door.

She stared at her phone. "I'll call and if it goes to voicemail, he's busy. It's Friday night. He might be out. He sure as hell doesn't need a crazy woman bothering him at ten o'clock."

She dialed Declan's number.

"Hey, babe. What's up?"

The calm, casual way he spoke made all of her resolve crumble. She inhaled deeply, but her breath hitched.

"Renee, what's wrong?"

She swallowed. "I know it's late. And I tried to fix it myself but the back door is stuck. I can't get it to move. I've watched a ton of videos showing me what to do, but I think I might've made it worse. And Sadie is afraid bad guys are gonna come in—"

"I'll be there soon."

"If you can just tell me what to do to get it to close. I'll call someone to fix it tomorrow."

"The hell you will. I'm on my way."

Then he hung up.

DECLAN RACED OVER TO RENEE'S HOUSE. HE'D NEVER BEEN SO glad to be a truck owner in his life. He didn't have to wait for a ride or figure out how to get his tools there. Everything he needed was in his truck.

He grabbed a bucket of tools and went to the front door. He used his key to get in.

"Renee?" he called quietly, assuming Sadie was in bed.

"In here," she called.

He went to the kitchen and saw her sitting on the floor,

surrounded by a mess of mismatched tools and a glass of wine.

She looked up at him and it was the most pitiful thing he'd ever seen. She got up from the floor.

"I told Sadie to stop slamming the door. I think today was one time too many. It won't budge. I tried to shove it. I tried to adjust the rollers. Then Sadie wanted to help and I snapped at her and she's worried about bad guys. And then I kicked the fucking thing."

Damn. She was freaking out. He didn't know what else to do, so he pulled her into a hug.

"I'm sorry I bothered you on a Friday night."

"You're not bothering me. You should've called me as soon as it happened."

"It's not your job anymore. You moved out. Moved on."

He pulled her away from his chest. "I didn't move on from you. I moved on from my life of nothing. I want to build a business with Ronan, but I'm not leaving you."

Her eyes were glassy and he wasn't sure if it was the wine or tears. "We agreed—"

"We agreed we'd give this a real try. I moved out to be able stay with you."

"That doesn't make sense."

"As long as I was living here, rent-free, I could never be the partner you want and need. I'd be a fun cabana boy."

"Declan, that's not how I see you."

He smiled. "Kind of. Not in a bad way. I know that. But I want more. I know I need to prove to you I can be more. Part of that is building this business with my brother."

"You don't need to change your life for me."

"I'm changing it for me. And I can't do that here. But we're not done. I told you that weeks ago."

"I thought you were easing away quietly. Slow ghosting

the relationship. No conflict. No trouble. I haven't seen you. And even when you came to Sadie's Halloween show, you were there and then gone."

"I haven't been around as much because I've been busy running around and setting things up for me and Ronan. He's still working full-time, so it's on me to get things moving. And when I came to the Halloween show, I came in a couple of minutes late. I was literally in between jobs. I wanted Sadie to know I showed up, but I didn't want to cause a problem for you if Graham saw me there. So, no, I'm not ghosting you."

She looked startled. "Oh."

"In fact, I'd planned to take you out next weekend."

"What?"

"On a date, Renee. Let's go out."

"I don't—"

"Ty said he'd babysit if Graham flakes on taking Sadie."

"You arranged a babysitter?"

"He's my best friend and her uncle. It wasn't a hard ask."

She blinked up at him.

"You got some other objection?"

"I thought..."

"I know what you thought. I just cleared that up, didn't I?"

"Okay. Let me know when."

"Friday night. Pick you up at seven." He leaned in and gave her a quick kiss. "Now, let me figure out the door."

"At the risk of making you mad, can you show me how to fix it, so if it happens again, I'll know what to do?"

"I'll show you, but you won't need to do it."

"It's my house."

"I'll handle it. And anything else that needs to be fixed."

He watched as her shoulder muscles relaxed and a slow smile spread across her face.

"Do you know how sexy those words are?"

"What?"

"*I'll handle it.* Because I believe you will. It's been a long time since I've been able to depend on someone like that."

"To think that's all I had to say to get you naked." He lowered his mouth to hers. Kissing her was the best feeling. Like coming home after a long day.

It had been too long since he'd held her and tasted her. He had a hard time pulling away. He rested his forehead against hers. "For the record, if I have my way, you'll never be without that again. I want to be that person for you."

She wrapped her arms around his neck and pulled him close again. "What do you get out of this? It feels like you're always doing for me. That's not much of a partnership."

He didn't have to think, but he wasn't sure of the right words. He knew what she was for him, but no matter how he thought about it, it sounded corny as hell. "You make me a better person just by being around you. I like who I am with you. You give me someplace to belong."

He kissed her again and then tapped her ass. "Now move it. I have manly things to do here."

She snorted and laughed, which was what he was going for.

"Watch close, and I'll flex my muscles for you."

"You're in fine form tonight, aren't you?"

"You ain't seen nothin' yet."

As he propped the door up, he tried to explain what she should look for and how to turn the screwdriver to adjust the roller. Mostly, she listened and drank her wine, which was how it should be.

A WEEK LATER, RENEE KISSED SADIE GOODBYE WHEN GRAHAM showed up to take her for the weekend. Then she changed into a dress and heels. Her stomach tumbled.

Why the hell am I nervous? This is Declan.

He rang the bell when he arrived. She answered the door with a smile. "It's okay to use your key."

He lifted a shoulder in that careless way he had. "I figured since this is a proper date, I should treat it like one."

He handed her a bouquet of flowers.

"Thank you." She accepted them and ushered him inside. "You don't need to do anything special. We can keep it low-key."

She was trying to keep her own expectations in check, and she knew it.

"You deserve to have someone spoil you a little. You look gorgeous, by the way." He pointed a finger up and down the length of her. "This doesn't look so low-key."

"I wasn't sure where we're going."

"Anywhere you want."

"Can we go to the bar and dance?"

"You want to go to a bar?"

"I had a lot of fun that night we went out and danced."

"You got it."

They took her car because according to Declan, his work truck was too smelly for her. At the bar, they ordered food and drinks and talked. They talked about everything. Little things that happened over the week and big things like what they wanted. It was almost like he hadn't left her life at all.

And when he pulled her into his arms on the dance floor, she felt safe and relaxed. Like she belonged there. "I wish you hadn't moved out," she whispered in his ear.

"Rennie—"

"First, don't call me that. Second, I understand why you did, but it's lonely without you there. I got used to your noise."

"Turn on the radio."

She chuckled. "You laugh, but after you were gone for like a week, I almost went out and got a dog."

He stepped back, twirled her away from his body and tugged her back. "Are you saying I could be replaced by a dog?"

"No. Not really. But it would be another presence in the house. I don't think you realize how big your personality is. I miss it." It was tough to admit it, but she wanted him to know.

"I miss you, too, Rennie."

"I will *never* miss that."

His chest vibrated under her hand with his laugh. "I want to get this right. That means I have to build up my life so I can be your equal partner. In the meantime, we date."

"Are you going to spend the night?"

"Is that an invitation?"

"Consider it an open invitation."

"Are we going to tell Sadie about us?"

Her heart lurched and she licked her lips. "I don't know if I'm ready."

His jaw set, but he said, "Okay."

"It's not you. This is new. Us. Me dating."

"I get it." He stopped dancing and held her face, his gaze

boring into her. "But hear this. I'm not going anywhere. I love you and I love Sadie."

She froze.

"Ah, fuck. I freaked you out, didn't I?"

She gulped in air and a smile filled her face. Her whole body. "You do?"

"Of course I do, you big dummy."

"I love you, too. I just thought we weren't there yet. Or shouldn't be there yet. I don't know. It's fast, right?"

"I've known you most of my life. We lived together for months. It feels right to me."

"It does, doesn't it?" She pressed close and kissed him again. "Take me home."

"Don't gotta tell me twice." He grabbed her hand, slapped cash on the table, and hustled her out the door.

"We don't have to run. We have all night."

"I have time to make up for. Plus, Sadie will be home next weekend, so I won't get this chance again for at least two weeks."

"We'll see. Maybe we can tell Sadie and see how she reacts."

He opened the car door for her. As she sat down, he winked at her. "I got this in the bag. Sadie loves having me around."

"We both do," Renee admitted.

Epilogue

Brendon stared at the copies of the ledgers Chloe had given him. He knew what Renee had said about money laundering. Now he just had to find enough to make a case. He knew if he pushed the right buttons, he could get Danny Cahill to admit what happened to Michael Doyle. Even if Danny had nothing to do with his father's death, he was sure Danny's father Alan would've shared those secrets.

If for no other reason, to keep him safe.

The problem was, that his basic knowledge of finance and financial crimes wasn't enough to figure this out. He needed to find out why Cahill was laundering money.

So in an effort to figure this out, he'd asked for help. The bell rang and he hit the buzzer to let his family up to his condo.

His family.

It had been forever since he thought about his siblings that way. He usually interacted with them one-on-one. But in recent months, it felt more like it had when they were kids.

Kind of a pack mentality.

He had to admit, he didn't hate it.

A few minutes later, he was reassessing. Ronan and Declan both pushed through his door, with their women trailing behind, chatting with each other.

"What are you doing here?" he asked Declan.

"Nice to see you, too, bro. If you involve Renee in your shit, you involve me."

"I told him he didn't need to babysit me," Renee said as she took off her coat. "I want to help if I can."

Everyone gathered around his dining room table. He slid his whiteboard over so everyone could see it. He'd been trying to create a timeline of everything, but there were too many gaps.

"As you can see, I've put everything we have on here. I added the dates of the fake invoices from the Rose. Payments to Alan. Where did they come from?"

Renee raised her hand. "Um...We don't know for sure the payments went to Alan—"

"I'm sure."

"But," she continued, "the money could've very well come from him, too. Let's say he came into extra money and needed a way to explain it. He'd give it to the Byrnes, and they could pay him a legitimate bill. Well, legitimate-looking anyway."

"Why would he need to hide his own money? He was in construction. It's easy to hide money there," Ronan said.

"Speaking from experience?" Brendan asked.

"Am I talking to a fed or my brother?"

Declan looked at the board. "It's dirty money from a dirty politician. You guys said Dad used to handle the money pickups for side jobs. Cahill might've done construction, but he was known for his politics."

Brendan froze. It was almost too obvious. "So he was hiding his kickback money. Did Dad want a cut? And Cahill got rid of him?"

Ronan shook his head. "You know that wasn't Dad."

"I'd like to think so. But he was under a lot of pressure. Seven kids. Another on the way. It could push a man."

"Not Dad. Something else happened."

"Is there any way to find out where the money came from?"

They all looked at Renee.

"Not without knowing where to look. You saw the books. Alastair Byrne kept it old school as long as he could. There was nothing too outrageous in his taxes. Nothing to raise a flag to cause an audit."

"I think he was doing a favor for a friend," Chloe added. "He and Alan went way back."

"Speaking of way back," Declan said. "I've been listening to this podcast."

Ronan gave him an incredulous look. "You listen to podcasts?"

"I read, too, go figure. Anyway, I only caught one episode. This chick is doing a deep dive into the Cahill dynasty."

Brendan waved a hand. "I doubt I'm going to learn about the Cahills from some fluff piece."

"It didn't sound like fluff to me. I'm just sayin'. She might have sources."

Brendan stopped short of rolling his eyes. "This isn't a TV movie."

"Whatever, man."

Brendan took a deep breath and blew it out. "I'm sorry I'm being a dick. I've been trying to keep this investigation quiet and every time I turn around the circle is expanding." He pointed around the table.

Ronan nudged his shoulder. "But with every expansion, we learn more. Neither of us was getting too far on our own."

"Point taken." Looking at Declan, he said, "Send me the name of it. But so help me God, if this is a joke and I turn on some porn-worthy audio, I'm gonna hurt you."

Declan burst out laughing. "Hadn't even crossed my mind, but now it has."

They didn't make much progress on the investigation, but it was good having other people to bounce ideas off. As shitty as things had been between him and his brothers, he finally felt like they were a family again.

Now, it was time for them to work together to find the answers they needed.

***

I hope you enjoyed reading about Declan and Renee. If you missed Ronan and Chloe's story, pick up *In Too Deep*. Keep an eye out for Brendan's story next, where the Doyles will finally get to the bottom of what happened to their dad.

If you want to keep up-to-date on all my new releases (and get freebies sent to your inbox), go to my website and sign up for my newsletter. www.ShannynSchroeder.com

Also by Shannyn Schroeder

The O'Leary Family

The O'Malley Family

The Doyle Family

Daring Divorcees Series

Stand Alones

Meeting His Match

Hot & Nerdy

Her Best Shot

Her Perfect Game

Her Winning Formula

His Work of Art

His New Jam

His Dream Role

Sloane Steele's Books

The Counterfeit Capers

Origin of a Thief (The Counterfeit Capers 0)

It Takes a Thief (The Counterfeit Capers #1)

Between Two Thieves (The Counterfeit Capers #2)

To Catch a Thief (The Counterfeit Capers #3)

The Thief Before Christmas (The Counterfeit Capers #4)

Milton Keynes UK
Ingram Content Group UK Ltd.
UKHW041322300624
444823UK00005B/2

9 781950 640638